I0762767

A HOUSE OF VIPERS

EMMA JACKSON

Delacorte Press

Delacorte Press
An imprint of Random House Children's Books
A division of Penguin Random House LLC
1745 Broadway, New York, NY 10019
penguinrandomhouse.com
getunderlined.com

Editor: Kelsey Horton
Cover Designer: Ray Shappell
Interior Designer: Michelle Gengaro-Kokmen
Production Editor: Colleen Fellingham
Managing Editor: Tamar Schwartz
Production Manager: CJ Han

Library of Congress Cataloging-in-Publication Data is available upon request.
ISBN 979-8-217-02698-2 (hardcover) —
ISBN 979-8-217-02700-2 (ebook)

Manufactured in the United States of America
1st Printing

The authorized representative in the EU for product safety and compliance is Penguin Random House Ireland, Morrison Chambers, 32 Nassau Street, Dublin D02 YH68, Ireland, https://eu-contact.penguin.ie.

Random House Children's Books supports
the First Amendment and celebrates the right to read.

For Grammy and Fifi,
who are a part of all my favorite stories.
It was a joy to be your granddaughter.

CHURCHILL HALL
PARRISH HALL
BARNABY BOATHOUSE
MORLAND HALL
BELL TOWER
SIMON THATCHER MEMORIAL LIBRARY
ACE AVERELL SPORTS COMPLEX
MEDDLEHART MANOR

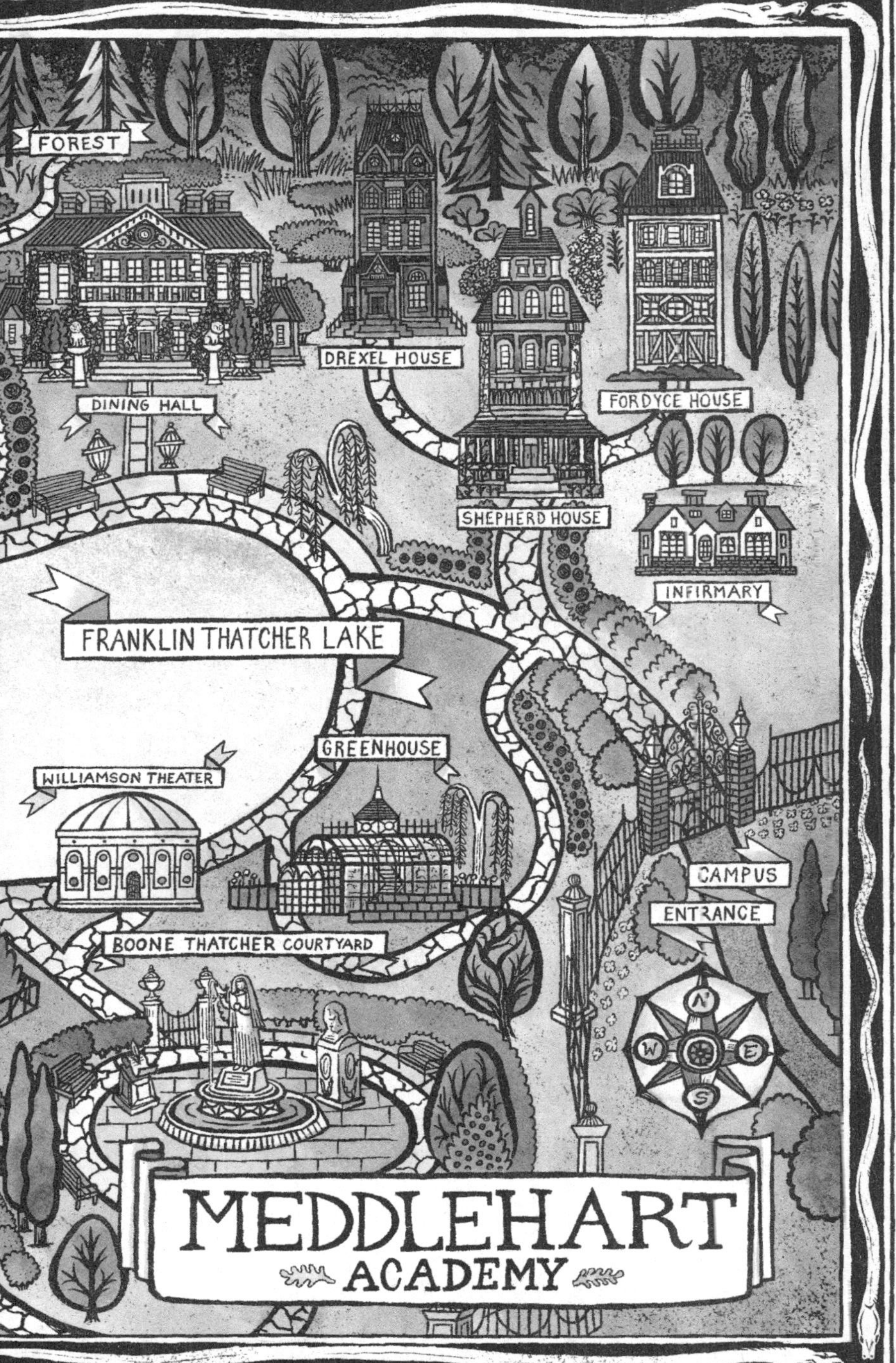
FOREST
DREXEL HOUSE
DINING HALL
FORDYCE HOUSE
SHEPHERD HOUSE
INFIRMARY
FRANKLIN THATCHER LAKE
GREENHOUSE
WILLIAMSON THEATER
CAMPUS
ENTRANCE
BOONE THATCHER COURTYARD
N
W
E
S
MEDDLEHART
ACADEMY

MARCH 2025

Lawson swore he could hear voices in the rainstorm outside his window.

Torrents of water pounded the rooftop of Drexel House against the backdrop of a sky bound for nighttime. The storm was a roaring chorus in Lawson's ears, punctuated by blinding lightning strikes that lit up the wilderness.

With every gust of wind, the voices of the rain pleaded with him, an angry desperation reflecting the fears in his own mind.

This is a mistake.

Lawson's muscles tensed tighter with every clap of thunder. His hands shook violently as he raced back and forth across the cramped space of his dorm, stuffing objects into his backpack without much thought.

Flashlight, map, phone, pocketknife . . . and the notebook, the leather-bound one that had belonged to his father, the one he'd given him before the school year started. The one Lawson wished he'd never opened, never read, never written in himself.

He couldn't take it with him. If things didn't go his way tonight . . .

Lawson grabbed a pen and scratched a message in the notebook for the one person who would understand. A last-ditch effort, just in case.

Lawson stowed the journal away with a hot rush of disgust and took one last glance around the room. He'd packed everything he could think of. He wasn't sure exactly what he would need, but he knew he wouldn't be coming back to Drexel House. Not tonight, and maybe not ever again. He hadn't even graduated, but maybe . . . maybe he wouldn't have to.

Because you're going to find it, he told himself. *You won't have to come back here again, because you'll have finally found it, and you'll end the Vipers once and for all.* But the words felt false, even whispered privately in his thoughts.

He couldn't be sure of anything now. All he could do was hope he was right, that his carefully laid plan would work.

His hand strayed to the viper pendant hanging at his neck, and he realized with a surge of anger that he wanted nothing to do with it anymore. He tore the necklace off with a sharp *snap*.

By the fangs of greed. The words echoed hollowly in his mind, a final refrain, as the chain broke and landed softly on his bed. He realized the irony of what he was doing—that others might believe *him* to be the greedy one, when it was all over.

He supposed that was something he would just have to accept.

Footsteps thundered down the hallway, and Lawson froze. They grew louder with each passing second. His throat tightened.

He's coming, Lawson thought. *He's going to stop me before I ever find it. Everything I've done will be for nothing.*

There was no time to grab a weapon. Lawson braced himself, raising his fists—if he couldn't escape, he would go down fighting.

But the pounding on the other side of his door was accompanied by a small, familiar voice.

"Lawson, open up!"

"Sutter?" Lawson reached for the doorknob and pulled it open to reveal his freshman brother, soaked to the bone and grinning like an idiot.

"Ready for your last dance, Lawson?" Sutter asked, but his grin disappeared before he'd uttered the last word. "Wait, why aren't you in your tux yet?"

"Sutter, what the hell are you doing here?" Lawson grabbed his collar and dragged him through the doorway, slamming the door shut behind him. He wasn't sure how Sutter had gotten this far—he was supposed to be safe in his room at Shepherd House, and the prefect at Drexel was never supposed to let freshmen past the common room this late.

"Laney asked me to come find you, since you're supposed to meet her at the dance," Sutter said. "She's waiting for you."

Laney. At the start of his senior year, Lawson had wanted nothing more than to ask Laney to prom. Now the concept of prom was meaningless. Everything about high school was pointless, and Laney was just a girl he didn't know, and who certainly didn't know him. He could only count on himself now.

Sutter frowned at him. A little dimple appeared between his knit brows, the same dimple their dad had every time he frowned, the same one Lawson himself had. "What's going on, Lawson? You seem—"

"Nothing," Lawson snapped.

Sutter flinched slightly at the outburst. Lawson squeezed his eyes shut briefly to steady himself. Normally he wasn't this tightly wound, this temperamental. But he had reached the end of his rope, only to find it frayed and useless, with nothing to grab on to.

It will all go away if I find it . . .

Lawson reached for his letterman jacket, which hung on the coatrack by the door, and pulled it off the hook.

"I forgot to pick up Laney's corsage," he told Sutter, "so I have to sneak into town to get it." The lie felt stiff on his lips, but it didn't matter. Sutter would believe anything he said, just like he always had. "Can you cover for me? Tell her I'm on my way. I'll be back before she knows it." He slipped the jacket over his shoulders and stepped toward the door.

"But the dance is starting," Sutter said. "You'll miss the whole thing if you—"

"Damn it, Sutter, just do what I say, okay?" Lawson cried.

Sutter's mouth hung slightly open like he'd been slapped, but then he clenched his jaw and balled his fists. "Why are you yelling at me? I didn't do anything."

Lawson caught sight of the clock on his bedside table—7:02. *Shit.* "I don't have time for this," he said, slinging his bag over his shoulder and reaching for the doorknob.

"Lawson, wait," Sutter said. His hand locked around Lawson's wrist. "Let me come with—"

Lawson's mind was blank as he shoved his little brother hard in the chest. Sutter toppled backward and hit the worn wooden floor with a thud.

For a moment, they just stared at each other. Sutter's eyes glistened, and Lawson suddenly realized how young his baby brother was. His features were still soft, his limbs scrawny, on the brink of a growth spurt. He'd never looked more like a child than he did at that moment, staring up at Lawson from the floor.

Guilt seized Lawson's chest in an iron vise, and for a second—just a second—he considered throwing everything away, lifting his brother off the ground and saying he was sorry, that he'd never hurt him again. He wanted to tell Sutter everything—about the

Vipers, the treasure, all the horrible things he'd discovered because of them.

But he knew he couldn't. He was in too deep now. He had to do this alone.

Maybe one day, when this was all over, Sutter would understand. Lawson was simply doing what older brothers exist to do—protect their younger brothers, look after them. But right now, Sutter wouldn't get it. He'd never had to protect anything or anyone in his life, not like Lawson had.

"I'll be back," Lawson said, hoping it was a promise he could keep. "Cover for me."

Without another word, he tore his gaze away from Sutter, then dashed out of his room and into the hallway. He hustled for the window leading to the fire escape and shoved it open. A bitter wind rushed in immediately, and rain pelted his face before he'd even eased himself through the gap. *Some weather for a dance,* he thought numbly.

His hands shook, but he gripped the ladder tight as he climbed out the window and made his way down. Rain soaked his hair, dripped from his eyelashes, ran into his mouth, but he didn't let it slow his pace. He was already behind, and he couldn't risk a single second. He felt bare without the small silver viper thumping against his chest as he moved, and disappointment sank like a stone from his throat to the pit of his stomach.

He'd hoped for a thrilling, sweeping, all-encompassing sense of freedom with the absence of the necklace. But as he ran across the lawn of Meddlehart Academy, the wet ground splashing beneath his feet, he only felt a hollow emptiness that seemed to echo the thought he'd been trying to ignore for hours.

It ends tonight.

AUGUST 2026

ONE

Sutter

Everyone had their reasons for attending Meddlehart Academy.

There were many things that drew people to this place. For some, it was the snowcapped mountain peaks cocooning the campus. For most, it was the prestige bestowed upon Meddlehart graduates. For a few, perhaps it came down to the age-old mystery that haunted the grounds—the promise of buried treasure yet to be found.

Sutter's reason was ever evolving. He only hoped it wouldn't change again this year.

It had been simple in the beginning: Sutter's father had attended Meddlehart for his high school years, as had every one of his uncles and grandfathers for generations. There wasn't a question as to whether Sutter and his older brother, Lawson, would attend Meddlehart as well. It was simply a fact.

Now, it was much more than that for Sutter. His parents couldn't have kept him from this campus if they tried.

But he wondered if his parents would change their minds, if they could turn back the clock. If they had only known what the future held, maybe they wouldn't have sent their two sons to this boarding school.

Sutter was fairly certain what his mother's choice would have been. As he and his parents approached the campus gates, he spared his mother a glance. Her lips were pursed the same way they'd been all day yesterday during the long drive up to the Colorado campus, her displeasure completely stifling.

His dad hardly seemed to notice, though. As usual, he was focused on his own feelings, his own priorities, rather than anyone else's. His mouth was turned down in a frown, but he still walked onto the campus with his chest puffed out with pride, like he owned the place. Even today, of all days. The day they placed a permanent memorial for his firstborn son in the campus courtyard.

Sutter shook his head. This wasn't how his first day back at Meddlehart was supposed to feel. He should have been waking up in his dorm room, getting breakfast with his friends, catching up on what had happened during their summer apart, preparing for his first classes of the semester. He should have felt the relief of finally being back here after surviving a slow, lonely, brutally hot summer with his parents at their house in Texas.

Instead, he felt a simmering anger in his gut, dread weighing down his shoulders. This shouldn't be happening. They shouldn't be doing this. Didn't anyone else see that? Why was everyone on board with memorializing someone who was still alive, for all they knew? They'd never found Lawson's body; they hadn't even found a trace of where he'd gone, and yet—

"Something wrong, champ?" Sutter's dad asked with a sidelong glance.

Sutter halted his thoughts, flexing one hand into a fist and then releasing it as he pondered what to say. Because *everything* was wrong, but if there was one thing Sutter had learned since Lawson's disappearance, it was that he couldn't be honest with his father about that. Not without setting him off.

With his father's next step, Sutter spotted a glint of silver in his jacket pocket—a flask, something he probably thought no one would notice.

But Sutter certainly did.

"No," he said in response. "I'm fine. This just . . . doesn't feel right." And it truly didn't. The day was too bright, too cheerful for the occasion, the campus as beautiful as ever—a beacon of light in a sea of misery. Elegant redbrick buildings with immaculate white pillars flanking each wall surrounded the massive pond, commonly referred to as "the lake." White flowers lined the edges of the pathway that wound toward the south side of campus, to the courtyard. An academic fortress on the hillside, the hidden gem of West Fork, and the only place that felt like home to Sutter anymore.

His father gave a slight nod. "You're right, it doesn't. We wish Lawson was here, too. But try not to look so hostile, champ—there'll be press at the ceremony, cameras. We need to look like a united front. Can't have anyone seeing that surly look on your face and thinking you're not on board with this memorial. Understood?"

White-hot anger flashed through Sutter's chest—he *wasn't* on board with this memorial, but that clearly didn't matter to anyone else. His father was only concerned with the way they were perceived by the outside world. It was probably because of the rumors that had swirled at the time of Lawson's disappearance—rumors that Lawson had a bad relationship with his parents, which prompted him to run away.

Which . . . was entirely true. Lawson didn't get along with their dad. But Sutter doubted that Lawson would have left Meddlehart in the middle of a torrential downpour because of it.

Sutter reached for the chain around his neck, for the weight of the viper pendant. The same one Lawson had left behind in his room that night. Sutter had stolen it from one of the many boxes of Lawson's things the school shipped back after his disappearance. Their father insisted that Sutter leave Lawson's things alone, but he just wanted to have something—*anything*—that would make him feel closer to his brother. Something to give back to him when he finally came home.

I haven't stopped looking for you, Lawson, he thought. *Even if the rest of the world has, I haven't.*

Nothing infuriated Sutter more than this—that their own parents had given up on finding Lawson so soon. It was as if they'd accepted—no, *decided*—their older son was dead.

And no matter how it looked to the crowd and the cameras, there was no "united front" as far as Sutter was concerned. Their family wasn't a family anymore and hadn't been for the past year and a half.

"Heyward!"

Sutter turned at the sound of his last name, and there was Carter Sterling barreling down the pebble walkway from where the student houses sat atop the hill. Despite everything, Sutter grinned as his lifelong best friend bounded toward him and pulled him into a one-armed hug.

"I'm sorry, Sutter," Carter said quietly.

To his surprise, Sutter found he had a knot in his throat. Lawson had been missing for a long time, and his friends had expressed their condolences many times before . . . but somehow, having a friend who knew how painful this was—who knew what this memorial would do to him—hit him hard, right in the chest.

His life felt unlucky in a lot of ways, but not in this one.

"It's good to see you, buddy," Sutter managed.

Carter let go and wiped off the sheen of sweat that had surfaced on his dark-brown skin. Even at this altitude, the late-summer air was too warm for the suits they were wearing. Then, as if just realizing Sutter's parents were there, Carter moved to hug them, too. Carter's father had met Sutter's when they were in high school at Meddlehart, and they'd remained friends all these years. Sutter had known Carter and his older brother, Scott, since they were in diapers.

Something about seeing Carter had broken the dam of tears his mother was holding back, because now she was dabbing at her eyes with a tissue. His dad's expression had taken a turn toward discomfort—he'd never been great at responding to tears.

"Hey, champ," Sutter's dad said. "Let's keep moving, or we'll be late."

Sutter turned wordlessly and led the way down the path, toward the courtyard. Carter fell into step beside him.

"Where are the others?" Sutter asked quietly.

"They'll meet us there. Grayson's late again. His dad screwed up the flights like last year. Fallon and Margot had to do their makeup and stuff—you know the drill," Carter said. He squeezed Sutter's shoulder. "But they're excited to see you."

Sutter sighed—yet another thing this memorial had robbed him of. Thanks to his parents, who had insisted he arrive on campus with them on the day of the ceremony—more of this "united front" nonsense—he was arriving two days after the rest of the student body. Classes didn't start until tomorrow, but his friends had already moved their belongings into their dorms and had some time to catch up with each other. He wished his reunion with them could happen anywhere else, on any other day.

But despite the weight in his chest, Sutter couldn't wait to see his friends. Margot and Grayson and . . .

Fallon. Hearing her name, knowing he'd get to see her again today, was almost enough to make him forget about everything else.

At the end of the path, Sutter could see the crowd already gathered in the courtyard—students and teachers dressed in funeral black, donors and camera crews, all starting the school year off by saying goodbye to his brother.

Sutter wondered numbly if he was the only person left on earth who believed Lawson was still alive.

Lawson's voice rang clear as a bell in his mind—the last words he'd said before he vanished into the night.

I'll be back.

Sutter swallowed the bile rising in his throat. *I know you will*, he thought. He willed the words to reach Lawson, wherever he was.

And he promised he wouldn't let the rest of the world forget his brother was still out there, no matter what.

TWO

Fallon

Fallon carefully studied herself in the wall mirror as Margot wound the final curls into her hair. Normally, she would do her own hair—something less time-consuming than meticulously curling it one lock at a time—but her hands were a bit too shaky today, and when Margot offered to help, it only made sense to take her up on it.

There were pieces of her reflection that looked authentic, but so many others that were not—her dress, all-black with an embroidered floral pattern that blended in with the smooth fabric and sleeves that cut off at the elbows, was something she would never have chosen on her own. The students had been instructed to wear black to the ceremony in lieu of their Meddlehart uniforms, a grim reminder of what today stood for.

And on top of that, she'd allowed Margot to do her makeup. Fallon didn't like wearing much makeup. She could never get it to settle right on her skin, and she didn't like the way it covered the light smattering of freckles on her cheeks. The ones that made her look most like her mom.

No—don't think about Mom and Dad. Not today. Instead, Fallon focused her eyes on the reflection of the wall behind her—the side of the room that was entirely hers, covered in fan art she'd drawn over the past couple of years. It was a direct contrast to the explosion of pink on Margot's side of the room, but Margot didn't seem to mind. Each rendering Fallon did of her favorite characters made this dorm feel like home in a way that nowhere else could.

Aunt Jennie had kindly asked Fallon not to pin fan art all over the walls of her room at their house (pushpins were choking risks for toddlers), and she had agreed, because . . . well, it wasn't her house, and she didn't want to cause Jennie any more stress than she was already dealing with.

In the four years she'd lived with Aunt Jennie and Uncle Fred in New Mexico, she had never felt at home there, no matter what they did to make it comfortable for her. As long as there were screaming babies and saggy-diapered toddlers running around, wreaking havoc on every clean surface in the house, it would feel like she was in the way of her aunt and uncle trying to raise their family. It wouldn't really feel like she belonged.

But *belonging* was what Meddlehart Academy had given her.

"And . . . there we go," Margot said, delicately releasing the still-hot curl so it dangled just above Fallon's collarbone. "All done."

Fallon smiled, relieved, and ran her fingers through the curls. "Thanks, Margot. What would I do without you?" This wasn't the first time Fallon had Margot to thank for helping her with the perfect outfit for an event at Meddlehart, and it likely wouldn't be the last.

"You would look beautiful with or without my help," Margot promised. "And besides, I can't take credit for that dress. It looks really nice on you."

Fallon smiled but couldn't bring herself to agree. She hated dresses like this—the kind you wore to funerals. She hated remembering the last time she had to wear one, on the day her parents were buried.

"Should we go?" she asked instead.

Margot nodded and led the way into the hall, her long blond hair swishing over her shoulders. Fallon and Margot had been roommates since freshman year, but this year was their first having a dorm on the third floor of Shepherd House. Somehow, the long trip down the stairs and across campus to the courtyard felt daunting.

Or perhaps it was just what waited for them that made Fallon feel ill at ease.

"This is such a strange way to start junior year," Margot said quietly as they cleared the first flight of stairs. "It doesn't feel right."

"I know," Fallon agreed. Her reunion with Margot on move-in day had been so exciting. They'd had hours to catch up on their summer spent apart—Margot told Fallon all about her family's trip to Paris (even though it had been thoroughly documented in vlogs on her YouTube channel), and Fallon vented about how much she'd missed her friends while she was stuck babysitting her little cousins.

But that excitement had waned leading up to the day of Lawson Heyward's memorial ceremony. Margot's usual giddy chatter had been dialed down, and all Fallon's energy had morphed into nervous anticipation that rattled through her bones.

She was finally going to see Sutter again, but she knew he wouldn't be himself today. She knew he would be against this memorial and all it stood for, and the thought made her stomach churn with anxiety.

Things will feel normal again once the ceremony is over, Fallon reassured herself as she and Margot entered the Shepherd House common room. *We just need to get through today.*

A handful of sophomore boys, also dressed in black, were milling around near the entrance before heading to the memorial ceremony. A WELCOME HOME, DRAGONS banner hung above the mantel of the massive stone fireplace. Deep-blue leather chairs and couches surrounded wooden tables and ornate rugs lined the floors.

The large-screen TV on the far wall displayed a slideshow of photos taken the year before, with smiling students participating in various school activities: studying at Simon Thatcher Memorial Library, playing kickball at the Ace Averell Sports Complex on field day, painting a new mural on the walls of Parrish Hall, skiing at Swallowtail Resort on the annual school trip.

Just then, Dr. Wilbur, one of their science teachers, burst through the Shepherd House front doors and eyed each of the stragglers in the common room. "Chop, chop!" she called out. "What is going on in here? You all should be with the other students and taking your seats in the courtyard by now!"

Fallon and Margot ducked past Dr. Wilbur, narrowly avoiding her wrath, and stepped into the crisp mountain air. They made their way past the student houses and toward the southern corner of campus. The houses were arranged around a manicured lawn, with Drexel House in the back, Fordyce House to the right, and Shepherd House in the front.

The framework of each house was much like the others—four stories stacked evenly atop each other, with square windows spaced at equal distances—but they were entirely individual outside of that. Fordyce House was surrounded with clean white paneling and a slate shingled roof. Drexel House was built with dark bricks and a black metal roof, the spooky, mysterious house next door. But to Fallon, Shepherd House was by far the most beautiful, with deep-blue front doors and stone walls scaled by ivy.

"Fallon," Margot said, reaching out to stop her. She took the moment as an opportunity to adjust the ruffled straps of her black dress. Hers was knee-length and more fitted than Fallon's flowy dress. "Are you all right? You've hardly said a word all day."

Fallon pursed her lips, considering her answer. "Well, I could ask you the same question. You're the talkative one of this duo."

Margot gave her a pointed look. "And *you* are avoiding my question." Then her expression softened. "Sutter will be okay, you know."

Fallon's cheeks heated against her wishes. This is why Margot was her best friend—she knew what was going through her head and heart before Fallon even knew herself. "I know he will. I'm just . . ."

"Worried about him," Margot supplied. "I get it."

Fallon nodded. Of course Margot understood—they'd all witnessed the depths to which Sutter's grief had dragged him during their sophomore year, the first semester they'd returned to campus since Lawson went missing. They all knew how much pain his brother's disappearance had caused him, no matter how well he tried to hide it.

"We'll be there for him," Margot said. "That's what counts. Besides . . . aren't you at least a little excited to see him?" She nudged her friend knowingly, though it was gentle.

Almost instinctively, Fallon glanced around to make sure no one could hear. Margot was the only person on the planet who knew how Fallon felt about Sutter, and even *she* wasn't supposed to, but . . . Well. This would be their third year as roommates. They knew a lot about each other.

Of course she was excited to see him. But she also wasn't

naive enough to think that he would be thinking the same thing about her—not today of all days. He had enough to deal with. Sutter's mind and heart would be focused on his brother's memorial, and that's how it should be.

Just then, the shriek of a microphone's feedback echoed from down the path—a sure sign the ceremony would start any minute.

"We can talk about this later," Fallon said, waving her hand. "Let's go."

Fallon tried to put her feelings for Sutter out of her mind as they picked up their pace, and she gazed around at the campus she'd spent all summer longing for. She felt like the beauty of Meddlehart's sprawling campus would never get old to her. It was the perfect retreat nestled in the mountains, surrounded by woods and wildlife. The still water on the lake guarded by the old bell tower that stood sentry over the school grounds reflected the quiet afternoon around them like a mirror. Fallon could almost hear the rushing currents of the river that flowed just past campus, to the west.

As they passed the greenhouse and approached the Boone Thatcher Courtyard, Fallon took in the unfamiliar rows of white chairs facing the circular space. Set before the chairs was a short structure covered in a sheet, waiting to be unveiled.

Fallon wondered where Lawson's memorial would be placed—there were other memorial plaques and benches in the courtyard to honor past students and teachers, most of which had been there long before Fallon became a Meddlehart student.

Margot led the way, weaving through the crowd of students toward the front rows. Fallon craned her neck to look for those familiar faces, the ones she'd missed all summer. She spotted

Headmaster Averell taking his place behind the podium and adjusting the microphone.

"Surely they're here by now," Margot said. "It's about to start."

"Looking for someone?"

Sutter's familiar voice was like a magnet. Fallon and Margot spun around, and he and Carter stood there, smiles on their faces. Neither of the boys had a chance to move before Margot threw her arms around both their necks in a double hug. It didn't matter that the girls had already reunited with Carter for dinner last night—he got another hug anyway. Fallon couldn't escape the group hug, either, because Carter reached out and pulled her into it.

When they finally let go, she was facing Sutter. He was looking at her with the crooked grin she knew so well. But there was a heaviness in his shoulders, weariness in his eyes. His chestnut hair stood up in places like he'd run his hands through it too many times.

"Hi," Fallon said, a little breathless.

His eyes softened. "Hey, Winthrop."

Fallon's heart raced, and she could have doubled over at the ache of longing that rocked her. She wanted to hug him, but before she could move, the podium microphone screeched. Everyone in the courtyard turned to look.

Headmaster Averell smiled sheepishly. "My apologies. If everyone could please take their seats."

Sutter's expression darkened. Just like that, it was time for the memorial ceremony to start. Fallon spotted Sutter's parents in the front row, waving him over.

He turned to his friends again, brows furrowed in a frown. "Will you sit with us?"

The three of them hesitated. Most of the other students had been relegated to the back rows, behind the teachers and school staff. Would Sutter's parents appreciate them all taking the row that was reserved for family?

Sutter's voice took on a note of desperation. "Please," he said. His eyes locked on Fallon's, and she saw the plea in them: *Don't make me face this alone.*

So she nodded, and Margot said, "Of course." The four of them shuffled toward the first row of seats, but Fallon stopped before they could sit down.

"Wait, where's Grayson?"

Carter shrugged. "He's late. His dad messed up the plane tickets again, remember?"

Fallon's chest tightened. "Yeah, but he should have shown up by now." Did that mean something was wrong? What if something had happened to him on his way here? Images flashed in Fallon's mind—cracked windshields, screeching tires, sirens wailing from much too far away—

Sutter touched her arm. "He'll be okay, Fallon. Don't worry."

She looked at him, his hazel eyes locked on hers. His hand was warm on her skin, reassuring.

Fallon nodded and stepped into the row, taking her seat. She looked at the courtyard entrance, certain that Grayson would arrive any minute now. She pulled her phone out quickly, before the ceremony began, and sent him a text.

You ok? Almost here?

She waited for him to respond. And even after Headmaster Averell started to speak, she watched the courtyard gates and waited for Grayson to show.

THREE

Grayson

Grayson's chest grew tighter with every passing minute as the limousine wound along the mountain pass leading to Meddlehart Academy. He adjusted the sleeve of his black suit jacket and checked his watch.

"Sir?" he called out to the driver, straining to keep his tone polite. "Can you go any faster?"

The driver glanced at him through the limo's privacy barrier, which he'd left open for most of the drive. "We'll be there shortly, Mr. Hendricks."

Grayson clenched his jaw. He was definitely going to be late for the memorial ceremony.

Maybe this shouldn't come as a shock to him. Grayson's father had never given a damn about getting him anywhere on time. He'd already missed move-in day, thanks to his dad booking the flight for the wrong date, and to top it all off, the limo driver had been told the wrong pickup time.

Whatever. At least he was *here*, moments away from being back on campus with his friends. Anything beat being in California with his dad, always hiding out from anyone who might recognize who he was . . . or rather, who his parents were.

Grayson wasn't the famous one, after all. He was famous by association.

When his father first informed Grayson four years ago that he'd complete his secondary education at Meddlehart Academy, Grayson wasn't sure how to feel. Damon Hendricks had attended Meddlehart himself as a teenager, and he told Grayson the school would "make a man out of you." Because apparently Damon was too busy acting in Hollywood blockbusters to raise his teenage son himself.

At first, all Grayson could do was numb himself to the fact that his dad wanted him out of his hair so badly, he was willing to ship him off to become someone else's problem. It hurt like hell that he'd made the call without giving Grayson any choice in the matter.

But then Grayson realized he *did* have a choice. When he first set foot on the Meddlehart Academy campus, he immediately thought of his mother. He saw her in the towering mountain peaks surrounding the immaculate ivy-covered buildings, shielding the campus from the outside world as though it were a hidden treasure.

Grayson saw a place that might make him feel as safe as she once had, and he realized he could choose this place for himself. He could choose his own path here, separate from his father's plans for him.

Just then, there was a loud *pop*. The limo slowed to a stop, right in the middle of the road.

Grayson froze, watching as the driver stepped out of the vehicle and returned with an apology written across his face.

"Mr. Hendricks, I'm sorry," he said. "We have a flat tire."

"What?" Grayson asked. Without another word, he shoved the limo door open and stepped onto the gravel road. He took in the punctured tire, and his chest deflated.

"Don't worry—I can have roadside assistance here in an hour," the driver promised, already on his phone.

Grayson thought of his friends, waiting for him at the memorial ceremony, and shook his head. "I don't have an hour." He peered at the road ahead—one more steep incline that would get him to the Meddlehart gates. "I can walk from here."

The driver raised an eyebrow, studying Grayson's dress shoes, suit jacket, and tie. "Are you sure?"

Grayson ignored the doubt on the man's face—he was already moving to the trunk to retrieve his luggage.

The driver rushed around the limo. "Do you want me to—"

"No," Grayson said, probably too quickly. "Thank you. I've got it, really."

He just wanted to see his friends. Everything would be better once he saw his friends.

Grayson fished in his pockets for cash, handed the driver a tip without looking at the bills, and began his trek up the incline to the Meddlehart entrance gates.

As he hiked, blisters forming on his heels from his dress shoes, a surge of anger pulsed to the surface—anger at his dad, for insisting on putting him in a stupid, flashy car for no reason other than optics. A car that wasn't remotely cut out for steep, winding mountain passes.

Well, the joke was on him—now no one would see Grayson arrive in a limousine. Instead, he'd show up covered in dirt and smelling like he ran a marathon.

He closed his eyes for a moment. *Breathe.* The mountain air was cooler and cleaner than it was in LA, and even though he'd have plenty of time to savor it, he felt like this was a good opportunity to breathe. Just breathe and maybe the raging sea of emotion in his chest would subside.

That's what his therapist was always saying—breathe, breathe, *breathe*. And Grayson did. He'd tried breathing a hundred different ways with no real results.

But what did his therapist know, anyway? Not a lot, even after all these years. Grayson had made sure of that—he said just enough to satisfy her without really admitting anything major.

The only reason he had a therapist was because ages ago school officials had recommended he talk to someone about his mother's overdose, and God knows Damon Hendricks wouldn't say no to getting his son therapy when he had all the money in the world to pay for it. It would make him look bad if he didn't get Grayson the help he needed.

All his therapist had ever been able to focus on was the loss of his mother, and Grayson just went along with it, because it was the easiest thing to do. *Yes, my mom dying when I was little is the source of all my problems.* That's what everyone wanted to hear—the public wanted to know what he remembered about his mother before her final overdose, what really happened that day, what he'd seen.

As if it was any of their business.

But the world felt entitled to it, because they felt like they knew her. They'd watched her in all their favorite movies. It was the same with his dad. *Rachel Hill. Damon Hendricks.* Star-crossed lovers, a modern tragedy.

If only they knew.

Grayson focused his energy on the hike, each step bringing him closer to the people who *did* know him.

To the friend who would need his support today, as they memorialized his older brother.

And to the girl he'd missed all summer.

Grayson didn't bother dropping his bags off at Shepherd House when he arrived on campus, sweaty and breathless, leather shoes caked in mud. He made a beeline to the courtyard. It wasn't a place he visited often, but it was just as serene as he remembered, surrounded by expertly trimmed hedges and willow trees. Grayson abandoned his luggage at the courtyard entrance and stepped into the aisle to find his seat.

The rest of the staff and student body were already seated, and Headmaster Averell was speaking. Everyone was dressed in black, an unfamiliar sight compared to the usual sea of navy Meddlehart uniforms.

"Honoring Lawson Heyward's memory is a privilege we . . ." Averell hesitated for a fraction of a moment when he saw Grayson, long enough for the crowd to turn and train their eyes on the latecomer.

Grayson's neck flushed with warmth, another spark of frustration lighting in his chest as he scanned the crowd for his friends, or an empty seat, *anywhere* for him to—

And then he saw her, giving him a little wave.

Fallon. She was there in the first row, next to Margot, Carter, and Sutter. The row had clearly been reserved for the Heyward family, but his friends were there, with an empty seat saved for him.

Grayson's throat tightened at the sight, because he remembered his life before this place. He remembered when he had no one who would bother to do a thing like save him a seat, no one there for reasons other than his famous parents, nowhere that was meant for him.

But looking at his friends now, those old hurts melted away.

It almost felt as though he'd always had this, like he'd always been meant for Meddlehart.

Quickly, Grayson walked down the aisle toward the front row. He made it halfway before his foot caught on something hard. He pitched forward, only just catching himself before he hit the ground, and turned to see what had tripped him.

Alex Harker stared back at him, a satisfied gleam in his gray-blue eyes, as he pulled his foot back from where he'd stuck it into Grayson's path.

Grayson straightened, his fists already clenching, as white-hot anger boiled in his bloodstream. Alex was one of his football teammates, and he'd never liked Grayson. Probably because Grayson had taken the last varsity spot on the team when he was only a sophomore—leaving Alex to ride the bench for another year—and then went on to become quarterback this year.

Grayson wanted to give Alex a piece of his mind right then, for all to see . . . but he couldn't—*wouldn't*—do that. Today was too important to Sutter, and Alex was not worth the trouble.

Ignoring the stares of those around him, Grayson strode forward and took his seat beside Fallon. His heart practically leaped out of his chest when she reached for his hand and squeezed it.

"You made it," she whispered. Her voice was so low, he could barely hear. "I was worried."

For a moment he was confused—what was there to worry about? Then he saw the remnants of fear fading from her eyes, and he remembered.

Her parents. The day she'd told him about, when she'd waited and waited for them, and they never came home.

He and Fallon had become that for each other—confidants of sorts. She was the kind of friend he'd never been lucky enough to have until Meddlehart. The fact that he wanted it to be more was one of the handful of things he kept close to his chest.

But Grayson wondered if she saw through it, the way she saw through so many other things about him.

He squeezed her hand back. "I'm here now." *I'm home*, he thought.

God, he'd missed her. Grayson would never admit it to anyone—it was hard enough to even admit it to himself—but she was the one he was most excited to see. That was true every day, every time he woke up and knew he would see her at breakfast or in class. But it was especially true today.

Too soon, she let go and tucked a strand of hair behind her ear. Looking at her now, the afternoon sunlight catching hints of gold in her light-brown locks, Grayson wasn't sure if she'd ever been more beautiful.

". . . Lawson left a meaningful legacy on our campus thanks to his natural leadership, dedication to academics, and admirable conduct," Headmaster Averell went on. "We are incredibly proud of the example he set for all Meddlehart students, and it is our honor to unveil his memorial plaque, which will remain here in the Boone Thatcher Courtyard. Now, I would like to invite the Heyward family to join me at the front for the reveal."

Grayson glanced down the aisle at Sutter, whose jaw ticked with tension, eyes stony. It was clear as day—he did *not* want to be part of this. He remained frozen in his seat for several moments after his parents stood, unmoving until his father discreetly nudged his shoulder.

"Get up," he whispered, his voice practically a hiss.

Sutter stood, face pale, and followed his parents to the podium, his every movement stiff with reluctance. Grayson's chest tightened when he saw Sutter's hands trembling as he brushed his hair out of his eyes. Suddenly, he wondered whose idea it was to do this—to force his friend to stand in front of the entire school and put his anguish on display.

Just then, Sutter's father stepped in front of Headmaster Averell at the podium, adjusting the microphone to his height. "I'd like to say a few words."

A hush fell over the crowd as they waited with bated breath to hear Mr. Heyward speak. The quiet was only interrupted by the clicking of cameras at the back of the courtyard, where members of the press greedily documented every detail of the memorial.

"My name is Sam Heyward . . . I'm Lawson's father. Our family would like to thank everyone for being here today," Mr. Heyward said. "Your presence is the ultimate show of support for our Lawson, and he would be so happy to see all of you gathered in this courtyard."

Grayson couldn't help but notice the way Sutter was staring daggers at his father. No one else seemed to notice, though—teachers dabbed tissues at the corners of their eyes, and Headmaster Averell nodded solemnly, sniffling himself. Grayson glanced over his shoulder at the news cameras, which were eating it all up.

Mr. Heyward stepped back, allowing Headmaster Averell to do the honors. The headmaster pulled away the black sheet, revealing an intricate wreath made of stone. At the center of the wreath was an etching of Lawson's face.

The crowd immediately reacted with a collective gasp. Sutter's mom choked back a sob. His father put a hand on her shoulder, nodding in approval of the plaque. Suddenly everyone was applauding, students and teachers alike.

The applause turned to surprised murmurs, though, when

Sutter shook his head and said, just loud enough for everyone to hear, "Total bullshit."

Grayson's stomach knotted. *Oh, no.*

Without another word, Sutter stormed down the aisle and out of the courtyard. His cheeks were red, eyes ablaze. His face was a mask of fury meant to hide the kind of heartache you could only see if you knew what it looked like in the mirror.

"Sutter," Fallon murmured. She had stood up when he passed by. Grayson risked a glance at Sutter's parents, who looked stunned. The cameras were clicking wildly now, almost frenzied.

Margot stood, too. "Where's he going?"

Carter shook his head. "I don't know, but we're going, too."

The four of them didn't hesitate. Without sparing a thought for the crowd turning their heads to stare, they shoved out into the aisle and bolted from the courtyard, toward the student houses, to find their friend.

FOUR

Sutter

Sutter's friends caught up with him right as he was charging up the front steps to Shepherd House. He'd just rested his palms on the deep-blue doors when a hand landed on his shoulder.

"Hey, man," Carter said. "Wait up!"

Sutter shrugged his hand off. "I'm fine."

"We know you're not," Margot said breathlessly. She was panting as she came to a stop at the bottom of the steps. Fallon and Grayson jogged up behind her.

Sutter ground his teeth. He was minutes away from falling apart, his anger the only thing holding him together, and he didn't want anyone—not even his friends—to see that. He tried to focus every ounce of emotion down to a point, but his chest heaved with each breath, like his heart couldn't keep up with the pain.

"This was just . . . the most *colossal* waste of time in the world!" he bit out. He jabbed a finger in the direction of the courtyard. "All those people memorializing someone whose body they *never even found*."

"It's all right, man," Carter murmured.

"It's not," Sutter said. He couldn't meet any of their eyes. He hoped to God they couldn't see that he was shaking. "It won't be okay until I find my brother and tear that memorial down. You can't memorialize someone who isn't dead."

Sutter's friends didn't speak. They just stared at him in silent understanding, concern etched into their faces. Sutter recognized the worry in their eyes, and he knew they were probably thinking about last year—about how he lost himself looking for Lawson, lost his shit and got sent home like he was—

He squeezed his eyes shut for a moment, willing that line of thinking to stop. Slowly, he shook his head.

"It's all fake," he growled under his breath. "The memorial, everyone squeezing out tears for the cameras, putting on a show . . . if any of them truly cared about Lawson, they would be *searching* for him. Because he *is* still out there, you know?"

Margot nodded, and the others murmured their assent. "We know."

And Sutter knew they did. But what they *didn't* know was how amazing Lawson was. They didn't know Lawson like Sutter did—they never had the chance. But knowing Lawson the way Sutter did made the entire ceremony even more of an injustice.

Sutter's first memories were made with Lawson. He remembered toddling after his brother at the playground across the street from their house while their mother watched from a nearby bench. Lawson had showed him how to pump his legs on the swing so he could go higher, higher, higher.

When Lawson got a little bit older, he would walk Sutter to the park on his own. Along the way, he would make up funny acrostics and recite them to Sutter with the goal of making him laugh. He'd try to incorporate strange words he'd learned from the books he read at school, like *uvula* and *catawampus*, and Sutter usually wound up laughing until his stomach hurt, even though he didn't know what half the words meant. Sutter would beg for another poem until they got to the park and raced to the swing set, acrostics momentarily forgotten.

For Sutter's entire childhood, Lawson was the one who was always around. When their dad was off drinking with his buddies on weeknights and missed Sutter's T-ball games, Lawson was the one cheering from behind the fence. When Sutter fell and broke his arm at the skate park, Lawson was the one who ran for help. When the family dog died, Lawson was the one who consoled Sutter. When Sutter had a nightmare and couldn't calm down, Lawson would give him a piece of candy from his secret stash—the one he kept hidden behind the air vent in his room, the one only the two of them knew about.

And these memories may not have aligned with Sutter's final memory of his older brother—when he was angry for no reason at all, when he shoved Sutter out of his way and disappeared into the dark, letting the rainstorm wipe him off the face of the earth. But that didn't matter to Sutter, because he knew in his bones that Lawson wasn't himself that night.

No . . . something was *wrong*.

Suddenly, Sutter's parents came bounding up the path—his mother tearful, his father fuming.

"Sutter!" Mom cried. "Sutter, dear, please—"

"Got anything to say to your parents, champ?" Dad called out as they neared.

Carter cleared his throat. "Hey, let's all give Sutter a minute with his parents, all right?" He nudged Sutter with his elbow as they trickled past him. "We'll wait for you upstairs."

"What exactly was that?" Sutter's father snapped. He was close enough that Sutter could smell the liquor on his breath.

"Storming off, leaving your mother and me to take the family photo without you? Quite the performance. You *humiliated* us!"

Sutter sighed. All he wanted now was for his parents to leave, and the only way to accomplish that would be to act agreeable and defuse the situation.

"I'm sorry," he said. "Today was just . . . a lot."

His mother stepped forward. "See, Sam? This has been hard enough. Let's *drop* it, for heaven's sake."

Slowly, his father's puffed-out chest lowered, and he adjusted one of the buttons on his jacket. "I understand. It's a hard thing to accept. But we wouldn't have wanted you to leave the ceremony without saying goodbye. We won't see you for weeks after today."

Sutter held back a snort. Dad's words said *We miss you when you're away,* but his voice lacked inflection. It almost sounded like a flight attendant's safety speech before takeoff. *Please turn all electronic devices to airplane mode, remember I love you, and we'll see you at Thanksgiving.*

"I know," he replied instead, mirroring his father's flat tone. "I'm sorry."

That seemed to be satisfactory for them. His mother brushed a piece of lint off his sleeve.

"Sutter, remember what we've talked about," she said, peeking over her large, round sunglasses. "You go to class, and you return to Shepherd House well before curfew every night, okay? Don't pull any more funny business with your professors, understand?"

"Yes, Mom," Sutter grumbled, even though he knew he would consciously break both of those rules, and his mother would never know. It was exhausting, the way she'd smothered him since Lawson disappeared. She acted like Meddlehart might swallow him whole or something. Little did she know Sutter felt safer at this school than anywhere else.

"Make sure if you take the bus into town on the weekends that you call me first," she added. "I don't want you going anywhere without someone knowing. That way—"

"That way I won't disappear off the face of the earth and leave you with no one to pester," Sutter snapped before he could think better of it. His cheeks heated instantly, and his mother's jaw dropped.

"Sutter Thomas Heyward," Dad barked, but Mom laid a hand on his arm, and he quieted.

"I'm sorry," Sutter muttered. "I shouldn't have said that . . . it's just . . . you guys need to trust me a little bit, all right? I'm not Lawson, and I'm not going anywhere. I can take care of myself."

Mom's lips were pursed again, but she nodded. "I know, honey." She gave him a stiff, quick hug and stalked away, her bleached hair bobbing with each step.

Dad gave Sutter a one-armed hug around his shoulder. Sutter carefully hugged him back, his hand resting near his father's jacket pocket.

"You say you're not like Lawson, eh, champ?" Dad murmured in Sutter's ear. "Best keep it that way."

Sutter wasn't sure what his father meant, but in that moment, he didn't care. He extricated himself from his father's grasp and waved as his father strutted down the path.

In a fluid motion, Sutter slipped his father's silver flask into his own pocket and stepped through the doors of Shepherd House.

FIVE

Fallon

The boys' dorm was a mess.

Carter led them to room 211 while Sutter said goodbye to his parents. Grayson lugged his belongings up the stairs, resisting help no matter how many times his friends offered.

"I've got it," he insisted as he carried his suitcase up one step at a time, precariously balancing his bag on his shoulder. Fallon couldn't help but notice a small bead of sweat dripping from his dark, tousled hair.

"You don't have to refuse our help just to prove your strength," Margot told him, which earned her a glare. She held her hands up in mock innocence. Fallon couldn't help but giggle.

That's when she noticed the dirt Grayson left behind with each footstep. "Gray, where did all this mud come from?"

Grayson sighed heavily. "That's a story for another day."

When Carter opened the door, what they found was a sea of half-unpacked boxes, two unmade beds, and a disconnected TV surrounded by a slew of cords and loose plugs.

Fallon said a silent prayer of thanks that her roommate was someone as neat and organized as Margot.

Margot gasped. "What have you been doing the past two days? I thought you said you unpacked!"

"I *did*," Carter said, indignant. Then he gestured to what was supposed to be a bookshelf, but instead was stocked with cookware and utensils. It was the only part of the room that was even remotely assembled. "See?"

Carter was a budding chef, and he would do anything to keep his culinary skills sharp, including cooking in his dorm.

His endless quest to perfect his recipes had gotten them all into trouble more than once. Fallon remembered the day sophomore year where the five of them had devised a plan to break into the dining hall pantry because Carter needed vanilla bean to make his famed crème brûlée—*real* vanilla bean, not the extract. After determining there was no way they'd be able to get in through the pantry door, Sutter decided that hoisting Grayson—the most athletic member of the group—through the window was the best course of action.

That ended with Grayson getting stuck in the window and accidentally kicking Fallon in the face. She wound up in the infirmary with a bruised nose—nothing major—and the rest of her friends earned themselves two weeks of detention.

Despite the kick being accidental, Grayson had felt so guilty, he could hardly look at Fallon until she begged him to forgive himself. She'd missed history class while Nurse Fran tended to her nose, and she returned to find that Grayson had taken class notes for her, even though he didn't bother to take notes for himself half the time. Fallon remembered how surprised she'd been—how the boy with the steely exterior could be so tender with her.

She watched him now as he picked his way through the

room, dropping his luggage onto one of the unmade mattresses. "So did you bring any clothes?" he asked Carter. He picked up a ladle. "Or just . . . spoons?"

"In what world is that a spoon?" Carter asked, his voice uncharacteristically stern. He snatched it back from Grayson and said, "Don't touch my ladles."

"It's a glorified spoon," Grayson muttered under his breath.

"You're like Fallon with her books, Carter," Margot said. "She brought, like, seven boxes of books and only one duffel bag of necessities!"

Fallon shrugged. "Books are *entirely* necessary to my survival. And besides, half the time we wear uniforms here! It's not like I need a lot of clothes."

Margot looked momentarily horrified by this statement but shook it off quickly. "That's why I bring plenty you can borrow. Carter, however . . . this amount of culinary equipment is borderline ridiculous." She picked up a skillet off the shelf and inspected it. "Also, weren't you banned from cooking in your dorm after setting off the fire alarms last year?"

Carter took the skillet back, handling it like a precious artifact, and placed it delicately on the shelf. "I don't know what you're talking about."

The door opened then and Sutter stepped into the room. For a moment, they all went quiet. Fallon's breath caught, and she studied Sutter's face. His eyes locked on hers.

Margot broke the silence. "Everything okay?"

Sutter managed an unconvincing smile. "It is now."

Before anyone could say another word, Carter put an arm around Sutter's shoulders. "You're right, my friend, because we are *back*. It's going to be one hell of a year!"

They grinned, a collective sigh of relief moving through the group. With that, Carter started trying to connect the TV cables, pulling Grayson in to help him and proposing ideas for how they'd spend the night—video game tournament, movie marathon . . . the possibilities were endless.

And while Sutter nodded along to each idea as though they all sounded fine, Fallon saw the shadows lingering behind his eyes. She knew he wasn't all right—not by a long shot.

Fallon and her friends spent the evening doing whatever they could to make Sutter feel better.

They played cards in the common room. They visited the snack bar in the dining hall and were pleased to find fresh, melty chocolate chip cookies and milk awaiting them. They had a video game tournament, in which Margot won several rounds of *Fortnite* before the boys gave up trying to beat her and resorted to watching a new Netflix comedy.

One minute, Fallon was curled up on top of Carter's new beanbag, watching the first ten minutes of the film. The next, she was opening her bleary eyes and peering around the dim room, wondering when it had gotten so quiet.

The bright, warm movie had cast a comforting glow over the room, and it must have lulled them all to sleep. Margot was asleep on the floor. Grayson was bundled in a comforter at the foot of his bed, and Carter was snoring.

The space Sutter had occupied was empty.

Fallon stood, shaking off her sleepiness, and crept to the door. The hallway was empty and quiet—no sign of Sutter.

Before she could surrender to the panic rising in her chest, she reminded herself that she knew Sutter. She knew exactly where he'd gone, tonight of all nights.

Fallon slipped her shoes on, careful not to wake the others. She tiptoed out of the room and toward the fire escape window at the end of the hallway, which she silently prayed Sutter had left open a smidge. They weren't the easiest to open, despite being meant for escape—the locks were old and tight, and the windows themselves were heavy.

Fallon and her friends knew better than to use the fire escape often. It was the easiest way to sneak out past curfew, but it wasn't foolproof. A prefect could easily hear feet clanging on the metal stairs or see you through one of the windows.

They'd never been caught, though. They were careful. And as much as Fallon hated taking risks like this, hated bending the rules in any scenario, she didn't like the idea of Sutter crossing campus alone right now. Not after the day they'd had.

Besides, Sutter and the others brought out a rebellious side in her. She was only just now getting used to it, after two years of friendship. She was still the voice of reason in their group, but lately that voice had been a bit . . . quieter.

She found the window left slightly ajar. *Bingo.* As quietly as she could, she shoved it open, slipped out into the night, and descended the ladder.

The courtyard wasn't far, and when she made it there, she saw Sutter approaching from the opposite direction. He had a baseball bat resting on his shoulder, and a silver flask clutched in his other hand glinted in the moonlight. Fallon was pretty sure she'd seen it peeking out of Mr. Heyward's pocket at the ceremony.

Sutter stopped short when he saw her, swaying a little on his feet.

"Hey, sleepyhead," he mumbled.

"Hey, you," she said, her heart skipping a beat.

"That movie sucked." His words were runny, leaning into each other.

Fallon managed a smile. "So I didn't miss much?"

He shook his head. "Nope."

She kicked at a rock on the ground. "Didn't know you played baseball."

He glanced at the bat in his hand. "Oh, yeah, well . . . I don't."

"Did you take that from the Ace?" He'd come from the direction of the school sports complex—it wasn't hard for Fallon to put two and two together.

He lowered the bat and let the tip of it touch the ground. "Maybe."

"What are you going to do with it?"

He sighed, turning to the stone wreath with the etching of his older brother at its center. Lawson's smiling face looked so much like Sutter's. Lawson's face was rounder than his brother's narrower features. His hair was a little lighter, closer to blond than to Sutter's brown, stick-straight hair. But Sutter kept it neatly combed, a lot like Lawson had, and that alone made them look almost exactly alike.

There were dozens of flowers and teddy bears, small gifts people had placed around the plaque. Sutter stared at them with disgust.

"I'm gonna smash this stupid fucking plaque until it's dust," he said.

"Sutter," Fallon murmured. She stepped toward him, and only then could she see the tremble in his hands, the glisten in his bloodshot eyes. He didn't look so angry anymore. He just looked heartbroken.

Fallon knew good and well where Sutter's head was, where his heart was. He fully believed his brother was alive. He always said things like *Lawson's a fighter* and *Lawson knows how to take care of himself*. He looked at his older brother the way a little kid might look at a superhero, even after all this time.

Even though Lawson had shoved Sutter to the floor and left him there, confused and hurt.

Sutter didn't talk about that night much unless he was tracking down clues, searching for answers, laying out evidence. That was the only reason why Fallon knew about the brothers' interaction that night before Lawson left campus for the last time. If Sutter hadn't actively searched for Lawson and tried to determine where he disappeared to, she wasn't sure Sutter would've ever admitted how callously his brother had acted, how coldly. Sutter didn't want to admit that hurt to anyone—maybe not even to himself.

But Fallon knew better. Beneath Sutter's simmering rage was an untamed grief dealing damage she could only imagine. She knew because while she'd endured her own losses, she couldn't fathom not knowing what had happened to her parents, not knowing where they'd gone.

"Fallon," Sutter said, his voice wavering. "I have to do something. If they're putting memorials up for him, that means they'll . . ."

He trailed off, but Fallon knew what he would have said.

Putting memorials up meant people were moving on. People were forgetting and needed a way to keep Lawson's memory alive. People thought he was dead.

"I know," she said. She was right in front of him now. Slowly, she reached for the bat, gripped it with her fingers, and gently pulled it from his hand. Sutter let go, shoulders wilting. The flask fell to the ground with a hollow *thunk*.

"He's not dead," he murmured. His eyes overflowed.

"I know," she whispered again.

She put her hands behind his neck, pulled him close. His head rested heavily on her shoulder, and his chest shuddered against hers. His hands moved up to hold her back, so she hugged him tighter. The pressure of his fingertips sent shivers dancing across her skin.

Crickets chirped and sang around them. The starry night was like a cocoon holding them together, tucked away from the rest of the world. Only for a moment did Fallon wonder how many times she'd longed to hold him—but not like this, not when he was in so much pain. She couldn't wish this grief upon anyone, especially not him.

Gently, she pulled back and cupped his face in her hands.

"Look at me, Sutter," she whispered. "You're going to figure this out, one way or another, and we'll all be with you. I'll be right there the whole time. I promise."

He looked back at her, tears streaming down his cheeks. But there was something different in his gaze now, something new.

It looked a lot like longing. Like desire.

Then he was leaning in, and Fallon's heart stuttered in her chest—what was he doing? But she couldn't move, wouldn't move, because this . . . with him . . .

His lips pressed against hers. Soft, warm, and so gentle. He tasted like the spice of the liquor he'd been drinking. She kissed him back, and her heart flipped in her chest. Her entire body ached for him, yearned for him.

Sutter. Sutter. Sutter.

He kissed her again, and again. His fingertips grazed her back, climbing toward her hair, and then—

She remembered where she was, what was happening.

Sutter was in pieces right now. He was completely vulnerable, and while she wanted nothing more than to let him keep kissing her, to let his hands travel across her body, to let this moment last as long as it possibly could . . . it wouldn't be right for it to be *this* moment, of all moments. It wouldn't be fair to either of them.

"Wait," Fallon whispered, pulling away.

Sutter's face fell. "What . . . ?"

"You're upset, Sutter," she said. Her voice shook, nervousness shooting through every inch of her body. "You've been drinking . . . I . . . wouldn't feel right if . . ."

Realization dawned on his face, and Fallon's stomach dropped, because that look—it wasn't the one she wanted to see.

It was embarrassment. It was doubt and confusion.

It was regret.

"I'm an idiot," he said. "I'm an *idiot* . . . I'm so sorry, Fallon, I shouldn't have—"

"No," Fallon said quickly. "Sutter, no, I wanted to—"

"We can forget about it," he murmured, his words layering over hers before she could finish. "Really, I'm . . . so sorry. I mean . . . we're friends . . . you're my best friend. I wouldn't . . . I'm *so* sorry."

Fallon's heart sank as she realized what he was saying. *Friends.* That's what they were. That's what they should be, what they *had* to be.

That's what Sutter really wanted. This moment never should have happened.

Fallon nodded numbly, turning her head so she didn't have

to meet his eyes. "It's okay," she promised, her voice nearly a whisper. "You're right, let's forget about it. We should get back before a prefect notices we're gone."

He stared at her for a moment, his eyes still glistening, but it looked like all the life—the anger, sadness, everything—had left them.

"Yeah, okay . . . okay." Sutter glanced at the baseball bat now lying on the ground. "I should take that back to the Ace, or I'll have the wrath of Coach Hamilton to deal with." He tried to laugh, but it was a broken sound. He took a few steps and grasped the bat with one hand, but then he froze, his eyes locked on the memorial plaque.

Fallon frowned. "Sutter?"

"What's that?" he asked. He dropped the bat again, and it rolled at his feet. He walked toward the plaque surrounded by gifts and reached behind it. When he turned to face Fallon, he held a small parcel wrapped in brown paper. She could barely make out the wax seal holding the wrapping in place.

"Maybe we should just leave it there," Fallon said hesitantly. "It might not—"

But the words died in her throat when Sutter stepped closer and turned over the tag attached to the parcel to reveal the words there, written in block letters.

For: Sutter Heyward

SIX

Grayson

"Guys, wake up."

A flash of light dragged Grayson from sleep. Confusion flooded his brain as he took in the sight of his dorm, now lit by Sutter's desk lamp. Both Sutter and Fallon stood by the door, like they'd just come in.

Grayson noticed then that Fallon was shivering. She looked . . . rattled.

"What the hell, Sutter?" Carter groaned. "It's the middle of the night! Turn that light off!"

"That was extremely inconsiderate," Margot mumbled, pushing herself upright.

Grayson got out of bed and grabbed the jacket he'd been wearing earlier. He put it around Fallon's shoulders, and she looked up at him.

"You look like you're freezing," he murmured. "What's wrong?"

For a moment, she just shook her head. "Sutter—"

"We found something," Sutter cut in. He sounded tense, urgent. Then Grayson noticed the package in his hands—a small, wrapped box. "Someone left this for me at Lawson's memorial."

That caught their attention. Carter and Margot both stood, and the four of them gathered around Sutter to see what he was holding. Grayson reached out, and Sutter passed the box along so he could see it. Though not heavy, it was weightier than it looked like it would be. There was a wax seal pressed over the folds of the wrapping, but the pattern in the seal looked smudged—Grayson could just make out a coiled shape, almost like . . .

"A snake?" he asked, confused. Then he studied the tag. "It doesn't say who it's from."

"Wait, what were you doing in the courtyard this late?" Margot asked. "You were both down there—you and Fallon?"

The two of them went still, like deer caught in the headlights. Something about it made Grayson's chest sink, and his cheeks went hot. He'd seen the way Fallon and Sutter looked at each other sometimes, and it had always made him wonder . . . was there something between them no one else knew about?

"I, um," Fallon stammered. "I woke up and he was gone. I just went to look for him, that's all."

Margot had a questioning gleam in her eye that Grayson didn't miss. But she let it go, and Carter grinned, his momentary anger at being woken up forgotten.

"What are you waiting for?" he asked. He nudged Sutter's arm. "Open it!"

Sutter hesitated for a moment, but then he nodded. Slowly, he pushed one finger beneath the wax seal and lifted it. He peeled the paper away to reveal a white box. When he lifted the lid, the world seemed to slow to a stop.

"Holy shit," Carter murmured.

There was a cell phone inside. It was clearly used—the plastic case was dirty, scuffed and scratched all over. Sutter lifted it from the box with trembling hands, revealing a cracked screen. On the outside was a sticker—the Meddlehart crest, complete with the outline of a dragon surrounded by tangled, leafy vines. And beneath the crest were the words *Class of 2025.*

"This is Lawson's phone," Sutter said, a bit breathlessly. He tried to turn it on, but nothing happened.

"You're joking," Margot murmured. "I thought no one ever found his phone!"

"They didn't," Sutter said. He was frantic now, searching through the moving boxes in a panic. "The police were unable to track it after he went missing—they said its last known location was Meddlehart's campus, but after that it must've been wiped. They're not even sure if it was with Lawson when he disappeared. But it definitely wasn't in his dorm—all his things got shipped back to our parents, and it *wasn't there*." He opened his desk drawers, which were still empty, and then moved on to his backpack. "I need a charger!"

"Wait, Sutter," Fallon said. "This counts as evidence, doesn't it? Shouldn't we take it to the police?"

"What, so they can keep doing nothing like they've done this entire time?" he cried. "Not a *chance*."

"Here," Carter said. He pulled his charger out of the outlet by his bed. "Use mine."

Sutter's hands shook as he plugged his brother's phone into the charger and slumped into his desk chair. With bated breath, they all watched as the screen lit with the dimmest glow and the battery began to charge. It seemed to take ages, and while they waited, Grayson glanced at Fallon. She looked like she was about to crawl out of her skin.

He wanted so badly to talk to her, to tell her everything was going to be all right. But even he wasn't sure what this meant.

Who would have left Lawson's phone for Sutter to find? And how had someone gotten it in the first place? And . . . why now, after Lawson had been missing all this time?

Finally, the screen lit up. The lock screen was blank. When Sutter tried to open the phone, Grayson expected it to request a passcode, but it didn't. There were no apps, no cellular connection, no SIM card, nothing. The phone had been completely wiped.

Except for the Photos app.

Shakily, Sutter tapped it, and a video began to play.

It took Grayson several moments to make out what they were seeing. At first, it was just darkness, punctuated by movement and wobbly shapes. The audio was full of rustling leaves and chirping insects, the midnight sounds of the wilderness. Then a beam of light flashed across the space—a flashlight cast over dozens of trees. The camera turned, and Lawson's face filled the screen.

Grayson saw Sutter startle at the sight of his brother. Though the footage was dim, it was clearly him. His arm was extended—he was filming himself—and just behind him, the silhouette of Drexel House stood high, staring down at him like a giant.

Margot gasped. "Oh my God."

Carter's eyes were wide and his jaw hung open. "Was this *that* night?"

Sutter shook his head. "No," he croaked. "He's not wearing his letterman jacket. And it's not raining."

Grayson's breath hitched. Being friends with Sutter, he'd met Lawson a handful of times during their freshman year at Meddlehart. Grayson hadn't known him very well—he didn't think the others had, either, except Carter—but hearing his voice, seeing his face . . . it brought the memories flooding back.

And Sutter was right—this footage wasn't filmed the night he disappeared, but that didn't answer the question on Grayson's mind: What was Lawson doing out in the woods in the middle of the night?

In the video, Lawson moved forward, the camera trained on his face.

"This is Lawson Heyward," he said. "It's just past midnight on April third, 2025 . . . and maybe it's stupid for me to be recording this, but if I don't, I might forget where I buried this thing."

Margot jolted. "What's he burying?"

"Not only that," Lawson went on, "but if I don't get to come back one day and dig it up myself . . . I need to know it's not lost forever. Time capsules are kind of useless if they get lost."

Margot sighed in relief at the confirmation of what Lawson was burying, but his words sent a chill down Grayson's spine. *If I don't get to come back one day and dig it up myself . . .*

The way he said it almost sounded like he knew he wouldn't.

Suddenly, the camera stopped moving as Lawson set it down and took several steps back. He stood in a small clearing near a ledge of rock jutting out of the earth. He had a shovel in his hands, and he began to dig.

"Sutter," Lawson said. "Listen to me."

The very air in the room seemed to evaporate. Grayson looked at Sutter. His friend's chest was rising and falling rapidly, sweat beading on his forehead.

"You'd better not be watching this," he said as he shoveled dirt. "But if you are . . . you're probably mad as hell at me. And I get it. But there's something you need to know."

Grayson pretended not to notice the tear that dropped down Sutter's cheek.

"If anyone ever asks you how Franklin Thatcher died," Lawson said, "tell them he died by the fangs of greed."

Grayson couldn't help but wrinkle his nose. That name—Franklin Thatcher—tickled at the back of his mind. It was familiar. What the hell was Lawson talking about?

He looked down at Sutter, and a sour feeling wormed itself into his chest. Then he glanced around at his friends and saw their emotions plain as day in Carter's tense jaw, Margot's distant eyes, the worried purse of Fallon's lips.

This discovery could send Sutter into a tailspin, just like sophomore year, and they all knew it. Grayson refocused on the video, which was nearing its final moments.

Lawson stopped digging. Carefully, he lowered something barely larger than a shoebox into the hole he'd dug. He smoothed the dirt back over it, packing it in with his hands. He reached for the camera once more.

"And then," he said, "I want you to tell them to fuck off."

The screen dimmed . . . but the video didn't stop.

Maybe Lawson thought he'd stopped the recording, but he hadn't. The audio crackled with the rustling sounds of Lawson's movements. As he hiked back down the mountain, he was muttering to himself, words Grayson could barely make out . . .

"It'll all be okay once I find it."

Then it was truly over. The footage froze on a frame of Lawson's face cast in shadow, taken from below, his eyes searching the night before him.

Sutter jumped up from the desk chair. "Fuck, is that it?" he asked, voice gravelly. He tried scrolling, looking for more, but there was nothing. With a grunt, he threw the phone across the room, and Grayson startled. It clattered against the wall and landed on the floor.

"Sutter," Fallon murmured.

Sutter didn't respond. He started grabbing things—his backpack, shoes, phone.

"What are you doing?" Carter asked.

"I'm going to find it," Sutter said.

"Sutter," Fallon said again, louder now.

"It's dark out, man," Grayson spoke up. "We'll get—"

"I'm going now," Sutter said, pulling his shoes on.

"You can't," Margot said. "You're not going alone, first of all, but we don't even have a *shovel*, Sutter. Where are we going to get one?"

"The greenhouse," Sutter said, like it was simple.

"The greenhouse is locked up every night," Fallon said.

Sutter ignored that, which didn't surprise Grayson—Sutter had never let a locked door stop him from doing anything before. He made for the door.

Carter jumped in front of him. "Sutter, hold on. Take a breath."

"Carter, move before I—"

"Sutter, *stop*."

Sutter stopped and stared at Carter, dumbfounded. Then he dropped everything, stumbled back to his desk chair and plunked down in it, burying his face in his hands. They all watched in stunned silence as Sutter pulled the top of his shirt over his eyes and wiped tears away with it. Fallon stood beside him and rested her hand on his back. He trembled slightly, and Grayson looked away.

After a long, painful minute, Sutter stood up, scrubbing one hand across his blotchy face.

"Sorry," he muttered.

"It's okay," Margot told him. Carter and Grayson both murmured their agreement. Fallon still stood behind him, chewing on her lower lip.

"I haven't heard his voice in a long time," he told them quietly.

"We know," Fallon whispered.

Another moment passed quietly, and then Sutter cleared his throat. "Tomorrow night, I'm going to see if that capsule is still there. You guys don't have to come with me."

Carter shook his head. "I'll go with you."

Margot stepped forward. "Me too."

Fallon just nodded, which didn't surprise Grayson. Of course she would go, no matter how big a rule follower she was. She'd go for Sutter.

Grayson wasn't letting them all go without him. "Count me in." Whether it was a good idea or not didn't matter. He'd be there to support Sutter. But if he was being one hundred percent honest, he wanted to see that time capsule, too.

For one more moment, they stood around their friend, a silent circle of support. Grayson wasn't sure what the others were thinking, but he had a feeling they had as many questions as he did. So many questions, he wasn't sure where to start.

But they wouldn't voice those questions tonight. For now, they'd let the quiet swallow them whole. They would stay there in the silence until Sutter was ready to crawl back out again, and then they would follow, because that's what they did.

Thank God, that's what they always did.

SEVEN

Fallon

After a nearly sleepless night, Fallon headed to the dining hall on the official first day of classes. She and Margot barely made it in time for breakfast after dragging themselves out of bed and navigating the maze of boxes and bags in their half-unpacked dorm room.

They'd been too tired to talk after leaving the boys' room—all they could do was stumble into bed with a mumbled "good night." Fallon hadn't told Margot any of what had transpired between her and Sutter that night, and part of her didn't want to. It was too humiliating to relive it herself, and to confess it to someone else? She wasn't sure if she'd ever be ready for that.

And she felt like the entire incident was a good sign she needed to let Sutter go. He didn't share her feelings, and he likely never would. But that truth was almost too much to bear right now.

They arrived at the high-ceilinged, warmly lit dining hall in a haze of exhaustion and joined the line of sleepy students to make their breakfast plates. Margot got the same thing she always did—two eggs, sunny-side up, and a blueberry bagel. That morning, Fallon chose a cinnamon roll. Tomorrow, she might choose something else, but it would probably also contain cinnamon.

The boys had heavy bags under their eyes, but they were at their usual table on time, and that was impressive enough to Fallon. Grayson had piled his plate high with scrambled eggs, sausage, and bacon, and was shoveling it in without really chewing.

"Please don't choke on that," Margot told him. "I'm begging you."

"Sorry," he said around a mouthful of food. "Protein. Football."

"Cholesterol," Carter added. Grayson punched his arm.

Just then, a group of younger girls walked up, eyes locked on Grayson.

"Hey, Grayson," one of them said, waving. "How was your summer?"

He managed a smile. "Oh, uh, it was all right. Yours?"

"Good," she answered, smirking. "I went swimming most days. We went to Hawaii, too. I've got the perfect tan now."

"Cool," Grayson said, and then the girls hurried off, chattering to each other. Fallon glanced at Grayson.

"Who were they?" she asked.

He shrugged. "I have no idea."

"They're probably just looking for a piece of that Hendricks fame and fortune," Carter said, nudging Grayson with a smirk.

Grayson laughed weakly. "Shut up," he muttered, shoving Carter back, but his face had fallen. Fallon eyed him for a minute but didn't say another word.

Across the table, Sutter was quiet. He wasn't even eating the French toast in front of him. Instead, he studied a wrinkled sheet of printer paper, brows furrowed.

"Whatcha got there, Sutter?" Margot asked.

"And what's the plan for tonight?" Carter asked, leaning forward and lowering his voice.

Sutter glanced up as if he'd only just realized he wasn't alone. "That's what I'm trying to figure out," he said. "As Margot astutely pointed out last night . . . we need a shovel. I can grab one from the greenhouse, and I'm trying to find an opening in my class schedule today when I'll be able to make that happen."

A light bulb went off in Fallon's head. "Botany is my first class today. I'll be in the greenhouse all morning."

Grayson's eyes flashed at her and he said, "Me too." Fallon smiled. Grayson nudged Sutter and said, "We'll take care of the shovel. You focus on figuring out where to dig."

"You'll have to watch out for Dr. Wilbur, though," Carter pointed out between bites of a buttered biscuit. "She'd probably skin you alive if she saw you stealing garden tools."

Margot groaned. "I have her for homeroom this year, and I heard she gives out homework. Who does that?" Then she brightened. "Wait, we haven't compared schedules yet, have we? Who else has Wilbur for homeroom?"

"I do, unfortunately," Grayson grumbled.

Margot patted his arm. "We're in this together."

Sutter brandished his class schedule triumphantly with the first hint of a smile Fallon had seen on him all morning. "I got Whittaker, thank God."

"What about Whittaker?" a voice said from behind them.

They turned, and there was Mr. Whittaker, strolling down the aisle between tables, his cane tapping lightly on the floor with each step. They all waved at him, and he smiled. "If it isn't my favorite students!" Then he lowered his voice. "I'd better be careful admitting that out loud."

Fallon couldn't help but smile. Mr. Whittaker was the history teacher at Meddlehart, and if they were truly his favorite students, the feeling was mutual.

"I was telling everyone I'm in your homeroom this year," Sutter said.

"I saw you on the roster," Whittaker confirmed. Then he patted Fallon's shoulder. "As well as Ms. Winthrop here!"

Sutter glanced at Fallon, then averted his gaze quickly. "Awesome."

Fallon's heart dropped. He could hardly look at her.

"But the rest of you don't need to worry, because you'll see me for history. And you'll all be on your best behavior, correct?"

They glanced at each other, no one willing to commit to such a thing.

Whittaker sighed. "I expect nothing less."

That's when Fallon spotted the tiny, crumpled leaf in Whittaker's wispy hair.

"Sir," she said, gesturing toward it. "You've, uh, got a leaf."

"Oh!" Whittaker reached up and pinched it between his fingers. "Thank you. I took a nature walk before breakfast."

"I figured," she said with a laugh. Whittaker took a lot of walks around campus, between almost every class and on every weekend. He blamed it on the fresh mountain air—*I can't get enough of it*, he always said.

"Well, I'd best be going. Be ready for a fun history class today," he told them. "We'll be starting off with the most interesting lesson of all . . . the history of our wonderful school! And of course, we'll have a special guest to provide some announcements."

They waved goodbye as Whittaker strolled off, and Margot frowned. "Well, now I feel salty. Having Whittaker for *two* of your classes? No fair." She turned to Carter. "Who's your homeroom teacher? You never said."

Carter glanced sideways at her. "To be honest, Margot, I haven't even looked at my schedule yet."

Margot gasped, and Grayson spluttered a laugh, nearly choking on his bacon.

"What is the matter with you?" Margot cried. "Classes start in less than an hour, and you have no idea where you're supposed to be? Hand it over!"

Carter fished around in his bag until he found his crumpled class schedule. As Margot unfolded it, Carter muttered a silent prayer of "Please be Whittaker, *please* be Whittaker . . ."

Margot smiled. "You're with me in Wilbur's class!"

"Shit!" Carter cried, prompting stares from surrounding tables.

A distant voice called out, "Language, Carter! I'm only warning you once!"

Frowning, Fallon turned around to see Scott Sterling, Carter's older brother, eyeballing their table. "Did your brother just scold you for using foul language?"

Carter groaned and dropped his head onto the table in despair.

"With everything going on, I forgot to tell you all. Something terrible has happened."

Fallon leaned forward, heart rate rising. Even Grayson and Sutter frowned, concerned.

"What's wrong?" Margot asked.

"My brother . . . he's a . . ." Carter squeezed his eyes shut, like whatever news he had to deliver was just too awful. "He's . . . a *prefect* this year."

Grayson snorted in response, and all the tension evaporated.

Fallon let out a relieved breath. "Carter, don't scare us like that!"

"Next time, please be *more* dramatic when you deliver such world-ending news," Margot said, rolling her eyes.

"You don't get it," Carter said, whispering across the table like Scott might hear him. "He's a *Shepherd House* prefect. Which means my life is over."

"Hey, maybe it won't be so bad," Sutter said. "Who knows—this might be an advantage for us."

"Only if he's too busy kissing the teachers' asses to hound us about curfew," Carter mumbled. "Which . . . wouldn't be shocking, now that I'm thinking about it."

Margot's eyes widened. "Warning, Carter—he's coming this way."

Not a moment later, Scott approached their table, prefect badge gleaming on his chest. Without preamble, his gaze on Carter, he said, "You're already pushing the boundaries. Don't make me issue you a demerit."

Carter gripped his fork tight. "Did we die?" he asked in a low voice. "Is this hell?"

Scott moved along to the next table, unfazed and looking quite satisfied with himself.

Just then, the dining hall speakers crackled, and the warm, familiar voice of Nurse Fran echoed in the spacious room.

"Students, the first classes of the year begin in just thirty minutes. We wanted to remind our Meddlehart veterans to be mindful of new students who may need help finding their way around campus . . ."

Sutter's expression turned serious. "All right, guys—the plan is to meet up at our dorm tonight after Grayson is done with football practice. We'll sneak out after curfew and find the time capsule then. I think that gives us the lowest risk of getting caught."

The group nodded, and Carter said, "You got it, boss."

With that, the five of them dispersed. Grayson matched Fallon's pace and said, "Ready to steal a shovel?"

The early-morning sunlight filtered through the greenhouse walls and cast a warm glow over Fallon that made her long for her bed. Fallon enjoyed school, but she wished more than anything she'd gotten more sleep before the first day. Blearily, she stared at the packet of seeds Dr. Wilbur had tossed on the table in front of her and Grayson.

Mustard.

Grayson sighed. "I was really hoping for the ketchup seed."

Fallon bit her lip, fighting a smile. "Grayson."

"Yes?" His grayish eyes were intent on hers.

"That was not your best joke."

He smirked, and Fallon felt something loosen in her chest. When Fallon had first met Grayson, she had no idea what he would come to mean to her. She remembered that day clearly—she and Margot at the start of freshman year, brand-new roommates walking together to homeroom in Parrish Hall. Fallon had just taken the greatest leap of her life—turning a new leaf after losing her parents, starting over at a boarding school far from home—and she was a jumble of nerves.

Fallon was relieved to be going to class with someone she'd already befriended, and she planned on sticking close to Margot . . . until their homeroom teacher had instructed them all to find a seat next to someone they hadn't met yet.

Fallon only had a moment to panic before a tall boy with dark hair, grayish eyes, and a square jaw pulled up a chair next to her and introduced himself as Grayson Hendricks. It was almost as if he'd known she was terrified, that her shyness was going to drag her under if someone didn't throw her a lifeline.

He asked her about her drawings and smiled when she showed him her art. He talked to her about how he liked football, how he'd come to Meddlehart Academy from California. It wasn't until later that she realized who he reminded her of, the features of his face so like those of his famous parents.

Through him, she was introduced to Sutter and Carter, the boys who lived in the dorm next to his. The five of them sat together in homeroom for the rest of the year, but eventually, it turned into more. They started sitting together in the dining hall. They'd pile into the stands at Grayson's football games to cheer him on, and Carter would practice his cooking for them on weekends. They'd have movie nights and crash on the floors of their dorms.

But her bond with Grayson felt particularly special to Fallon. That first day in homeroom, she had no idea she'd just met someone who'd become one of her best friends—someone she knew forward and backward, and who knew her, too. Someone she trusted wholeheartedly. Someone who made her feel safe in a world that had only ever wounded her.

Dr. Wilbur spoke, snapping her out of her reverie. "Among other assignments, you and your lab partner will have a semester-long project: growing and caring for a plant together," Dr. Wilbur explained in the brisk tone she was known for. "But the catch is this: You must grow the plant in your dorm room. This will require careful attention, and your grade will depend on the condition of your plant by Christmas . . . plus a fifteen-page paper and a brief presentation of your findings."

A low chorus of groans rumbled through the greenhouse,

and Dr. Wilbur threw the class a glare Fallon feared might turn them all to stone. The groans ceased.

"I suggest you spend some time discussing this with your partners now," she said warningly. "Obviously, I will be giving weekly lectures to help you with this project, but much of it will require studying on your own time. The care of plants is not as simple as you may think."

She turned away, leaving the students to talk to their lab partners.

Grayson snorted. "Sun, water, soil. How hard can it be?"

Fallon stared doubtfully at the packet of mustard seeds.

"Are you sure, Gray?" she asked. "Have you ever grown *mustard* before?"

"I mean, no. But I always put it on my burgers and stuff."

"And that helps us how?"

He rattled the seed packet in his hand. "It means I know what it tastes like when it's done?"

Fallon groaned. "We're doomed. I can't even keep a succulent alive. And I've tried multiple times."

"How do you kill a succulent?"

"You leave it within reach of your three-year-old cousin."

"Well, that was a pretty obvious mistake."

She shot him a look, and he smiled, but it was gentle.

"You look tired," he said.

She rubbed at the bags under her eyes. "Thanks for noticing."

"Did you sleep much?"

She shook her head. "Not at all, really."

"Me either." He looked down, pushing his pencil up the table and back down again. "At least, it doesn't feel like I did.

Every time I woke up, I kept thinking about last year . . . what happened with Sutter."

Fallon pressed her lips together. She'd be lying if she said she wasn't worried about Sutter, too.

Before the start of their sophomore year, Sutter had spent his entire summer poring over the evidence connected to Lawson's disappearance. He'd searched for holes in the police findings, grasped desperately at anything to point him in the right direction. His search didn't end once he'd arrived back at Meddlehart, either—he let it consume him, day in and day out, until he wasn't himself anymore.

By the end of the first semester, Sutter had reached his breaking point. He wasn't eating or sleeping nearly enough, and one day Carter found him on the floor of their dorm, inconsolable. After, Sutter had gone home for a while and come back a calmer, steadier version of himself. He saw a counselor on campus, and things had seemed better since then.

Fallon wanted to believe he was doing better, but she couldn't be sure. He hadn't looked well last night, and while the memorial ceremony was a perfect explanation why, she couldn't ignore the gnawing feeling in her chest.

It had been scary and upsetting to see Sutter fall apart sophomore year. He'd dropped into a bad place following Lawson's disappearance—a dark, dangerous place. What if it happened again? And if it did, what if it was worse this time?

Grief is complicated. It doesn't just disappear. The thought echoed in Fallon's mind, and her parents' faces surfaced there, foggy and blurred, like figures from an old dream. She shut her eyes, urging them away.

"We just need to be there for him," she said quietly. "That's all we can do. We're his friends—we'll listen and take care of him, like we all do for each other. Like he would do for us."

But when she looked at Grayson, he was staring at his phone, brows furrowed.

"You okay?" she asked. When he didn't answer, she said, "Gray."

He looked up at her, eyes hazy, distant.

"You okay?" she repeated.

He nodded and stuffed his phone in his pocket. "Yeah, I'm good." He offered her a watered-down version of his usual smile, and she frowned.

The bells chimed outside, and Grayson started packing his bag along with the rest of the class. Then he was gone, off to whatever class he had next.

Before he left the greenhouse, though, Fallon saw him snag a small shovel from beside the door and walk away like it belonged to him.

If anyone else saw, they didn't say anything.

EIGHT

Grayson

When Grayson held the door for Fallon on their way into history class that afternoon, Headmaster Averell was already in the classroom, chatting with Mr. Whittaker and waving hello as students trickled in to find their seats.

Grayson barely suppressed a groan. When Whittaker had mentioned having a "special guest" for their first history class, he'd forgotten about the yearly tradition of the headmaster telling the story of how Meddlehart Academy came to be.

"Think we'll get the CliffsNotes on this now that we're juniors?" Grayson whispered as they picked two empty desks toward the back.

Fallon smirked. "I don't want the CliffsNotes. I like hearing the whole story every year."

Grayson grinned. "Of course you do."

She huffed. "What? It's really interesting—the tragedy, the *treasure*. The story never gets old."

"Yeah, but Averell doesn't even acknowledge the treasure." The Meddlehart administration knew they couldn't keep students from the rumors of the school's lost fortune, but they certainly didn't encourage them to hunt for it. There were some kids Grayson had heard of being expelled for treasure hunting on campus, which scared off most others from even trying it.

The only acknowledgment of the treasure the school had ever given was a single rule, in small print, in the student handbook: *Students are strictly prohibited from participating in any pursuits of rumored artifacts, bounties, or valuables that involve leaving school boundaries, defacing campus grounds, or other potentially dangerous and harmful actions.*

"Do you even think it's real?" Grayson asked Fallon. "It's always sounded made-up to me."

"I don't know. There probably isn't any treasure, because someone would have found it by now, right? But I still love that our school has this history. It's fascinating."

"Well, aren't you quite the historian," Grayson said.

"Everyone loves a hidden treasure story," Fallon said with a shrug. "If you say you don't, you're lying."

He started to speak, but his phone buzzed in his pocket again, sending a nervous jolt through him. His dad had received a stern message from the school when Grayson missed move-in day. Now he was blowing up Grayson's phone with texts—he'd decided it was Grayson's fault, somehow.

Grayson ignored the messages. He couldn't think about his dad right now.

"All right, class, settle down," Whittaker called. "You are juniors, so most of you know me—and if you know me, you certainly know our fearless leader, Headmaster Greg Averell. He'll be sharing the history of our school with us today. The stage is yours, sir!"

"Thank you, Mr. Whittaker," Averell said, smiling. He was tall and his hair was still thick, with only a few hints of gray hidden in the brown tufts. The projector screen behind him was lit up with the Meddlehart crest—elegant vines woven around a majestic dragon. Grayson remembered the sticker on Lawson's phone and shuddered.

Grayson noticed Fallon quietly reach into her backpack and remove a notebook and purple roller pen.

"What are you doing?" Grayson asked under his breath as she opened the notebook to a blank page.

"Taking notes," she whispered.

"You're not being tested on this, you know," he said, smirking.

She flushed, sending a dizzying warmth through Grayson, and the freckles on her nose bunched up as she gave him the kind of dirty look he wouldn't mind seeing every day for the rest of his life.

"Now, I know the story of Meddlehart Academy might not excite students who have heard it year after year," Averell said. "But lucky for us, Meddlehart has rather fascinating and mysterious origins . . . I suppose I'll start there rather than leave you hanging."

The image on the screen changed to an old black-and-white photo of two men in suits standing in the woods, a shovel stuck in the ground between them.

"Meddlehart Academy was founded in 1919 by the two men in this photograph: Jacob Meddlehart and his friend and business partner Franklin Thatcher."

That name. Grayson shot a look at Fallon—a look she returned. Lawson's words from the video echoed in his mind.

How did Franklin Thatcher die?

By the fangs of greed.

Suddenly, Grayson was much more interested in this history lesson.

"They had earned quite a fortune between the two of them

from the coal mining industry in Colorado," Averell went on, "and they decided they wanted their children to earn proper educations . . . and who better to provide that than their parents?"

That earned a hearty laugh from Whittaker.

"The campus was built one piece at a time," Averell said. "They started with Meddlehart Manor so they could live here on the mountain. It's now the home reserved for headmasters, like me." The photo shifted to the map of Meddlehart that Grayson had seen a hundred times. It was printed in all the new-student pamphlets. To the west of the lake was a house labeled *Meddlehart Manor.*

"The academy thrived and was quickly considered a prestigious institution," Averell stated. "Meddlehart's daughter and Thatcher's twin sons attended the school together. One of the twins, Boone, served as headmaster for many years. And believe it or not, he was my grandfather. My parents met here as students, and I also attended high school here. So you could say this school runs in my blood."

Grayson had known this much. It was easy to remember because Averell's father was Ace Averell, who the school sports complex was named for. He'd been a star athlete who went pro, and the Ace Averell Sports Complex—fondly referred to as "the Ace" by most students—was named in his honor. Grayson saw that name on the side of the building every time he went to football practice.

In terms of Meddlehart history, Headmaster Averell was legendary—great-grandson of the school cofounder, son of a well-known athlete.

A student up front raised her hand. "What does this have to do with the treasure?"

Averell went quiet, the smile falling off his face. For a moment, the room was so quiet, you could hear a pin drop. Even Whittaker, brows raised, seemed interested in what Averell would say.

Finally, the headmaster cleared his throat.

"Jacob Meddlehart's treasure is just a rumor, and we certainly won't be entertaining rumors like that in class," he said evenly. "I suppose this is as good a time as any to move on to other topics. First, a reminder that you're all invited to attend the junior class dinner at Meddlehart Manor later this week . . ."

Averell continued talking about activities and events coming up—he reminded them about Parents Weekend and the Halloween dance, which were the next festivities on the calendar, and the annual school ski trip to Swallowtail Mountain in the winter.

But Grayson wasn't listening anymore. Once he was confident Averell and Whittaker weren't looking, he leaned across the aisle to Fallon, dropping his voice to a whisper.

"I forgot Franklin Thatcher was one of the founders of the school," he said.

"Me too," she whispered back, almost ashamed. "I should have realized. I didn't even think about it last night, after . . ." She trailed off, her cheeks pink.

Grayson only briefly let his mind wonder about the rosy blush in her face, about why she and Sutter had been in the courtyard together.

"So . . . what do we do now?" he asked.

She met his eyes with determination. "There's a book I read that I think might help . . . Will you come with me to the library?"

Grayson couldn't say no to that. He wondered if Fallon had a clue that he'd follow her anywhere.

The Simon Thatcher Memorial Library was a building Grayson didn't visit often. It was stationed right beside the bell tower, set apart from the classrooms and the sports complex.

It was the kind of place that seemed to exist specifically for Fallon Winthrop. She looked right at home among the tall wooden shelves, a maze she navigated with ease.

"I don't know how you avoid getting lost in here," Grayson said, which was followed by a stern *"Shh"* from somewhere in the massive space.

Fallon grinned. The light seeping through the stained glass windows cast a purplish glow over her that made her look almost ethereal. "Getting lost in here's kind of the goal," she murmured.

She led him to the back of the library, to a section of shelves labeled BIOGRAPHIES. Without hesitation, she began climbing one of the rolling ladders to reach the very top.

"Be careful," Grayson whispered, watching as she made her ascent.

Fallon studied the shelf, fingers trailing along book spines, until she finally gestured to the right. "Gray, give me a push."

Gently, Grayson took the base of the ladder in his hands and moved it over a foot. Fallon found the book she wanted and removed it with a flourish. One step at a time, she climbed down and let Grayson read the title: *Jacob Meddlehart: A Legacy Worth Its Weight in Gold.*

"You've read this before?" Grayson asked.

Fallon led him to a long table lined with lamps. "My first semester here, I wanted to learn more about the treasure, but I was too shy to ask anyone about it . . . so I came here. I'm pretty sure this book mentions Franklin Thatcher too . . ."

She opened the book, blew off a thin layer of dust, and began flipping the pages. Grayson watched her skim past the sections covering Meddlehart's early life and coal mining business until she reached one titled "Tall Tales: Meddlehart's Missing Fortune."

"The rumor of Jacob Meddlehart's hidden treasure is fascinating, but stems from tragedy," Fallon read aloud, her voice hushed. *"Jacob and his wife, Florence, had a daughter named Amelia, who was a student at Meddlehart Academy before passing away at the age of sixteen in a drowning accident. The location of her death is not confirmed in historical records, but many speculate that she died swimming in the small body of water located at the academy."*

Grayson nodded; he remembered this part of the story. Some students liked to joke that Amelia haunted the campus, blaming her ghost for things like missing homework assignments.

"Florence Meddlehart became unwell in the years after Amelia's passing," Fallon went on. *"Representatives of the family reported she couldn't stand to live on the same grounds where her daughter had died. Florence left to recover in the countryside, where she ultimately passed away. Jacob never saw her again."*

"Damn," Grayson murmured.

Fallon nodded in agreement. *"For the final years of his life, Jacob was alone, consumed with grief, without a child or any other surviving relative to pass his fortune down to. When he passed away in 1950, he was found alone in his home, sitting at his favorite place: his writing desk, where he often composed poetry. But his fortune was missing, aside from the small amount of spending money he left in a bank.*

There was not a single thing of value left in Meddlehart Manor—every piece of gold, every jewel, every cent he had was gone. It initially appeared as though he'd been robbed. But in his hand was a poem in his own handwriting."

Fallon shifted the book so Grayson could see the image on the page—a cryptic message written in loopy cursive that must have captivated and confounded treasure hunters for decades.

For you, protector of the wood,
I hide my worth in my legacy
As my one final act of good
To provide for future family.
With love and regret,
J. Meddlehart

"Jacob was a lover of poetry and was known to write poems as a pastime. But this poem was different—it was a message," Fallon continued reading. *"Historians believe this was Meddlehart's way of telling the world his fortune was out there, waiting to be found—though its true meaning has been analyzed and dissected, but with little success. The poem implies he hid his treasure for someone in particular—the mysterious* protector of the wood. *And his choice of words—*I hide my worth in my legacy*—has led people to believe he buried it somewhere on the campus he founded."*

Goose bumps rose on Grayson's arms. Then Fallon let out a gasp.

"What is it?" Grayson asked, leaning forward.

"Many treasure hunters have ventured to Meddlehart Academy to uncover the fortune, but no one has ever been successful, and several have lost their lives in the fruitless search," Fallon read. *"Even* Franklin

Thatcher *searched for the treasure after Jacob's passing, but failed to locate it.*"

Grayson's mouth went dry. "Holy shit. Franklin Thatcher hunted for Meddlehart's treasure?"

Fallon shook her head, dumbfounded. "What does this mean? It can't be a coincidence."

"Maybe we'll know more tonight," Grayson murmured. "After it's done."

After they dug up Lawson's time capsule.

After they finally found out what he had been hiding before he disappeared.

NINE

Sutter

"Are you sure that's where it is?"

Sutter had spent the past hour rewatching Lawson's video and drawing a map that would lead them to where the time capsule was buried. The sun had set, and it was almost time to go.

Grayson sat in the corner of their dorm, fiddling with the strings of his hoodie. He'd just finished filling them in on what he and Fallon discovered at the library—the connection between Franklin Thatcher and Meddlehart Academy. Carter stood over Sutter's shoulder, watching him draw the path.

"I mean, yeah," Sutter said. "Unless someone already dug it up." He still wasn't sure who'd left Lawson's phone for him, but he hoped no one else knew the capsule was out there. He wanted to be the one to find it. He wanted to see what his brother had put inside.

"Look," Sutter said. "You can tell in the footage—he's near that ledge in the woods behind Churchill Hall." He pointed at the screen, where the paused video showed the time capsule's resting place. "See? It's the same place those guys got busted smoking last year."

You could barely see it in the background, in the upper left corner of the screen: the short wall of rock sticking up from the ground, covered in dead leaves, dirt, and brush.

Carter nodded. "Yeah . . . so this won't be that hard to find?"

"It shouldn't be," Sutter murmured, rolling the map up.

"As long as we get out of here without Scott knowing," Grayson chimed in.

Carter grunted at the mention of his brother. "Scott would be *thrilled* to catch me sneaking out past curfew. It would make his freaking life."

Just then, their door opened without so much as a knock. Margot strolled in, followed by Fallon, both dressed in hoodies, jeans, and hiking boots. Fallon's hair was pulled into a bun, revealing her cheekbones. She tucked a stray lock behind her ear, and the gesture struck Sutter with familiarity and comfort. Her eyes searched his face hesitantly.

His cheeks heated with embarrassment as he was once again dragged back to the night before—him kissing her, the spin of alcohol throwing any sensible thoughts out of his mind.

How she'd pushed him away.

What was he thinking? He'd replayed it in his head, trying to figure out where he'd read her wrong, what he'd missed. The only thing he knew for sure was that he felt lucky she was still willing to be in the same room as him.

"Bad news," Margot said, snapping Sutter out of his train of thought. "Scott is still patrolling the halls. He'll be making rounds on this floor any minute."

"Damn it," Sutter muttered. "We need a distraction."

The others turned to Carter.

He shook his head. "I hate you guys."

"Can you do it, though?" Sutter asked.

He sighed. "Yeah, fine. I've got this."

Sutter slapped him five, and Carter stepped into the hall, leaving the door slightly ajar. Grayson pressed Play on a video game stream on his laptop, so whoever passed by would hear the sounds of *Fortnite* rather than the suspicious hum of silence. The rest huddled against the wall by the door, waiting for their moment.

After a minute or so, Carter's voice echoed from down the hall.

"Scott! Hey, Scott."

"What are you doing out of your room, Carter?"

"Is it a crime to leave my room? I wanted some water."

"There's water in the—"

"Yeah, yeah, I know where the water is. Listen, I heard someone puking upstairs."

"Puking?"

"Puking."

"Upstairs?"

"The air vents here carry sound very well."

"Ew," Margot murmured, wrinkling her nose.

Sutter elbowed her. "It's not real," he hissed.

"Yeah, but just the thought of it . . ."

Scott sighed heavily. "Carter, if this is one of your—"

"I swear it's not a joke. You should go check on them. Come on, I'll show you. I think it's the room right above mine."

"No," Scott said firmly. "I'll go check it out. I can find it myself. You just get back in your room. It's past curfew."

"Yes, sir," Carter said with an enthusiasm so false, Grayson snorted. Sutter elbowed him, listening intently as the sound of Scott's footsteps retreated. The stairwell door opened and clicked shut.

"Scott's gone," Carter hissed. *"Move!"*

They all shoved through the door, nearly toppling over each other in the process, and hurried to the fire escape. Sutter held the window open, and one by one, they climbed through. Fallon went last, and Sutter followed, hustling down the steps behind her.

The moment they reached the ground, they bolted for the woods surrounding campus. It wasn't until they were past the tree line that they slowed and glanced at each other. Nighttime was settling in quickly, the sky a canvas for a slowly bleeding sunset that would soon give way to millions of stars.

Sutter always missed that when he went back to his crowded neighborhood streets in Texas at the end of each school year—those starry skies that could only be seen from the mountaintops in West Fork.

Some nights, you could see meteor showers and milky strips of galaxy stroked across the deep sky, and on those nights, students would lay blankets out on the lawns by the lake to watch late into the night. Those were among the few nights the teachers hung around after dark and curfew hours were extended. The views from the windows weren't the same as they were there on the grass, right beneath it all.

"Everyone good?" Sutter asked.

They nodded, muttering "Good" through panting breaths.

"Grayson," he said, "you got the shovel?"

Grayson held up the tool for the others to see. It wasn't the heavy-duty shovel Sutter had in mind, but it was better than nothing.

Sutter pulled out the makeshift map and led the way forward. They waited until they were farther into the woods before clicking their flashlights on. The hike wasn't long—the ledge they were looking for was on the northwest corner of campus, almost to the point where the river flowed down from the mountain.

The crew moved in silence until the ledge was in sight, and by the time they reached it, Sutter's hands were trembling. He squeezed them into fists and released them a few times as he paced, trying to picture where his brother had stood in the video.

He walked to the center of the clearing and brushed some pine needles aside with his foot. It was dark, but in the beam of his flashlight, he could just see a slight disturbance in the earth.

"Shovel," he said. Grayson passed it to him, and Sutter dropped to his knees. Without hesitation, he plunged the shovel into the dirt and pushed until the soil lifted. He flung it to the side and dug again, and again.

There was nothing but dirt.

"I don't see anything," Margot said carefully.

"It can't be gone, can it?" Carter asked.

Panic flooded Sutter's chest. "There's no way. It *has* to be here." He shoveled faster, tossing chunks of earth over his shoulder. He felt tiny specks of dirt falling down his shirt, catching in his hair, but he didn't care. He pushed the shovel harder. His arms ached with the effort, his heart hammering, and then—

Thump.

The shovel struck something hard. Sutter reached down, feeling for what he knew must be there, and touched cool, smooth metal.

Frantic, he began scooping mud away with his hands, unearthing the object one handful of dirt at a time. The corner, then the side, then the metal latch . . .

The box. The time capsule.

Sutter gripped the capsule in his cold fingers, wriggling it out of the hole. He stood, covered in soil and bits of brush. The box in his hands was dented and caked with dirt, but there. It was there.

Sutter's friends gazed at the time capsule with wide eyes.

"Holy shit," Carter mumbled.

"Should we open it now?" Fallon asked. "Or take it back to Shepherd?"

Margot shook her head. "We have no idea what's in that thing. We might not want to take it back with us . . . Let's see what's inside first."

Sutter nodded. His heart stumbled over each beat to get to the next, and he wasn't sure he could speak if he tried to. He knelt and set the box on the ground, then placed his fingers over the latch and flipped it open. He had to pry at the lid for a moment, but it finally came off, revealing the contents of the capsule.

Sutter brushed his dirty hands on his jeans before removing the items one by one. At the top was a small collection of photographs. The first was a black-and-white photograph of a young woman, probably near their age at the time it was taken, with round, pale eyes and hair pinned intricately to her head. She wore a dress that ruffled at the neck, a style Sutter figured had to be from ages ago. Fallon took the photo and held it under her flashlight.

"That's Amelia," she said quickly.

"Who?" Grayson asked.

"Amelia," she said again, like it was obvious. "Meddlehart. Jacob Meddlehart's daughter. I recognize her from the pictures in the biography . . . but this one is new."

Sutter held up the next photo, just as old as the first—two men shaking hands, their smiles wide. This time, he immediately recognized the subjects of the picture.

"It's Jacob Meddlehart and Franklin Thatcher," he said.

The others gathered around to peer over Sutter's shoulder at the photograph, and he squinted to get a closer look. It looked like Meddlehart and Thatcher were standing on a stage, holding a plaque between them—some sort of award, maybe. There were people in the background, clapping. Off to the side, standing behind Meddlehart, was a short, brown-haired woman, smiling up at him fondly.

Sutter pointed her out. "Is that Meddlehart's wife, Fallon?"

Fallon studied the woman for a moment. She shook her head. "In all the pictures I've seen, Florence had blond hair, and she was taller. Almost as tall as Meddlehart."

The final photo was another black-and-white portrait, but this one showed a newborn baby swaddled in a white blanket. The letters *TJH* were embroidered on one edge of the blanket in chunky yarn.

"Do you recognize that baby?" Fallon asked Sutter, pointing at the photo.

Sutter shook his head. "No."

"What's *TJH* stand for?" Carter asked, snatching the photo from Sutter's hands.

Sutter shook his head. "I don't know." Confusion twisted his thoughts. What were these old pictures doing in this time capsule that was supposed to hold Lawson's belongings?

Below the stack of photos was a faded, wrinkled piece of paper. He quickly recognized the map of Meddlehart's campus—the official one still used by the school. There was a big, fat X in blue ink, right over Meddlehart Manor.

"What the hell?" Carter asked as Sutter passed the map to him.

And then, at the bottom of the box, something glinted in the flashlight beam. Sutter reached in and took it between his fingers. Silver metal, cold to the touch, curving in a slithering shape, scales etched into the gleaming surface . . .

A viper pendant.

Instinctively, he reached for the viper hanging around his neck and pulled it against the chain so he could see it. It was clear the two pendants were not the same—the one in the box had a pin attached to the back, something you might fasten on your lapel. It was slightly larger than his pendant, with tiny red jewels for the snake's eyes. And it looked older, the silver a bit tarnished.

But they were both vipers. Sutter held them up.

"Look at this," he said. "The necklace I'm wearing—it was Lawson's. He left it in his room the night he disappeared."

His friends frowned, sharing puzzled glances.

"Does it mean anything?" Grayson asked. "The snake?"

Sutter shook his head. "I didn't know before, but now . . . it *must* have some significance."

Something clicked in his brain, like magnets snapping together, satisfying and sure. Sutter stood and snatched the map back from Carter.

"It'll all be okay once I find it," Sutter murmured, repeating the words Lawson had said at the end of the video.

"What?" Carter asked, cupping his hand around his ear. "Speak up, buddy."

"He was looking for it," Sutter said. "Meddlehart's treasure. Lawson was *looking* for it." It all made sense now—the mention of Franklin Thatcher in the video, someone who they had proof was a treasure hunter. And the photo of Amelia Meddlehart, the dead heiress, the reason Meddlehart had no one to leave his fortune to . . .

This is what Lawson wanted Sutter to find. *This* is what Lawson was hiding before he disappeared.

He turned to Fallon. "What else do you know about the Meddlehart treasure, beyond what you read in that biography?"

"I m-mean," she stammered. "That's a really broad question, Sutter. I've read some articles online, but . . ."

"But what?" he pressed.

She hesitated. "But I never thought it was real or anything. It's just a story. Right?" She turned to the others, her voice rising in pitch in a desperate sort of way. "There's no way it could be real."

But the others were silent. Because *of course* it was possible. The school prohibited treasure hunting because they couldn't risk students prowling around campus, sneaking off to hunt treasure in the woods on their own—that was too dangerous, a liability for the school. The administration would say what they had to, to convince students there was nothing to hunt for.

But these clues practically confirmed it for Sutter. The only questionable parts of what they'd found were the viper pendants and the photo of the baby whose identity was unknown.

Sutter pointed at the X on the map. "This must be where Lawson thought the treasure was hidden," he said. "That's got to be what this is—a treasure map."

Grayson was shaking his head, dumbfounded.

"This is a lot to process," Carter mumbled.

Fallon's brows were furrowed. "We can't hunt for the treasure, though—that's a recipe for disaster. Not only could we get hurt, but we could face expulsion, and—"

"Hold on a second," Margot said, waving her hands. "How much is the Meddlehart fortune worth? Like, a million?"

"More," Fallon said numbly.

"How much more?" Margot asked.

"I don't know," Fallon answered, shaking her head. "I mean, I'd need to do more research, but . . . millions, plural. At least."

"Shit," Carter murmured.

"Did you guys hear me, though?" Fallon asked. "We can't hunt for the treasure. You all understand that, right?"

No one replied, and Sutter knew why.

Because they *could hunt for it.* And wherever the treasure hunt led . . .

Lawson would be there, too. He was sure of it.

"Can you find them again?" Sutter asked, eyes on Fallon. "Those articles you read online?"

She hesitated. "I'm sure I could . . . It's all easily accessible information. But—"

"Good," Sutter said. "Because we are finding it."

"Finding it?" Grayson asked. "The treasure?"

Sutter nodded. "During the junior class dinner tomorrow night."

TEN

Fallon

Fallon sat in the desk next to Sutter's in homeroom the next day, and she managed a tight smile. He returned it, but even at this hour of the morning, she could see the wheels turning in his brain.

Last night, she'd made it very clear she thought hunting for treasure in the headmaster's home—during the class dinner, no less—was a terrible, terrible idea.

"We won't do anything stupid," Sutter had promised.

"We'd never do that," Grayson agreed, though his voice dripped with sarcasm.

"We're just going to look around," Sutter went on. "We won't dig a hole in his backyard or anything."

"You say that, but I know you," Fallon argued. "You won't dig a hole in the headmaster's backyard, *until you want to*."

Sutter merely shrugged, and Fallon groaned. She turned to Margot.

"Students are *not* allowed to treasure hunt. Do you see where I'm coming from here?" she asked her roommate, the one who would surely give her support. "Do you see the point of view of a student who doesn't want to get expelled?"

"Yes," Margot said. "But, I mean, Fallon . . . this is our best chance at finding out what happened to Lawson, right? And think about if we did find that treasure."

"It's *not real*," Fallon argued.

"But if it *is*," Margot countered patiently, "our lives would change *forever*. I could finally ditch my parents."

"I could go to culinary school," Carter said. "Hell, I could *buy* culinary school."

And I could move out of my aunt and uncle's house for good, Fallon thought hollowly. But she shook her head to rid her mind of the idea, because that wasn't the point. The treasure was a story, a rumor, and nothing more. Aside from finding Lawson, hunting for it was pointless—she didn't care what the others said. Searching for buried treasure, especially at the home their headmaster *lived* in, was just an easy way to get in big, big trouble. Bigger than they'd ever been in before.

This wasn't just sneaking into the kitchen to find fancy ingredients for Carter, or breaking curfew to hang out, or any of the other silly things they'd done in the past. And that voice in Fallon's head—the voice of responsibility—had broken its streak of silence and was speaking out now. *Danger—beware!*

She'd turned to Grayson. "And you? Why are *you* pro–treasure hunting?"

He flashed that classic Grayson smirk. "We've come this far, haven't we? Why stop now?"

But when Fallon just stared back at him, his smirk faded. Gently, he nudged her arm.

"Lawson left these clues for a reason, right?" Grayson murmured. "If we don't follow them, who else will? It'll be all right, Fallon. Promise."

She sighed, knowing Grayson was making a promise he

couldn't keep. Finally, she looked at Sutter, who stared back at her with an earnestness that stole her resolve.

She knew finding the treasure, to him, meant another shot at finding Lawson. And no one could talk him out of that.

So she'd let it go. Now she sat in stony silence, waiting for Whittaker to show up and start class. Her phone dinged with an Instagram notification—another shared reel from Carter, who was notorious for sending an unreasonable number of social media DMs despite never reading his texts.

"This story of a golden retriever saving a starving kitten will break your heart," Sutter read from his phone. He'd gotten the reel, too.

Fallon managed a smile. "No one loves a motivational story more than Carter."

Sutter grinned, but it faded quickly. He turned toward her slightly.

"Look, Winthrop . . ."

Fallon went still. Her heartbeat ticked up a notch. Did he want to talk about what happened between them the other night? She braced herself, waiting for him to say—

"I know you're not totally on board with this whole treasure hunt thing."

She felt a rush of relief, but then had the urge to respond sarcastically, *Who, me? Not on board? Where'd you get that idea?*

But she didn't. She was a little too groggy from another restless night to be anything other than honest.

"I get you all probably think I'm a stick-in-the-mud," she said. "The rule follower who ruins all your fun. But just know it's only because I care."

And if she was honest with herself, she couldn't stop replaying the words Margot had said the night before: *Our lives would change forever.*

After Fallon's parents died—a car accident—she'd been shoved into a life that wasn't really hers. Her aunt and uncle were starting their own family, and suddenly, they had a teenager in the house.

She felt like a burden in every way, dropped on her relatives with hardly any warning. She knew they loved her, and she loved them. But they were out of their minds if they said they wanted Fallon to be there, just like Fallon knew she didn't want to be there, either. She didn't want to be woken every single night by a screaming infant. She didn't want to feel remorse for the way she decorated her bedroom, knowing the walls didn't truly belong to her.

She wanted her parents back, more than anything. She wanted their Saturday movie dates, oldies music in the car, and homemade ice cream cakes on her birthday. She wanted her father's lame jokes and her mother's endless lectures on finances.

But they weren't coming back. The next best thing would be the freedom to be, to just *be*, without feeling like she was infringing on someone else's life.

So out of desperation to get out of their house, Fallon had asked—or rather, begged—her aunt and uncle to let her enroll at Meddlehart. And it was the one positive thing change had ever done for her. She finally had a life she could feel happy in for the first time since she lost her parents.

Which made the thought of finding the treasure and changing everything . . . oddly unpleasant.

What if Fallon didn't *want* her life to change? What if she was completely sick of change waltzing in and ruining her life, one piece at a time? Change had taken her parents away and shoved her into a new life, like a puzzle piece jammed into the wrong place, forced to fit.

And now that she'd found a place where she belonged, she could hardly bear the idea of anything—even buried treasure—changing that. She couldn't stand the thought of her and her friends getting rich and famous and leaving Meddlehart, fracturing into separate pieces that never quite fit together the same way again.

She knew friendships never stayed the same after high school, or after college, or after *anything* changed. Just like her old friends had never treated her the same after her parents died.

Plus, Fallon had heard stories of people winning the lottery and their lives falling apart in the aftermath. Finding this treasure might mean some form of fame and fortune, but what if it turned into a curse, too?

But the softness in Sutter's eyes washed these thoughts out of her mind.

"What?" he whispered. "No, Fallon. I don't think you ruin our fun at all."

Her cheeks warmed. And maybe because she was tired—maybe because she was confused and just wanted the truth—she asked, "What *do* you think about me, then?"

Sutter froze, and for a moment, Fallon was stunned she'd asked him the question out loud. But then he cleared his throat, leaning slightly closer to her across the aisle.

"I think you're smart," he said, his voice nearly a whisper. "And creative. I think you're the most loyal person I've ever met—the kind of person you only meet once, and if you lose them, no one else will ever quite measure up." He met her gaze.

"I don't think you've ever ruined a thing in your life, Fallon . . . I think you're irreplaceable."

Fallon's heart was in her throat, and her eyes prickled as his words settled over her. Suddenly, she was alone with him in the courtyard again, and he was kissing her like he was hungry for it, like he'd waited ages to be able to feel her lips on his.

His eyes searched her face now, almost as if he could see the memory playing back in her eyes. Warmth flooded her cheeks, yet it wasn't from embarrassment—she could see it in his eyes. He was thinking about the kiss, too.

But Fallon wondered why he would say these things now when he never had before.

Before either of them could say anything more, the classroom door opened and Mr. Whittaker appeared, his cane in one hand and a tray of doughnuts in the other. Sutter leaned away from her, and the moment was broken.

"Good morning," Whittaker said with a warm smile. He tracked in dirt on the soles of his shoes, probably just returning from another nature walk around campus. "Doughnuts at the snack bar today, so I made sure to stop by before I came here. I think this will be a great way to start off homeroom, don't you? Come help yourselves before we get started." Whittaker carefully set the tray down on his desk, selected a dry-erase marker, and began writing on the whiteboard in big, square letters.

The other students smiled at the sight of the doughnuts, and Fallon's chest relaxed. Whittaker really was the best. And then something occurred to her.

Maybe she would feel better about this plan if she had confirmation that the treasure was real in the first place. And who better to ask than a history expert?

Sutter cleared his throat again. His cheeks were slightly pink, and he couldn't quite meet Fallon's eyes.

"Want one?" he asked her. "Cinnamon sugar, right?"

She smiled, warmth spreading through her chest. "Yeah . . . thanks, Sutter."

He stood to get in the doughnut line. Before he could walk away, though, she grabbed his wrist. His brows furrowed in confusion.

"Let me do my research," she said in a whisper. "Before we do this tonight, let me look into it, all right?"

He sighed. "Fallon—"

"I just need to figure out if the risk is worth it," she told him quietly.

He stared at her for a long time, lips pressed firmly together, before he gave a slight nod. Then he walked away, leaving Fallon to her thoughts.

She wasn't able to catch Whittaker alone until after history later that day.

When she approached his desk, he was stacking papers and setting them aside. A steaming cup of tea rested beside his gold nameplate—MR. JENSEN WHITTAKER—and he looked at her over his glasses.

"Ms. Winthrop," he said fondly. "What can I do for you?"

"Would you be the right person to ask if I have questions about Meddlehart's history?"

He nodded, somewhat bashful. "I *am* something of an expert on the topic. But I kind of have to be, don't I? I'm the history teacher." He chuckled. "Take a seat, Fallon."

She did, and he took a lemon juice packet from his desk while he waited for her to speak.

"Well," she began, her mouth suddenly dry. Maybe she should have prepared questions. She racked her brain for a moment, thinking about what she had read in the biography. "Truthfully, Mr. Whittaker, I'm just trying to figure out if the rumor about the treasure is real."

For a moment, he looked too stunned to speak. Then he recovered with a smile and a chuckle. "Ah. That is the question, isn't it?"

Fallon was relieved—his smile seemed genuine, like he was going to entertain this conversation without shutting it down the way Averell would. "I don't know why the story would have been told if it wasn't true, but to me, it's always seemed like just a rumor."

"Well, let's start there. Why do any rumors spread?" Whittaker asked, squeezing the lemon juice into his tea. "What's the purpose of a rumor?"

Fallon could think of several, but what would make the most sense in this case?

"To liven things up?" she asked.

"Precisely," he said, pointing one finger in the air. "People get bored. High school students stuck on the side of a mountain get *very* bored—or at least, they used to. You and your friends seem to have plenty of fun."

Fallon managed a dismissive shrug, and he laughed.

"So does that mean you agree with me?" she asked. "The treasure isn't real?"

To her surprise, he stretched his lips into a strange grimace. "I didn't say that."

She sat up straighter. "You *do* think it's real?"

"Fallon," Whittaker said carefully, leaning forward. "I am not supposed to be honest with students about my opinion on the Meddlehart treasure. But I trust you not to take this information and do something irresponsible with it. Understand?"

She nodded. A speechless feeling had taken her tongue captive.

He gave a little shrug. "I think the treasure is out there. There's no record of the Meddlehart fortune going to anyone else after his death in 1950—not to mention Franklin Thatcher was hunting the treasure when he died. And by that, Fallon, I mean *when he died*. Do you know much about Franklin Thatcher—his life, his death?"

Fallon shook her head, waiting for him to go on.

"Well, he was not an outdoorsy, do-it-yourself kind of guy, the way Meddlehart was. He was the type to take his money and pay someone else to do the hard work. He spent most of his time inside, at his desk, and when he wasn't at his desk, he was drinking tea by the fireplace. But when he died," Whittaker said, "he was hiking in the wilderness surrounding the campus, and he was bitten by a venomous snake." Whittaker's eyebrows were raised. "Why do you think he was hiking on his own?"

"He was looking for the treasure," Fallon mumbled.

And what Lawson had said in the video . . . *he died by the fangs of greed.*

"He was," Whittaker said. "He told everyone he knew he was looking for it—that was no secret. And I find it hard to believe the person closest to Meddlehart, the one who knew him best, would be treasure hunting if it wasn't out there to find."

Fallon's head spun. It took her a long moment to think of something else to ask.

"What about the poem?" she asked. "The message Meddlehart left right before he died. What do you think it means?"

Whittaker smiled. "Well, I think it serves the purpose of telling the world his fortune is hidden for someone. But who *is* that someone? Finding the *protector of the wood* . . . that's the key, Fallon."

Fallon frowned. "Would that person even be alive today?"

Whittaker answered her question by posing a new one. "Does it matter if they aren't?"

Fallon pondered this, turning the information over like a puzzle piece with nowhere to fit. Meddlehart lost his daughter and his wife. He had no family to leave his fortune to . . . so he left it for someone else. And his poem suggested he had a certain someone in mind.

Who was it? And had they known what Meddlehart intended for them?

The thought of Meddlehart's daughter spurred Fallon to ask another question. "Do you think Amelia drowned in the lake? The one on campus?"

At that, Whittaker leaned back in his chair, eyes on his folded hands. "No. The lake is in the middle of campus. Someone would have witnessed it." He chuckled, but his voice was low now. "Her ghost does not haunt this campus."

Fallon managed a weary smile. Students had reported on-campus ghost sightings for years, claiming it was Amelia searching for her father.

Fallon didn't believe in ghosts. She did, however, believe in howling, whistling mountain winds and foggy mists rising off the lake in the morning.

Students began arriving for Whittaker's next class, so Fallon gathered her things and left in a daze. She wasn't sure what she'd expected her history teacher to say.

But now she knew there was no stopping the plan her friends had set in motion.

Hours before the junior class dinner, Fallon was walking back to Shepherd House with Margot, who was filming the final clips for her latest vlog.

". . . and that will be it for this video, but I promise a dorm room tour is coming soon. Fallon and I finished unpacking, and our room is absolutely *adorable*!"

Fallon couldn't help but smile thinking about the opposite sides of their room. When Fallon had moved in with Margot their freshman year, it was obvious they had very little in common. Fallon was a shy bookworm and devoted artist. Margot was an outgoing vlogger, theater kid, and three-time student body president. But somehow—Fallon still wasn't entirely sure how—the two of them clicked with a near-instant friendship that had magnetic force.

Margot pressed the power button on her camera and stuffed it in her bag. Since starting her YouTube channel freshman year, Margot had developed a solid following, enough that she made a little bit of money. She did makeup tutorials occasionally, but the videos with the most views were her vlogs covering her days at Meddlehart.

"Will the subscribers approve?" Fallon asked as their pace slowed.

Margot swished her hair over one shoulder. "Of *course*. Now, let's talk about the junior class dinner, since you're officially on board with the plan. What are you wearing?"

Fallon had already filled Margot in on her conversation with Whittaker, and she planned on telling the boys when they made it back to Shepherd. She hadn't even thought about an outfit for that night.

Sheepishly, she shrugged. "I don't know."

"Good, because I do." Margot grinned. "I've got a dress in my closet with your name all over it. And a certain someone won't be able to resist you. Here, I think I have a picture of it on my phone . . ."

Fallon's stomach dropped. She still hadn't told her roommate what happened. "Margot . . . I have to tell you something."

Margot looked up, blue eyes twinkling. "Yeah?"

Fallon hesitated. "Don't kill me. I would've told you sooner, but things have been so hectic, and—"

"If you're going to tell me you already picked out a hoodie to wear to the dinner, don't even start. I won't accept it. I don't care *how* cold the temperature will—"

Fallon rolled her eyes. "It's not about clothes!" She hesitated, lowered her voice, and ripped off the proverbial Band-Aid. "Sutter kissed me."

"What?"

Her scream might as well have echoed all the way across campus. It was not an exaggeration to say every single student in the vicinity turned to stare at them in confusion.

"Shh," Fallon hissed, lurching to cover Margot's mouth with her hand. Her cheeks were practically ablaze as she pulled Margot off the path, away from any passing students.

"Listen . . . it was a mistake," Fallon explained in a whisper.

"It was after the memorial—he was drunk, and really upset, and it . . . just . . ."

"Happened," Margot finished for her. "It finally *happened*! Fallon, don't you get what this *means*?"

"Nothing," Fallon urged her. "It means absolutely nothing. We both realized immediately it shouldn't have—"

"Hold on, *what*?" Margot trilled. "Why would it be a mistake?"

Fallon backtracked—explained the night in detail, the things they'd said to each other. The memory barged in like a wave breaking on the shore, vivid and visceral, and then retreated to the ocean of her thoughts just as quickly. Fallon shuddered at the thought of the kiss—shivers across her skin, unbearably intoxicating—and the way it ended, so uncomfortably it made her stomach turn.

She was beginning to wish the part of her heart that longed for Sutter could be surgically removed, because all it did was cause her pain and disappointment.

"The way I see it," she told Margot, "Sutter's feelings are still a question mark. One drunken kiss in the courtyard doesn't prove he feels the same way I do."

"That's because you haven't talked to him about it," Margot said plainly.

"I just . . . don't think that will ever happen," Fallon told her after a long pause. "I think I should let it go. Save myself the heartache." The heartache she was already very much feeling.

"Fallon, you know what I always say," Margot said simply. "You don't—"

"Get to choose your feelings," Fallon finished for her. "Yeah, I know. But maybe I should . . . you know . . . try."

"*Or* you could tell him how you feel," Margot countered. "Have an honest conversation—"

"And risk ruining our friendship and destroying the dynamic we have with all our mutual friends?" Fallon scoffed. "No *thank* you."

"*Why?* Fallon, he obviously has feelings for you!" Margot cried. "He *kissed* you—"

"And made it clear he thought it was a mistake," Fallon said, fighting the way her voice wanted to break. "He said so himself."

"Bullshit," Margot said with a confident, matter-of-fact shrug. "I call bullshit! Mark my words, Fallon—this is the year Sutter Heyward is going to wake the hell *up*."

Fallon shushed her again, glancing fearfully over her shoulder to see if anyone had heard them.

Margot sighed, leaning her head back in exasperation. "Okay. I can see you're still processing all this, and for that reason, I'll drop it. *For now.* Either way . . . I've made it my personal mission to ensure you feel gorgeous tonight. Because you are, and the whole world should know it. *Especially* a certain boy."

Fallon smiled, and they resumed walking. "It's just the class dinner. Knowing you, we'll probably be the best dressed people there by a mile."

"As we should," Margot said with a knowing grin.

They were passing the Ace then, as the football team was leaving practice.

"Hey, maybe we can wait for Grayson to walk back with us?" Fallon said. "That way I can tell him what Whittaker had to say."

Margot checked her watch. "You go ahead. I need to fulfill a few class president duties before we get ready for dinner. See you at Shepherd?"

Fallon nodded and watched her friend go. She took a moment to compose herself, breathing in and out until the mountain air cleared her mind, and then rerouted toward the complex.

As Fallon approached, most of the players were filing in and out of the locker room, some lazily tossing a football back and forth on the field. She scanned the crowd but didn't see Grayson.

Maybe he's still in the locker room. She started in that direction but then saw someone standing hidden behind the bleachers. They were wearing a pair of blue cleats just like Grayson's.

"Gray?" she called, rounding the corner. Then she stopped short—Grayson wasn't there. It was Alex Harker, a fellow junior and one of the football players, all by himself. He had a phone pressed to his ear.

"I'll figure it out," he muttered, then ended the call. When he turned and saw Fallon standing there, his eyes lit up with anger.

"What the fuck are you doing back here?" he snapped. "Were you eavesdropping?"

Fallon's chest seized with a rush of anxiety. Her mind went blank as she searched for an answer.

"*Hello?* Are you going to answer me?" Alex pressed, reading the panic on her face. He moved closer, and Fallon stepped backward. "You're *not* going to get away with doing that to me, you get that? Or are you too stupid to understand?"

Grayson was there in a flash, still in his football pads and uniform, hair matted down from his helmet. His jaw ticked, and his eyes had gone dark. He shoved his hands firmly into Alex's chest, forcing him to step back, away from Fallon.

"Watch your mouth," Grayson bit out.

Fallon saw the tension in his shoulders, his clenched fists, and she knew where this was going. Her heart rate rose. "Gray—"

Alex's eyes lit up. Without a second's hesitation, he charged Grayson, throwing a wild punch that struck him in the temple.

Grayson showed no shock. He swung at Alex like he welcomed the fight. His fist struck Alex's jaw, sending him reeling and only making him angrier.

"Grayson, *stop*," Fallon said, moving in to pull him away, but there was no need. Some other players had heard the commotion and rushed over to break it up. Coach Hamilton was there, too—his whistle shrieked through the chaos.

"Stop this *now*!" he bellowed.

Fallon's heart was in her throat as she was shoved to the outskirts of the small crowd, only able to watch as Grayson was pulled in one direction and Alex in another.

"You pathetic little *bitch*!" Alex shouted. "The hell's wrong with you?"

"Don't talk to her like that!" Grayson shouted back.

"What are you, in *love* with her?" Alex taunted. "Is that it?"

Humiliation washed over Fallon so fast she could hardly keep up with what was happening. But she was unable to stop herself from looking at Grayson, still being held back by his teammates.

Of all the things that had happened in the last minute, that was the one that made Grayson's face blanch.

And yet, he barely hesitated before saying, "So what if I am?"

Fallon's world stopped.

She stood still as Coach Hamilton herded the boys into the locker room. She watched them go, head spinning as Grayson's words echoed in her ears.

So what if I am?

Grayson turned to look over his shoulder at her, craning his neck to lock eyes with hers through the crowd of football players.

He was still looking at her when the locker room door shut behind him.

ELEVEN

Grayson

Stupid. So unbelievably *stupid*.

Grayson stood in front of the mirror in his dorm, tousling his wavy locks with his fingers and carefully avoiding the tender spot on his temple, which was already bruising. Nothing he couldn't handle—unlike the hurricane of thoughts in his head.

So what if I am?

What the hell was he thinking? Grayson squeezed his eyes shut, but no matter how hard he tried, he couldn't unsee the look on Fallon's face when he said those words.

She'd looked . . . shocked. And she certainly hadn't looked like someone who felt the same way.

Why'd he say it? Why'd he say anything at all? He could have just left Alex's taunts hanging in the air . . . but he couldn't let him have the last word.

Of course he couldn't. Grayson never left a fight until he'd *won*—or gone down swinging, at least. And Alex had been asking for it for a long damn time.

But still, he heard the words in his father's voice: *So fucking stupid*.

Carter came up behind him. He was wearing his faded blue Meddlehart Dragons hoodie.

"Well, you're dressed to impress," he said. "You know there's no dress code for class dinners, right?"

Grayson shrugged. "I like ties."

Carter eyed him, like he didn't buy it. "You sure there isn't someone you're dressing up for?" Grinning, he nudged his friend.

Grayson went still, his face flushing hot. He turned to eyeball Carter, whose smile fell right off his face. Had he already heard what happened on the football field?

"I'm kidding, dude," Carter said. Then his eyes widened. "Whoa, what happened to your face?"

That answered his question. Grayson turned back to the mirror. "Don't want to talk about it."

Carter raised a brow, but just then Sutter walked into the room, saving Grayson from further questioning. Sutter doused himself generously in cologne until Grayson's nose burned from the smell, then glanced at him and Carter.

Sutter raised a brow, but he must've gotten the hint from Grayson's expression that he didn't want to discuss his bruises. "Let's go," he said. "The girls already left."

Grayson's stomach churned. He wanted to check on Fallon before they left Shepherd House, but it sounded like he had missed his chance. He just needed to make sure she was all right. His heart pounded against his ribs so hard it hurt.

Calm down, he told himself. It wasn't as if he had confessed anything real.

He'd only done what he needed to do to defend Fallon from that prick. And he would *never* regret that.

The three of them ventured out of Shepherd House into

the crisp evening air. Normally, Grayson and his friends were chattier, but Sutter was silent, his gaze darting back and forth as they walked.

Grayson sighed quietly. In all the commotion of that afternoon, he'd nearly forgotten what their objective was this evening. Sutter Heyward was a man on a mission, and nothing would stand in his way. Grayson couldn't help but feel like his friend would be disappointed by what they found . . . or didn't find. But he wouldn't say that out loud.

As they approached Meddlehart Manor, Grayson could see warm lights shining from the tall front windows. Really, the class dinners were special because they were one of the few times students were allowed inside Meddlehart Manor. The house was old and, though well maintained, had that ancient mansion look on the outside. But inside, it had been remodeled with every fancy thing Grayson could think of—high ceilings, white marble countertops, sleek appliances, real wood floors, plush sofas, polished furniture.

Some of the original features of the house had been left in place, according to Averell, to "maintain the historic elements of the structure." Among those elements were the photographs documenting the Meddlehart family and the history of the school that lined the staircase wall.

The highlight of the house for most students was the game room. It had the most space for everyone to be together, and it also had the most stuff to do—air hockey and Ping-Pong and pool tables, a projector screen for movies and video games, a small bar for people to chill at (complete with a locked liquor cabinet—every year someone checked, and every year they were disappointed).

They entered through the front door, where Headmaster

Averell greeted students. He smiled broadly and shook their hands as they walked in.

"Grayson, looking sharp!" he said. "Hey, everything okay? Looks like you took a knock to the head."

"Just your average bruises from football, sir," he managed, relief washing over him. Coach Hamilton had given Grayson a warning but had also implied he wouldn't tell Headmaster Averell what happened. *You're a good player, and I need you on this team,* he'd said. It appeared Hammy had kept his word.

Averell nodded in understanding, seemingly satisfied. "Food and drinks are in the kitchen," he told them. "Head on in—I think most students are already upstairs. It'll be a fun evening!"

Grayson followed Sutter and Carter into the immaculate house. In the kitchen, the headmaster's wife greeted them warmly, offering food from the dozens of trays stationed on the counters—massive dishes of baked ziti and lasagna and carbonara, stacks of garlic bread, and displays of cookies for dessert.

And near the back door, Grayson spotted Margot and Fallon.

Margot's shirt was cropped just above the waist of her flared jeans, and her lips were painted a dark shade similar to that of her eye shadow. But Grayson's gaze stayed on Fallon, in a knee-length dusty-blue dress with a floral print. Her short hair was curled just above her shoulders, and she smiled at something Margot was saying.

Grayson's knees went weak.

Margot rushed off to the drinks table. As if she could sense him there, Fallon turned and looked at him. Her eyes softened with concern.

"I'm going to get a cannoli before they run out like last year," Carter said, oblivious. "Come on, Sutter."

"I don't want a cannoli," Sutter said. He was already scanning the room in a way Grayson would generously describe as unsubtle.

"That's something someone who's never tried a cannoli would say." Carter dragged him off without allowing time for protest.

Grayson didn't wait. He strode toward Fallon, who sucked in a little breath as he approached.

"Hey," he murmured. "Are you okay?"

She swallowed. "I feel like I should be the one asking you that question. Look at your face."

"It doesn't hurt."

She gave him a disbelieving look. "Gray."

"I'm fine," he said, forcing evenness into his voice. "Hammy let me go with a warning."

She barely concealed the shock in her expression. Then she averted her gaze. "You shouldn't have done it, Grayson. It was risky and could have gotten you in a *lot* more trouble."

"Fallon," he said in a low voice, hoping she couldn't hear the tremor in his voice, "there's not a chance in hell I was going to let him get away with talking to you like that."

The rage had not left him. It was still coursing steadily through his veins, getting faster and spreading further as he recalled the way Alex had spoken to her. The way he'd *rattled* her for no good reason.

Quickly, he scanned the room for any sign of Alex—as a junior, he was probably there somewhere—but Fallon grabbed his arm, like she knew exactly who he was looking for.

"It didn't matter enough to *fight* him," she said. "You can't just punch your way out of everything. That's never the answer, and you could've—you could've gotten kicked out!" But she still couldn't quite meet his gaze, and it was only then he saw the glisten in her eyes.

The sight cleaved Grayson's chest, and fury flared in his heart anew—no matter what she said, Alex's words *had* hurt her.

Desperate to do something, *anything* to comfort her, Grayson put his hands on her shoulders, lowering his head so he could look her in the eye. "Fallon, hey. Look at me."

She did. Her face was so close to his, he could count the freckles on her cheeks.

"I don't care if they punish me. I don't care *what* they do. You are worth it," he whispered. "*All* of it. You get that, don't you?"

He thought she might say something, but all she did was stare. Suddenly, he felt as though there was a live wire between them, sending a charge through his hands where they rested on her shoulders.

His words from earlier echoed between them. *So what if I am?*

He knew she was thinking of that, too—what he'd said on the football field, for all to hear. He could see her wheels turning, the way her gaze darted from his eyes to his mouth and back again. Like she was trying to read him.

And he wanted her to. For a split second, he wanted her to read him, to see it, to *know*. In a way, he wasn't sure how she *didn't* know—not when it was so loud in his own heart, in his every waking thought.

But in that instant, Margot approached, and Fallon was the first to step backward. The air felt cold around him. Grayson's arms fell at his sides, the moment disintegrating into nothing.

"Look at you!" Margot cried. "You put on a tie!"

"I like ties," Grayson mumbled. The tie now felt like it might cut off his airway.

"Wait, what the heck happened to your face?" Margot shrieked.

Grayson's roommates strolled up behind him. "He won't say," Carter said through a mouthful of cannoli.

Grayson looked at Fallon once more, but her eyes were on her feet.

So he cleared his throat, ignoring the ache in his chest. "It doesn't matter."

Sutter eyed him with quiet curiosity for a second before he abandoned the topic. "Okay, guys. We can't forget why we're here tonight," he said. "I double-checked the map, and the X is right over Meddlehart Manor. I say we start scoping things out now. We need to use our time here as wisely as possible. Once it's gone, there's not going to be an easy way to get back in here."

"*Back* in here?" Fallon hissed, jarred out of her momentary silence. "I'm sorry, Sutter, but I am not breaking into this house. *Ever.* I don't want to have to explain that in my college interviews one day."

"Who says we'd get caught?" Sutter asked, but even Carter and Margot were shaking their heads.

"No, buddy. Fallon's right. It's now or never," Carter said, clapping him on the shoulder. "And you know I love you, but I will not be doing any treasure hunting until I've eaten."

"I second that," Grayson muttered half-heartedly. Suddenly, he wasn't in the mood for any of this—the party, the treasure, none of it.

Sutter's jaw clenched, but he said nothing as the group dispersed, making their way toward the buffet. Right as Grayson took his place in line, his phone buzzed in his pocket. His stomach dropped immediately, like he already knew who it was.

And he was right.

Are you on the starting lineup for game 1? His dad.

Grayson paused. His dad wasn't thinking about coming to watch, was he? Normally he was too busy filming—that was always his excuse for never attending Grayson's games.

But Damon Hendricks was a Meddlehart alum—not to mention that he had played on the football team while there—and he knew what a big deal the first game of the season was. Every year, game one was against West Fork High, their biggest rival, and Meddlehart's football stadium was always packed to the gills for the occasion.

Maybe that's why he was asking. Maybe, for once, he planned to be there—on the condition that Grayson would be the starting quarterback.

Grayson tapped out a quick reply. *Yes, I'm varsity QB this season.* It bothered him that his father needed confirmation, but at least he was asking. It was more than he'd ever done before.

He sent the text, hesitated, then typed out one more. *Will you be there?*

He'd stuffed his phone back in his pocket before the reply came but pulled it out when he felt the vibration.

I have a break from filming, and it's the rivalry game. Wouldn't miss it.

Grayson turned his phone off with a trembling hand. His dad *was* coming. He'd wanted that to be his father's answer, despite everything. Even if he made it seem like he was coming for the rivalry game and not because he wanted to see Grayson, it didn't matter.

Grayson wanted his dad to see him play. He wanted to *prove* himself.

Grayson's throat was still thick when Fallon tapped him on the shoulder, and he had to clench his jaw to keep it together.

"You sure you're okay?" she asked quietly. Her eyes were locked on him with that intense concern that always ruined him.

He nodded quickly, furrowing his brows with faked confusion. "Why wouldn't I be?"

But his hands still shook a little even after he turned away from Fallon. He stuffed them in his pockets. His chest was tight, and it ached. God, it ached.

Breathe, Grayson. If you could just get a damn breath in, maybe things will be better.

Or maybe, just maybe, everything would stay exactly the fucking same.

TWELVE

Sutter

Sutter pushed his dinner back and forth on his plate, gazing around the Meddlehart Manor dining room and waiting for his friends to finish stalling.

"This ricotta," Carter said, scooping another bite onto his fork. "It's so *fresh*. I can tell this was made in a scratch kitchen—wanna know how you can tell?"

Sutter did *not* want to know. The food was divine, as it was every year, but he shoveled it in without bothering to pay attention to the flavors or textures or quality of the cheese. He just wanted to be done eating so he could do what he'd come to do.

Carter was the last one of his friends still eating, taking his sweet time and savoring every bite.

Finally, Sutter couldn't take it. He stood and made his way out of the room, toward the staircase. "We're wasting time, Carter."

"All right, all *right*," Carter said, shoving the last bites into his mouth. "I'm done."

Sutter led the way upstairs to the game room, where the rest of their classmates were chattering over games of air hockey and

Ping-Pong. Old-school arcade games lined one wall, creating a chorus of tinny music that rivaled the students' laughter in volume. There was a VR system that seemed to be the highlight, in addition to a game of flip cup using Coke that was probably spiked with something someone had smuggled in, if Sutter had to guess.

Sutter scanned the room to see where his friends had scattered. Grayson was surrounded by a bunch of girls, probably talking to him about his famous dad. His expression was one of supreme boredom. Margot was piling a plate high with sugar cookies at the minibar. And Fallon had gotten pulled away by some of her art classmates.

Carter clapped his hand on Sutter's shoulder. "Don't worry, man. We'll look for it. It's just been a long day. We're all decompressing for a minute."

"A long day" was an understatement. It had been a long *week*, and though he'd never admit it out loud, Sutter was exhausted. But he couldn't stop thinking about the video, the time capsule, the sound of his brother's voice like a ghost from a distant memory.

I'll find you, Lawson, I swear it.

Just then, someone passing by tripped over Sutter's foot, though it felt more like a kick. He stepped back to see Quincy Stiles peering at him as though he hadn't noticed Sutter at all.

"Hey, Sutter," Quincy said. His voice had a slow, drawling rhythm that made Sutter's skin itch. His lips twisted into a smirk. "Sorry about that."

"It's fine," he muttered as Quincy moved along. Every year, Meddlehart assigned graduating seniors as "mentors" to incoming freshmen to help them acclimate to campus, and Quincy had been Lawson's mentee. Back when Lawson was around, he'd tried to convince Quincy and Sutter to hang out and get to know each other, but they never quite gelled.

And Sutter was fine with that. Because even though Quincy had never done anything wrong to him . . . Sutter just didn't like the guy. Maybe because Quincy acted like a spoiled snob all the time, but Sutter wasn't keeping track.

As if confirming his sentiments, Quincy strolled over to the flip cup game and began speaking in a low voice to none other than Alex Harker, whose jaw sported an angry red mark. Alex listened intently, bowing his head slightly in concentration.

Sutter smothered a scoff. Figures that people like those two would have plenty to talk about.

That's when Sutter noticed Fallon's eyes were on him from across the room. She gave him a reassuring smile before turning back to the people she was talking to. She looked really pretty in that dress. He'd nearly let the thought slip past his lips when Margot walked back up to them and offered them cookies she'd stacked on a plate.

"We should start our search now," she said quietly. "One of my drama class friends just told me Averell is giving a speech soon."

"Let's get going," Sutter said. He caught Grayson's eye from across the room and signaled to him with a nod. Grayson broke away from the girls and strode over, and Fallon made it back to them before he did.

"I say we split up," Sutter whispered. "The game room and the kitchen are rooms to avoid—too many people, and I doubt there's anything there for us."

"We can sweep the downstairs," Fallon offered, gesturing to Margot. "The sitting rooms, their personal library, and the laundry room."

"Mrs. Averell is still down there," Margot said. "We can start a conversation with her, buy some time."

"Great," Sutter said. "We'll cover the upstairs, then." That meant the bedrooms and Averell's study.

They split up, and the girls went downstairs. Sutter nodded at Grayson and Carter, and they dispersed into the hallway. A group of girls passed by whispering to each other, and the boys waited for them to leave before ducking into different rooms.

Sutter pushed the first door open, and there he was, in Averell's study.

It was pristine. The dark wooden furniture was matching—desk, chairs, everything—and polished perfectly. A bookcase stood tall and wide across the back wall beside the window. There were framed photos on the wood-paneled walls, a signed football in a glass case, crystal paperweights, and bookends made of marble.

Sutter's heart skipped. This was the room that interested him the most by far, but was *not* a room he wanted to be caught snooping in.

Too late to turn back now. He moved toward the desk first, briefly scanning the neatly sorted documents and loose papers before testing the top drawer.

Locked. He tried the others—all locked.

Grayson hurried in just then.

"The master bedroom door is locked," he said. "Which, you know, makes sense."

"Help me search this one," Sutter said, and they both continued looking. Grayson turned to the closet on the other side of the room and opened it to reveal nothing but filing cabinets and storage boxes. As he started peeking through each one, Sutter got on his knees and tested the floorboards beneath the desk. He checked under the rug and the bookcase, but the floorboards were all solid.

And that's when he spotted it.

Sutter's back was to the door, so he didn't see Carter come in—he only heard his footsteps.

"The other room is a spare," Carter said. "A bed, an empty closet. Nothing. The furniture even smells like it came from the nearest Pottery Barn."

"Closet's got nothing," Grayson said back. "This was a bust."

"Guys," Sutter said.

"Maybe Margot and Fallon have those little hair things," Grayson said. "We could pick the locks with them."

"Little hair things?" Carter asked.

"The little *things*," Grayson said desperately. "The tiny sticks that hold their hair in—"

"Would you two shut up?" Sutter hissed. "I found something."

Carter's and Grayson's footsteps felt like thunder in Sutter's ear, which was resting on the floor in front of the bookcase. The two of them came to a halt by Sutter's head, and he could practically feel their questioning looks.

"Yes, Sutter. That's the floor," Grayson said sarcastically.

Sutter ignored him. "Look."

They eased onto the floor beside him.

"Not sure what we're seeing here, buddy," Carter said.

"The wall," Sutter told them. He reached under the legs of the bookcase and pressed his fingertips against a cold, rough surface.

"The other walls are paneled wood," he said, "but behind the bookcase . . ."

"It's brick," Carter murmured.

It was then they heard Headmaster Averell's voice, growing louder with each word until it sounded like he was just outside the door.

Sutter's heart clanged with panic. "Closet," he hissed. *"Closet, now!"*

The three of them scrambled for the opposite side of the study. Carter stepped on Grayson's hand in the chaos, and he barely bit back a choked yelp. Sutter stumbled halfway there, his knees slamming into the floor, and he crawled the last few feet to the closet.

Grayson shut the closet door behind them a mere second before the door to the study opened, and Headmaster Averell's chiding voice filled the room.

". . . sure how you got this," he was saying, "but I must say, I'm disappointed."

"Someone's in trooouble," Carter whispered. Grayson and Sutter both elbowed him, and Carter hugged his ribs.

"Ow," he muttered.

"I'm sorry, sir," an easy, drawling voice replied—one that didn't sound very sorry at all.

"Oh my God," Sutter whispered as recognition dawned on him. "Open the door."

"Are you nuts?" Grayson hissed.

"That's Quincy Stiles," Sutter insisted. "I want to see. *Open. The. Door.*"

Grayson took the knob gingerly and eased the door open the slightest bit. Sure enough, Quincy had taken the chair across from the desk, where Averell sat in the leather swivel chair. On the desk between them sat a flask, small enough to fit in someone's pocket.

"Quincy," Averell said carefully, "I know you're well aware alcohol is strictly prohibited on campus."

Quincy nodded, eyes on his shoes.

A glint of silver at Quincy's feet caught Sutter's eye, and he startled.

Oh my God. The world swayed slightly under Sutter's feet.

Quincy was wearing an ankle bracelet, and the charm that dangled from it . . .

. . . was a viper pendant.

Sutter's mind reeled. What the hell did it mean? There was only one thing he knew for sure—there was no way it was a coincidence.

"I'm going to let you off with a warning because you're a good student and we've never had an issue like this with you before," Averell went on. "But please remember if this happens again, there will be greater consequences."

Sutter held back a snort. He was pretty sure Quincy's father's net worth had more to do with him getting away with this than his supposed record of good behavior.

"Understood, Headmaster," Quincy said as Averell stood and ushered him out. "I'm truly sorry. It was foolish of me."

Averell chuckled lightly, and the door to the study swung open. "Well, I can't say I didn't make similar mistakes back in my . . ." The roar of the party filled the room for one brief second, drowning out Averell's voice before the door shut with a soft *click.*

The three of them burst from the closet. In nearly the same moment, the study door flew open again; thank God it was only Fallon and Margot standing in the doorway, eyes wide, mouths agape.

“Oh my God, we thought you guys got caught,” Margot whispered.

“Did you find anything?” Sutter asked them.

Fallon shook her head. “Nothing at all. You?”

Sutter nodded, barely able to catch his breath. “Quincy is wearing a viper pendant.”

“What?” his friends chorused, including Carter and Grayson—they must not have noticed.

“On an ankle bracelet,” Sutter told them. “But we’ll talk about that later—we’re running out of time. And there’s something else we found.” He strode toward the bookcase.

“What are you doing?” Fallon asked, but Sutter was already bracing his palms against one side of the bookcase and pushing hard to the left. Grayson rushed to help him and pulled from the other side. Slowly, carefully, they slid the bookcase away from the wall.

“Holy shit,” Carter breathed.

Behind the bookcase was a section of wall filled in with brick. It was uneven in places, about the size of a small door.

“What is this?” Margot asked, her voice rising slightly.

Sutter knocked against the bricks a few times.

“There’s something behind this,” he said, feeling all the confidence in the world. “We need to get through here.”

“Sutter,” Fallon said warningly. Worry laced her tone. Sutter opened his mouth to reassure her everything would be fine, but a muffled shout interrupted him from the hallway. It was Mrs. Averell.

“Students!” she called. “Please gather in the game room for a word from the headmaster!”

Grayson shook his head. “No time, Sutter,” he said, bracing against the bookcase again. “On three. One, two . . .”

Together, they slid the bookcase back in place and filed into the hallway and to the game room right as Headmaster Averell was calling for everyone to settle down.

Sutter gazed around the roomful of students oblivious to what he and his friends had just done, searching until his eyes locked on Quincy. His brain itched with questions, one louder than all the rest.

What are you hiding, Quincy Stiles?

THIRTEEN

Grayson

Weekends at Meddlehart meant something different for everyone. For Grayson and the rest of the football team, weekends meant early-morning practices.

Grayson hauled himself out of bed and down to the dining hall in a stupor of exhaustion, puffy-eyed and disoriented. To his surprise, he found his friends at their usual table, bright and early, each with their own plans for the day.

"Didn't expect you all to be here so early," Grayson said as he joined the group, his plate piled high with eggs, bacon, and hash browns.

"I doubt any of us slept much last night," Fallon said quietly, buttering a slice of cinnamon raisin toast.

"I had to get here early to make sure I can track down Quincy," Sutter said firmly. He had no food in front of him, and his knuckles tapped an antsy rhythm on the table.

"My head is still spinning," Margot said, rubbing her temples. "Why would Quincy have a viper pendant?"

"What if it's a friendship bracelet type of thing?" Carter asked. He stabbed a fork into the last bite of his omelet. "Lawson was Quincy's freshman-year mentor."

“I don’t know Lawson well,” Grayson said, scratching the back of his head, “but I don’t see him being a friendship bracelet kind of guy.”

“He wasn’t. But we won’t have to wonder for long,” Sutter said. “I’m going to ask Quincy myself.”

“Why does that sound like a horrible idea to me?” Fallon asked.

“Most ideas sound horrible to you at first,” Carter said, “but then you warm up to them, right?”

“Wrong,” she muttered. “I just follow along because I’d rather be there to supervise than to *not* supervise.”

“That’s called FOMO,” Grayson informed her.

“It’s not FOMO.”

“It’s probably at least thirty percent FOMO.”

Her lips curled at the corners the tiniest bit, and that felt like a victory to Grayson. He smiled to himself and dug into his food.

“Are we going to talk about the weird bricked-up part of Averell’s wall?” Carter asked. “Because that seems extra sketchy to me.”

“It looked like there was something there he didn’t want anyone to access,” Margot said. “It’s like he was trying to block off part of the house. A secret room or something.”

Fallon shifted anxiously in her seat. “The problem with figuring out what’s behind that wall is we don’t have the means to knock it down without getting in a lot of trouble. We need to think of another way.”

They all paused, considering her words. She was right and they knew it.

“I’ll track Quincy down today and figure this out,” Sutter promised, breaking the silence. “The first thing we need to do is figure out why he has a viper pendant like Lawson's, and then maybe we'll know what to do next. I'd better confront him alone, though. If we all approach him, it'll feel like an ambush."

They split up after that. Fallon went to the library to see if she could find more information about Meddlehart's history. Margot left to get ready for a day of shopping in town. Carter headed to Dr. Wilbur's office hours for help on an upcoming exam. Sutter stayed right there in the dining hall, watching the doors, waiting for Quincy.

Grayson still felt tired as he made his way to the Ace for practice. He ambled into the locker room and sat to tie his cleats.

"Hey, Hendricks."

Alex Harker's voice sounded like nails on a chalkboard to Grayson. Alex walked over to Grayson's locker, smirking.

This could not be good.

"Leave me alone," Grayson told Alex warily.

"Hey, why the hostility? I just wanted to congratulate you on your new stepmom," Alex said, pushing a hand through his strawberry-blond locks. "Or stepmom-to-be, anyway. She's hot. Think you might be able to introduce all of us, maybe on Parents Weekend?"

Grayson's heart dropped into his stomach before Alex even showed him what was on his phone. He scanned the gossip article quickly, trying to take it with a grain of salt.

But there were pictures to back up the headline, ones even Grayson couldn't brush off as gossip.

ACTOR DAMON HENDRICKS CAUGHT CUDDLING HANNAH GRACE JAMES IN DOWNTOWN LA

Hannah Grace James. Grayson knew who she was. The girl who'd risen to fame from rom-coms Netflix had released a few months back.

And she was barely twenty-two years old.

The photos showed his father walking with his arm around Hannah's shoulders, fingers dangling near one breast. Her blond head was tucked against his chest, this girl who was young enough to be his daughter. They were both grinning like they had a secret, like they were oblivious to the camera snapping photos of them just yards away.

But Grayson knew his dad. He wasn't oblivious to cameras, not ever.

"What, hadn't you heard about this?" Alex said.

Before Grayson could respond, Hammy came in and called them out to the field. The players pushed through the doors. Grayson followed in a daze, anger simmering in his stomach.

The team ran through their warm-up routine, but Grayson's limbs felt like they were full of lead. The paparazzi photos imprinted behind his eyes—his father's smug expression was all he could see.

What was he thinking?

Hammy ordered them to line up and practice plays. Grayson took his position as quarterback. He nearly missed the snap, fumbling it, and then took off for a quarterback sneak.

One second, he was running. The next, he was flat on his back, the force of the ground so strong, his teeth rattled. Alex towered over him. Grayson's head spun with confusion, and he realized his helmet had flown off with the impact.

"Hendricks, what the hell are you doing?" Hammy called from the sidelines. *"Wake up!"*

"Better watch where you're going next time," Alex said smugly. He started to walk away, kicking a bit of dirt in Grayson's face.

Grayson shoved himself to his feet, fists already clenched.

"Back off, Harker," he snapped.

"Hey, man," Alex said. "All I'm saying is you shouldn't drag your daddy issues onto the field with you, all right? Really not the place for—"

Grayson's vision flooded with red.

His body moved before his mind could catch up. He charged Alex, throwing his shoulder into his gut, and they toppled to the ground. Alex didn't hesitate before he started punching. His fist connected hard with Grayson's jaw, then his right eye, and though Grayson saw stars, he didn't stop swinging. Grayson shoved Alex's arms away and threw a punch to his side.

Mere seconds passed before other players burst in to separate them. Multiple hands gripped Grayson's shoulders and dragged him backward, restraining him as he struggled to go forward, back to Alex. The coppery tang of blood flooded his mouth, and he spat on the ground.

Hammy was between them now. He was red in the face, and veins pulsed in his forehead.

"Enough!" he bellowed. "Who the hell do you two think you are, fighting during practice? You're both gonna end up on the sidelines this Friday if you keep it up! I swear—"

"I'm sorry, Coach," Grayson muttered, and Alex grumbled something along those lines.

"I don't want to hear it," Hammy growled. "I don't want to see your faces. Get your asses off my field. *Now.*"

Grayson didn't wait. He stormed off, and Alex went the other direction, staying far away from him.

"My office in three hours, both of you!" Hammy shouted as he retreated.

Grayson didn't bother to turn around. He left the sports complex without a clue where he intended to go—he just needed to get away.

Out the corner of his eye, he saw Fallon making her way up the path, coming back from the library with a few books tucked under her arm.

"Grayson!" she called. There was a note of concern in her voice, like she could tell just from looking at him that something was wrong. "Hey, wait up! Gray, *stop*."

She grabbed his arm. Her hand was warm and soft. He pulled his arm away before her touch could bring him back down to earth.

"What's wrong?" Her eyes clouded as she took in the fresh bruises on his face, his bleeding lip. "What *happened*? You didn't get into another fight with Alex, did you?"

Grayson didn't answer. In response, Fallon shook her head.

"You can't let him get to you like this," she insisted. "I know he's always been jealous of you and that's why he targets you, but—"

"I don't need another lecture, Fallon!" he snapped.

Her face flashed with a confused kind of hurt, and all at once, Grayson felt like the worst person in the world. But her expression shifted as she studied his face.

Suddenly, it felt like she could see right through him—see the gaping wound in his chest. The one that had been festering, unhealed, for as long as he could remember. And he couldn't let that happen.

"Talk to me, Gray," she said. Her voice was gentler now, so gentle it made his throat tighten.

He wished he could. He wanted to tell her everything. If there was anyone in the world who would understand it—understand *him*—it was Fallon.

But she doesn't, that voice in the darkest part of him whispered. *No one does.*

"There's nothing to talk about," he told her, and stormed away.

She didn't come after him, didn't call his name again, didn't argue. She just let him go.

And Grayson supposed he might have done the same. It was what everyone else in his life had done, after all. He shouldn't expect anything different from her.

Grayson wanted nothing more than to go straight to Shepherd House and bury himself in bed, block the world out for as long as he could, but he couldn't face any of his friends right now. He made a beeline for the locker room—he needed to dump his shoulder pads and helmet there, anyway.

His pace slowed as he trudged into the room, praying he wouldn't run into Alex or Hammy, but the coast was clear. He reached his locker and let the door swing open.

It wasn't until after he'd unloaded his gear that he saw it—a small piece of thick, creamy paper stuck in the door. He pulled it out and studied the blocky handwritten letters in black ink:

Time is lost, bridges are burned,
All are ways you come to learn.
To play the game of Hot or cold,
Your next move must be brave and bold.
Don't lose hope, please take heart—
Maybe it's time to go back to the start . . .

Grayson frowned, a chill dropping down his spine. *A poem.* He pored over the paper for a moment more, then glanced over his shoulder.

The locker room was empty. No sign of who might have left this message, or why.

Could it have been from the same person who left Lawson's phone for Sutter to find?

Carefully, Grayson stuffed the poem into his pocket. He had a feeling he and his friends might need this message, wherever it might lead.

FOURTEEN

Sutter

Sutter hadn't planned on taking the weekend bus into West Fork. But after waiting an hour for Quincy Stiles to show up for breakfast, he finally saw him strut into the dining hall, only to grab a croissant to go and then make his way toward the parking lot.

Quincy was heading into town. And if Sutter wanted to confront him about his viper pendant, that meant he was joining him.

When Sutter boarded the bus, he found Margot there. She was wearing a chunky knit sweater and round sunglasses and applying burgundy lipstick. She peered over her hand mirror and shot him a surprised glance as he took the empty seat beside her.

"What are you doing here?" she asked with a smile. "I didn't think you wanted to be my shopping buddy today."

Sutter wrinkled his nose as the bus started to roll forward. "I will never want that, Margot."

Margot's smile dropped. "Well, you sure do know how to make a girl feel special," she deadpanned.

"I'm here because I saw Quincy heading this way." He glanced around the bus, looking for his target, and spotted him in the very back. *Bingo.* "Where is there to shop in West Fork, anyway?"

"There's a little family-owned boutique on Main," she told him. "It's officially sweater weather, and I'm in need of some new warm clothes. Plus, it's good vlog material—advocating for small businesses while showing off my weekend shopping haul. Win-win."

She pulled her phone out of her bag and held it up, lens facing them.

"All right, guys, so I brought Sutter along to go shopping—"

"I'm not going shopping," he clarified, eyeing the camera lens.

"—and it's a beautiful fall day here in the mountains! I'm so excited to be dressed in my cutest autumn outfit and hit up my favorite store in town. Feeling good, and ready to shop small!"

Margot continued as the bus rumbled down the road. When Sutter glanced over his shoulder, he saw no one was sitting next to Quincy. Carefully, he stood up and wedged his way into the aisle, knocking into Margot in the process.

"Sutter, watch the camera!"

"Sorry, Margot," he muttered. He moved quickly to the back of the bus, hanging on to the headrests to keep his balance, and took the empty seat next to Quincy.

He was listening to something on his earbuds, and he yanked one out, glancing at Sutter with a raised brow.

"Heyward," he said in a steady tone. "Can I help you with something?"

Sutter shrugged slightly. "Just thought I'd drop by and say hello. Figured you could use some company. You looked lonely."

Quincy's eyes narrowed. "What do you want?"

Sutter sighed—no point in beating around the bush. He

glanced around, reached for his neck, and slipped the viper pendant from under the collar of his shirt.

"This look familiar to you, Stiles?" he asked coolly.

Quincy's eyes widened slightly, the only thing to betray his even expression. He recovered quickly, though, giving Sutter an easy grin and running a hand through his black hair.

"I figured this would happen eventually."

"You gonna tell me what this means?" Sutter asked, hardening his voice.

"I don't know, Heyward," Quincy muttered. "Answer this first: How did Franklin Thatcher die?"

Sutter's mouth went dry, his vision narrowing to a point. It was suddenly harder to breathe as Lawson's words from the video echoed in his mind. He remembered what his older brother told him to do if anyone ever asked him that question.

Tell them to fuck off.

But he couldn't. Not if he wanted to get the answers he'd been looking for.

He could hardly hear the response leave his mouth over the blood pounding in his ears. "By the fangs of greed," he responded.

Quincy nodded slowly. He leaned back, smirking.

"If you want to talk, then we'll talk," he told Sutter, gaze focused straight ahead. "Just not here."

"Where, then?"

"Beanstalk Coffee," Quincy said.

Sutter could just barely smell the sharp tang of alcohol on Quincy's breath.

Sutter didn't respond. Wordlessly, he stood and made his way back to the seat beside Margot. She'd put her camera away and turned her stern gaze on him.

"What did he say?"

"Nothing yet," Sutter responded. "But he will. I'll make sure of it."

Sutter wasn't much of a coffee drinker. He texted Margot from the line at the counter and ordered exactly what she recommended.

"An iced caramel macchiato," Sutter muttered to the barista. He was pretty sure he completely destroyed the pronunciation, but the barista didn't seem fazed.

When he sat down across from Quincy and took a sip, he scowled at the bitterness.

"Didn't know you were a cold coffee guy," Quincy said, stirring his steaming cup of frothing, foaming whatever-he-had-ordered.

"First, you don't know anything about me," Sutter said, "and second, I'm not a coffee guy at all."

"Might want to stir it," Quincy said. "Get the caramel mixed in so it's sweeter."

Sutter glared at him but gripped the straw and swirled it around a few times. To his dismay, the drink tasted much better.

"I came here to study," Quincy said, "but clearly that's not going to happen, so . . . I'm going to need some context, Sutter."

"Context?" he repeated.

"What do you want to know?" Quincy asked. "Or rather, what *do* you know?"

For a moment, Sutter debated how to answer the question. He didn't want to tell Quincy he didn't know anything about the viper pendant and what it meant—that would give him the upper hand. Because it was clear Quincy knew *something* significant.

Sutter cleared his throat. "I know my brother was your mentor. I know he disappeared the year he met you. And I know this snake pendant has something to do with it."

Quincy's grin looked lethal, his teeth gleaming like fangs. "Awfully accusatory of you."

"Can you blame me?"

Quincy pondered this for a moment. "The pendants have *something* to do with it," he echoed. He tapped his chin. "What do you think that *something* might be?"

His lips had twisted into a knowing smirk that Sutter did not like. He could feel his frustration mounting, so he took a steadying breath. He wasn't here to let Quincy toy with him like a cat playing with its prey.

"I know something else, Stiles," he said. "I know you're in hot water with the headmaster."

Quincy's stare darkened. "Is that right?"

Sutter nodded. "*Someone* was stupid enough to sneak booze into the class dinner. And I have a feeling there's more where that came from, isn't there?"

Quincy glared at him for a long moment, and Sutter's heart galloped the entire time. Finally, though, Quincy leaned forward.

"Listen, Heyward," he said in a low voice. "I think you're getting the wrong idea here. You're right—your brother was my mentor, but I have no idea where he went. He was my friend, and I want to know what happened that night just as much as you do. We're not enemies, understand? I've actually been hoping this would happen for some time, whether you initiated it or I did."

Sutter wasn't sure what he meant, but he nodded in response. Whatever it took to keep him talking.

"It sounds to me," Quincy went on, "like you found out about this the same way I did—your brother left something for you to find."

Sutter's mind whirred and clicked. Had Lawson been the one who planted his phone for Sutter to find? Was he hiding out somewhere nearby, lying low, waiting for Sutter to find him? The thought sent a rush of sweet adrenaline through his veins.

In response, Sutter nodded. "He did."

"That guarantees your invitation, then," Quincy said. "If a past head of the order deems you worthy to compete for membership, no one can turn you down. You're a smart guy, Sutter. And so was your brother. He was the best shot we had at finding it, and I'd be stupid not to bring you in. We can be the group that changes everything."

Sutter went still. "What?"

"I can't say more right now. Not here."

"Not here, in this half-empty coffee shop?" Sutter pressed.

Quincy dismissed this, turning a hard gaze on him. "Look for the invitation in the next few days, but if you breathe a word to anyone else, you're in deep shit, and so are they. Not a word." He smiled. "It'll all start to make sense soon. Trust me when I say this will be the best decision of your life."

Sutter could hardly absorb what Quincy was saying. "I'm not—"

"At this rate, Heyward, you really don't have a choice. You know too much. Think of this as . . . destiny. Just wait and it will all fall into place. Now, if you'd excuse me," Quincy said, "I have a lot to get done today."

A long moment of silence passed between them before Sutter

realized Quincy was waiting for him to leave. Sutter stood, dumbfounded. He left his coffee and made his way to the exit.

"Heyward."

Sutter turned. "What?"

"Do your friends know, too?"

Sutter frowned. "Which friends?"

"You know who I'm talking about," Quincy said, rolling his eyes. "It's not like the five of you hang out with anyone else."

Sutter just stared at him. What was the right answer to that question?

But Quincy simply nodded after a beat. "That's what I thought." He turned back to his coffee and stirred it, clearly done talking.

Sutter walked out numbly and went straight to the bus stop, trying desperately to understand what he'd just gotten himself into.

FIFTEEN

Fallon

Grayson would hardly look at Fallon. He sat across the table in the dining hall, right eye blackened and nearly swollen shut. His lip was split in the middle, a bloody line barely scabbed over. She tried to meet his eyes, but he kept avoiding her gaze.

She knew why now. It had been impossible to avoid overhearing Grayson's teammates talking in the buffet line moments before about what Alex did. And she felt terrible for pressing Grayson on the topic when she should've been able to see the hurt radiating off him, the same way it was now.

Dinner had been quiet so far, with Margot and Carter making small talk, and Sutter absent. He'd texted that he was running late and not to wait on him.

So the four of them sat, forks tapping audibly against their plates as they ate. Fallon was starting to wonder if anyone was going to acknowledge Grayson's bruises, when Margot spoke.

"So, when are you going to tell us what happened to your face?" Margot asked, stabbing a fork into the last bite of her salad. "We've been sitting here for fifteen minutes in silence,

Grayson, pretending not to notice. And we aren't going to accept 'it doesn't matter' as an answer this time."

Carter started waving his hand near his neck, a signal for Margot to cut it out, but it wasn't quite subtle enough, because Grayson turned and glared at him.

Carter let his hand drop and looked away, eyes wide. He took a massive gulp of tea—some herbal variety he claimed Whittaker had recommended to him—and then cursed quietly under his breath. "Shit, that's really hot."

"Got in a disagreement at practice," Grayson answered bluntly. "Both times."

"With a brick wall?" Margot asked.

"Margot," Fallon whispered warningly.

She turned to Fallon, eyebrows raised, but Fallon didn't say a word.

Margot huffed. "You won't tell me, either?"

Guilt wormed around in Fallon's stomach. She hadn't told Margot about any of it—not the punches Grayson had thrown on her behalf, not what he'd said, the words she'd been unable to stop thinking about since they left his lips.

So what if I am?

And she certainly hadn't told Margot about the way she felt when Grayson saw the tears in her eyes later that night, when he put his hands on her shoulders, when he told her he didn't care what happened after he'd defended her.

You are worth it.

No, she couldn't tell Margot about how her stomach had flipped twice, how her heart had lurched into her throat, because to admit those things out loud would upend everything Fallon thought she knew.

Margot turned back on Grayson, snapping Fallon from her

thoughts. "Will you at least confirm you didn't get in trouble? You're not going to be suspended or anything?"

Grayson shook his head. "Hammy's making me mop the locker room as punishment. That's it."

Fallon barely hid her surprise. It was a miracle he'd be allowed to play. Then again, the game against West Fork was around the corner, and Hammy probably knew he'd need his star quarterback on the field to win.

"Speaking of brick walls," Carter said, clearly trying to change the subject, "does anyone have any ideas of how we're going to figure out what's behind the one in Averell's office?"

Fallon sighed. This wouldn't have been her subject change of choice, but . . . maybe she could speak her mind honestly while Sutter wasn't with them.

"What if there *isn't* a way for us to find out?" she proposed, choosing her words carefully. "Even if we manage to get back into Averell's office undetected . . . what then? We can't dismantle the wall."

"Maybe we don't have to fully dismantle it to find out what's behind it," Carter countered. "There might be a clue in Averell's office."

"But you guys searched that room top to bottom and didn't find anything like that," Margot pointed out. "Right?"

Carter pinched the bridge of his nose, exasperated.

Grayson cleared his throat. "Sutter's not going to stop until we find out. If it has something to do with Lawson . . . we *have* to know. Maybe he found out something useful from Quincy—let's wait and see what he says."

A moment of silence fell over the group. Fallon glanced around the dining hall with a sinking feeling, wondering where Sutter was. It looked like he might skip dinner altogether.

"All right. I'm going to get dessert." Margot got up and started to strut away from the table without another word. She wasn't the best at hiding her frustration.

"Wait," Grayson said, and Margot stopped short. "There's . . . actually something I need to show you guys. Something I found. I was going to wait for Sutter, but . . ."

Fallon perked up, straightening in her chair. She watched as Grayson fumbled with his pocket until he pulled out a crumpled piece of paper. He unfolded it and smoothed it on the tabletop.

Time is lost, bridges are Burned,
All are ways you come to learn.
To play the game of Hot or cold,
Your next move must be brave and bold.
Don't lose hope, please take heart—
Maybe it's time to go back to the start . . .

"What the hell does that mean?" Carter asked.

"No idea," Grayson muttered. "And I didn't see who left it, either. It was just . . . there, in my locker."

Fallon grabbed the paper and held it up to the light. What exactly she was looking for, she didn't know—anything to make the message clearer.

"There are randomly capitalized words," she said. *"Burned* and *Hot*. That has to be intentional, but why?"

"Maybe it's a sign that we're on the right track," Carter said, excited. *"The game of hot and cold*. Whoever left this is trying to say we're getting warmer—we're close to finding out the truth."

Fallon nodded—that could be it, but something was still

scratching at the back of her mind. The ellipses in the last line of the poem almost made it seem like the poem was incomplete. She set the paper down on the table, considering the possibility.

Margot's lips twisted in concern. "Okay . . . this is starting to creep me out. First we're given Lawson's phone and now a poem? Who's doing this?"

Carter leaned forward to get a closer look, only to knock his tea over, spilling it everywhere. Fallon gasped as the steaming liquid flooded the table. Grayson snatched the paper up and shook it off, but it was too late. It was soaked, the black ink already bleeding.

"Carter!" Margot yelped.

"Damn it!" Carter cried. "Stupid clumsy genes!"

Grayson pressed the paper flat on a dry part of the table. "It's whatever. We read it, we know what it says. We can tell Sutter about it later."

Margot sighed. "On that note . . . I was serious about getting dessert. I'll be back."

"I'm gonna follow her," Carter said. "It's cake tonight. Anyone want a slice?"

Fallon and Grayson shook their heads, and their friends walked off. She glanced across the table at him, worry nagging at her. He was still avoiding her gaze, eyes downcast.

"Gray," she said carefully, her voice quiet. "Are you all right?"

He nodded. His voice was low when he responded. "I've been in a few fights before. Just some bruises. I can take it."

"I didn't mean . . ." She stopped herself. "I heard about what Alex said . . . what he *did*, and—"

"It's not important, Fallon," Grayson interrupted. "This is just how my dad is. He's always been this way. It doesn't bother me, okay? I can handle it."

She stared at him, lost for words. It clearly *did* bother him, but she couldn't say that, not when he was closed off like this. It would only push him further away.

So Fallon stood—to do what, she wasn't sure, but she couldn't sit there any longer. She stopped before she passed by him.

"You can talk to me," she whispered. "You know that, right?"

He kept his eyes on his food. After a long pause, he nodded. Then she walked away, past the dessert cart and out the dining hall doors.

She marched straight to Shepherd, went to her room, and plopped down on her bed. For a long time, she just stared at her dozens of drawings—all the characters who had been her friends when she had none—and tried to melt into the covers.

She tried not to think about Grayson. She tried not to think about the walls he had up, and how much she wished he'd let them down. He'd always been someone who made her feel seen. From the moment he'd pulled up a chair beside her in homeroom on their first day and made sure she didn't feel alone, and every day since.

It made Fallon's chest ache to think he might not feel the same way about her.

Fallon wasn't sure how much time passed before she forced herself to move. Her first major art assignment was due Monday, and she'd hardly started on it.

Right as she reached for her sketch pad, a few hollow knocks sounded at the door.

Carefully, she padded across Margot's furry pink rug to the door. When she opened it, she was met with an empty hallway. Confusion swirled in her brain until she looked down at the floor.

There, in a plastic to-go container, was a perfect slice of cinnamon streusel cake.

She glanced both ways down the hallway and didn't see anyone. But she smiled knowingly as she picked up the cake and closed the door behind her.

SIXTEEN

Grayson

The last thing Grayson remembered before waking up was his mother's open eyes, staring blankly at him.

He shot upright in bed, gasping for air. For a long, painful minute, none came. He stumbled to the floor, sweaty and trembling, and just made it to the trash can before he coughed up the meager contents of his stomach. Finally, he managed a breath and wiped his mouth with the back of his hand.

Grayson didn't have nightmares all the time, but when he did, it was always when he was stressed about something. And the nightmares were always about the same moment, the one he'd spent his entire life trying to forget.

It hardly occurred to him Sutter's desk lamp was on, and he was sitting at it. Carter was passed out in bed, snoring, but Sutter was wide awake, looking at him. The alarm clock on Grayson's nightstand read 2:34 a.m.

"What are you doing up?" Grayson asked roughly.

"Can't sleep," Sutter answered. He had a pencil in his hand, and he tap-tap-tapped the eraser on the surface of the desk. "You all right? Are you sick?"

Grayson shook his head. His damp hair hung in his eyes,

and he brushed it off his forehead. "No, I'm good. Just . . . ate something bad, I think."

"Hope it wasn't the fish of the day."

Somehow, Grayson managed a smile. "No, never that. Learned the first time."

Sutter grinned. "I only tried it because Carter insisted. Possibly the only time he was wrong about food."

To Grayson's surprise, Carter rolled over and murmured, eyes still closed, "I'm never wrong about food."

Grayson laughed. In that moment, he felt a rush of thankfulness to be rooming with Sutter and Carter.

"The chef has spoken," Sutter said. "Sorry, Carter. We'll be quiet." Carter pulled the covers over his head in response.

Grayson climbed back into his bed. "You sure you're good?"

Sutter nodded, rubbing at his swollen eyes. "We'll see."

Grayson slumped down under his comforter, his brain too foggy to try to decipher what Sutter meant. He spent what felt like hours battling the image of his mother's eyes before exhaustion pulled him into sleep again.

It felt like mere moments later that their door rattled and shook. Grayson's eyes flew open, and bright morning sunlight shocked him.

Sutter sat up in his desk chair, his cheeks creased where he'd rested his face on his notebook. Carter emerged from under the covers, frowning.

"Who's at the door?" he grumbled.

Sutter stood, stumbling a little before he reached the door and twisted the knob.

Fallon and Margot were still in their pajamas, hair pulled haphazardly into buns. Fallon held up two thick white envelopes, each with their names printed on it.

"Did you get these, too?" she asked, though it sounded like a demand.

That's when Sutter looked down at his feet. Grayson followed his gaze and spotted them, too.

Three thick white envelopes, stacked atop each other, resting under their door.

Grayson crossed the room and grabbed the envelopes off the floor. He tore into the one labeled *Grayson Hendricks* and read the letter inside:

Mr. Grayson Hendricks,

You have been selected to pursue entrance into the Order of the Vipers.

This is not a matter to be discussed with any outside party.

If you wish to reserve your place with us, please arrive at Barnaby Boathouse no later than 11 p.m. tomorrow with this invitation in hand.

We appreciate your discretion.

There was a seal at the bottom of the page—a hissing snake encircled by the words *BY THE FANGS OF GREED.*

Grayson took Fallon's letter and scanned it, then Margot's. They were all the same, the only difference being their names.

"The Order of the Vipers?" Grayson asked.

"Sutter?" Fallon said, alarm lacing her voice.

Grayson looked at Sutter. He was pale as a sheet.

"Oh, shit," he murmured.

"What did you *do*?" Fallon cried.

"Look," Sutter said carefully, holding his hands up in surrender, "I talked to Quincy, and he started saying all this confusing shit about—"

"About a secret society?" Margot hissed.

"Shh!" Sutter hissed. He ushered the girls in and shut the door, then slumped back down in his desk chair.

"It is way, way, *way* too early for this," Carter said, but his voice was taut, his eyes wide. He took his own invitation and started reading.

"He didn't say it was a secret society," Sutter explained desperately. "He was being so vague—I didn't understand what he was talking about. And I *swear* I never said your names! He just assumed you guys were involved."

They all glanced at each other. It wasn't a wild assumption to make.

"He must have figured out we dug up the capsule with you, or else he wouldn't have included us in . . . whatever this is," Grayson said.

"He doesn't know about the capsule," Sutter corrected. "I didn't tell him everything, just that I knew something was up. Next thing I know, he said he'd be sending me an invite."

"Is this why you were MIA at dinner last night?" Carter asked.

"I needed to think," Sutter muttered.

"Wait, so you guys haven't told him about the poem?" Fallon asked, looking first at Carter and then at Grayson, who felt a jolt run through him when her gaze met his.

Sutter looked back and forth between them, a wrinkle forming between his brows. "What poem?"

"Oh, damn—totally forgot to show you," Carter said. He started searching his backpack, which was under his bed. "Where is it?"

"I have it," Grayson said. He reached for the paper on his nightstand—he'd put it beneath his lamp to dry after the tea spill. The ink had gone runny, but the words were still legible.

But his legs nearly buckled when he saw that a new set of words, pale as a ghost, had surfaced on the bottom of the page.

"Holy shit," he breathed, and then his friends surrounded him, reading over his shoulder.

Time is lost, bridges are Burned,
All are ways you come to learn.
To play the game of Hot or cold,
Your next move must be brave and bold.
Don't lose hope, please take heart—
Maybe it's time to go back to the start . . .
Where a brother departs.

"Whoa," Margot said.

"That last line was *not* there yesterday!" Carter cried. "Grayson, how did you do that?"

Grayson opened his mouth to respond, but he saw the light bulb go on in Fallon's eyes before he could manage a word.

"Invisible ink," Fallon murmured. She pointed at Carter. "When you spilled the tea, the heat must have activated it! That's why *Hot* and *Burned* had capital letters—it was a hint."

Carter's brow furrowed. "How do you know that?"

"The experiment in Dr. Wilbur's chemistry class last year," she said. "Don't you remember? She was teaching us about how the organic compounds in invisible ink break down when exposed to heat, and—"

"Nope, you definitely dreamed that," Carter interrupted. "Dr. Wilbur has never taught us anything cool or interesting."

Sutter took the paper and read it over and over. "You guys get what this means, don't you?" He held it up so they could see. "*Where a brother departs.* It's telling us to go back to Lawson's room in Drexel House—that's the last place I saw him!"

They all fell silent for a moment. Grayson was hesitant to be the one to break it.

"Who would want you to search Lawson's dorm, though?" Margot asked. "Who would write this in the first place?"

"Dr. Wilbur," Carter said pointedly.

"That theory makes no sense," Grayson replied.

"She knows the invisible ink trick!" Carter cried.

"So does *anyone* who took her chemistry class. Or anyone with Google," Margot countered.

"Sutter," Fallon said carefully, "Lawson's room is occupied by another student now. There's nothing of his left there. We can't just—"

"Break in?" Carter finished for her. "Would it be that far off from things we've done in the past?"

"We *can*," Sutter challenged, "if we find out who's rooming there now and make a plan—go while they're in class, or—"

"Sutter," Fallon said firmly. *"No."*

He stared at her silently, disbelieving, long enough that Grayson squirmed with discomfort.

"What does any of this have to do with the capsule, though?" Grayson pressed. "The poem . . . these invitations . . . I'm having trouble connecting the dots here, man."

"I don't know," Sutter said, pressing one hand to his temple. "I don't have all the answers."

"But you do think this is connected to the treasure somehow?" Carter asked.

Sutter looked at the invites, then nodded. "The thing Lawson said in the video . . . the fangs-of-greed thing . . . it's on the seal. And when I said it to Quincy yesterday, it felt like he was testing me. So . . . yeah. I think it's connected. But we'll find out for certain tomorrow night."

Fallon barked out a laugh. "Assuming we're all *going*?"

The others looked at her, then back at Sutter.

Fallon threw her hands up. "No. You guys *can't* be serious. Is anyone thinking about the consequences of being a part of this?"

Sutter sat up straighter, and Grayson saw the spark of frustration in his eyes. "I never said anyone *has* to join me, but I'm going. I think Lawson was part of this—Quincy said he was the head of it, so . . . I'm going."

The implication of his words was crystal clear. *With or without you.*

"This is becoming a pattern," Fallon said, hands on her hips. "Sutter says he's going somewhere, and we all follow?" She turned to Carter first.

"Sutter and I are a package deal," he said with a shrug.

She turned to Margot next. "You too? Really?"

Margot folded her arms. "I'm . . . intrigued."

"She's intrigued," Sutter repeated with a shrug, like that was that.

Finally, she looked at Grayson.

All he could do was nod. Yes, he was going with them. At the end of the day, it came down to curiosity. He couldn't help it—he wanted to know what this was all about . . . but he hated the stress in her expression. Hated feeling like he was the cause of it.

Fallon looked like she might burst into either tears or flames. Grayson couldn't be sure which. Before either could happen, though, she turned and stormed out of the room. Surprise rolled over him in a wave—he wasn't sure he'd ever seen Fallon so mad before.

"Fallon," he said, starting to go after her, but Margot put a hand on his chest.

"Just give her a minute," she mumbled.

Grayson nodded reluctantly, stepping back.

Carter looked at each of them. "Are we really doing this . . . *Order of the Vipers* thing?" Even he sounded somewhat unsure, intimidated by what they were about to do.

Grayson felt it, too—that uncertainty. Like they were standing on the edge of something bigger than themselves, about to free-fall.

No one jumped in to answer, and they were silent for a moment. Finally, Grayson shrugged, if only to put his friends at ease.

"It's a club," he said. "What's the big deal? If we go and don't like what we see, we leave."

When he put it like that, it sounded simple. Harmless.

He could only hope he was right.

SEVENTEEN

Fallon

Fallon made herself scarce for most of the day. She went to Parrish Hall and spent the day sitting and drawing by the massive windows.

By dinnertime, she was still there, hiding out. Her phone dinged with one notification after another, so she silenced it. She worked on her art assignment for a bit, then found herself turning to blank pages and sketching her mother's smile, her tortoiseshell glasses, the necklace she used to wear with the silver swirl charm.

Her eyes burned with tears, and she shoved the sketchbook away.

You would know what to do, Mom, she thought. *You would know exactly what to say.*

Fallon longed for both her parents often, but in different ways. She longed for the smell of her dad's woodshop, the constant presence of fresh sawdust from his projects. She missed when he would hand her a paintbrush and let her turn his newest woodworking piece into her own art. She missed the background noise of the football games he watched on weekends.

She wished for the feel of his rough hand encompassing hers, sure and sturdy and the one true definition of safety.

But she longed for her mother when she was sick, and when her eyes were full of tears, when her heart was shattered to pieces. She longed for her mother's soothing words and her off-key singing and her tender touch as she smoothed her hair down.

She needed her mother's guidance. Her mother was the best kind of person, exactly the kind Fallon wanted to be. She was never supposed to grow up—to learn how to be part of this world—without her mom.

She shook her head, ignoring the tears that fell freely. *No.* If she thought about them like this, she would spiral back into the grief she'd managed to claw her way out of, and she wouldn't do that. Not here. Not in the one place she felt happy.

"Fallon?"

She startled even though the voice was so familiar, her heart ached.

Grayson stood across the otherwise empty Parrish common room, leaning against the wall opposite the mural they'd painted last year. When he saw the tears running down Fallon's cheeks, his soft expression twisted with concern. Brow furrowed, he hurried to where she sat by the window.

"Hey," he said, gentler this time, kneeling beside her. "Fallon, what's going on?"

She tried to turn away, her cheeks flaming with shame, but then his hand was on her shoulder, and her stubborn front wilted. When he pulled her against his chest, she let him. And she felt herself melting into him—his comforting warmth, the cocoon of his arms. He smelled clean and familiar, like every safe place she'd ever been, and she closed her eyes.

"Fallon, we didn't mean to upset you," he said. His words were nearly a whisper, but the cadence of his voice still hummed through her. His heartbeat was steady against her ear. She huffed out a sigh.

"I know," she whispered. Of course they didn't. They were doing what had to be done—to uncover the truth, to follow the breadcrumb trail that would lead to Lawson. She couldn't blame them for that.

She just wished there was another way—one without risk. One without a secret society they knew nothing about beckoning them to join.

"What's the worst that can happen?" Grayson whispered. "We've been in trouble before. There's always a way out."

"Not if we go too far this time," she mumbled against his chest. "All this could be taken away—us being at Meddlehart, together."

He paused, then pulled away to look at her. "You know we wouldn't lose this even if we got expelled, right? We would still have each other."

She wanted to argue—wanted to bring up all the people she'd lost touch with since her parents died, people who'd moved on and stopped reaching out after she moved in with her aunt and uncle in New Mexico.

But Grayson was staring back at her with such calm, reassuring confidence, she couldn't bring herself to say any of those things. He was looking at her like he would never let this world and its circumstances pull her away from him.

She broke from his gaze, from the warm feeling it was giving her, and glanced at her sketchbook. "I always miss my mom when I'm feeling like this," she said.

Grayson frowned, but there was something unfamiliar about

the expression on his face. There was an understanding there, so raw it made her throat ache with a fresh wave of tears.

"That's the worst feeling in the world," he murmured.

She searched his grayish eyes for a moment. Grayson rarely spoke of his parents, especially his mother. Fallon never asked—she was sure he was sick and tired of being asked about them—but she'd wondered, more than once, what they were like. What *she* had been like.

She hated to admit that curiosity, but it was there, though it didn't feel like a hunger for celebrity gossip. That wasn't something Fallon cared for, anyway.

It felt more like a hunger for Grayson. To know him.

"I didn't get much time with my mom," he said quietly, eyes focused on the distance, "but she used to do this thing where she'd bundle me up in blankets . . . even when I was in kindergarten, right before everything got bad . . . and she'd hold me close to her chest and sing this song . . ." He wrinkled his nose, and Fallon's heart twinged with fondness.

"What was it called?" she whispered.

"I don't know. It went something like . . . *turn around and you're two, turn around and you're four, turn around and you're a young man, going out of the door.*" He smiled a little. "I think it's a song about someone's daughter, so she may have changed the lyrics a little for me." His smile faded, and he looked away again. "I know all moms probably do that, but it's what I miss the most."

Fallon managed a smile and shook her head. "No. Not all moms."

His thumb traced circles on her back, and she found herself relishing the feeling. She yearned for more of it and leaned closer to him.

Grayson's eyes were steady on Fallon, but his gaze had softened, almost hazy now. Slowly, so slowly it felt like the earth was halting on its axis, he lifted his hand and pushed a lock of hair behind her ear.

A shock of lightning wound its way down her spine. It raised a chill on her skin while simultaneously warming her from the inside out.

She recognized this feeling, and the realization sank heavily in her stomach, fogging her brain. Quietly, she cleared her throat. He sat back, alertness returning to his eyes.

"You don't have to come with us," Grayson told her carefully.

She shook her head. "Of course I do. Any of you would do it for me."

He held her gaze, quiet. He wouldn't deny that, and she knew it.

"I want Sutter to find Lawson as much as anyone," she said. "I just . . . don't want us to walk the same path he did. I don't want to step into whatever quicksand he got himself into and couldn't get out of."

"We won't," Grayson whispered.

"How can we be sure? He was part of this . . . thing," Fallon said. "The order, or whatever it's called. What if it had something to do with his disappearance?"

"I doubt it," Grayson answered. "It's a silly club. A way for kids to feel cooler. It's dumb, but"—he shrugged—"probably harmless."

"*Probably* being the key word."

He sighed, a small smile playing on his lips. "Come on. Have we ever steered you wrong before?"

She paused for a moment before she answered. "Yes."

Grayson frowned. "When?"

Fallon reached up and tapped her nose.

Grayson's face splintered with a smile at the memory of their ill-fated Meddlehart pantry scheme and her bruised nose. And then they were both laughing.

"Well, you've got me there," he managed between laughs. "I'm still so sorry about that, by the way."

"You don't have to be," Fallon promised. "You've made up for it since then."

His smile softened. "If you say so."

Then silence fell between them, and he offered her his hand.

"Dinner's still on in the dining hall," he said. "I haven't eaten yet, if you want to join."

Fallon looked down at his proffered hand, hesitating. Thinking of his jacket around her shoulders when she was cold. Thinking of the bruises still coloring his face like little galaxies under his skin, and what he'd done to earn them.

Thinking of the heat still pulsing through her veins.

She wasn't sure what it meant when she took his hand and let him lead her outside. She wasn't sure at all.

EIGHTEEN

Sutter

The nights had grown colder since the start of the semester. Sutter pulled his jacket tighter around him as he walked alongside his friends toward Barnaby Boathouse on Monday night, invitation in hand.

He still felt uncertain about what they were walking into. He'd done enough Google searches seeking answers about the Order of the Vipers—what it was, what it did, who was part of it—to kill his laptop battery the night before. But he hadn't found anything.

He asked Fallon if she'd ever come across it in any of her research. Her response had been a flat, resounding no.

Even as she joined them in crossing campus to the boathouse, there was an icy silence between her and Sutter. He knew she had reservations about what they were doing, and he kept replaying what she said the night before.

Sutter does something, we all follow.

It didn't sound like an outright insult, but it left a sting that hadn't quite worn off. Sutter wondered if the sting was from the words themselves, or from the fact it had been Fallon who'd uttered them.

Sutter had told them all they didn't have to follow him, hadn't he? He hadn't pressured anyone into joining him in this search for the treasure, the search for Lawson. They'd *chosen* to. He couldn't be blamed for that.

But he wouldn't deny he fully expected them to help him. He never really questioned whether his friends would stand beside him in this search, no matter where it led. He just knew they would, because they always did. It's who they were. They never abandoned each other.

That had always been true between Sutter and his friends. If only it had been true with Lawson.

Despite the hurt Sutter felt over the secrets Lawson kept from him, it didn't change who his older brother was to him. Lawson was the glue, the hero, the guy who made everything make sense. And nothing had made sense in a long time, especially not what had turned Lawson's heart so cold those last months before he vanished—what had made him push Sutter away.

So Sutter would *make* it make sense, no matter what it took. He'd take a page from his brother's book and fix what was broken.

The crew approached the boathouse, which was stationed by the river running down from the mountain. Sutter shone his flashlight around, searching for signs of activity. The rowing team's boats were stowed alongside the building, and the boathouse was dark and locked tight.

"So, I'm starting to think we were set up," Carter said. "Am I the only one?"

"What time is it?" Grayson asked.

"Eleven o'clock on the dot," Margot said, her phone screen casting a glow over her face. "And not a soul in sight."

"Are we missing something?" Fallon asked. Her voice was tight. Sutter glanced over and saw her eyes locked on him.

Sutter shone his flashlight on his invitation and read it again. No clues as to where exactly this meeting was happening.

A low whistle broke the silence. Their heads turned toward the sound. A lone figure stood, a hooded jacket concealing their face. A rowboat was pulled to the edge of the water beside them.

"Oh, shit," Carter whispered. "Is this the part where the stranger in a hoodie kills us all?"

"Shut up," Sutter murmured. He led the way forward, and when they got closer he recognized the face under the hood. It was a senior named Jeffrey Price who lived in Drexel House. He was a quiet guy who mostly kept to himself, but Sutter knew him because Lawson had tutored him in algebra. Sutter noticed the silver viper pinned to his jacket, glinting in the moonlight.

"Jeffrey," he said.

"How did Franklin Thatcher die?" Jeffrey asked in response. His voice was much deeper than Sutter remembered.

Sutter cleared his throat and glanced at the others. "By the fangs of greed."

"I'll need proof of invitation." Jeffrey held out his hand, and one by one, they handed over their envelopes. Jeffrey looked them over, nodded, and gestured to the rowboat.

"One at a time." He took Margot's and Fallon's hands as they stepped in, holding them steady. Sutter followed next.

"We've been waiting for you, Sutter," Jeffrey said. "Your brother's legacy with the order was notable. It's fitting you would follow in his footsteps."

Throat dry, Sutter nodded as if he knew what Jeffrey was talking about. The others eyed him with stony glares, and Sutter looked out at the water as Jeffrey stepped into the boat and started rowing. The boat moved down the river, the current carrying them slowly away from the boathouse.

Sutter saw Fallon was gripping the side of the boat, her knuckles white. He had the strange urge to reach out and rest his hand over hers, to reassure her, but then her eyes met his, and the ice in them forced his gaze away.

He turned right in time to see what appeared to be the mouth of a small cave looming out of the mountainside on the opposite side of the river. Jeffrey rowed the boat to the rocky shore and climbed out. Wordlessly, he started toward the entrance, and Sutter followed, but the closer he got the less it looked like a cave. It was too perfectly round and hidden by a draping curtain of ivy that somehow struck him as unnatural, like it hadn't grown there on its own.

"Welcome to the Order of the Vipers," Jeffrey said. "They're waiting for you inside."

NINETEEN

Fallon

The farther they walked down the tunnel, the colder and darker it became. It was wide enough for Fallon and Margot to walk side by side, and it sloped downward slightly, enough that Fallon felt the soles of her shoes slide a little with each step. Margot grabbed her wrist at one point to steady herself.

"Is it just me," she whispered in Fallon's ear, "or does this look like a horror movie scene in the making?"

"Oh, definitely," Fallon agreed. Her voice had a sarcastic edge, but her heart was mere beats away from shattering her rib cage.

Margot glanced at her. "Are you still mad at Sutter?"

Fallon kept her gaze focused ahead. "Who says I was ever mad at him?"

"So you stormed out of the room yesterday because you were happy?"

Fallon sighed. She wasn't sure what her feelings were toward Sutter right now. She knew it wasn't anger. She was just . . . concerned. And frustrated, no doubt. She was frustrated with him in a million ways—how stubborn he was, how determinedly he worked toward things that might hurt him in the end. How sometimes his noble pursuits consumed him, absorbed every ounce of his attention, blinded him to everything and everyone else.

Blinded him to her.

And most of all, she was frustrated with how their kiss haunted her thoughts like a specter, taunting her with a thing that was never meant to be, and Sutter acting like it had never happened at all.

After a long moment, Fallon shook her head. "No, Margot. Let's talk about it later."

Grayson glanced back at them before turning around again. Fallon caught sight of his bruised face, a ripple crossing the hard line of his jaw. For a moment, she was back in Parrish Hall with him, his arms wrapped protectively around her.

The memory offered her comfort as they descended underground. If they were going to walk down a dark, secret tunnel toward complete uncertainty, at least they were doing it together. At least she'd have him right there with her, the person who made her feel safe.

The thought was sudden and somewhat unexpected, and Fallon frowned a little, forcing her gaze away from him.

There was a sudden turn in the tunnel, and warm light cast from around the corner. Fallon followed her friends around the bend, and what she saw stunned her.

The room before them wasn't large, but it was much bigger than she would've expected an underground room to be. The walls looked to be made of stone, but there was only so much she could see in the dim space. A few candlesticks burned in the corners, dripping wax onto the floor. On the left was an ancient metal door, like the door to a vault, with a massive wheel-like contraption anchored in the center. There were shelves filled with old books—the kind with leather covers and silky ribbon bookmarks—and on the far wall was a massive old map.

It took Fallon a moment to realize the map was one of Meddlehart. It wasn't updated with the newer buildings and facilities, but that made it all the more impressive.

Three rectangular tables were pushed together at the ends to form an open square in the center of the room. Mismatched chairs lined each one. Some were occupied by students Fallon recognized, all of whom looked as confused and anxious as she felt. Quincy stood in front of the map, flanked by four other guys all wearing black. Little silver vipers were pinned to their chests or hanging around their wrists or necks.

"Take your seats," Quincy said as Fallon and her friends walked in. Jeffery followed behind them and pulled another large metal door shut after they'd all entered the space.

Just like that, they were closed in.

Fallon shuddered as her eyes roamed the seats at the tables, each marked with a place card. She found hers in the southeast part of the room, right by Sutter. Carter and Margot were at the opposite side, and Grayson had a lone seat near the front of the room, at the end of the first table.

Including them, there were ten people seated at the tables. Fallon took note of the crowd. There was a girl named Haley from her and Grayson's botany class—she shot glares around the room with a hostility that surprised Fallon—and a guy named Ken who she knew from her art classes.

And then there was Alex Harker, glaring at them with a hungry gleam in his eyes.

Fallon hated the way her stomach dropped when she saw him.

She glanced at Grayson, whose jaw was clenched. She knew Grayson would be watching Alex like a hawk, but still . . . Alex was unpredictable. The fact that he'd always had a chip on his shoulder when it came to Grayson, and that he'd been so angry at her for supposedly eavesdropping on his phone call, put her on edge.

Glancing around at the other initiates, Fallon couldn't help but wonder how they'd been selected. Had they known about the secret society before this? Had they sought the order out? Or had they been handpicked for some other reason?

Jeffrey joined Quincy and the four other guys at the front of the room, interrupting her thoughts.

"This is everyone," he told Quincy.

"Excellent," he murmured, stepping forward. His gaze passed slowly over every single one of them, and he smiled.

"Welcome to the Order of the Vipers," he said proudly. "The new order. The first to exist since the abolishment of the original order in the summer of 2025."

Fallon could practically feel Sutter tense up beside her. *That date . . .* She forced down the urge to grab his hand.

"You probably have questions, so allow me to explain. We're a collection of students dedicated to discovering the treasure buried by Jacob Meddlehart himself, and we follow in the footsteps of decades of Meddlehart alumni before us," Quincy said evenly. "The order was founded not by students, however, but by Franklin Thatcher, cofounder of Meddlehart Academy."

Fallon's brain was firing as the pieces suddenly fell into place. The Vipers were treasure hunters—a secret group of students doing exactly what the school forbade them to do.

But the fact that Franklin Thatcher had founded the order was what surprised her most. What would the cofounder of their school have to gain from forming a secret society under the rest of the administrators' noses?

"It started out simpler than you might think," Quincy explained. "Thatcher was obsessed with finding the treasure. He felt entitled to it, since the riches Meddlehart possessed were ones he'd gained from business ventures with Thatcher himself. He had multiple private tunnel systems, like this one, dug beneath the campus when students and staff were gone over the summer so he could search for the treasure without others knowing. He enlisted a select group of students to help him—students who knew the campus grounds as well as he did, backward and forward—but then he died from a snakebite while searching on his own. The students called themselves the Order of the Vipers in his honor, and agreed they would divide the fortune evenly between them should they find it. That's the deal we stand by to this day."

The students seated around Fallon exchanged glances, as if considering the idea of sharing the Meddlehart treasure with these people. She suddenly felt like the oxygen in the tunnel was disappearing slowly, one molecule at a time.

"Some of us here tonight are legacies," Quincy said. "Others have earned their place through their own means. The closest the Vipers have ever come to finding the treasure was under the head of the 2025 order, Lawson Heyward."

Quincy's eyes locked on Sutter. Other students turned to stare at him, too. Fallon refused to look at him, though. Margot, Carter, and Grayson did the same, gazes focused firmly ahead of them.

"And the elephant in the room tonight is most definitely his younger brother," Quincy finally said, lips quirked into a wry smile. "Sutter."

"You must know something, Heyward," Alex said from across the room, breaking the spell Quincy had cast with his speech. "Where'd Lawson go that night? He was hunting the treasure. Did he leave because he found it?"

Fallon's cheeks flushed hot, and she clenched one fist—what was Quincy doing, putting Sutter on the spot like this? Was he trying to start conflict with the others? But her anger shattered into surprise when Sutter's warm hand rested atop hers. She met his eyes, burning hazel even in the dim light.

It's all right. She could see the message in his eyes.

"I don't know anything," Sutter said evenly.

"Bullshit," Haley spat, and Quincy stepped forward.

"Enough," he said, raising one hand. "Lawson was head of the order and worked on highly classified operations that year. Hardly anyone knew what his plans were, and to my knowledge, no one knows what happened to him that night, not even other members of the order."

Haley glared at him. "Oh yeah? Then who decided you were in charge, if the order disbanded and its leader is gone?"

Fallon couldn't help but study the reactions of the members of the order standing behind Quincy. One shifted slightly from one foot to the other, and another fidgeted with his pin. She could see the question caused them discomfort—maybe even nervousness—though they were trying not to show it.

But Quincy smirked, like he'd expected precisely this question.

"Lawson was my mentor. Before he disappeared, he left this for me." He held up a black leather notebook, stuffed with pages and bookmarks and notes. "I'd just been initiated to the order. Lawson was the one who invited me to join. I became the secretary of the order that year, and I documented every meeting of the Vipers. The week before Lawson disappeared, he asked to borrow my journal so he could review the notes from our last meeting. Then he vanished, and I wasn't sure I'd ever get the notebook back. But it was left in my dorm before I went home for the summer, and here, on the last page . . ."

Quincy pointed to a few words hastily scrawled in bold black marker. Fallon squinted, and she could just make out the message, the letters squat and square:

Q,

KEEP GOING. BY THE FANGS OF GREED . . .

L

"When Lawson went missing," Quincy said, "the remaining members of the order made the decision to disband. They were convinced his disappearance was linked to the treasure and felt it was too dangerous to continue operations. But then I found this, and I knew. Lawson wanted the Vipers to live on, and he wanted *me* to make sure of it."

Fallon risked a glance at Sutter, and her heart sank. His face was ashen, and he looked entirely wounded. He glanced at her and clenched his jaw, but he couldn't hide it from her. She knew what he was thinking.

Lawson could've invited Sutter to join the Order of the Vipers, but he didn't. Quincy had just said that he was initiated as a freshman, so age clearly didn't disqualify students from joining. Why would Lawson exclude his own brother from the secret society he'd become the leader of?

Why hadn't Lawson brought Sutter into the order, too?

A chill settled over the room. Quincy set the notebook down and gestured to the others behind him.

"The people standing here with me are fully initiated members of the order," he said. "The ones who returned. We are the executives—the ones you must convince you belong here."

"Initiated," Margot spoke up. "Which means . . . ?"

Quincy nodded, smirking. "You must earn your place in the order through a series of tests. Legacy or not, no one joins without first proving they have what it takes."

Fallon's stomach turned. "And why would we?" she asked, surprising herself with her boldness. "What's in it for us, exactly? I could go search for the treasure on my own and keep it for myself, couldn't I?"

Quincy's icy gaze fell on her. She wanted nothing more than to crawl under the table, but she held still and waited for his response.

"You could," he said with a slight shrug. "Of course you could try to find it yourself. Anyone can. Clearly, some have already tried . . . unsuccessfully." Quincy's gaze flitted briefly to Sutter, which resulted in looks from almost everyone else in the room.

Fallon burned with anger toward Quincy, knowing how the barb must have stuck in Sutter's heart. It was obvious that no matter how much the Vipers respected Lawson as their leader . . . there was some resentment harbored among them. Lawson kept his plans hidden, and that wasn't part of the deal each member of the order had agreed to.

"There's power in numbers, isn't that what they say?" Quincy went on. "The chances of finding this fortune without help—without resources—are slim to none, and Franklin Thatcher proved that by dying alone on this very mountain. It's dangerous to do this on your own. We're here for each *other*. At the end of the day, this is a team. A family."

Fallon glanced around at Haley, Alex, and all the other hostile faces. She wondered if they were here to be part of the "family," too.

But she'd never heard of snakes living their lives in groups. She'd only ever known them to be solitary creatures, out for themselves. She struggled to believe the Vipers would be any different.

"However," Quincy said, drumming his fingertips slowly on the table, "there *is* something 'in it' for you, as you so sweetly put it."

He turned and knocked on the vault door. It rang hollowly with each rap of his knuckles.

"This is the information vault," he said. "Many of Franklin Thatcher's belongings . . . and perhaps a few things he stole . . . now belong to us."

Fallon leaned forward slightly. *Franklin Thatcher's belongings?*

"Hundreds of documents," Quincy said, pressing his palm against the metal door. "Thatcher's journals, letters from Jacob Meddlehart, maps of the campus, and recordings of past orders . . . all the history no one else knows about, no one has access to but us, the Vipers. It's all ours."

Fallon was nearly salivating at the thought. There was a treasure trove of information about the history of Meddlehart right behind that door.

To get to it, all she had to do was become a Viper.

"The tunnels," Grayson spoke up. "You said there are more of them."

Quincy nodded slowly, like he was weighing his answer. "Yes, but . . . we haven't had access to them since Lawson disappeared. He had possession of the keys. Wherever he went, the keys went with him."

"We're working on finding ways in," Jeffrey chimed in. "The tunnels are one of our greatest assets. They're priceless to us. We'll find a way."

Quincy nodded. "Jeffrey's right. We have more information, more resources, than any other order in history. Those before us—they couldn't find the fortune. But we will."

"By the fangs of greed," Jeffrey said.

And then the other members repeated it in unison: "By the fangs of greed."

Fallon was already sick of that phrase.

"What happens if you don't pass the tests?" Carter asked.

Quincy crossed his arms. "You leave. You won't be welcome when we assemble. You won't gain access to the vault. And you'll be held to secrecy, of course. There are consequences for anyone who spreads information about the Vipers. That's a rule you don't want to break. The order will be watching, and we *will* know if you talk."

Fallon met Grayson's eyes across the room. His jaw was clenched, and he averted his gaze.

"When are the tests?" Sutter asked.

"You'll know when the time is right," Quincy said.

He didn't elaborate. They didn't get another ounce of information about the tests before the meeting ended and they left the cave. There was no way of knowing what the tests would entail, when they would happen, or what they might cost Fallon and her friends.

That was what worried her the most.

TWENTY

Grayson

Grayson's mind should've been on football. Instead, mere hours before the first game of the season, he was planting mustard seeds on the windowsill of Margot and Fallon's room and trying not to dwell on what awaited his friends in the first test of the Order of the Vipers.

Carefully, Grayson poured water into each of the three tiny clay pots they'd planted the seeds in. He eyed the overcast sky. September brought colder weather with little warning, and the temperature dropped further each day. He wore a letterman jacket with his number 29 jersey under it, just like the team all wore on game days. But for some reason, the layers couldn't quite keep the chill off today.

"You won't be getting much sun today, little guys," he said quietly as he finished watering. He turned to Fallon, who sat on the edge of her bed. Her arms were folded, her eyes distant, as they had been ever since they left the cave after the meeting with the Vipers.

"Are you sure it's okay to keep the plants in here?" Grayson asked. He'd suggested keeping them in her and Margot's room rather than in the chaos of his own.

She nodded, snapping out of whatever thoughts held her captive. "Yeah. I think they're safer in here, like you said."

She smiled a little, and he smiled back. Her cinnamon candle was burning on one of the shelves, and for a moment, Grayson had to remind himself it wasn't Christmastime, but rather several weeks away from Halloween. Meddlehart always held a dance for the students on Halloween, and he'd never taken a date before. There was only ever one girl he wanted to ask.

"You hanging in there?" he murmured.

Fallon nodded. "Yeah, just . . . anxious. I feel like I'm on pins and needles, waiting for Quincy and his dudes to come around the corner. But the sooner the tests are over, the sooner we can access the vault."

Grayson felt the same way. There hadn't been any sign of a test yet, and he wished they'd been told something, *anything*, about what to expect. A time, a place . . . anything would do.

But there was nothing. It had been radio silence from the Vipers since the meeting, and every passing day added to the tension. Carter had been stress-cooking on his camping griddle (the one Scott, not to mention the entire Meddlehart administration, had specifically told him not to use in his room). Margot was engaging in online retail therapy.

Sutter had started biting his nails, a habit Grayson hadn't seen him do since freshman year. He hadn't said anything about the poem in days. Grayson kept expecting him to cook up some plan to break into Lawson's old dorm and look for clues, but so far, he hadn't breathed a word about it.

Grayson was a little relieved, if he was being honest. It still bothered him that they didn't know who had left those things for them to find—Lawson's phone, the poem. Could it be someone on the football team who would've been able to enter the locker room undetected? Or Quincy? Or another Viper initiate? But why would any of them do it?

And Fallon . . . she was just quiet. So, so quiet, always staring into space. He hadn't spent much time with her since the day he found her crying in Parrish Hall, but he thought about it almost constantly.

Her body leaning into his. The look in her eyes when he'd brushed her hair out of her face, hoping she didn't notice the way his hand trembled slightly at their proximity.

He wondered if she thought about it, too. He wondered if she had even the slightest idea how he hung on her every word, every look. And he wondered if she knew how terrified he was of that—of her, and the power she held over him without even knowing it.

Today, though, Grayson's stress was divided. Today, he had more on his mind than most days. Sure, he was concerned about the order's test looming over their heads. But most of all, he was worried about that night's football game.

Maybe *worried* wasn't the right word. Maybe it was just fear. It was the first game of the season, yes. But also his dad would be there, and that fact alone had tied an intricate knot in his chest he couldn't untangle.

"At least football starts tonight," Fallon said with a smile, like she'd been reading his mind.

He managed a smile, but he couldn't meet her eyes. "Yeah."

"You should be excited," she said. "You're one of the best players, Gray. And I'm not just saying that."

He shrugged a little, though the words warmed his chest. "My dad's coming tonight."

It was only after the words left his mouth that he realized he hadn't told anyone that yet, not even Sutter or Carter. He wasn't sure what made him say it, or why his chest squirmed immediately after. He played with the bottom button of his jacket, brushing his thumb over the smooth top.

Fallon stood and walked toward him. "That's good, right?"

Grayson nodded, running a hand through his hair. He hadn't told Fallon much about his dad—in fact, he avoided the topic with just about everyone in his life. But when he glanced up at her, there was a depth in her gaze. Like he was a window, and she was looking right into him.

Her hands rested on her upper arms, hugged around herself. For a moment he wondered what it might be like for her arms to hold him, for her hands to tangle in his hair and stay there for a while. He couldn't remember the last time anyone had truly held him, ever.

His chest ached to the point he could feel it in his fingertips, and he cleared his throat.

"My dad has a break in filming," he muttered. "He doesn't usually have a chance to come, so, you know . . . it'll be nice to have him here. For sure. Yeah."

Fallon reached out and squeezed his arm.

"You're going to be great, just like you always are," she told him. "And I'll be right there in the stands, cheering you on."

Right then, her phone buzzed from the nightstand. Grayson could see the name on the screen from where he stood.

Sutter.

Suddenly, he was dragged back to the night in the tunnel, when Margot had been whispering to Fallon and he heard Sutter's name. And then, in the meeting, how Fallon had looked at Sutter and how he'd rested his hand over hers. Grayson had watched it all from the other side of the room.

And maybe none of it meant anything. But what if it did?

Grayson's heart dropped, and before he could think it through, he was headed for the door.

Fallon looked up from her phone as he passed. "Gray?"

"Gotta head to the Ace," he said quickly. "I'll see you later, all right? After the game."

He shut the door behind him before she could say another word.

The team didn't leave the locker room until after dark that evening, and Grayson kept his earbuds in until the moment Coach Hamilton gathered them into a huddle. Nerves rattled through his bones, unsettled his stomach.

"Harker, Sanchez, and Johnson, you're on offensive line tonight. We start our season off with a big win tonight, boys—heads in the game!"

The team shouted in response, "*Heads in the game*." Then they made their way to the edge of the field, to the inflatable tunnel for the players to run through—the grand entrance, the one meant to hype everyone up for the game—but all Grayson felt was nausea.

Before he crossed the threshold of the locker room, a hand gripped his shoulder pads and yanked him back. Alex Harker's stony eyes stared into his.

"You must live an easy existence," Alex said in a growl. "Living your cushy life in the hills. Winning every game you play."

Grayson grappled against Alex's chest to shove him off, but the lineman's grip was tight. "Despite what you may think," Grayson said, "we're on the same team. I've never been against you, Alex."

"I'm not talking about *football* anymore, Hendricks," Alex whispered. "I'm talking about a much, much bigger game. And this time, I'll make damn sure that no one takes my spot—especially not you."

Alex released him and jogged easily out of the locker room as though the interaction hadn't happened. A hot flash of fury rippled through Grayson, but he shook it off. *Focus on the game. Focus on what's happening now.*

Grayson joined his team as they charged onto the field. Music blared through the stadium speakers, and the crowd in the stands roared. Most were students, but there was a section designated for the parents dedicated enough to make their way up the mountain for the games every Friday night.

Grayson found himself scanning the bleachers as the team stood along the sideline for the national anthem, searching for the faces he knew would be there. He spotted Sutter and Carter standing with Margot and Fallon. Both girls had #29 painted on their cheeks in blue glitter.

He was searching the parents' section again as they jogged onto the field to start the game, wondering if he'd missed him the first time.

But his dad wasn't there.

The kickoff passed in a blur, and then the Dragons had the ball. Grayson lined up on the offensive. His eyes were supposed to be on the game in front of him, but he kept glancing at the bleachers.

He's late. He'll be here. He said he'd be here.

Grayson missed the spike. He surged forward to secure the ball, but his brain was scrambled. His footing was off. The next thing he knew, he was on the ground, clumps of grass and dirt wedged in his face mask.

"Hendricks!" he could hear Hammy bellowing from the sideline. *"Head in the game, damn it!"*

His dad wasn't there. He hadn't come.

Stupid, Grayson thought. *So stupid, Grayson. You are so fucking stupid.*

He knew better than to believe a word his dad said. And now here he was, looking like a fool on the field, head spinning, eyes blurred, chest aching.

Breathe, if you could only breathe, just breathe.

He took his position for the next play, eyes on the bleachers once more.

The center spiked the ball. Grayson grasped it in his fingertips, barely hanging on. He looked forward, where the line was breaking for the quarterback sneak—but Alex veered in the wrong direction. He left it wide open, and Grayson couldn't think, couldn't react, couldn't—

The hit was hard and fast, and he heard the bones break in his arm before he felt it.

TWENTY-ONE
Fallon

Fallon watched as the defensive lineman plowed Grayson into the ground. Then he was screaming, his voice raw and untethered. He writhed on the field as the whistle blew and the players stopped to stare.

The stadium went quiet, so quiet that Fallon could hear the blood roaring in her ears.

Had the coaches seen what just happened? Alex Harker—he'd blocked the wrong player, left an open gap for the lineman to take Grayson down. It was clear as day, even to Fallon, he'd done it on *purpose*.

But she couldn't dwell on what that meant, not right now, because the pain in Grayson's voice was enough to set her free. She didn't wait another second before she shoved her way out of the bleacher seat and onto the stairs.

"Fallon, wait!" she heard Margot call after her, but she didn't stop. She charged down the bleachers until she reached the grass. Fallon pushed by the coaches on the sidelines and ran onto the field, past the players who had already taken knees, all the way to Grayson's side.

Fallon's stomach turned when she saw the way his arm was

bent. His eyes were squeezed shut, tears streaking down his cheeks, and his teeth were clenched.

"We need Nurse Fran out here," Coach Hamilton said, waving to the sideline. "We need to get him off the field and to the infirmary!"

Grayson's eyes, wild with pain, locked on Fallon's as Coach Hamilton pulled his helmet off. Coach talked to him, trying to get him to calm down, but Grayson was focused only on Fallon.

"Fallon," he gritted out.

She knelt beside him. "I'm right here, Gray," she said. Her eyes burned with the threat of tears, but she gritted her teeth—she had to keep it together. She touched the top of his head in a feeble attempt to comfort him. "I'm right here, okay?"

"*Fallon*," he said again. The other coaches were rushing around—one gathering the other players into a huddle, one guiding the stretcher cart onto the field. Fallon was the one by his side, running her hand over his hair and waiting for them to get him off the field.

"I didn't know it was a sneak," Fallon heard Alex saying. She turned and saw him several yards away, explaining himself to the offensive coach. But his eyes met hers, and there was a gleam of satisfaction she did not miss. She could almost hear him saying *Good luck with the order's tests now.*

Fallon trembled with anger, but before she could say or do anything, the cart pulled up and they began helping Grayson into the back. The infirmary was near the student houses, too far to walk while he was in this much pain.

"You want to go with him?" Coach Hamilton asked Fallon. "Get him to Nurse Fran and let her know what happened."

Fallon nodded, unable to speak past the knot in her throat. She climbed into the passenger seat, and the coach driving the cart stepped on the accelerator. The crowd in the stands clapped as they drove into the dark quiet of campus.

Fallon had only visited the infirmary a handful of times—once when she got the flu freshman year, another time after her nose was bruised during their Meddlehart kitchen heist. Nurse Fran was always able to crack a joke or do something to make everyone smile, despite whatever was wrong.

This time was different, though. When they arrived with Grayson, Nurse Fran's brows knit with concern. She would have to take him to the hospital for X-rays, she said. He'd need a cast, maybe more.

"I can't let you come along, dear," she told Fallon. "You'll have to wait here. I'm sorry."

"It's okay," Fallon said, though her eyes prickled with unshed tears.

Fallon watched them drive away, but she didn't leave the infirmary. She sat on the front steps and waited for them to come back, even after her friends showed up and tried to convince her to go with them.

"They might be a while," Margot said gently, putting her hand on Fallon's shoulder.

"Come with us," Carter said. "We're ditching the game to get ice cream. If Grayson's not playing, it's not worth watching."

"We'll come right back after," Margot promised her.

Fallon shook her head. The thought of ice cream made her

stomach churn. "I'm not . . . I can't. Go ahead. I'll see you guys later."

Quietly, they turned to go. But Sutter hung back for a moment and said, "He'll be okay, Fallon."

She looked up at him. He was watching her with the faintest curiosity in his expression.

All she could do was nod. He walked away, and she kept waiting.

It felt like hours passed before they returned. Nurse Fran helped Grayson inside. His arm rested in a cast and sling, his eyes bleary, his hair disheveled. He looked disoriented, and his gaze passed over Fallon without much recognition. Nurse Fran helped him to a bed in the back of the infirmary, a quieter area where no one else was around.

"He's very lucky," she told Fallon quietly once they got Grayson settled. "It was a serious break, but he won't need surgery if he takes care of it. He might be a little loopy for a while, though. They gave him some medication for the pain."

Fallon nodded. Grayson had fallen asleep almost as soon as he lay down, and Fallon sat in a chair by his bedside, not moving. Nurse Fran started to leave the room, but she paused.

"Are you coming, dear?"

Fallon looked up at her. "Could I, um . . . could I stay for a while? I . . ." She trailed off.

I don't want to leave him here alone.

Nurse Fran smiled. "All right. I'll be just out here, in my office."

Fallon nodded, and then they were alone. Grayson's chest rose and fell slowly. His face was still dirty and streaked with tears, his eyes swollen. His hair was stiff with sweat, and little strands stuck to his forehead.

Somehow, even though Grayson was tall and strong and practically towered over Fallon when standing, he looked small here, asleep in the infirmary cot. Her eyes traveled over his damp lashes, the curve of his lips, the hard line of his jaw.

They were features she knew. She saw them every day. But she let her gaze linger over them tonight.

Fallon wasn't sure how much time had passed before Grayson stirred. She grasped his hand, the one not bound with a cast, and held it. It was warm and rough, and she gripped it tight as he blinked open his eyes.

"Fallon?" he murmured. His eyes widened with confusion.

"Hey," she said. She reached for his hair and smoothed it down. "You're okay. Your arm is broken and you're in the infirmary, but you're okay. It's all right."

"It's you," he mumbled.

She smiled a little. "Yeah, Gray, it's me."

He relaxed against the pillow again, eyes hazy. "It's really broken?"

Nurse Fran was right—he was confused. "It'll be okay, Gray."

"But how will I play this season? Or . . . complete the tests for the Vipers? I'm screwed now, aren't I?"

"Shh." She hushed him gently, glancing over her shoulder to make sure Nurse Fran hadn't come back in and overheard him. But they were still alone. "We'll figure it out, I promise."

"But when did I . . . ?" He looked down at the cast.

Fallon leaned forward slightly. "During the game, a linebacker tackled you, and you landed wrong. Grayson . . ." She hesitated. "I think Alex let him tackle you on purpose."

A light bulb seemed to turn on behind his tired eyes. He blinked sleepily. "Oh, yeah . . . that makes sense. He threatened me before the game. In the locker room."

Fallon's heart stuttered. "Alex did?"

He bypassed her question, eyes focused on some point in the distance. His tongue stumbled around the words he spoke next, slow and thick. "And then I went onto the field, and . . . he didn't come."

She didn't have to ask who he was talking about now. She knew as soon as the team had walked onto the field, as soon as she saw that dejected look on Grayson's face. His dad hadn't shown.

"I know," she whispered. "I'm so sorry."

"I'm so stupid, Fallon."

"No," she said. She brushed her hand over his cheek. "No, Gray, you're not stupid."

"I am." Her gut wrenched when she saw his eyes brimming with tears—she tried to remember a time she'd seen him cry, and she couldn't.

"I should've known," he went on, his words slurring. "He *hates* me, and I know it, and I should have *known* he wouldn't come."

Fallon's throat tightened. Grayson hadn't ever said things like that before.

"It's my fault," he murmured. "He says so."

"What?" she asked. "What's your fault?"

"My mom," he said. "She did the things she did . . . she *died* because of me."

Fallon frowned. "That's not true."

"He says so," Grayson repeated. "And sometimes I believe him, and . . . I understand why he hates me so much." He swallowed thickly. "I would hate me, too."

"Gray," she whispered. She brushed a tear off his cheek with her thumb.

For a long, quiet moment, the only sound was the hum of the infirmary lights.

"I found her," he mumbled. "I found my mom, Fallon, when she died . . . she was on the bathroom floor, and . . . she was already gone. I tried to save her, but I couldn't."

It was like his words sucked the air right from Fallon's lungs.

"He doesn't believe me." Grayson took a shuddering breath. "I tried to . . ." His chin trembled. "I begged her to wake up, I tried to help her breathe, but he doesn't believe me, Fallon . . ."

"*I* believe you," she whispered.

"It's my fault," he murmured again. "It's my fault, it's *my* fault . . ."

"Come here," she said, because she couldn't find any more words to say. She sat on the edge of the bed and reached for him, and he dropped his head to her chest. His shoulders shook, and she held him tighter. She was glad he couldn't see the tears falling down her cheeks.

"It's not your fault," she told him quietly, fighting to keep her voice from shaking. "Don't listen to him, okay? Don't you *ever* blame yourself, Grayson. Never. You didn't do anything wrong."

The tremors in his chest slowed. He murmured something into her shoulder, something she didn't catch.

"What, Gray?" she asked.

But he didn't answer. His muscles relaxed and his breathing became deep and even.

Fallon wiped her eyes, but the tears kept coming. Her chest ached as she grieved for him, for what he'd endured, for what he'd lost. For what he'd been carrying all on his own for so long.

He'd chosen to share it with her.

She rested her hand against his cheek, brushed at the

remaining tear tracks lining his face. Pushed a few stray curls behind his ears. He didn't move.

He was fast asleep in her arms. Peaceful, his pain momentarily forgotten.

She stayed there, holding him like that, for what felt like hours. And somewhere in the quiet, she realized she would have stayed there with him forever if he needed her to.

TWENTY-TWO

Grayson

Grayson woke up alone in the infirmary Saturday morning. There was a stack of clothes on the table beside his bed, and his arm was in a sling, broken.

"Fallon brought those," Nurse Fran told him, gesturing to the clothing. "She was very worried about you."

Grayson's chest ached hollowly. He remembered. His memories of the night before were murky, like he had been underwater the whole time, but he remembered enough. He remembered spilling his guts to Fallon, all the things he'd never said before, just . . . there. Right out of his mouth and into the air between them.

What would she think of him now? What would she see when she looked at him?

Broken. Pathetic. Humiliating. A burden.

By the time he got to the dining hall for breakfast, the others were already done eating. But they still stood and welcomed him back, concern in their eyes.

Carter's hand landed on Grayson's shoulder as he plunked into the empty seat, the one across from Fallon.

"You all right, man?" he asked.

"Yeah," Grayson mumbled.

"It was a nasty tackle," Sutter said with a grimace.

Grayson remembered Alex's threats, his deliberate push in the wrong direction. "Harker sabotaged me. He let that lineman in on purpose. He practically admitted to me before the game that he'd do anything to keep me from joining the Vipers."

Margot's jaw dropped. "You're *kidding*. He can't get away with something like that!"

Fallon cleared her throat. "I heard him playing dumb on the field, explaining himself to the coaches. But he looked satisfied with himself. It was intentional."

Carter shook his head. "We need to tell someone."

"What's the point?" Grayson asked. "There's no way to prove it."

Sutter's eyes darkened. "This won't stop you from joining the Vipers, Grayson."

"It will if it prevents me from passing their tests," Grayson murmured. He focused his gaze on the table—anywhere but on his friends' faces.

"Does it hurt still?" Margot asked gently.

Grayson nodded. "They gave me meds, though. *Strong* meds."

The others laughed a little. Fallon was the only one who stayed silent, eyes locked on him, mouth pressed into a firm line.

"Nurse Fran is making me eat before I take them," he added.

"I'll go make you a plate, all right?" Margot said.

"I'll help," Carter said, standing to follow her. "Eggs, bacon, sausage . . . maybe a pancake or two?"

Grayson couldn't bear the thought of eating all that, but he just nodded. "Thanks, guys."

Sutter stood, too, stacking their empty plates and then heading to the dish drop-off. That left Fallon and Grayson alone at the table.

"Hey," she said.

"Hey," he murmured. He suddenly felt nervous, and his heartbeat flickered. "Thanks, um, for . . ."

"Of course," she said. "I'm just glad you're okay."

He looked down at his cast and sling.

"Listen, Fallon," he said quietly. "About . . . the things I told you last night. You won't say anything, right? To the others, or . . . anyone at all?"

"No, Grayson," she said, reaching for his good hand across the table. She took it in hers, and her skin was soft. "Of course not. I won't say a word."

And he knew she was telling the truth. He knew it without having to ask—it was Fallon. But he had to say the words. He had to know last night had really happened for her, too, beyond his drug-infused memory.

It had. She'd been there. She'd held him. She'd told him it wasn't his fault, and she meant it.

Fallon was looking at him with tenderness in her eyes, and something in his chest loosened.

They sat there like that for a while, Fallon holding his hand, her eyes burning into his, until Margot and Carter came back with plates of food. She let go of his hand suddenly, sat up straighter, and smiled at them. The moment between them snapped, and Grayson picked up his fork to take a bite.

But he caught the look Margot shot Fallon from across the table. And somehow, that was enough to make him smile.

TWENTY-THREE

Sutter

Sutter found himself on the front steps of Drexel House after dinner that evening.

Many nights recently, he'd found himself staring out the window of his dorm room. From there, he could watch the leaves turn in autumn, the first snowfall in the colder months, the sunset glinting off the face of the lake, the throng of students bustling back and forth from the houses to the classroom halls on the northwest side of campus.

And he could also watch the windows of Drexel House, the fire escape on the back of the building, the window of Lawson's old room. Watch the lights turn on in that room, watch the shadow of someone else moving across the cramped space. Watch and remember the last time he saw Lawson.

That moment was like a little room in the back of his brain, an attic no one ever entered. He could walk in and visit any time he wanted, and it was all right there, waiting for him, untouched. Each piece of that night would come to life effortlessly in visceral, painful detail, and he didn't even have to try—his wet clothes clinging to his skin, back flat against the floor as he stared up at his brother's face for what would be the last time.

The rainstorm. The prom. The bag Lawson slung over his shoulder before he left. The stone wall behind his brother's eyes, hiding something.

He was hiding something. Sutter knew it like he knew the sun would rise tomorrow morning. There were so many questions about that fateful night, and Sutter knew there was more to it than what the police had to say.

That's why the poem left in Grayson's locker haunted him. If Lawson had left something behind—something the police missed, any remnant that could crack the case wide open—what if he could be the one to find it?

He knew his friends might not agree. He knew he should be spending his time searching for who left the poem for them to find in the first place, or finding out what was behind the brick wall in Averell's office, or even seeking out answers about the pictures in Lawson's time capsule—they still didn't know who the unnamed woman was, or the baby.

But instead, he was thinking of ways to get into that dorm room.

He found himself reaching for the front door. If he could just go upstairs, he might be able to—

Suddenly, the doors of Drexel House burst open and startled Sutter from his thoughts. The person emerging ran right into him, and before he could even register Mr. Whittaker's familiar face, the contents of his briefcase spilled onto the ground.

"Shit," Sutter muttered. Then he amended, "I mean—shoot. Sorry, sir."

Whittaker gave a nervous laugh as he knelt to gather his things, still clutching his cane. "That's a dollar for the swear jar, Mr. Heyward."

"Here, let me," Sutter said. He scooped up what Whittaker

had spilled—a couple of ink pens, a tin of Altoids, some lemon juice packets.

"What might you be doing at Drexel House this evening?" Whittaker asked as he hastily shoved the items back in his briefcase. "You're a Shepherd House resident, aren't you?"

"I was just, uh," Sutter stammered, ". . . reminiscing."

Whittaker smiled sadly. "Drexel is an awfully mystifying house, isn't it? I was in Fordyce when I was a student, but I always did love this one. It's always looked so . . . *sinister* compared to the other two."

Sutter nodded numbly, feeling as though he'd been caught somehow. He wasn't even sure if he'd known Whittaker was a Meddlehart alum. "I, um, could ask you the same question, sir. What are you doing here on the weekend?"

Whittaker chuckled. "Oh, just meeting a student for some tutoring. Dr. Wilbur and I often visit campus on weekends—I ought to tell Headmaster Averell to construct teachers' quarters at this rate." He nodded toward Shepherd House. "You should get to your room before curfew, young man."

Sutter nodded, relieved he hadn't been caught doing anything truly stupid. He hurried back to Shepherd and into his room before he could give another thought to breaking into Drexel House after curfew.

Before he turned out his lamp and crawled into bed, he looked at Carter. "Where's Grayson?" His second roommate was notably absent.

Carter was wrapping up an episode of *The Great British Bake Off*. Yawning, he switched the TV off.

"Finishing his checkup with Nurse Fran. He'll be back."

Sutter nodded. He tossed his T-shirt into the hamper, ignoring that it landed on the floor instead, and settled into bed.

"Night," Carter said.

"Good night," Sutter mumbled. The last thing he saw in his mind was the lit window on the third floor of Drexel House, aglow in the darkness like a single watchful eye, taunting him with its hidden secrets as he drifted off.

In the groggy haze of sleep, Sutter heard the door open and thought he might've been dreaming.

Then he felt hands on his shoulders, dragging him from bed. He'd hardly opened his eyes when a cloth was folded over them and tied at the back of his head. It knotted in his hair, pinching at his skull. Someone shoved his hands behind his back and bound them tight enough that he could feel his pulse in his fingers.

"What the hell?" he managed, but before he could speak another word, a dry cloth was shoved in his mouth and tied tight, pulling at the edges of his lips.

"Shut up, Heyward," that awful drawling voice said. "Keep quiet, or I swear you'll regret it."

Quincy. This was the first test.

Sutter was pulled to his feet and led blindly out of his room. "Quiet," Quincy hissed, hand firm on the back of Sutter's head. Quincy pushed him down into a crouch, and a familiar nighttime breeze pinched his cheeks.

The fire escape, Sutter realized. He squeezed through the open window like he had a hundred times before, and for a moment he felt safer, because he could picture his surroundings there.

But his muscles strained uncomfortably and cold air snapped at his skin as Quincy guided him down. The terrain changed from metal stairs to manicured grass to uneven mountain ground, and with every step, Sutter grew more disoriented. He felt dizzy, stumbling haphazardly up the side of the mountain, sleep still fogging his brain. He swore he could hear other voices, but the rest of his senses were numb. He couldn't tell who was speaking, which way was up, or what time it was.

Where were his roommates? Had they been taken, too? How had he not heard?

And what about the girls? The thought of someone breaking into their room, blindfolding and gagging them, infuriated him. He suddenly had the urge to swing for Quincy, to kick and punch and scream.

But that would be a terribly stupid move, considering he couldn't move his hands, couldn't see, couldn't even *speak.*

Lawson, he reminded himself. *You're doing this for Lawson.*

It felt like they hiked for hours. Finally, Quincy shoved Sutter to his knees and growled, "Don't move."

Sutter stayed like that, silent, knees aching against the unyielding earth, for a painfully long time. He could hear quick breathing to his left and muffled cries to his right. The gag had dried out his mouth, dozens of tiny fabric fibers sticking to his tongue.

Had Lawson gone through the same thing during his initiation? Or worse, had he done this to other students, other aspiring Vipers? Sutter's heart raced uncomfortably at the thought, and he couldn't help but picture Quincy as a freshman, being invited by his older brother to be part of the order.

Lawson hadn't done that for Sutter. He hadn't said a word about it. And as much as Sutter wanted to ignore that truth, he couldn't. It had plagued his thoughts every day since the meeting. It made him feel like a child again, knowing he'd been excluded from something so important to Lawson. Something he could've been a part of.

Maybe I could've stopped it if you'd told me, Sutter couldn't help thinking. *Maybe I could've helped, and maybe you'd still be here.*

"All right."

The sound of Quincy's voice was like the flip of a switch. Someone tore Sutter's blindfold off, and his vision returned in a nauseating rush. Flashlights lit the space enough for him to see the circle of initiates on their knees, bound and blindfolded, and Quincy watched from the center as the other Vipers unmasked them one at a time.

Sutter spotted Carter first, nostrils flared, glaring at Quincy. Margot was next to him, her long hair tangled around her face.

Sutter turned his head to the left and saw Fallon just two spaces away, but she didn't look at him. Her eyes were scanning the group frantically, like she was searching for someone.

It hit him then. *Where was Grayson?* Was he being excluded from this test because he was injured, just as he'd feared? And Sutter realized he didn't see Alex Harker, either.

"Welcome," Quincy said. "This is your first test. Tonight, you'll participate in a little game we like to call Vipers and Mice."

Sutter strained against the ties around his wrists, blood boiling. He wanted nothing more than to free his hands so he could untie his friends and take the gags from their mouths. But his wrists were bound tight, and he couldn't move.

"Treasure hunting is dangerous business," Quincy said, arms folded. "It's scary. Sometimes treasure is hidden in plain sight, but by the time you realize it, you're already in deep, deep shit. We Vipers have been there a time or two—not *all* the items in our vault were passed down to us. Some, we had to take."

Again Sutter pictured his older brother, giving speeches like this, stealing things for the sake of a treasure hunt. He wanted so badly to understand Lawson's motives, but he feared he never would.

"Sometimes," Quincy went on, "the only way to survive when you're in a pinch is to find your own way out. So in Vipers and Mice, we've combined two little games to mimic the process: Hostages and Capture the Flag. Ever heard of them?"

Sutter wrestled against his restraints. He could tell Quincy found himself funny, asking them questions when they were gagged and unable to respond.

Jeffrey stepped forward. "This is a test of your navigational skills," he said. "We've hidden a green flag for you to find. Your task is to locate it and return it to us by sunrise. We'll be waiting in the campus courtyard. If you can't find the flag, your only chance at passing the test is to find your way back here by sunrise. How you choose to do this—alone or in groups—is up to you."

"I know what you're thinking," Quincy said. "How can you find your way back if you don't know where you are?"

"That's precisely the point," Jeffrey said. "Prove you can. Show us you're cut out for this."

A game. Is that what the Vipers called this? It felt too twisted to be a game—being dropped on the side of a mountain in the middle of the night.

The Vipers were quiet for a moment, and Sutter could hear the whimpers of fear coming from Fallon.

"Here's a little motivation for you," Quincy said. "You might notice some familiar faces are missing. That's because they're a bit . . . tied up, and in need of your help. I suppose that's where this game turns into a hostage situation."

Sutter went rigid. *Grayson.* He was one of the hostages.

Quincy laughed darkly. "If you find the missing initiates, you'll notice they hold a clue to help you locate the flag. I highly advise you find them before the sun comes up, and maybe they'll help you see the light."

Sutter startled when someone stepped behind him and slid a cold knife blade between his wrists. The Viper cut the ties swiftly and moved to the person beside him. Sutter's hands flew to his mouth and he tore the gag from it, coughing and sputtering.

Before Sutter could regain his composure, the Vipers dropped their flashlights on the ground and took off running. Their footsteps beat against the earth and faded to nothing within seconds. He didn't see where they went, and he didn't think anyone else had, either. The night absorbed them, hid them from sight the moment they dropped their flashlights.

He lunged across the ground for one of the flashlights and snatched it up. Margot lunged for one too and grabbed it right as Ken took the last one, kicking dirt into Sutter's face. Sutter watched as Ken and Haley and the other initiates bolted into the dark.

It had barely been thirty seconds, and Sutter and his friends were the only ones left. He looked around at them. They were all in their pajamas, shocked and shivering.

Fallon stood and stumbled forward, eyes scanning the dark forest. Her panicked breaths practically echoed. She appeared to be on the verge of tears.

"It's Grayson," she panted. "They took *Grayson*."

Sutter swallowed thickly. He shone the flashlight around to try to gain some sense of direction. It only left him feeling more disoriented.

"I can't believe that dick," Margot said bitterly, a frantic note in her voice. "It's already psychopathic enough to kidnap us, but doing it to *Grayson*, when he's hurt?"

"Grayson never came back to our room last night," Carter said, eyes wide as the realization hit him. "They've probably had him for hours, since before we went to sleep."

"That's probably why they chose him," Sutter said numbly. "He's injured. It makes him an easy target. He couldn't fight back when they took him, not like he normally would."

"That is so *fucked*," Margot said. "If they led us deep into the forest and left us here, where do you think they took Grayson?"

A wave of hot panic washed over Sutter at her question, because he didn't know. He had no idea how far the Vipers would go, what they were willing to do.

"They do this every year," Carter spoke up. "That's what Jeffrey told me on the way up here. Every Viper must do this to join."

Sutter gripped the flashlight tighter. He found himself wishing Carter hadn't told them that. That meant Lawson did this, too. Sutter's whole freshman year, Lawson was running this group and he had been oblivious.

Sutter shook his head. *Stop, stop, stop.*

"We need to get going," he said. "We've given the others a head start by standing here talking."

"We have to find Grayson," Fallon cried. "I don't care about anything else—not the flag, not the order—none of that matters until we *find him*!"

"We *will*, Fallon," Sutter promised. He put his hands on her shoulders and squeezed them tightly. "Just breathe."

"How about we try to figure out where the hell they dumped us first?" Margot said, a chill to her voice. "We have *no clue* where we are. They led us up the mountain in the middle of the night with no directions on how to get back to the school."

Sutter cast the flashlight over their surroundings. Thick pine and spruce trees covered the mountainside, and the rocky ground was blanketed in fallen needles and shrubs. The only light they had other than the flashlights was the pale glow of the moon.

"They're trying to get us killed, aren't they?" Carter asked. "There are *bears* out here."

"Maybe they're hibernating by now," Margot suggested.

"It's not cold enough for that yet, is it?" Carter asked. "Does anyone know the hibernation calendar for bears?"

Sutter shook his head. "The fact is, to get back to campus, we need to go south. The mountain is north of campus. All we need to do is hike down and we'll get back, one way or another."

"Yeah, unless we hike *around* campus and wind up on the mountain pass leading to West Fork," Margot said. "And is Grayson out here in the woods? Do we need to find him before we try to get back to Meddlehart? A bunch of teenagers on the side of the road in the middle of the night with no idea where their missing friend could be—what could go wrong?"

"Everything," Carter replied. "The answer is everything."

"No," Fallon spoke up. "Not everything."

They turned to look at her, flashlight beams aimed in her direction. She held up her hands to shield her eyes, squinting a little.

"Quincy said if we find the missing initiates, they might help us *see the light*," she said. "And then they cut us free, dropped their *flashlights*, and ran."

It clicked in Sutter's brain then, too.

"The flashlights," Sutter said quickly. He began twisting the top off his. The bulb flickered out and submerged them in partial darkness. Margot aimed her flashlight beam at Sutter's hands as he worked, removing the batteries until . . .

A tiny folded piece of paper fell out. Hands trembling from the cold, he unfolded it and revealed letters written in a blocky script.

WHICH ONE IS THICKER?
OUR HEARTS PUMP BLOOD LIKE WATER
AND ANSWERS LIE HERE

"Okay," Carter said. "Most unhelpful clue ever. Who's with me?"

"It's a haiku," Fallon said. "Another poem."

Margot pursed her lips. "Definitely seeing a pattern here with the poems. What's up with that?"

Sutter shook his head, mind reeling. "Jacob Meddlehart loved poetry. His final message about the treasure was in the form of a poem." It felt like the founder's hand was in all of this, even beyond the grave.

"But what if this one is connected to the poem Grayson found?" Carter asked.

"No, this is part of the test," Fallon insisted. She took Margot's flashlight, unscrewed it, and an identical note fell out. "All the flashlights the Vipers left will contain this clue. We can only hope the others don't figure it out in time to beat us."

Sutter agreed, but it was clear to him that Meddlehart's interest in poetry had influenced whoever left them the other clues the same way it influenced the order's games. It seemed reasonable to think that person might be a Viper, too.

"Okay, this poem must be telling us a location," Margot said. "So what are the key words? I'm choosing to believe *blood* is not one of them."

"Water," Sutter murmured.

"The river," Carter said, snapping his fingers. "The river *pumps* water, doesn't it?"

Margot nodded. "That could be it. The only problem is the river covers a *lot* of ground . . . Fallon, what do you think?"

Fallon's voice was shaky as she said, "We don't have time to second-guess. We need to find Grayson. Let's go."

And then she took off down the mountain, hardly waiting a single second for the others to follow.

Sutter raced after her, weaving between the trees. The incline was a little steep, but no more so than the Shepherd House staircase, and it got less steep with each passing minute.

Doubt ate away at the back of his mind. What if they were wrong about the clue? What if they wasted time trying to get back to the river, but Grayson wasn't there? Would they find him in time? Would they even have a chance at finding the flag?

But there was no time to dwell on his doubts. They had to move.

The four of them descended the mountain as quickly as they could. Sutter wanted to believe they were going in the right direction, but it was dark, and there were no landmarks or clues to guide them.

"Stop," Margot said after a long stretch of silence. They halted in their tracks near the top of a ledge, and she pointed.

"We're off track," she said. "Look, over the trees. It's the houses."

Peeking over the trees, to the west, were the roofs of the student houses.

"If we keep hiking down from here, we'll hit the highway," Margot told them.

"She's right," Sutter said. "We need to move west."

Carter nodded wordlessly, and they adjusted their course.

Fallon was rushing, barely able to catch her breath. Sutter wanted to comfort her, but he knew no words would help right now. None of them would feel at ease until they found Grayson.

As they traversed in the opposite direction, Sutter wondered at what point they would reach the river. He was only familiar with the stretch that ran alongside the western border of campus, but this far up the mountain? He hadn't the slightest clue where the river started.

Sutter was just beginning to wonder if they would ever find it when he heard the telltale rushing of water.

"I hear it," he said, hoping it would give Fallon some peace of mind. "We're close."

Sutter's flashlight caught on an opening in the trees, and then a beaten path emerged ahead. He hurried forward, his breath hitching.

The mountain gave way to a small ravine with a footbridge extended across it. Below, the river rushed with a current much stronger than near campus.

"Whoa!" Carter cried. "I didn't even know this was here."

"I don't think any of us did," Margot said. "Did you, Sutter?"

Sutter shook his head. Just when you thought you knew every secret Meddlehart had to offer, there was always one more.

"There he is," Fallon gasped. Then she was running onto the footbridge, the wood creaking with every step she took.

"Fallon, be careful!" Margot cried, dashing after her. Sutter and Carter followed. Up ahead, Sutter saw someone—a figure, shrouded in the shadows, tied to a post at the midpoint of the bridge.

We found him, Sutter thought. He ran faster toward his friend . . . but his flashlight beam didn't reveal Grayson.

It was Alex Harker on the bridge, hands and feet bound

with rope. A cloth was tied across his mouth, barring him from speaking. He glared at them with venom in his eyes, straining against the binds around his wrists.

Sutter and his friends froze. A sick feeling settled in Sutter's gut. They'd been right about the clue . . . but it had led them to the wrong person.

"What does this mean?" Fallon asked. Panic laced her every word. "He's supposed to be here. If Alex is a hostage and he's here, why isn't Grayson?"

Margot pressed one hand to her forehead. "I—I don't know. Maybe the poem has a double meaning."

Alex tried to shout something, but it was unintelligible.

"Are we letting him go?" Carter asked Sutter, voice low.

Sutter approached Alex hesitantly. Knowing what he'd done to Grayson, he had half a mind to leave him like this . . .

But Quincy had promised the hostages would have a clue. They had to free Alex, if only to get the clue from him so they could end the test.

"We need his clue," Sutter said with finality. He knelt before Alex, eyeing him warily, and yanked the cloth from his mouth.

"You fucking—"

"Where's your clue?" Sutter cut him off.

"I don't have one," Alex growled.

"You're lying," Sutter snapped.

Alex nodded toward his bindings. "Untie me and I'll give it to you."

Sutter stared at him for a long moment before he began untying the rope around Alex's ankles. He didn't have another choice.

"Is Grayson out here with you?" Fallon asked, her voice wavering.

Alex's eyes glinted with curiosity—he hadn't known Grayson was a hostage, too. "No, they brought me here alone. I don't even know how to get back—they blindfolded me."

"Where is he, then? Where could they have taken him?" Fallon started to cry now, tears running down her face.

Sutter stopped for a moment, turning toward her. He felt stunned. He'd never seen her like this before.

"Hey," Margot said. She pulled Fallon into a hug. "We've got this, all right? We'll find him."

Carter reached out and squeezed Fallon's shoulder as she cried, shooting a concerned look at Sutter.

His chest was aching something fierce. It was *his* fault they were in this mess—he had to fix it. *Where the hell did they take Grayson?*

Sutter worked faster, untangling the rope until Alex's feet were free. Alex pushed to his feet and held his wrists out. Sutter undid the knot, loosening the loops until—

Alex's head slammed into Sutter's jaw, and his vision burst with dazzling darkness. He felt Alex's fists lock in the fabric of his shirt, felt the wooden rails of the bridge dig into his spine.

Alex shoved him up until he hung over the edge, nothing protecting him from the drop into the frigid currents below.

TWENTY-FOUR

Fallon

Fallon watched in shock as Alex headbutted Sutter, whose eyes glazed at the impact. Alex hauled Sutter up, and he was going to do it—he was going to throw Sutter off the bridge if they didn't do something.

"Stop!" Fallon screamed, her voice shredding her throat. She grabbed Alex's left arm, and Carter grabbed his right. They dragged him backward, but Alex held fast to Sutter.

"What do you know, Heyward? Where'd your brother go?" Alex bellowed, even as Fallon and Carter dragged him away from the railing. There was a shine in his eyes, a sort of desperation. "He found the treasure, didn't he? *Spit it out!*"

"I don't know *shit*, Alex," Sutter grunted.

Carter wrapped one arm around Alex's neck and pulled until Alex finally let go. Sutter slumped to the ground, heaving in giant breaths. Carter couldn't keep hold of Alex, though, and he wrestled free.

"What the hell is *wrong* with you, Alex?" Margot cried. "You're a *monster.* We saw what you did during the football game, by the way—we know what a pathetic *coward* you are!"

This renewed Alex's anger, and he surged forward. "You don't have a *clue* what you're dealing with! You have *no idea*!"

Sutter jumped to his feet, tackling Alex before he could get to Margot—but Sutter was unstable, and Alex threw him off with ease. Fallon pulled Margot away as Alex regained his footing. Before anyone could move, he bolted across the bridge in the opposite direction from which they'd come. They watched until he made it to the other side and the trees devoured him.

"Asshole!" Margot called after him.

"And there goes Alex's clue," Carter said grimly.

Fallon helped Sutter to his feet. Her body hummed with adrenaline, heart pounding so hard she feared it might burst. It made her feel numb all over.

"Are you okay?" She held on to Sutter's shoulders, studying him.

Sutter nodded, but he looked shaken, and his jaw was already purpling. "I'm fine, promise. What's our next move?"

Fallon swallowed thickly, still fighting tears. "We . . . we must've missed something in the poem. Something that would lead us to Grayson."

She recited it in her mind. *Which one is thicker? Our hearts pump blood like water . . .*

"Heart," she murmured, turning to her friends. "Could it mean the heart of campus?"

Sutter's eyes flashed. "And the heart of campus is water. The lake."

"That has to be where he is," Margot said. "Let's go."

They started walking back across the bridge, but Sutter was wobbly. They moved slowly for a moment until he seemed more stable. Margot's flashlight beam shone ahead, lighting the way.

It crossed over one of the bridge posts, and Fallon froze.

"Margot, stop," she said, pointing. "There's a carving—look."

They all paused to look, and Margot steadied her light on the post. Two names were haphazardly carved in the wood—worn with age, but still readable.

Amelia + Boone

Forever

Fallon sucked in a breath. "Amelia Meddlehart?"

"And Boone," Sutter murmured, "as in Franklin Thatcher's son."

"Wow," Margot said. "They were a couple?"

"Probably while they were students," Sutter said. "When she was still alive."

Carter's eyes went wide. "What if this river is where she drowned?"

A chilled silence settled over them before Sutter prompted them to keep moving. "We need to hurry."

The four of them veered off the path and back into the woods, hustling down, down, down the mountain. Fallon's heart thundered as she silently urged her friends to move faster toward campus—toward the lake, where Grayson would surely be.

An eternity passed before they saw the dining hall through the trees, washed in pale moonlight. Cautiously, they stepped back onto campus grounds and paused, searching for signs of anyone who might bust them for snooping around in the woods past curfew.

"Coast is clear," Sutter said.

"To the lake!" Carter whispered, and they crept onto the path circling campus. The closer to the lake they got, the faster Fallon ran, tears still prickling the corners of her eyes. Her only thought now was of finding Grayson.

When the lake was in sight, its still surface a mirrored

reflection of the moon above them, Fallon scanned the area for disturbances but saw none. The benches facing the massive pond were empty. The grassy lawn was clear.

Panic seized her chest for a moment—but then, as if the night was begging her to see it, a movement to the left caught her eye. A phantom wind rolled over her, and with it, she saw the groundskeeper's shed a handful of yards from the path.

Its door was hanging open on its hinges and swaying slightly in the breeze.

"*There*," she said. She charged for the open door, heartbeat thudding in her ears with every step. Her eyes brimmed at the thought—the *fear* that Grayson wasn't here, despite the clue's promise that he would be.

"Grayson?" she called as she approached. His voice didn't call back to her.

"Gray?" she said again, desperation lacing her voice. She reached for the door and pulled it fully open.

And he was there, slumped on the floor against a wall—eyes closed, dark hair stuck to his forehead with sweat. His uninjured arm was bound to a steel bar behind him, and his mouth was gagged, just as theirs had been.

"Oh my God," Fallon cried, kneeling in front of him. She took his face in her hands and pulled the cloth from his parted lips. "Grayson, can you hear me?"

He didn't respond. His body was limp, his skin clammy.

"Is he breathing?" someone said from behind her. Margot.

Fallon didn't answer, because she couldn't tell. The world tilted on its axis. Panic flooded her chest in a nauseating rush. She pushed the damp, disheveled hair off Grayson's forehead. She shook him gently.

Her memories drowned out every rational thought like a bloodcurdling scream. Screeching tires, blood on the dashboard, lungs that would never breathe again—

"Please wake up," she begged. *"Gray, please!"*

It seemed like an eternity passed before his eyes fluttered open and he looked at her, disoriented. "Fallon?" he murmured.

She couldn't have spoken if she tried. Sobs racked her chest as she flung her arms around him, hanging on to him for dear life. For a moment, he just sat there, too stunned to move. Then, finally, she felt his uninjured arm wrap around her. His hand stroked her hair.

"Shh," he whispered. His voice was gravelly. "It's okay, Fallon. I'm okay."

Fallon wasn't sure how much time passed with her clinging to him, unable to stop her tears. Finally, she let go, and Margot and Carter stepped in to help Grayson up. When she looked at Sutter, he was glancing back and forth between her and Grayson, his brow furrowed.

Her stomach dropped at the look in his eyes. Was he . . . jealous?

No, Fallon told herself. *Don't give that a second thought.*

But Sutter continued to watch them in stony silence as Grayson got his bearings. His broken arm was still in its sling. He was pale, and the sweat on his skin glinted in the flashlight beams.

"Someone grabbed me," he told them. "They had masks on. I was kicking, trying to fight back . . . I think I hit my head when they shoved me in here. That's the last thing I remember."

"It's the first test," Margot told him. "It was the Vipers."

Grayson swallowed thickly and reached up to hold his forehead. "I don't understand."

"There's no time," Sutter said. His swollen lip made his words thick. "We'll tell you everything after we get back to Shepherd. There's supposed to be a clue with you—do you have anything?"

Fallon glanced at Sutter, wishing he would slow down and give Grayson a minute. Her chest prickled with frustration. She was about to voice her thoughts when Margot pointed at Grayson.

"Your sling," she said. Carefully, she reached for his broken arm, where a small slip of paper was tucked under his cast. Margot unfolded it and held it under her flashlight, frowning.

IF YOU LOOK EAST, YOU MAY BE RIGHT:
SOMETIMES TREASURE'S HIDDEN IN PLAIN SIGHT.

The words sounded familiar. Fallon thought back to the things Quincy had said just before cutting them loose . . .

"Okay, east," Carter said. "What's on the east side of campus?"

"The student houses," Margot said, counting off on her fingers. "The greenhouse—"

"The courtyard," Fallon said, like it was simple.

"But that's where Quincy is waiting for us to bring the flag," Carter said.

Sutter was staring at her, like it made perfect sense. "She's right. The flag is already there. *In plain sight.*"

The others pondered this for a moment.

"I wouldn't put it past the Vipers to pull a trick like that," Margot agreed.

"Let's go, before the others figure it out," Sutter said. He hustled through the door of the shed, followed by Carter and Margot.

Fallon stayed beside Grayson as he stepped out. She noticed

he was trembling slightly and holding his arm gingerly at his side. She knew he must be in pain, not to mention cold. As the adrenaline rush wore off, Fallon shivered harder herself. Her pajamas weren't enough to keep her warm out here, and her toes steadily grew numb, her legs aching.

"Did they hurt you?" she whispered to Grayson as they walked.

He shook his head unconvincingly. "I'm okay."

Of course Grayson would say he was okay, no matter how clear it was that he was lying. Fallon wanted nothing more than to get back to the warm safety of Shepherd House as fast as possible, and that alone motivated her to move faster. She watched the others as they raced across campus.

Fallon saw the green flag, hoisted above Lawson's memorial, before she spotted the Vipers. They watched with grins wide enough to be snarls. Fallon scanned the area surrounding them and nearly breathed a sigh of relief—they'd made it back first.

"Well," Quincy called out as they approached, "you solved the riddle. Looks like you and your brother have a lot in common after all, Heyward."

Sutter took it upon himself to snatch the flag and thrust it into Quincy's hands. "I suppose we do."

Carter leaned over on his knees, sucking in big gulps of air. Margot brushed dirt off her pajamas, and Grayson slumped to the ground, pale and panting.

A hot rush of anger washed over Fallon at the sight of Quincy's smug face. He could see the toll the night had taken on them, but he didn't care one bit.

It doesn't matter, she tried to tell herself. They had passed the test. They were one step closer to becoming Vipers—one step closer to seeing inside that vault.

Sutter glared at Quincy. "Well? Is that it?"

Quincy nodded. "Congratulations. You qualify for the next test. If I were you, I'd get back to your dorms before sunrise."

As they turned to go, Sutter's eyes met Fallon's. Despite everything, there was a glint of triumph in his eyes. A sense of pride at their victory.

But Fallon didn't feel as though they'd won anything at all.

TWENTY-FIVE

Sutter

When Sutter awoke Sunday morning, it didn't matter that he had been up all night wandering through the forest, or that he'd taken a blow to the jaw. He was restless, thinking only about last night's test and what it revealed.

There was a lot he didn't know about his older brother.

Lawson had a whole life under the cover of the order that Sutter knew nothing about. Places he'd gone. Things he'd stolen. Students he'd led through initiation, where they may have experienced horrible, dangerous nights like the one Sutter just had.

All the while, Sutter was clueless. And Lawson must've wanted it that way.

Sutter rubbed his aching face tenderly, wondering when the pain would ease. His bruises would fade, but he feared the loss of his brother never would. Maybe the gaping hole Lawson left in his life would never be filled, not even if he found the answers he so desperately sought.

After Sutter had stared at the ceiling for what felt like hours, his stomach growled its demand for food. He decided he'd head to the dining hall to see if there was any French toast left.

He wondered if Fallon was already in the dining hall. His

few hours of sleep were broken up by thoughts of her, mixed in with all his other questions. He couldn't shake it—the way she'd looked at Grayson last night, and how badly he wanted her to look at him that way instead.

But she does look at you that way, he thought. *Doesn't she?*

Sutter thought back to that night when he drunkenly kissed Fallon in the courtyard. His memory was fuzzy, but the moment their lips had met was crystal clear. Halfway through freshman year, he'd realized how he felt about her, and that kiss . . . it was something he'd wanted for a long time. He remembered the look on her face when she pulled away, the word that broke his heart. *Wait.*

Since then, he'd done everything he could to hide that kiss away in his memory, hide his feelings for her, as though none of it had happened.

Maybe he shouldn't have hidden it so well. In the moments Sutter had allowed himself to look back on that kiss, he wondered if there was something missing—something he misremembered or misunderstood. There were so many moments that made Sutter wonder if he was wrong and friendship wasn't all Fallon wanted with him.

Maybe you should ask her.

A cold sense of dread seeped through Sutter's limbs. Maybe one day he'd work up the courage to talk to her about it—maybe even soon—but not today. Not until they'd recovered from the Vipers' first test and figured out a plan for what came next.

Sutter tried to shove it all from his mind as he pulled on sweatpants and a hoodie. Grayson and Carter dragged themselves from bed to follow him, looking as though they hadn't slept a wink. The three of them lumbered out of Shepherd House and into the chilly fall air.

French toast, Sutter thought. *Don't think about anything else. Think about French toast, sustenance for the day ahead.*

They joined the line of students stacking their plates with food. Sutter took the last slices of French toast, dusted with a perfect snowfall of powdered sugar, and doused them in syrup.

He was the first to arrive at their usual table, only to find a folded piece of paper—that thick, creamy stationery he already recognized.

Sutter snatched it up before he could think twice and read the familiar blocky handwriting:

Each day another grain of sand,
But no closer to completed plans.
The sand runs out,
Your end draws near,
And chances slowly disappear.

Sutter's arms were covered in gooseflesh. *What the hell?*

Carter and Grayson set their plates down. Wordlessly, he handed them the paper and watched them read.

Grayson's face blanched. "Does this one have invisible ink, too?"

Carter gestured to his mug of tea. "Shall we?"

"Maybe don't completely spill it this time," Grayson said, which resulted in an exaggerated eye roll from Carter. Carefully, he held the paper over the steaming cup and waited for the heat to reveal a hidden message.

But none appeared. Sutter's chest deflated.

"This one seems less like a clue," Grayson mumbled, "and more like a warning."

"Does it feel to either of you like we're being watched?"

Carter asked. His normal easygoing tone was replaced with a note of fear.

Sutter swallowed thickly. He agreed, and he didn't like the feeling of unease settling in his gut. Who was watching them? And what could this warning be for? He thought of the Vipers—Quincy and Jeffrey and the others. Could one of them be leaving these poems for them?

To Sutter, the only clear message was this: They weren't looking hard enough. They weren't working *fast* enough.

Just then, Fallon and Margot entered the dining hall, waving at the boys as they got in the breakfast line.

"I hope Fallon's all right this morning," Carter whispered.

Grayson frowned. "What do you mean?"

Carter sucked his teeth. "You didn't see how she was last night when we couldn't find you. I've never seen her so upset."

Inconsolable would have been the word Sutter used. But something about the new softness in Grayson's eyes put a sour taste in his mouth.

Just then, the girls joined them with their plates. Sutter cleared his throat and said, "We need to make a plan."

Margot and Fallon stopped short, staring at him. Finally, Margot snorted and took her seat beside him.

"Good morning to you, too, Sutter."

Even Fallon smiled a little as she sat beside Grayson, who smiled back at her. She murmured a greeting to him, and he started to respond.

Sutter ignored Margot's sarcasm. "We just got a new poem." He slid the paper across the table for the girls to read, watching as fresh dread dawned on their faces. "I've been thinking about the first poem—the one with the clue about Lawson's room. I don't think we should wait any longer to get in there and look around. Every day that goes by without answers is wasted time."

"And do you have a plan for how to do that without getting in serious trouble?" Margot asked pointedly. "Sutter, I think the chances of finding something in Lawson's old room are slim to none. He hasn't lived there in ages."

Irritation prickled in Sutter's chest at Margot's dismissal of his idea, and the way Carter nodded along like she was automatically right. But Fallon and Grayson . . .

They weren't even listening. They were having their own whispered conversation as if they were the only two people at the table.

Jealously flooded his veins, taking him over like a fast-moving poison.

"Hey, are you two lovebirds going to join us, or should we just leave you alone?" Sutter snapped.

The words left his mouth before he'd even considered them, and his skin flushed hot almost instantly. Grayson and Fallon looked up at him silently. A stunned sort of anger dawned on Fallon's face. The sight made Sutter's stomach clench.

"Did you really just say that?" she asked.

"Yeah, what the hell?" Margot pressed.

"All right," Carter said, holding up his hands. "Now's not the time to start throwing jabs at each other, okay?" He lowered his voice, leaning in Sutter's direction. "Dude, chill. We're all on your side here."

Carter's eyes had taken on an uncharacteristic seriousness. The hidden meaning in his words was clear. *We're doing this for you. We're searching for the treasure, joining the Order of the Vipers, all of it* for you.

Sutter clenched his jaw, barring himself from speaking again.

He felt like a complete asshole. Immediately, he wanted to apologize, but Fallon's eyes were like daggers, and Grayson's were stone cold. If he opened his mouth, Sutter worried he might only make it worse.

And despite his regret, he still felt angry. He was pissed off they'd received a clue, a tip in the right direction, that all his friends chose to ignore.

Didn't they understand the gravity of all this? His brother was *missing*. At this point, they were Lawson's only hope of being found. There was no room for picking and choosing which clues to follow.

Sutter didn't have time for this, so he shoved up from the table and made for the doors.

He didn't need them. He could do it himself.

Before he made it outside, though, a hand caught his arm. He spun around to see Fallon, her eyes ablaze with anger and shining with unshed tears.

"You do *not* get to do that to me," she said.

Sutter just stared at her for a moment, trying to find words. "What?"

"You don't get to embarrass me like that," she said. "Or punish me. Not when you *kissed* me at the beginning of the semester and have done nothing since then but pretend it never happened!"

Her words were like a barb to his heart. "Fallon, I—"

"No." She blinked the tears out of her eyes. "Not right now. Not here."

She turned and went back to the table, where all his friends were eating without him.

Sutter pushed through the dining hall doors and into the cold morning air. His mind reeled as he tried to piece together what the hell just happened.

He hadn't meant to collide with Dr. Wilbur as he rounded the corner, and the moment their eyes met, he knew he should've just stayed in his dorm that morning. She stopped him in the middle of the pathway, brows furrowed.

"Mr. Heyward," she said sternly. "What on earth happened to your face?"

He reached up to the tender skin at his jaw, swollen and bruised.

"I fell," he said.

"Fell where?"

"Outside."

She narrowed her eyes. "And I expect it's been treated by Nurse Fran?"

He gave a slight shrug.

Her frown deepened. "I'll escort you to the headmaster's office."

Damn it. This day could not get any worse.

Meddlehart Manor felt warm and welcoming. The fireplace roared in the living room, and Mrs. Averell was playing the piano on the other side of the house. Sutter wondered if Headmaster Averell ever regretted having his office there—it was hard to feel like you were in trouble, like a typical walk to the principal's office might.

But when Averell took his seat at his desk, he seemed perfectly content, sipping coffee from a dark-blue mug. Even with the headmaster sitting right across from him, Sutter couldn't keep his eyes off the bookcase, knowing there was a brick wall behind it concealing *something*.

What is this house hiding?

"Coffee, Sutter?"

"No, thank you," he said. "Not much of a coffee guy."

"There's hot chocolate, too," Averell said with a smile.

Sutter couldn't say no to that.

Moments later, Averell set a mug of hot chocolate, complete with dozens of tiny marshmallows, before Sutter. He resettled into his chair.

"So," he said. "What happened to your face, Sutter?"

Sutter took a sip of hot chocolate, relishing the way the marshmallows melted on his tongue.

"I fell." Might as well stick to his original story. "Outside."

Averell nodded, and kind as his eyes were, Sutter knew he wasn't convinced.

"As difficult as this may be to believe," he said, "I got in my fair share of fights when I was your age. I know what it looks like."

Sutter kept his expression even and ran through possible responses. *What, you can tell these bruises are in the shape of knuckles?* But Averell went on before he came up with anything.

"Violence is not permitted at Meddlehart, as you know," he told Sutter. "It's in your best interest to tell me what happened. Who did this to you?"

Sutter cleared his throat. He couldn't rat out Alex, even if he was a complete dick who deserved it. Quincy had made it very clear—the Vipers didn't tolerate narcs. Telling Averell he got into a fight with Alex was too great a risk.

"The ground," Sutter said. "I fell. That's all, I swear."

Sutter knew it wasn't a convincing story. He wished he'd thought of something better when Wilbur put him on the spot.

Averell sighed. "Sutter . . . I know it's been a rough time for you. Have you felt any better since your break last year?"

Sutter didn't know why the words stunned him. He'd been in this office with the headmaster more than once, having this same conversation—*How are you doing, now that your brother is gone?* It shouldn't have come as a surprise Averell would take this opportunity to check up on him—attribute his swollen, bruised jaw to the loss of Lawson.

But it is *about Lawson,* Sutter couldn't help but think. *Isn't everything?*

Sutter tried most of the time to forget the "break" he experienced during sophomore year. He remembered all the hours he spent poring over news stories, interviews with investigators, his own memories from the night Lawson disappeared, until something snapped inside him. He felt unhinged, like the very thing holding him to the earth had loosened and there was nothing tethering him anymore.

He remembered Headmaster Averell sitting him down in this very room and suggesting he spend some time at home, since the school had so many memories tied to Lawson. That suggestion was Sutter's undoing—he hated thinking about it, how he'd cried in Averell's office, begging the headmaster not to send him away. *If Meddlehart reminds me of Lawson, home is a thousand times worse. My* parents *are a thousand times worse.*

But his parents showed up by the time the sun set that evening, and they took him home. His father could hardly look at him. His mother shut down his phone, TV, and internet access. She tucked him into his bed like a little boy and told him to let the police do their job.

A few weeks passed. And somewhere, in the time spent deliberately avoiding his brother's case, Sutter found a sense of stability strong enough to return to Meddlehart.

Now, though, he sat in Averell's office again, battered and

bruised, friendships falling to pieces, and unable to slow his racing, roaring mind. What if the headmaster had other reasons for wanting Sutter away from campus? What if he hadn't appreciated the way Sutter was sniffing around, looking for answers?

"Sutter?"

He cleared his throat. "To answer your question, Headmaster, I'm better than ever."

Averell nodded slowly. "Are you still actively searching for your brother?"

"No." Sutter hoped the lie was as easy to believe as it was to speak.

Averell watched him carefully for a moment, like he didn't buy it. He swiveled his chair to the left a little, then the right.

"I can't imagine what it's like to be in your position," he told Sutter. "I've tried many times to picture it, but I can't. The situation is painful even without the . . . strange circumstances."

Sutter's ears caught on the word. "Strange?"

Averell shrugged a little. "A young man due at his senior prom, and he decides to leave, gone without a trace." He shook his head. "Many strange things have happened here, but that night is surely one of the strangest nights in Meddlehart's history."

Sutter was tempted to argue a few of those points, but something about the look in the headmaster's eye, the words he spoke . . .

"Just be careful, Sutter," Averell said in a low voice. "High school students tend to find themselves in many troublesome situations, even if they didn't mean to. Don't be one of those students."

Don't be Lawson.

Then Averell smiled, and the moment slipped away. "I'll let

Nurse Fran know you're on your way to have that jaw looked at. In the meantime, stay the course with your studies. Your grades are good so far this semester."

Sutter nodded and stood. As he made his way out of the study, he grappled with what Averell had said.

The photos lining the wall next to the staircase stared down at him like a gallery of watchful eyes. Photos of the Meddleharts and Thatchers through the years—a photo of the Thatcher twins smiling in a rowboat at Barnaby Boathouse, another of Jacob on skis at the Goliath slope at Swallowtail Mountain. Sutter had skied that run a dozen times on the annual school trip, and he'd know it anywhere.

Sutter wasn't sure what to make of everything Averell had just told him, but there was one thought dominating all the rest.

It seemed like the headmaster knew something.

And it was as this thought crossed his mind that one of the dozens of photos caught his eye. Sutter stopped and looked up at it, his heart going frozen when he studied it.

A photo of Jacob Meddlehart standing on the front steps of a newly constructed Fordyce House, smiling proudly at the camera . . . but he wasn't alone. His hand rested on the shoulder of a short woman with brown hair and a warm smile.

The same woman from the photo in Lawson's time capsule.

TWENTY-SIX
Fallon

Fallon returned from breakfast with a pounding headache and a knot in her throat. She hadn't recovered from losing so much sleep the night before, and she collapsed into bed as soon as she and Margot got to their dorm. She'd intended to work on her art class project, but her brain felt scrambled, her eyelids heavy.

So she bundled herself in a blanket and tried to read a book instead of thinking about the way Sutter had snapped at them. But her heart still pounded from the rush of anger-laced embarrassment that had washed over her.

Lovebirds. She knew Sutter meant it as a jab, but it struck a nerve with her in a way she hadn't expected.

At some point, Fallon fell into a fitful rest. When she finally managed to crawl out of bed, achy and puffy-eyed, orange evening light trickled in through the blinds.

Margot was awake, too, but barely. She sat in her bed, laptop in her lap, surrounded by used Keurig pods and empty coffee mugs.

"Rise and shine," she mumbled as Fallon stumbled to her closet.

"I feel like a zombie," Fallon croaked.

"Same," Margot said. "I fell asleep and barely made it to my class officer meeting, and now I'm trying to learn my lines for rehearsal tonight. But it feels impossible at the moment, because I have a migraine coming on." She winced. "Forget the Vipers—Parents Weekend planning might be the death of me."

Fallon pulled a Swallowtail Mountain hoodie over her head, dread filling her stomach. "Is that . . . *this* weekend?"

She'd forgotten about it in all the stress over the first initiation. Not that she cared to take part in Parents Weekend, anyway—how could she?

"Oh, Fallon," Margot said, and the sympathy in her voice made Fallon's chest ache. "Did you invite your aunt and uncle? Will they make it?"

Fallon shook her head quickly. "I intentionally didn't invite them." She'd invited them freshman year, but it was kind of a nightmare. The teachers were totally clueless and spoke to them like they were her parents, calling them *Mr. Winthrop* and *Mrs. Winthrop*.

And as if that hadn't been painful enough, Jennie and Fred's sitter backed out last minute, so they had to bring the littles along. The baby cried through every assembly, and the toddlers wreaked havoc during the family games on the lawn. Fallon ended that weekend near tears, embarrassed and wishing more than ever her parents had been there instead.

Sophomore year, she didn't bring up Parents Weekend to her aunt and uncle at all, and they didn't ask about it. It came and went, and they were none the wiser. That was her plan this year, too, because spending it alone sucked, but not as much as freshman year.

Margot sighed. "Well . . . I don't think my parents are going to make it, either."

Fallon looked up, and the tears in Margot's eyes startled her. Margot hardly ever cried, and it pained Fallon when she did.

"What?" Fallon asked. "Why not?"

"They booked a trip to meet with investors in New York," Margot mumbled, lips quivering. She wiped under her eyes and sighed. "Mom said she didn't have the dates in her calendar, but I know that's not true. I mean, I'm class president—I *planned* the damn thing. Obviously I gave them the dates ages ago. They both knew, and they booked the trip anyway."

Fallon walked over and sat on the edge of Margot's bed. She took her hand and squeezed it.

It wasn't the first time Margot's parents had made decisions like this. Margot's family was wealthy, and most people assumed she wanted for nothing. But that wasn't really the truth. Her parents weren't around much, so she and her younger sisters were often on their own, aside from their drivers and butlers and other Cashton staff who made sure they were taken care of. Margot brushed it off most of the time, but today . . . she was hurting. And though their circumstances were different, Fallon understood.

Maybe that was partly why she and Margot got along so well. Fallon knew better than anyone what it meant to miss your parents.

"I'm so sorry, Margot," she said. "That just . . . sucks. It really sucks."

Margot sniffled, shaking her head. "It's whatever. I'm used to it by now, you know? I'm just sad for my little sisters. They deserve better."

"You *all* do," Fallon said. Then a light bulb turned on in her head. "How about we spend the day together, all four of us?"

Margot sat up straighter and smiled. "We can do all the family activities together! Who cares if our parents aren't there?"

"I'll be an honorary Cashton sister for the day," Fallon said, and the idea lifted her spirits in a surprising way. She'd always wondered what it might be like to have a sister.

Margot threw her arms around Fallon and squeezed her tight. "That's what I love about this place," she said. "We get to choose our own family."

Fallon's eyes prickled, and she blinked to fight the feeling. "I chose the best one."

And even though things felt different now—even though she was more worried for her friends than she'd been in a while—she meant it.

TWENTY-SEVEN

Sutter

Sutter hadn't visited the Drexel House common room in a long time, but it was like nothing had changed. The dark leather furniture, the old wooden beams crossing the ceiling, the massive elk antlers mounted over the roaring fireplace.

There was no time to waste. The sun was dropping quickly below the horizon, and students weren't supposed to visit other houses after dark. He only had an hour to burn before a prefect might catch him and kick him out.

Sutter studied the students milling about the common room, unsure how to avoid looking out of place. A couple of senior girls gave him a weird look as they made their way toward the exit.

"Are you lost?" one of them asked, sending the other into a fit of giggles.

Thinking quickly, Sutter smiled. "Actually, yeah. Jeffrey Price lives here, doesn't he? I'm looking for him."

The girl nodded. "Yeah, on the third floor. First door on the right."

Sutter grinned, feeling like he'd struck gold with an excuse to go to the third floor. If only Jeffrey's was the room he needed to get into.

Sutter took the stairs two at a time until he reached the third floor. Carefully, he peeked around the corner at the door almost at the very end of the hall, just feet from the window leading to Drexel's fire escape.

Lawson's dorm.

For a moment, Sutter felt frozen in time, transfixed by the familiarity of the place. If he closed his eyes, he could almost hear the rain beating down on the metal roof. He could almost picture his brother opening the door and looking at him like he was the last person on earth he wanted to see.

"What the hell are you doing here, Sutter?"

His heart nearly stopped until he turned around and saw . . . Grayson. His friend stood at the landing of the stairs below, staring at him with a knowing look.

Sutter sighed. "How did you—"

"I saw you," he interrupted in a whisper, taking the next few steps up. "I was heading to dinner, and I figured you were, too, until you made a *very* wrong turn."

Sutter clenched his jaw. "You should go. All of you made it abundantly clear you have no interest in helping me."

"Come on, Sutter, don't be a dick."

Sutter's chest sank with guilt. He swallowed thickly—he'd deserved that.

For a moment, Grayson just looked at him. Apologies weren't something that happened often between Sutter and his friends—most of the time, they weren't needed. And it was no shock Grayson didn't seem inclined to acknowledge the discomfort between them.

Sutter half expected Grayson to take a swing at him; that's likely what he would've done had another person talked to him the way Sutter did that morning.

But he didn't. And Sutter supposed he should've known Grayson better than that. Grayson may have tried to fight his way out of most situations, but when it came down to it, his loyalty won out.

Finally, Grayson sighed. "What you didn't consider is . . . you're going to need me for this. Have you thought about how you're going to get into that room? Do you even know who lives there? Because I do."

Sutter blinked. "How?"

Grayson didn't answer. Instead, he brushed past Sutter and walked straight up to the door of Lawson's old room. He took a deep breath, lifted his fist, and knocked.

Several moments passed before the click of the lock sounded and the door swung open.

Alex Harker stood on the other side, and his chest puffed up the instant he saw Grayson.

Sutter's stomach churned, and he edged as far behind the wall as he could while still being able to watch. *Ah, shit.*

"What do you want?" Alex spat. "Come back for more?"

Grayson's jaw ticked. "You and I have been summoned to Averell's office."

Alex's jaw dropped. "But why?"

"Why do you think, Harker? Did you really think you'd get away with all the shit you've pulled this semester?"

Alex groaned, shaking his head, and his face had gone ghost white. "This is such *bullshit*." Without another word, he shoved past Grayson and slammed the door shut behind him without bothering to lock it.

Sutter pressed his back against the wall as Alex brushed by, not even sparing him a glance. Grayson followed. He shot Sutter a look that said, *Now's your chance.*

Damn it, he owed Grayson big-time.

On swift feet, Sutter tiptoed down the hall to Alex's door and pushed it open. He knew the room wouldn't look the same as it did when it belonged to Lawson, but it still wrenched his heart to see it so changed—the red plaid bedspread replacing Lawson's blue one, the posters of sports cars that Lawson wouldn't have cared about.

Focus. Sutter blinked rapidly as he gazed around the room. He tried to look past the protein bar wrappers, the untouched homework assignments littering the desk, the laundry hamper full of unwashed football uniforms that stank up the room. Where to start?

There was no time to think about it. He dove to the floor and peeked under the bed, only to find dust bunnies and stale Cheetos. He turned to the closet and pushed Alex's clothes aside, but there was nothing.

Everything was Alex's. There was nothing of Lawson's, just like his friends had warned him.

Think, Sutter told himself, desperately trying to slow his racing heart. *What parts of this room are the same?*

The furniture. He inspected the wooden bed frame before moving on to the desk, where he looked through the drawers for any hidden compartments.

The only interesting thing he found was Alex's invitation to join the Order of the Vipers. The envelope was torn neatly and set beneath a silver letter opener with HARKER engraved on it, along with a delicate snake design.

It may not have been a piece of jewelry, but it seemed like

too much of a coincidence not to be connected to the order. *Maybe Alex was a Viper legacy, too.*

But there wasn't a trace of his brother, like he'd been erased. Like he'd never even *been* here.

Sutter could feel the tidal wave climbing up his throat, the pressure behind his eyes he hated so much. *No*, he told himself. *Not now. Not when you're so close.*

Where would Lawson hide something? If he were Lawson, what would he . . .

It caught Sutter's eye like a snag in an old sweater, a familiar thread coming loose.

The air vent high on the wall, its cast-iron cover welded into a pattern of squares. He thought of the slatted one in the floor of Lawson's bedroom at home, where he kept the secret stash of candy he only let Sutter dig into when he was upset.

Cautiously, he climbed onto Alex's bed and reached for the vent cover, only to find it screwed in place. Frantic, Sutter scanned the room until he remembered the letter opener. He snatched it from the desk, jumped back onto the bed, and used it to work the screws out of the wall.

The vent came free, and Sutter peered anxiously inside.

His breath caught in his throat when he saw a leather-bound notebook, well worn and faded. The pages were thick and bloated, but it seemed to be in one piece.

Heart hammering, he removed the notebook from the vent and gently peeled the cover back to the first page. He recognized the handwriting the second he saw it.

"This was our father's," he said breathlessly to no one at all.

But as he skimmed the pages, breezing through the words *Vipers* and *the order* and *Thatcher* and *Meddlehart*, he realized the handwriting shifted halfway through—clearly written by a different person, but still achingly familiar.

"Lawson." His voice cracked over the name. Lawson had taken their father's unfinished journal and used it as his own.

Sutter knew he needed to leave, but he felt as though he were anchored to this moment, unable to break free of it. He let his eyes pass over a few of Lawson's pages, but the entries were fragmented and scattered, as though his brother had written down dozens of incomplete thoughts, or like he was writing in code. One page near the end was a list of random words:

tiger
peacock
alex
zebra
goliath
lime
apollo
oregon

And the last page held only one sentence, written in a panicked, shaky scrawl:

we hear in the trees
a killer's every rumination

Sutter's head spun. Was this a lyric, or a line from a poem? The wobbling letters were enough to strike fear in Sutter's heart, and he couldn't help wondering why his brother's hand had trembled as he wrote this final message. But his mind remained blank as he stared at the words, another puzzle piece without a clear fit.

What were you trying to say?

Unable to help himself, he flipped back to where Lawson's pages started. And his eyes caught on something he hadn't seen the first time.

"Holy shit," he murmured.

In that instant, he heard footsteps thundering at the end of the hall. Quickly, he replaced the vent cover, not bothering to screw it in place, and bolted out the door.

He shut it behind him right as Alex appeared around the corner, thunder in his eyes and muttering to himself.

"Wasting my damn time—" He froze when he saw Sutter in the hallway. "Why are *you* here?"

Sutter swallowed. "Uh. Looking for Jeffrey."

Alex rolled his eyes and started past him. "If you think he's gonna give you hints about the next test, you're just as delusional as your buddy Hendricks. Get out of my way before I beat your ass again."

"Don't mind if I do," Sutter said, charging down the stairs of Drexel House with a spring in his step. He pulled out his phone and sent his friends a text:

Meet me at Barnaby Boathouse in 10.

TWENTY-EIGHT

Fallon

No one was at Barnaby Boathouse when Fallon arrived after dark. No one except Sutter, who was wrangling a rowboat into the water on his own. When he saw her approaching, he stopped.

Fallon's hands were in her hoodie pocket, and she fiddled anxiously with a loose thread inside. She'd been so close to not coming at all—her anger with Sutter was still too fresh—but she knew holding a grudge wouldn't do them any good. Not right now, with everything going on. And she was curious as to why he'd summoned them.

"Need a hand?" she asked.

He glanced down at the rowboat. "It's not a big deal," he said quietly.

But Fallon was already walking up to help. She lifted the other end of the boat and helped him lower it into the stream. Sutter knelt to tie the boat down, and Fallon lowered herself into the grass beside him, watching the water flow lazily past.

The two of them were silent for a moment as Sutter worked. Finally she asked, "So . . . why are we here?"

Sutter kept his eyes on the rope in his hands. "I'll explain once everyone shows up. Is Margot coming?" His words were stiff, but mostly because of his swollen face.

"Yeah," Fallon replied. "She's just finishing her makeup first. She has rehearsal tonight."

"Cool." They went quiet again as he finished his knot, and for a long moment, there was nothing to focus on but the stony silence between them. She glanced at him, and he glanced back, hazel eyes glinting.

"Fallon, I—"

"Your face looks terrible," she blurted.

He paused, taken aback. "How . . . *kind* of you, Winthrop."

"I didn't mean it like that," she said.

He tried to smile but winced instead. "Shit, that hurts."

"Don't smile," she said firmly. "And don't talk, either. That must hurt, too."

A wounded look passed over his face. "I know you probably don't want to talk to me," he said quietly. "And maybe it's better if I just keep my mouth shut, but . . . I'm sorry, Fallon. About this morning, and—"

"It's okay," she mumbled. "Really, you don't have to say anything. We're all right."

He looked down at his feet. The space between his brows was wrinkled, and she couldn't help the way her heart pulled in response. That expression was one of his little quirks, one of many that she'd adored for so long.

Fallon could almost see the wheels turning in Sutter's head. He was thinking, calculating, struggling for the right words. She was about to let him off the hook, when he shook his head, and then his eyes met hers, brave and fiery like she knew him to be.

"I'm sorry we haven't talked about it," he said. "That night."

Fallon froze. For a moment, all she could do was stare and wait for Sutter to clarify what he meant.

But he didn't. He stared right back patiently. He wanted her to respond, she realized.

"What night?" she finally asked, her voice nearly a whisper.

Something in his expression withered. "When I kissed you," he said. There was an ache in his voice. An insistence. "What other night could I be talking about, Fallon?"

Anxiety seized her. All this time, she thought that kiss was meaningless to him, nothing but a drunken, emotional mistake—insignificant enough to be ignored entirely, smothered by the booze and the burden that day had been.

But looking at him now, sitting in the grass by the boathouse, she realized she was wrong.

"I . . . thought I was the only one that kiss m-mattered to," she stammered. Her mouth was dry, her voice tight and wobbly. "You had too much to drink, and . . . it seemed like something you didn't mean to do."

The surprise that dawned on his face made her heart ache. He shook his head, and then he took her hand in his, clutching it tight.

"I think about it all the time," he said. "When I kissed you, Fallon . . . it's because I wanted to. It wasn't a mistake. For so long, I've wanted you."

Fallon's heart raced. This was it—this was the moment she'd dreamed of. This is what she'd longed for. Sutter's hand in hers, him telling her how he felt. Telling her he wanted her. All she had to do was say she felt the same way.

So why was she struggling to form the words?

"Hey!" Carter shouted. They turned and saw him approaching with Margot and Grayson close behind. "What's going on?"

Sutter quickly dropped Fallon's hand and cleared his throat.

"I found something, and I need your help," he said smoothly. "But first . . . I need to tell you all I'm sorry for acting like a jerk this morning. I've been . . . stressed out, I guess. Not that it's an excuse, but we're so close to figuring this out . . . and I think I have the missing piece."

He held up a notebook for the group to see.

"A journal?" Margot asked.

Sutter nodded. "It was Lawson's. And it was in his old room. I got in thanks to a diversion by Grayson—he's the only reason I didn't get caught."

Fallon's stomach nearly bottomed out. She looked back and forth between Sutter and Grayson in disbelief, both because Sutter had gotten away with his scheme, but also because Grayson had been willing to help after what happened in the dining hall.

"Listen," Sutter said, "we don't have a lot of time. I want you guys to see everything Lawson wrote in here, but the most important thing"—he opened to a page in the middle—"is this."

Margot already had her phone out, shining its flashlight over the words written in Lawson's messy scrawl:

if you wish to see the crypt
find a 5, a 2, a 6
if the path is still not clear
a snake will surely lead you here

Sutter stared at the others, waiting.

Carter clicked his teeth. "You're gonna need to spell it out for us, buddy."

"This is how we open the vault," Sutter said. "The door in the Vipers' meeting place has a combination dial on it. This is Lawson telling us the numbers we need. If we can get in there . . ."

Despite every warning bell sounding in Fallon's head, there was a spark of excitement in her chest at the thought of getting into that vault, at seeing all the things Franklin Thatcher and the Vipers had stowed away over the years. All the secrets about the treasure that had fascinated her for so long.

She wanted in, and she wanted in badly.

"If you're willing," Sutter said, "we can go now, while it's dark. We might have to sneak into Shepherd after curfew, but . . . we're all here. And we're running out of time."

Margot sighed. "Screw it, I'm in. I'll think of an excuse for missing rehearsal."

Carter clapped Sutter and Grayson on the shoulders. "Good work, fellas. Let's get in that vault!"

Grayson looked over at Fallon, hesitant. Waiting for her to speak.

Sutter turned to her as well. "Fallon—"

"Let's go," she said, heading toward the rowboat. "No time to lose."

Sutter blinked in surprise but nodded. "All aboard."

The others climbed into the boat after Fallon. Sutter took the oars, handing one off to Carter, and moments later, they were gliding slowly down the river.

Carter started singing a song about rocking the boat as he rowed, to which Margot reacted with a surprising amount of anger, demanding he keep the boat as still as possible. Grayson laughed, and Fallon found herself smiling at the sound of his laughter. She focused on it for a moment, willing her heartbeat to slow down.

She couldn't believe any of what had just happened. She

couldn't believe they were entering the Vipers' vault, and she couldn't believe after two years of wondering, she finally knew how Sutter felt about her.

And even more, she couldn't believe how conflicted she felt about it.

"Hey," Grayson murmured after a moment, leaning slightly toward her. She caught the clean scent of his cologne, and her heart fluttered. "You all right?"

Fallon spread her lips into a smile. "Yeah, why?"

"You seem quiet," he said.

"I'm good," she told him. "Promise."

But her head continued swimming as they approached the tunnel entrance. Carter hopped out of the boat and Sutter followed to help him anchor it.

All conversation ended as they stepped back onto dry land. The group made their way quietly through the tunnel to the vault. It was much darker than it had been when the candles were lit during that first meeting. Sutter shone his phone light around until he found a matchbox and lit the candles, illuminating the musty underground room.

Fallon knelt before the combination dial on the vault door. It looked like if they dialed the right combination of numbers, it would unlock the larger wheel of spokes they would turn to open it. But when she inspected the numbers, her heartbeat faltered.

"This doesn't look right," she said.

"What do you mean?" Sutter asked.

"The numbers . . . there aren't any single digits." She read off the ones on the dial. "124, 490, 52, 315, 28 . . ."

"Isn't there one for 326?" Margot asked.

Fallon shook her head. Her hopes were dying quickly.

"Fuck," Grayson muttered.

“This can’t be it,” Sutter said. “Search the room, guys. Look for anything that might have the combination.”

“We should be careful, though, right?” Carter asked hesitantly. “If we mess this room up, won’t Quincy know and, like, bury us alive or something?”

“*Please* don’t put thoughts like that in my head,” Margot said.

Fallon was already searching the tables and the shelves, unsure of what she was looking for . . . until she noticed the spines of the leather-covered books. Each one had a volume number.

“The books,” Grayson said, noticing at the same moment she did. He reached for the one with a 2 on the spine and then the one with a 3. Fallon grabbed number 6 and started searching the pages.

“What did Lawson’s journal say again?” she asked.

Sutter read the poem again. *“If the path is still not clear, a snake will surely lead you here.”*

Grayson jabbed his finger at a page in volume three. “This is a zoology textbook. Surely there’s a snake in here somewhere.”

He flipped the pages quickly, and Fallon watched each one go by until—

“There.” An anatomical diagram of a snake. “Page 124.”

“That’s on the dial!” Margot cried.

Fallon was tearing through volume two, her stomach in knots—there weren’t any pictures or diagrams in it, just pages of text.

But then she saw a name—*Edgar Allan Poe.*

“It’s an anthology,” she mumbled to herself. She flipped back to the table of contents and searched for what she knew had to be in the book . . .

“‘The Cask of Amontillado.’” She remembered their English class unit on Poe, and if she wasn’t mistaken . . .

She found what she was looking for on page 315. *The foot crushes a serpent rampant whose fangs are imbedded in the heel.*

She called out the page number, and then Grayson opened volume six, a slightly smaller tome, only to draw a gasp from Fallon.

The Poetry of Jacob Meddlehart.

Fallon couldn't resist the temptation to take the book from Grayson's hands.

"I didn't know Meddlehart's poetry was published anywhere," Grayson said as she flipped the pages.

"I don't think it was," Fallon said. The book appeared to be bound by hand, the ink on its pages smudged in places. She turned the pages frantically, skimming each stanza to find what they needed. And finally . . . there it was.

This world is a curse.
They'll ruin everything of worth.
They'll let silver and gold
Be buried under brick and stone?
The place that belonged to Mother
Nature
Now belongs to her ruinous children,
No better than hissing vipers
Lurking in the lion's den.

"Page 28," Fallon called, though her eyes stayed on the poem. This one had angry undertones in each line. *Silver and gold, buried under brick and stone* . . . Was he talking about his fortune, the treasure? Whatever he meant, it confused Fallon.

A hollow *thunk* pulled her mind back to the present. Sutter pushed the spoked wheel to the left, and the door unlatched.

The vault was open.

TWENTY-NINE

Fallon

Sutter stepped into the vault first and Fallon followed him, sucking in a breath when she saw the inside.

It was a small room—almost like a large closet—and every inch of the walls was covered in maps and photos. Mounted shelves held dozens of file folders and dusty glass cases containing artifacts Fallon knew *must* have belonged to Franklin Thatcher, or maybe even Jacob Meddlehart. From the doorway, she spotted a tarnished compass, a knife with a carved bone handle, and there, all on its own at the far end of the space . . .

An ornate viper pin, pressed into a velvet pillow and protected by a case of thick glass.

Carter rushed to the case and peered down at the pin. "Damn, I kinda want one!"

"You'll get one if we make it past the last test," Grayson said.

While Fallon could hardly move, transfixed, Sutter dove right in. He took a file box from one shelf and set it on the table in the center of the room. Then he grabbed another, and another, placing each one on the table and scanning the labels.

"Everyone should take a box," Sutter said. "Let's search everything—take notes, pictures, whatever we can. We can share what we found later. Wait, I almost forgot. There's something else I need to show you guys."

Sutter reached into his jacket pocket and pulled out a thin object. He unfolded it carefully to reveal an old photograph of Fordyce House, creased in the middle. There was a person on either side of the crease—one was Jacob Meddlehart. And the other . . .

"Holy shit," Carter whispered. "It's that lady from the time capsule!"

Fallon was breathless. "Where did you get this?"

"I saw it in Meddlehart Manor this morning," Sutter said. He gave a sheepish shrug. "I may have swiped it from the photo wall."

Grayson stared at him, dumbfounded. "You stole a photo from a frame in Meddlehart Manor and didn't get caught?"

"More importantly," Margot asked, "what were you doing in Meddlehart Manor this morning?"

Sutter raised an eyebrow. "That's definitely not more important. The point is, this is a clue. We need to figure out who this woman is and what involvement she had with the school."

"If she worked here, her picture might be in a yearbook," Fallon pointed out.

Sutter's eyes were alight. "I'll search for yearbooks," he said. "The rest of you, pick a box."

Fallon held the volume of poetry close to her chest. "I think I should read more of Meddlehart's poems. Maybe one of the clues we've already found will line up with them."

Sutter nodded. "Smart thinking, Fallon."

"News clippings," Grayson said as he claimed a box.

"Letters," Margot said.

"Maps," Carter said.

Fallon started turning the pages of poetry more slowly and reading more carefully. She realized the title page was dated: *Jacob Meddlehart, 1949*. Hadn't Meddlehart died in 1950?

Fallon hadn't read enough poetry to know if Meddlehart's was any good, but at first glance, most of it didn't make much sense. She skimmed through a few poems that were clearly about his wife until she came across one that caught her eye:

My Amelia, where are you now?
You used to dance in the starlight
On the mountainside, our
mountainside.
My Amelia, where have you gone?
I tried, my dear, to forget your smile,
But you are who I see in the mirror,
Your sins a reflection of mine.
My Amelia, I wished not to replace
you—
You are twin flames lit from the
same match,
Lights I could not live without.
And though it is the greatest regret
of my life,
I could never find you now.

Fallon shuddered. This was written some twenty-five years after Amelia's death, and still her father grieved her, pondering her afterlife through poetry.

And who can blame him? she thought. *He lost his teenage daughter.* It didn't matter how many years ago Fallon had lost her parents—it wasn't any easier today than it was then.

But the last part of the poem . . . *I wished not to replace you . . . twin flames lit from the same match . . .*

"Did Meddlehart have any other children?" Fallon asked.

Everyone stopped to look at her.

"We would probably know if he did, right?" Carter asked.

"Not necessarily," Margot said with a shrug. "Maybe he had a secret family. Maybe he had an affair."

Grayson's eyes went wide. "Wasn't there a picture of a baby in the time capsule?"

Fallon's stomach dropped the way it would on a roller coaster. "The baby could have been Meddlehart's."

"But the baby's initials were TJH," Sutter said. "The baby's last name wasn't Meddlehart."

"If Meddlehart had a *secret* family, then those children would be *secret* Meddleharts with different last names," Margot said.

Sutter looked like his head was spinning. "We should keep looking," he said. "We don't have much time."

"Any luck on the yearbooks?" Margot asked him.

Sutter sighed heavily. "Haven't found any yet, but . . . these photographs." He pointed out a row of black-and-white images on the wall. "They're of past orders, aren't they?"

Fallon craned her neck to see. There were dozens of photos—students lined up in dark passageways, probably the same tunnel they were sitting in right now, their cold stares pointed at the camera.

"See anyone you recognize?" Carter asked.

Sutter didn't answer. He moved to the more recent photographs, skipping over many until he reached the newest one.

From where she stood, Fallon could see Lawson's face, so much like Sutter's, peering from the back row of Vipers in the photo.

Carter clapped a hand on Sutter's shoulder.

Fallon looked away, back to Grayson. She watched him for a moment, his square jaw taut in concentration as he studied one news clipping after another, sorting them into piles. His dark hair hung over his forehead and a few thick, soft locks curled at the base of his neck.

She startled when his eyes darted up to meet hers and his lips quirked.

"What?" he asked.

She cleared her throat. "Find anything interesting?"

He looked back at the clippings. "Most of these are about deaths and injuries of people hunting for the treasure on campus," he said. "And . . . a *lot* of them are students."

Carter turned to join the conversation, frowning. "How many?"

Grayson sighed and dropped another clipping onto the pile. "A lot more than I expected. Most of these are older, but— you'd think we'd have heard about these, right?"

Margot raised a brow. "If the Meddlehart and Thatcher families are anything like the people my parents hang out with . . . they probably cover their tracks. Student deaths would tarnish the school's reputation, even if they were treasure hunting accidents, and back then . . . I bet they bent over backward to keep things hush-hush."

"Hold on a second," Carter said, reaching for one of the clippings. "James Clarkson, 1982 . . ." He held it up to the wall of photographs, scanning until he found one. He studied the photo for a moment before placing his fingertip on it.

"There," he said. "The kid in this article was a Viper that year."

Grayson picked out another clipping and moved to the wall

of photos. He pointed to one. "Here's another. Kirk Melton, 1997."

The boys continued, sifting through the news stories about student treasure hunters who'd been hurt or killed while hunting for the fortune. *Marcus Whitney. Larry Burton. Jack Preston. Martin Simpson.* Each one had a place on the wall.

"These kids are all Vipers, aren't they?" Fallon asked, looking at the stack of clippings.

Carter and Grayson fell silent and stared at the clippings. A shiver ran down Fallon's spine.

Sutter's face had gone especially pale. He'd been quiet for too long as he moved from one group photo to the next.

"Sutter?" Fallon asked. "Is everything okay?"

He swallowed thickly. "There's a Heyward in almost every picture."

Carter's eyes went wide. "Are you serious?"

Sutter walked to one end of the wall and pointed to a picture of the first order. "Thomas Heyward," he said. He moved a few paces down to another photo and pointed. "Malcolm Heyward." He pointed to another, and another. "Albert, Dennis, Lois, Jonathan. All Heywards. And then this one here"—he pointed to a photo from the eighties—"Samuel Heyward. My dad."

"Holy shit," Grayson murmured.

"Do you know any of the others, Sutter?" Margot asked.

Sutter shrugged and stepped back from the wall. "I mean, yeah. Jonathan's my dad's cousin, I think. We don't know him well, but . . . I know who he is. And Dennis was my grandfather. We weren't close either." He swallowed. "I know these names, and I know my family's legacy at this school, but . . . I didn't know they were Vipers."

He looked defeated. "It's not a coincidence all of them were a part of this, right? Why didn't anyone tell me about it?"

The group fell silent. The hurt look on Sutter's face made Fallon's chest ache. She scanned the photos of each order, pausing when she noticed one of the older photos had a blemish.

"This person," she said, pointing. "Their face is scratched out."

Sutter peered over her shoulder, so close she could smell his cologne, and her heart rate rose slightly. "What the hell?"

She scanned the list of names beneath the photo. Sure enough, the corresponding name was also aggressively scratched out. The only legible letters were *Je* at the beginning of the first name.

"Why would anyone want to be removed from this picture?" Fallon asked.

"If they had a reason to hide that they were a member," Sutter murmured, but he didn't complete the thought. Fallon noticed he had refocused on the very first photo, in which Thomas Heyward started the tradition of his descendants joining the Order of the Vipers.

"Well," Margot said after a minute, changing the subject. "Now that I've read half the letters in this box, I can confirm Franklin Thatcher wanted to find this treasure really, *really* badly. And he was pissed at Meddlehart for hiding it."

"Are there any clues in them?" Sutter asked, shaking the hurt from his expression. "Anything helpful?"

Margot shrugged. "Not that I can tell, but . . ."

"Photos and notes," Sutter reminded them, pulling his phone out of his pocket and taking pictures of the photograph wall, before turning to the news clippings. Grayson and Carter did the same.

Margot started taking pictures on her phone as well, and Fallon skimmed the next poem:

I'll go where the butterflies drift out west,
From the rabbit's home to the broken peak
I'll move along from the old giant's rest,
And seek the place where the snowflakes sneak
I won't look high, but I'll get down low
Though it's dark and cold, I'll knock on the door,
For my heart is hidden there below
Where the past will lie forevermore

Fallon turned the page—it was the last poem in the book.

"Guys," she spoke up, "this poem seems important."

The others gathered around to read it, and Sutter's eyes grew wide.

"Those sound like clues," he murmured. "Don't they?"

"If only they made *sense*," Carter grumbled.

Fallon took a photo of the poem and shut the book. The moment she did, there was a sound from outside.

Footsteps.

The five of them froze. Sutter whirled one finger in the air, a signal to *move*, and they all crept quietly to the door.

Grayson slipped out first and began extinguishing the candles. Once the others were safely out of the vault, Sutter pulled the door shut and turned the wheel to lock it.

The footsteps grew closer, and a voice echoed down the tunnel. Fallon pressed her back against the wall farthest from the entrance, deep in the shadows. Her friends followed suit.

". . . and I did," the voice said. "I've done everything you asked."

Silence. Then the voice spoke again, and Fallon realized whoever it was must be talking on the phone. "Of course not, it's too risky. I'm at the Vipers' den. I thought *you'd* be here, too, like you promised. How am I supposed to keep this going if you stop showing up to our appointments?"

It clicked in Fallon's brain, why the voice sounded so familiar. She looked at Grayson and mouthed, *Alex?*

He nodded, eyes wide.

"I know it's not my business," Alex said. "Which is why I haven't pried, all right? But I don't think you realize all I've done for you. I've been careful, going out of my way for your ass, and I feel like not enough is in it for me—not when I could tell *everyone* what you're—"

He stopped. Fallon was practically holding her breath, waiting for Alex to walk in and realize he wasn't alone.

"Don't you *dare*," Alex growled. "Leave her out of this. She doesn't know a damn thing about it."

A pause. Then, "What do you want me to say? I don't think they know it's me. Hendricks is just a weirdo—that stunt he pulled probably meant nothing. He's just mad about his broken arm and he blames me for it."

Fallon's heart nearly stopped. She heard Margot's breath catch in her throat.

"I already told you, there's no shit in my dorm!" Alex cried. "I looked, and there's nothing there. You can trust me. Haven't I proved that? I don't know what else you want!"

Fallon felt Sutter tense up beside her. She reached down and grabbed his wrist, squeezing it tight.

"Look, I'll come meet you there if that's . . . I just don't get why . . . All right, *all right*. I'm on my way."

A beat of silence. Then, retreating footsteps that faded until the tunnel was quiet again. Fallon released Sutter's arm.

"Let's get the hell out of here," Sutter whispered.

The five of them crept as quietly as they could out of the tunnel to where the rowboat waited for them. Alex was long gone—whoever was supposed to meet him there hadn't shown and he must've gone to meet them elsewhere. One by one, they climbed into the boat. Fallon dared a look at Grayson. His face had gone completely pale.

Sutter and Carter rowed, and once the group was out of earshot Margot asked, "What on earth was that? Grayson, do you know?"

They all turned to Grayson, who shook his head. "I have no idea. I was the one who lured him out of his dorm so Sutter could do his search, but . . . all I did was trick him into thinking he was in trouble with Averell. Once he realized I was lying, he cursed me out and went back to Drexel."

"Who could he have been talking to?" Fallon asked. She realized she was trembling and hugged her arms around her middle, trying to find a sense of calm.

"Someone that knows something," Sutter said darkly. "Someone who knows Lawson left his journal in his room."

"The same person who's been leaving us poems?" Carter pointed out.

They all fell silent. Fallon suddenly felt nauseated.

"I don't like this, guys," Margot said. "What are we supposed to do now?"

"Confront Alex?" Grayson proposed. "Ask him what he was talking about?"

"And reveal not only were we eavesdropping but we also snuck into the Vipers' den and broke into the vault?" Margot asked.

Grayson winced. "Never mind. I'm tired of fighting his ass anyway."

"Actually," Carter spoke up, "I found something else. I was about to show you guys before we had to bail, but . . ." He stopped rowing, reached for his phone, and held it up.

A photo of a map.

"What is it?" Fallon asked, leaning forward to see.

"I think," Carter said, "it's a map of the tunnels Thatcher dug beneath the campus. And one of them leads straight to Meddlehart Manor."

THIRTY

Sutter

The tunnels. Sutter had studied the map every free moment he had from the time they left the vault to the following Sunday, when he found himself stuck in the last place he wanted to be: at a table with his parents.

If it weren't Parents Weekend, he'd probably have already found a way into the tunnel leading to Averell's house. He had a gut feeling—he was almost *positive*—the bricked-in wall they'd discovered in his office was actually a tunnel entrance.

But why had it been blocked off? Was it Averell's doing? A headmaster before him? Or someone else entirely? Did Averell even know it was there?

He couldn't imagine Averell *didn't* know about it, especially after their chat in his office. Sutter had stewed over it all week, wondering what Averell knew, why he'd chosen to say the things he had. It was fishy in a million different ways.

What are you hiding, Headmaster?

"Don't look so sullen, champ," Sutter's father said from across the table. "We traveled a long way to be here."

Sutter sighed. "Sorry." Parents Weekend wasn't an occasion he looked forward to anyway, and he expected this one to be particularly unpleasant, because he wasn't letting the day end without confronting his father about the Order of the Vipers. He could feel the weight of the photographs he'd collected in his pocket—the photos from the time capsule, the one from Meddlehart Manor, and the photos of past orders, proving the Heywards had all been involved with the Vipers.

He needed answers. And if Lawson was the one to hide these photos . . . since his father had been a Viper himself . . . maybe he knew something about all of it.

The weekend so far had been spent doing one cheesy activity after another. First up was painting birdhouses with Carter and his parents, which seemed pointless because Sutter's father hated birds and would never use the one they painted. Next was a tea party on the lawn; Sutter wished hot chocolate had been served, or even one of those caramel macchiato things.

They participated in the family relay race before lunch, only to be absolutely demolished by the Cashton sisters, who beat every other team by a mile. Fallon took the last leg of the race, and when they won, Margot and her sisters hoisted her up on their shoulders. They all toppled to the ground, laughing hysterically.

That moment was the closest Sutter got to smiling, but then his father made a comment about the race being rigged, which ruined it.

Now they'd finally made it to lunch, which consisted of barbecue by the lake. As Sutter glanced around at picnic tables full of smiling parents and students, his stomach soured. He felt like he was trapped in a bad commercial—the kind where unnaturally happy people spent quality time with their families and laughed about how wonderful their lives were.

When Sutter was a freshman, Parents Weekend was actually

fun. They did all the goofy activities as a family of four, and at the end of the day, they left campus to get ice cream in town. They all knew it was Lawson's last Parents Weekend—he would graduate that year and go off to college.

They didn't know he'd vanish before he could even cross the stage.

Sutter's head ached—he couldn't think about that anymore. He stared down at the bratwurst on his plate. He couldn't have mustered up an appetite if he tried.

"You okay, honey?" Mom asked. "You're awfully quiet today."

Sutter shrugged.

"Come on, champ," his dad said. "Answer your mother."

Sutter cleared his throat. "Yeah, I'm fine."

His father stared at him for a minute. Then he leaned forward.

"I'm not sure where the attitude came from, Sutter," he said, "but I'm not a fan of it."

"No attitude," Sutter said. "I'm fine."

"Well, when were you planning on telling us what happened to your face?" his father asked pointedly.

Sutter folded his arms over his chest. He'd wondered why they hadn't brought it up sooner. The bruises had faded, but not entirely.

"We got a call from Headmaster Averell," his mother said quietly. "Will you talk to us, honey? Tell us what happened."

"I fell," he muttered.

"Likely story," his father said bitterly. "You think we're stupid, kid?"

"Sam." His mother's voice was quiet, and his father continued like he hadn't heard her.

"Sutter," he said in a low voice, "your mother and I have

been through enough. We're tired of this bullshit from you. Frankly, it's the last thing we have time for right now."

"Sam," Mom hissed.

"Oh, nice," Sutter said to his dad. Heat rose in his cheeks. "Glad to know I'm nothing but a waste of time to my own parents."

"Sutter," his mother begged. "Please."

"That's not what I meant, and you know it," Dad snapped. "But with everything that happened with Lawson . . ." He trailed off. "What's that around your neck?"

Sutter froze. "What?"

"That chain around your neck," he said. "Under your shirt. Show it to me."

Sutter's gut instinct was to argue, but he realized this was his opportunity to pin his father down. Slowly, he reached for the chain and drew the viper pendant out, watching his father's expression carefully.

The recognition in his eyes was immediate.

"You know what this is, don't you?" Sutter asked.

"It was Lawson's," his father said evenly, but his cheeks flamed. "I specifically told you *not* to touch it."

"But do you know what it *is*?" Sutter pressed. There was a tremor of anger and hurt in his voice he couldn't hide, the same emotions that had swelled up when he realized his relatives were in those photos.

"Sam, what's going on?" Mom demanded.

"Nothing," his father muttered, and then he stood. "Sutter, a word."

He stood and followed his dad away from the picnic area. They walked to the courtyard, far away from the festivities, and Dad extended his hand to Sutter.

"Take it off and give it to me," Dad said in a dangerously low voice. *"Now."*

"Why?" Sutter spat. "It's just a necklace, right? What does it matter?"

"Because it's *not* just a necklace, and you know that," his father growled, and Sutter's blood ran cold.

"You were a Viper, too." Sutter whispered the accusation with venom in his voice.

"It doesn't matter what I was," Dad snapped. "What matters is that you stop whatever you're doing, however you may be involved with the order, and *wise up*. You have no business being part of that group!"

The words felt like a slap in the face to Sutter. "Of course I do," he shot back. "Every single Heyward who attended Meddlehart joined the Vipers. Did you really think you could hide that from me?"

Without allowing his father to reply, Sutter pulled the photographs from his pocket and fanned them out like a hand of cards. He saw the color leave his father's face.

"Where did you get those?" he asked.

"Does it matter?" Sutter pointed to the unnamed woman in the photos with Meddlehart, and the photo of the newborn baby. "Do you know who these people are?"

His father swallowed, hesitating. A long moment passed where he just looked at Sutter. Finally, he bowed his head, resigned. Carefully, he pointed to the woman.

"This is Trudy Heyward," he whispered. "Your great-great-grandmother."

Sutter's heart nearly stopped.

"And this," he said, taking the photo of the baby, "is her son . . . your great-grandfather, Thomas Jacob Heyward."

Thomas Heyward. Sutter remembered the name and face from the old photograph—he was one of the people in the first Order of the Vipers.

But then something else clicked in his brain. He looked again at the pictures of Trudy and Jacob Meddlehart—the way she smiled up at him, his hand on her shoulder.

Maybe he had a secret family.

"Thomas *Jacob*," Sutter whispered. "As in . . ."

"Jacob Meddlehart," Dad confirmed quietly. "He's my great-grandfather. Your great-great-grandfather."

Sutter's head spun, and he ran a hand through his hair. "H-how?"

Dad took a deep breath. "Trudy Heyward was one of the first teachers at the school. She and Jacob Meddlehart were drawn to each other, and they began having an affair while Amelia was still alive. After Amelia died, Florence found out Jacob was cheating, and she left him. That's part of the story you've been told . . . that she was distraught about losing her daughter and needed space from the school, so she went to live with her family. But that's not the whole truth.

"Meddlehart was guilt-ridden and tried to win Florence back. He loved Trudy, but he didn't want to end his marriage. But Florence couldn't stand to stay with him, so he kept seeing Trudy in secret after Florence left to live in the countryside with her family. Then Trudy got pregnant with Thomas."

Sutter's father sighed. "Even after Florence left, though, Meddlehart had an image to protect . . . a legacy. He was highly respected by people in West Fork, and he did everything he could to keep his divorce covered up. Many people thought he was still married to Florence. If he publicly married Trudy, he feared the consequences he might face for his actions. So rather than claim Thomas as his son . . . he secretly supported Trudy and Thomas from afar. He wasn't a present father—Thomas probably didn't even know who his father was until after Meddlehart died."

Sutter tried to process this information as quickly as he could. "And what about Trudy? She just agreed to keep quiet?"

Dad nodded. "She loved Jacob. She knew what might happen to them both if word got out. They kept their relationship a secret, and it's been a secret kept by the Heywards to this day."

Sutter shook his head. "But . . . why? Why keep a decades-old affair a secret?"

A certain smugness crossed his father's face. "You don't know, do you?"

Sutter's cheeks heated, and he stayed silent.

Dad grabbed Sutter's shoulder. "Do you know the meaning of our last name, champ?"

Sutter's mind raced, and he searched his memory for any hint, any clue. But he had nothing. He'd never thought about it, never bothered to ask.

Dad pulled his lips into a strange smile. "Originally, *Heyward* was a word for someone responsible for protecting a certain area from any threats—wild animals, criminals." He paused. "Often, that area was a forest."

The realization hit Sutter like a thousand bricks.

"Protector of the wood," he murmured.

His father's grin turned greedy. "Meddlehart's fortune belongs to the Heywards," he whispered. "It was left for us, and us alone."

Sutter felt dizzy. He reached for his chest, as if that might stop the frantic beating of his heart.

Slowly, his father's grin turned into a sneer. "And your

brother took off with it," he spat. "Which is why you need to drop this . . . this *obsession* with Lawson and move *on*, Sutter!"

Sutter recoiled, struggling to understand what his father was saying. "You know where Lawson is?"

Dad rolled his eyes. "Damn it, Sutter—no, I don't fucking know where he is!" He pressed a hand to his forehead and released a long breath. "I did for Lawson what every father in our ancestry did for their children. Before he started school at Meddlehart, I told him the story I just told you. I explained his responsibility as a Heyward to search for the fortune and prevent anyone else from finding it. And because the Order of the Vipers exists . . . our responsibility has always been to join them. To infiltrate their operations and defend what's rightfully ours." Dad shook his head. "That's exactly what Lawson did. And I think he found the fortune, and he took off with it."

"What?" Sutter's eyes went wide. Was his father admitting he *did* think Lawson was alive after all?

But no—that wasn't how Sutter wanted it to happen. He couldn't bear the thought of his father believing Lawson was out there and choosing not to search for him.

"Are you out of your mind?" Sutter had to whisper the words for fear his voice would break.

His father glared at him. "You didn't know Lawson like I did, Sutter. He hated me deeply. And I think finding that fortune and running away, keeping it for himself . . . it was his final act of betrayal. It was his way of having the last word."

And suddenly, with those words, a theory formed in Sutter's mind. At the end of the day, Sutter knew his dad was a man who refused to own up to his mistakes, no matter what. He was selfish at his core. He had made the decision to rope Lawson into their family's history, into this insane mission to find

Meddlehart's treasure—their lost inheritance—and hide their plans from the rest of the world.

And if the order, the treasure, *any* of it had something to do with Lawson's disappearance, their father wouldn't accept that reality. He couldn't bear that responsibility. That *guilt*.

That's why he had never told Sutter about it. To protect himself.

"Your brother made mistakes," Dad said, "and those mistakes put us in the mess we're in now. You can't chase after him like you used to, Sutter—*not anymore*."

He was asking Sutter to drop it—to leave the Vipers and end his search. And Sutter knew, one way or another, he had to get his dad off his back.

So he swallowed his anger, reached for the chain, and tore it from his neck. He threw it on the ground and walked away.

"You're making the right choice, champ," his father called after him.

Sutter had to fight the urge to laugh. "I know, Dad."

He didn't need Lawson's pendant anymore. He could earn his own.

THIRTY-ONE

Grayson

Grayson couldn't stop himself from texting his dad before Parents Weekend. He knew he wouldn't come, and he wasn't sure he wanted him to in the first place. His dad's text the Friday before—*Busy filming in LA, but I'll be there next year*—was no shock to him.

Grayson tried not to let it hurt. He didn't need his dad here. He never had.

He avoided the Parents Weekend festivities for as long as possible. He went to the Ace and did as many exercises as he could without using his injured arm. But on his way back to Shepherd, he couldn't help stopping to watch the relay race. He saw Fallon cross the finish line, and when the Cashton sisters lifted her into the air in triumph, she spotted him. She waved, laughing.

He waved back, smiling. Fallon had gone through so many terrible Parents Weekends—she deserved to have a good one.

He continued toward Shepherd, but he hadn't made it far when he heard her voice.

"Gray, wait up!"

He slowed as Fallon approached, slightly breathless, eyes shining with the force of her smile.

He grinned and gave a little bow. "I didn't know I'd be in the presence of a champion today."

Grayson could've sworn her cheeks turned pink. "Where are you going?"

He hesitated. "Anywhere. Nowhere. You tell me, Fallon Winthrop."

The smile she leveled at him could've knocked him over. This girl had no idea how beautiful she was.

"There's a place I want to show you." She held her hand out to him, and nothing in the world had ever felt more right.

The hike to the footbridge was longer than Grayson had imagined it when his friends told him what he missed during the first test. He wasn't sure how they had managed it in the dark, with no sense of where they were going.

But Fallon climbed the trail with confidence today. The sun was out, and she knew where to lead him.

She showed him the names carved in the wood post, showed him where they found Alex. And then they sat side by side on the bridge, legs dangling over the edge, specks of water from the rushing river below landing on their feet.

"Are you okay?" she asked him quietly.

A part of him ached, deep and hollow. A part of him leaned toward her words extended like a lifeline, urging him to tell her the truth.

But he wouldn't open that door, wouldn't bring her down with his baggage today.

"I'm fine," he promised, looking around. "I wonder why we didn't know about this place before."

"Probably because it's dangerous," Fallon suggested. "The current, the old bridge . . . it felt dangerous that night, when we were looking for you."

Grayson looked at her. She was close to him, so close he could count each freckle on her nose. He could feel her warmth fending off the cool autumn air.

"I'm sorry it scared you so much," he murmured, so quietly he wondered if she was able to hear him. "That night."

She looked at him. "It wasn't your fault."

Grayson didn't answer. He couldn't quite find the words, because it felt like it *was* his fault, somehow.

Fallon must have seen it in his expression, because she turned toward him, drawing his attention solely to her. "That night . . . it reminded me of when I lost my parents. One minute they texted to tell me they were on their way home, and I knew they were fine. And the next . . . I called and called, but they didn't answer. They never answered." She closed her eyes. "I looked for you, I called for you, and you weren't there. You weren't *anywhere*. The feeling was the same, because . . . it would be so easy to lose you. And I *can't* lose you, Gray. Not you."

Grayson's heart could have stopped beating, for what the words did to him.

Fallon was gripping the edge of the bridge, her knuckles white. Gently, he rested his hand on hers. She turned her hand palm up and locked her fingers with his.

"I'm not going anywhere," he told her.

She smiled again, and Grayson decided he'd do anything to keep that smile on her face. He'd protect it with everything he had.

Just then, her gaze fixed on a spot over his shoulder. "Hang on—is that a blackberry bush?" Somehow, her smile got even wider. "I used to go berry picking with my parents every year and . . . hang on, I'm going to see."

Fallon stood and crossed the bridge, and Grayson took the moment alone to check his messages. He pulled his phone out of his pocket, but there weren't any new texts.

Instead, there was a news alert on his home screen that started with his father's name.

Grayson acted as if on autopilot. He ignored the voice in his head that warned him not to look. He opened the alert, and his heart dropped.

There were paparazzi photos. His father wasn't filming in Los Angeles.

He was on a beach in the Bahamas with Hannah Grace James.

Something withered in Grayson's heart. He could think of dozens of times when his father bailed on him, but this might have been the first time Grayson caught him in a lie about who he was *actually* spending time with instead of his son.

He knew it shouldn't hurt him anymore, but it did. It hurt like hell, because nothing would change the fact that Grayson's dad was the only family he had. Or that he would never have a dad who chose *him* instead of choosing himself.

The ache spread from Grayson's chest to his limbs and then to his head. His hands trembled. For a moment, he forgot where he was, until Fallon's voice jarred him back to reality.

"Hey," she said. He looked up, saw her expression stitched with concern, her hands full of fresh blackberries. "What's wrong?"

Grayson opened his mouth to lie, but the look on her face

stopped him cold. The photos were still on his screen, and she was looking right at them.

Slowly, she set the berries on the bridge and focused her gaze on him. He knew she was reading the pain all over his face. She was the only person who could do that with him, and he . . .

He couldn't do this to her today. His vision was already blurring, his chest tightening. He could feel the spiral of anger and loneliness and self-loathing rising to swallow him whole, and he could not—*would not*—take her down with him.

"I don't feel well. I need to head back." The excuse was stiff on his lips. He forced himself to his feet and started walking. Even without the sound of her footsteps behind him, he would have known she was following him. He could feel her the same way he could feel sunlight and wind and rain on his skin.

"Grayson." She grabbed his arm, pulling him around to face her. "*Please* don't push me away. Not right now."

"Why not?" He meant it as a challenge, but his voice broke over the words.

She stammered for a moment. "B-because you're hurting. I don't want you to be alone in it."

But that's what she didn't understand. He'd *always* been alone in this, and that was for a reason.

He clenched his fists, desperate to hide the way he was shaking. "I don't . . . I don't want you to look at me the way you're looking at me right now."

Her brow furrowed, but she didn't let go of his arm. "Like how?"

He ground his teeth. "Like I'm *broken*." He pulled his arm away from her—he couldn't handle her touching him, not when there was an earthquake happening in his heart. Not when the patched-together pieces of his life could fall apart at any second.

"I'm *not*," Fallon said, a new strength in her voice. "I could never look at you that way. But you deserve so much better than this."

"I don't think I do," Grayson murmured. Everything he touched turned to stone. Everyone he loved came to know the truth—he was a burden, and he always had been.

He turned to walk away again.

And again, she followed. She spoke as if she were reading his mind.

"Grayson, remember what you just said? *I'm not going anywhere.* Don't you see that I'm not, either? I'm *here*. I'm *with you*."

"Fallon," he gritted out. There was a roaring in his ears—he was barely hanging on—

"You're *always* there for me when I need you," she pressed. "Why can't I do the same for you? Why won't you let me in when—"

"Because I'm in *love* with you!"

There it was.

She stopped cold. Her hand fell from his arm. "What?"

Grayson's vision clouded. Fallon was the only person in the world who made him feel truly, wholly loved. She was the only person he trusted with the worst parts of his life—the worst parts of *himself*. Everything in him yearned to be with her, and in that moment, with the whole world falling apart around him, he didn't think. He just told her the truth he couldn't keep to himself any longer.

"I'm in love with you," he said, and though the fear he felt was dizzying, he forced himself to meet her eyes. "I've *been* in love with you. Ever since I met you, Fallon . . . it's never been any other way. Not for me. It's always been you."

He swallowed thickly, ignoring the way her face had paled, and went on. "I know we're friends, and it's the best thing about my life. I don't want anything to ruin that, because you mean the world to me."

You mean the world to me. That was the answer to all her questions—why he couldn't let her help carry his burdens. Why he couldn't let her see him for who he was.

He was floundering. His eyes welled, and he hated himself for choosing *this* moment, of all moments, to say the thing he'd been wanting to say for so long. It poured out of him like a rush of water bursting through a dam, so easy and so painful all at once.

"I'm not good with words, Fallon, you know that," he murmured. "But I wanted . . . I needed you to know. I can't go on without you knowing."

He closed his eyes. Any second now, she'd respond. *Any second now.*

But when he opened his eyes, she was staring at him like a deer caught in headlights. His heart sank in a whirlpool straight to his gut.

This was a mistake, his brain screamed at him. *You just made such a huge mistake. You just ruined everything.*

Grayson knew in his bones—that was all he'd ever done, all he'd ever do.

She'd been wordless for too long, and it was all the answer he needed. He started in the opposite direction of the bridge. He'd cut through the woods back to Shepherd—he didn't want to be seen.

"Grayson, no!" Fallon called after him. Her voice was strained. "Wait!"

"It's okay," he said, but he didn't turn around. He couldn't let her see his face.

"Grayson, please!"

He kept walking until it was just him and the trees.

It was dark when Grayson finally returned to the student houses. He avoided going back to Shepherd for as long as he could, until he knew the common room would be empty. He wanted to avoid running into anyone—anyone at all.

But as he passed Drexel House, he realized his timing couldn't have been worse. Alex Harker was sitting on the front steps.

Just put your head down and keep walking, he told himself. But Alex didn't look like his usual cocksure self—he seemed jittery, unsettled. There were dark circles under his eyes. A lock of his strawberry-blond hair was out of place and hanging in his eyes.

Grayson thought back to the things they'd overheard him say in the Vipers' den. *I don't think they know it's me.*

Ignoring the warning bells sounding in his head, Grayson stopped in front of Alex.

Alex looked up. Before he could mask it, Grayson saw a flash of fear in his eyes.

"Rough Parents Weekend?" he asked.

Alex shrugged. "Parents Weekend isn't a thing for me, Hendricks. Dad's dead and Mom . . ." He hesitated. "Doesn't travel."

Grayson was a little startled by that information—he hadn't known. "Sorry."

Alex spat on the ground. "Keep walking, Hendricks."

"You seem a little off," Grayson said evenly. "The Vipers getting to you, too?"

Alex scoffed. "You don't know the half of it."

"What do you mean?"

Alex wouldn't meet his eyes now. "Forget I said anything. Seriously, Hendricks, leave me the hell alone."

Grayson felt like he'd come to a crossroads of sorts. In that moment, something told him he needed to take a risk. He needed to push, just a little further.

He'd kept the poem from his locker folded and wedged in his phone case ever since they revealed the invisible message. He felt that was the safest place to put it. Without giving himself a moment to change his mind, he took out his phone, pulled the paper carefully out of the case, and unfolded it.

Alex was watching him closely now. "I said *go*, Grayson."

Grayson held the paper in front of Alex. "Look familiar to you?"

Alex blanched. Shakily, he stood. "Fuck *off*."

Grayson stepped toward him—he *knew* Alex was lying now. "Why'd you leave this for me and my friends? Are you trying to scare us out of joining the Vipers? You want the treasure all to yourself? Or do you know what happened to Lawson Heyward?"

"Listen to me," Alex said, holding his hands up in a show of innocence. "I swear to God I didn't write that. I didn't write any of them."

"Just tell the *truth*, Alex!" Grayson pressed.

"All right, all right—I will!" Alex cried. His voice had grown louder, higher than Grayson had ever heard it. "But not here, man. Not now. You gotta give me time."

Grayson shook his head. "I don't have time. The next test is coming up, and—"

"Shit," Alex said, shaking his head. "I gotta go. I'm late."

Grayson watched him jog down the path before he could ask what he was late for. But maybe it didn't matter—Grayson had got what he wanted.

He knew Alex was the one leaving them poems.

THIRTY-TWO
Fallon

Fallon hardly recognized her life anymore.

By the time the Parents Weekend festivities were over, she was emotionally drained. The week had been a roller coaster, and retreating to her dorm with Margot was the only thing she wanted to do.

She felt hesitant to tell her best friend what had occurred with Sutter and Grayson. She didn't want to create more awkwardness or share things they would have preferred to stay between them.

But she was in shock. She needed advice, and she needed it desperately.

When she told Margot what happened with Sutter, her roommate was ecstatic.

"Fallon!" she practically screamed. "Do you know what this means?"

"Margot," she said, holding her hands out. "I'm not even close to being done with this story."

Then she told her what happened with Grayson.

"He told you he's in *love* with you?" Margot cried, chucking one of her fuzzy throw pillows across the room. It struck a lamp, and Fallon caught it before it plummeted to the floor. "Whoops."

Fallon righted the lamp and sighed. "*Yes*, he said he's in love with me."

"And you didn't reciprocate?" Margot pressed. "To *either one of them*?"

"I—I was in shock!" Fallon groaned. "I had no idea what to say." She paused. "To either of them."

Margot's smile could have lit up the entire campus. "Fallon . . . you are in the center of a *love triangle*!"

Fallon groaned. "*No.* I hate love triangles!"

Margot laughed. "No one hates love triangles, and if they say they do, they're lying to themselves. They're too much fun."

"Not when you're trapped in one yourself!" Fallon cried. "You aren't allowed to enjoy this, Margot!"

"But it's exciting!" Margot squealed. "Okay, so who do we start with? I say Grayson. He's the wild card here." She adjusted her pillows and leaned forward, eager. "So you weren't expecting this from him at all?"

"I mean . . . *no*," Fallon said, throwing her hands up in frustration. "I don't think so?"

"Why did that sound like a question?" Margot asked.

"Because it kind of *was* a question?" Fallon dropped her head into her hands. Everything in her life was suddenly punctuated by dozens of question marks. "He . . . did kind of say something at football practice once . . ."

She told Margot about the first incident with Alex, what Grayson said in response. *So what if I am?*

Margot was quite literally on the floor now. "Oh. My. *God*."

Fallon covered her face with her hands. "I'm simply going to pass away."

"No, you're not. You're going to find *love*!" Margot sat up. "You and Grayson are close, though. He didn't address it with you afterward?" She asked another question, softer this time. "Do you have feelings for him, too?"

"I . . ." Fallon's cheeks were flaming red. She pressed her cool hands to them, trying to calm the heat, but to no avail. After a long pause, she stood and began to pace.

"All right, Margot, here's the thing," she said. "It's no secret our friends are very attractive young men."

"Absolutely," Margot agreed.

"Not to mention they're *wonderful* people. I'm not unaware of their charms," Fallon went on. "But I have chosen to ignore it, *mostly*, for the sake of our friendships!"

"*Mostly*, meaning Sutter?" Margot asked pointedly.

Fallon slumped into Margot's fluffy beanbag chair. "Yeah. Sutter."

"How do you feel about him?" Margot asked.

Fallon sighed. She was quiet for a long time before she answered.

"You know how I feel," she said. "How I've always felt. I adore him . . . I've always wanted this. But . . ."

If Fallon was honest with herself, Sutter had been . . . different lately. He was angrier, laser-focused on finding Lawson and the treasure and caring about little else. That ferocity and determination she loved about him was consuming him, and it worried her.

And though Fallon cared about Sutter just as much now as she had when they were freshmen—he was her friend, and nothing would change that—was he right for her, in a romantic way?

Fallon wasn't sure. She wasn't sure about anything now.

"This is so confusing," she murmured.

Margot reached out and squeezed Fallon's hand.

"It will work out, won't it?" Fallon asked her.

"Of course it will. And . . ." Margot trailed off, and she pressed her lips together.

Fallon widened her eyes. "And . . . what?"

Margot bit down on her lower lip. "Well."

"Well . . . *what*?"

"I was just going to say . . . maybe *you* haven't noticed anything between you and Grayson," she said slowly, "but that doesn't mean *I* haven't."

Fallon's jaw dropped. "You thought Grayson had feelings for me, and you didn't *say* anything?"

Margot shook her head. "Not just him, Fallon. I've seen the way you look at him."

Fallon shook her head. "No, no, no, no, no."

"I know you've always loved Sutter," Margot said. "But you know what I always say—"

Fallon was already onto her. "We don't get to choose our feelings," she grumbled. "But—"

"Sometimes, feelings *change*," Margot interrupted. "And sometimes . . . change is good."

Change. A wave of revulsion rolled over Fallon at the mention of it. If there was one thing she didn't want, it was change. She *knew* that—it had been established in her heart for years now, how badly she wanted things to stay the same, to stay the way they were now.

She couldn't handle any more change.

"I need to talk to them again," she decided. "Both of them. Talking this through will help me figure everything out."

"Okay," Margot said, though she sounded uncertain. "Fallon, just . . . be kind to yourself, okay? You don't owe anyone anything. This situation is weird, but . . . you've got to do what's right for you."

And in her mind, Fallon knew what that was. To preserve her friendships—to prevent anything from changing—was the right thing for her.

Her heart may not have agreed, but as she had a dozen times, Fallon shoved her heart aside.

"What if he doesn't show?" Fallon asked, hands fidgeting in the pocket of her sweatshirt. It was bitterly cold that Monday morning, the wind snapping around her and Margot like the jaws of an angry animal.

Margot bundled her thick, furry coat around her and sighed. "He will, Fallon. It'll be fine."

They'd agreed to meet the boys outside Shepherd before class so they could follow the map of the tunnel systems to whatever hid behind that wall in Meddlehart Manor. Hopefully.

Fallon's heart wasn't in it, though—she was more concerned about Grayson. She hadn't seen him since their conversation on the footbridge. He didn't even show up for dinner.

As for Sutter, she hadn't had a chance to talk to him about their feelings for each other. Sunday night at dinner, he dropped the bomb that he was a descendant of Jacob Meddlehart and it threw the others for a loop.

"So if we do find the treasure," Margot had said, "you have every right to it. It belongs to you!"

"Hell, maybe you could even say you own this *school*," Carter pointed out. "You're the damn heir to this place. Teachers can't tell you what to do anymore!"

"I doubt I'd be able to get away with that, especially considering I'm supposed to keep this a secret," Sutter said. He rubbed his forehead like he had a headache. "I don't even care about the treasure. I just want to find Lawson and prove our dad wrong."

Fallon could see the stress he was under, the toll the fallout with his dad had taken on him. She knew it wasn't the time to confront him with romantic woes.

Now, standing in front of Shepherd House in the biting cold, she waited and hoped Grayson would show. When Sutter and Carter arrived, each holding snacks wrapped in wax paper, she craned her neck to see if Grayson was behind them.

He wasn't.

"Is Grayson not with you two?" Margot asked the boys.

Carter shook his head. "Nope."

Sutter held up the food in his hand. "The snack bar has churros today."

Margot sighed. "Is Grayson coming or not, guys?"

"He said he'd be here," Sutter said, frowning at them. He glanced at Fallon. "What's going on?"

"Nothing," she and Margot said in unison. Sutter narrowed his eyes but didn't say another word.

With every passing minute, Fallon's chest grew tighter. This was exactly why she'd avoided acknowledging any of her romantic feelings for so long. Was her friendship with Grayson already damaged beyond repair? Her eyes had just started to prickle with tears when Grayson came walking down the pathway. His injured arm was still in a cast, but he'd ditched the sling. He waved at them, giving a tight-lipped smile.

"Hey, man," Carter said. "What took you so long?"

"I was looking for someone," he said, bumping fists with the boys. "Alex Harker."

Fallon couldn't help but raise her eyebrows.

"Uh. I believe I speak for the entire group when I ask *why?*" Carter pressed.

Grayson hesitated. "I confronted him last night when I got back to Shepherd." He quickly recounted their conversation, leaving them all slack-jawed.

"So *he's* responsible for the poems?" Carter asked.

"But . . . why?" Fallon asked.

Grayson's eyes briefly found Fallon's, then he looked down at his shoes. "That's why I went looking for him. He said he'd tell me the truth later, so I knocked at his dorm. No answer."

Sutter shook his head. "I bet he's avoiding you. We've gotta find him."

"Right now we should focus on the task at hand," Margot pointed out. "Before class starts."

"Agreed," Sutter said. "I studied the map, and there are three tunnel systems the order knows about—the one where they have their meetings, an unfinished tunnel near the dining hall, and one leading to Averell's house." He held up a copy of the map and pointed out the tunnel leading to Meddlehart Manor. "It's the longest one by far—the only other entrance is marked near the courtyard."

Carter let out a low whistle. "Long walk."

"Maybe not, though," Margot said. "The tunnel probably goes straight across campus. That means there aren't any turns to make—it's a straight shot."

"Only one way to find out," Sutter said. With that, he started walking south, toward the courtyard, and the others fell into step behind him. As the others moved ahead, Fallon walked beside Grayson.

"Hey, Gray," she said. "I wanted to talk to you so we could—"

"Fallon, it's okay," he said. He smiled down at her, though his face was too tight for the smile to be genuine. "I put you on the spot. I should've thought it through a little more, so . . . I'm sorry. We don't need to talk about it. Might be better to just"—he shrugged slightly—"move on, right?"

Fallon was surprised at how the words stung. "Oh, um . . . yeah. I just didn't want you to think—"

"I don't," he said, though she hadn't even finished her sentence. His gaze was as hollow as his words. "It was a mistake. I don't want to make things weird between us."

"Me either," Fallon agreed, but her throat was thick, and the words felt funny as they left her mouth.

"Cool," he said, nodding. "Let's just forget it ever happened."

With that, he forged ahead, leaving Fallon at the rear. Margot fell into step beside her.

"So?" she asked.

Fallon wasn't sure what to say. "We're okay."

Margot offered a smile. "That's good, right?"

Fallon nodded. It was what she wanted, wasn't it? To save their friendship, to keep things the same. But she couldn't shake one thought as they approached the courtyard.

Maybe okay wasn't good enough.

THIRTY-THREE

Sutter

Sutter hadn't expected to spend his morning crawling on his hands and knees through the courtyard, but there he was. The five of them split up so they wouldn't miss anything, but Sutter's hope waned with every second he continued searching the shrubbery.

He didn't know what the tunnel entrance looked like. The tunnel leading to the Vipers' den drove right out of the mountainside, like the perfectly round mouth of a cave. That couldn't be the case with a tunnel entrance located in the courtyard—there's no way it could be missed. No, this one had to be hidden, identifiable only if you were looking for it.

"Nothing over here, Sutter," Margot called from the opposite end of the courtyard.

"Keep looking," Sutter said as he pulled apart the leaves of a particularly prickly bush. "Think outside the box."

Carter sighed, rubbing his hands together. "This wind is ridiculous."

Fallon came to stand beside him, nodding. Her cheeks were rosy where the wind had whipped against her face. "No kidding."

Sutter stood, attempted to brush the soil off his jeans, and joined them. His eyes met Fallon's, and he offered a smile she didn't return.

"You okay?" he asked.

She nodded, but her expression left him unconvinced. "Just tired." Her eyes cut briefly to Grayson and then she looked down, kicking at a pebble.

Sutter felt a twinge in his chest. He glanced at Grayson, whose back was to them as he checked the stone memorials throughout the courtyard. *Was something going on between them?*

Carter walked away to make another lap around the perimeter of the courtyard, and Sutter cleared his throat. "Fallon . . . I know things have been crazy, and we haven't had much time to talk about . . ."

She smiled flatly. "I know. I've been meaning to bring it up to you."

His heart rate ticked up at the low inflection in her voice. He wished he didn't care, but he did, more than he ever thought he would. Sutter's feelings for Fallon had stirred into something complicated and unexpected. His heart was a tangled web he couldn't sort out. He crossed his arms over his chest, like maybe that would squash the feelings welling there.

"We don't have to decide anything now," he promised her. "I know there's a lot going on."

She nodded. "That's what I was thinking, too." She paused for a moment. "Our friendship is really important to me, Sutter. I just don't want anything to put it in jeopardy."

He nodded quickly. "Yeah . . . yeah, totally. I feel the same way."

And that was true. Sutter didn't want to risk losing Fallon—the thought scared him. But looking at her now—nose pink from the cold, stray locks of hair blown across her face—he had just one thought: *If only.*

"I'm not sure where else we can look, man," Carter told Sutter as he strolled over to one of the courtyard's benches. "What if the map isn't accurate?"

It was when Carter plunked down on the bench that Sutter saw it. The bench, anchored to the concrete pathway, lifted slightly with Carter's weight.

Sutter rushed toward Carter. "Stand up."

"What?"

Sutter shoved Carter off and he jumped up, eyes wide.

"Sutter, I *swear*—"

He ignored Carter, grabbed the right side of the bench, and lifted. The slab of concrete holding it to the ground gave a little. That's when he noticed the thick, rusted hinges attached to the concrete slab.

Realization dawned on Carter's face, and he moved to the other side of the bench to help lift. They hoisted the bench and leaned it on the hinges, tilting it until it was on its back.

There, a few feet deep in the ground where the bench had stood, was a set of square metal doors, like those of a storm shelter.

Margot jogged over, followed by Grayson.

"This is it," she breathed. "It has to be, right?"

"We've gotta open it," Sutter said. Before anyone could protest, he jumped into the shallow hole, his feet banging against the metal doors when he landed.

"Be careful!" Fallon cried, and Sutter couldn't help but grin.

"Always," he called back. With that, he gripped the door handles and pulled.

They clanged in protest, not budging. *Locked.*

"How the hell do we get in?" he grumbled, looking up at his friends.

"Didn't Quincy say Lawson had all the keys?" Fallon said. "They haven't been able to get into the tunnels since he went missing."

Sutter pressed a hand to his forehead, trying to tamp down his frustration. "We need to find another way," he said quietly.

Just then, a familiar voice called out, "Hello there!"

"*Shit*," Sutter hissed. *Whittaker.* "Help me up!"

Margot and Fallon reached down and hauled Sutter out as fast as they could. Carter and Grayson, with his good arm, pulled the bench back in place just as Whittaker rounded the corner into the courtyard.

"Look at you early birds," he said, his cane tapping along the paved pathway. "What might you five be doing out here?"

"Uh," Sutter said, thinking quickly. He gestured to Lawson's wreath. "Just paying a visit to my brother. And my friends are, um . . ."

"Moral support," Carter said matter-of-factly.

Whittaker smiled. "Just make sure you get the mulch off your pants before you come to history class."

Sutter looked down, barely holding back a curse as he dusted off the dirt he'd missed. Whittaker chuckled.

"Hey, Mr. Whittaker?" Grayson called.

Their teacher nodded, waiting.

"Have you seen Alex Harker today?"

A glint of surprise shone in Whittaker's eye. "Why, didn't you hear? Mr. Harker has withdrawn from school."

THIRTY-FOUR
Grayson

Grayson's nightmares were getting worse.

The occasional nightmare Grayson had grown to expect turned into nightly ones that rattled him to his core. Some were made-up scenarios; other times, he was reliving his worst memories, ones that had haunted him for years before he finally learned to lock them away in the deepest part of his heart.

This had happened a few times before—when he was stressed about school, when things were bad with his dad, on the anniversary of his mother's death.

He knew what caused them. He could still hear his therapist telling him his anxiety was manifesting itself through these bad dreams. He just had no idea how to get them to stop, not when there was so much going wrong in his life.

Every night he woke in a cold sweat and nauseated, his throat raw from screaming. Carter and Sutter had to shake him awake, and every time, their brows were furrowed with concern.

"I thought you were dying," Carter mumbled gruffly one night as he clambered back into bed.

"I'm fine," Grayson muttered, like he did every time. *I'm fine, I'm fine, I'm fine.*

But after a week of losing sleep, he was starting to wonder if there was any truth to that. His grades were slipping. He took a test in history class—the class he shared with Fallon and Quincy—after another sleepless night and failed miserably. When Whittaker passed the tests back, there was a note at the top of Grayson's: *Let's meet and discuss.*

Grayson didn't want to discuss anything, though. He dropped the test on his desk at the dorm and left it there with no intention of looking at it again.

"What's bothering you?" Sutter asked one day at lunch as he flipped through Lawson's notebook. He'd scoured the pages every single day since finding it, but he hadn't come up with anything else helpful yet.

"Nothing," Grayson said, but that was a lie. He'd hardly spoken to Fallon in days. None of them had found answers about why Alex left school, or how he was involved in all of this.

There were a thousand different emotions and fears crowding his mind, and he wasn't sure if it would ever stop.

At the end of the week, when the sound of his phone buzzing relentlessly on his nightstand dragged him from another nightmare, he was thankful for the interruption.

Carter's and Sutter's phones blared, too, and as Grayson blinked the sleep from his eyes, he saw them sitting up slowly, confused.

Grayson's hair was stuck to his forehead, drenched in cold sweat. He scrubbed a hand over his face before he reached for his phone and squinted against the brightness of the screen.

It was three in the morning, on the dot. There were several missed calls from an unknown number, in addition to one text:

Greenhouse in five minutes. By the fangs of greed.

"Oh, shit," Carter murmured, staring at his own phone.

Grayson's heart plummeted. It was time for the second test.

The boys barely had time to pull on sweatpants and jackets before they hustled down the Shepherd House fire escape. Fallon and Margot came out the window behind them, eyes swollen with sleep.

"Fancy seeing you ladies here," Carter said when they reached the bottom.

"I feel dead inside," Margot replied. "Does every Viper initiation have to happen in the freaking middle of the *night*?"

"The teachers would probably be onto us otherwise," Sutter replied.

Grayson's eyes met Fallon's, and for a moment, he wanted to hold her gaze. He wanted to hold *her*, more than anything in the world.

But then she looked away without a word, and he tried to ignore the bone-deep ache that rocked through him. He wondered if he'd ever get used to the wall of silence that now stood between them.

The five of them raced to the greenhouse and arrived out of breath but in the nick of time. Grayson looked around for the other initiates, but they were the only ones.

Quincy smiled. "Welcome, remaining initiates. You survived Vipers and Mice. Tonight, the stakes are higher. We aren't playing games anymore. The challenge will be dangerous, and the consequences are very, very real."

Grayson had grown to despise Quincy, with his low drawl and his cocky smirk. But the words still sent a chill down his spine. What the hell were they going to be asked to do?

"Sometimes," Quincy said, "treasure isn't simply up for grabs. Sometimes it's not a finders keepers situation, and in those cases, the only solution . . . is to steal."

Grayson closed his eyes. *Oh, no.*

Jeffrey stepped forward and handed Sutter an envelope.

"This is your assignment," Quincy said. "Retrieve what we asked for and return it to us in the courtyard by sunrise. If you can't, you've lost your chance."

Grayson felt his blood run cold as the words from the poem echoed in his mind. *Your end draws near, and chances slowly disappear.*

Alex had insisted he didn't write the poems. What if he'd simply been a pawn? What if *Quincy* wrote them?

Quincy turned on his heel. Jeffrey and the other Vipers followed wordlessly.

"Wait," Sutter called. "What happened to Alex?"

Quincy threw a glance over his shoulder. "Alex left me a note in the Vipers' den. It said his mother pulled him from school, so he was withdrawing from initiation. That's all I know."

Grayson shook his head slowly. He didn't buy it. He thought of the fear in Alex's eyes when he accused him of writing the poems, and the memory chilled him.

The Vipers kept walking until their group was left alone, still processing the news.

"Open it, Sutter," Margot said.

Slowly, he tore the envelope open and removed the note inside.

He let out a rush of air, and Grayson's stomach turned to lead at the sound. This wouldn't be good. He peered over Sutter's shoulder and read:

MAKE HASTE, AND IN A TIMELY MANNER,
TRAVEL TO THE HALLOWED MANOR.
TO ACE THIS TEST, USE WIT AND GUILE
AND BRING US LAWSON HEYWARD'S FILE.

"Lawson's file," Sutter said. "His student file. We have to get it out of Averell's office."

"You've got to be kidding," Carter said, raising his hands and resting them on top of his head. *"Shit."*

"We're supposed to break into Meddlehart Manor?" Margot asked in disbelief. "What are they trying to do, get us expelled?"

Fallon shook her head, a frantic look in her eyes. "No, no, no. Not a chance. I'm not doing this. *We* are not doing this."

Sutter glanced at her. "Fallon—"

"If we get caught, do you understand what will happen?" she went on, ignoring him. "We'll get shipped straight home, *all* of us, and Meddlehart—the five of us here, together, will be no more! This is by far the *stupidest* thing we could do, and—"

"*Fallon*," Sutter said again. This time, he took her gently by the shoulders, and she froze. "It will be fine. I'm not going to let any of us get expelled, especially not you. I've got a plan."

Grayson narrowed his eyes at Sutter, a flame lighting at his core that sent a bitter heat through him. The look in Sutter's eye, and the way he'd just touched Fallon . . . something was going on. And he knew he wasn't the only one to notice it, judging by the mild surprise in both Carter's and Margot's expressions.

Grayson opened his mouth to speak, but Sutter beat him to it.

"Fallon and Margot will stand guard outside," he said. "Carter will patrol the downstairs, and Grayson will watch my back upstairs. That way we'll have eyes everywhere while also having as few people in the house as possible. I'll do all the dirty work, and if I go down, I won't drag anyone else with me. I'll take all the blame—I swear it."

"Sutter," Fallon said, but he continued.

"We're so close," he said. "I can feel it. Just . . . trust me."

Suddenly, Grayson was acutely aware of the fact that maybe

he didn't want to trust Sutter this time. Maybe he didn't want to do this, either. The whole thing had gone from what felt like a fun adventure to a stupid, reckless game, and Grayson wasn't sure they were even on the right track.

How would they ever find Lawson or the treasure? They were just five high school students trying to solve a mystery, but now it felt like things were spiraling out of control.

Grayson didn't want to get expelled. That would land him straight on a plane back to his father, which was the *last* thing he wanted.

Or maybe it had more to do with the way Sutter was looking at Fallon and the way she'd always looked at him, even though Grayson didn't see that look in her eyes tonight. There was something different there instead. Something . . . sad. Confused.

It didn't matter. Grayson was suddenly angry—maybe more than angry, maybe even jealous—and he was moments away from speaking his mind.

But Carter stepped forward, as he always did when it came to Sutter, and said, "All right, man. Let's do this."

Margot shook her head. "If we get caught, you'll be the one explaining it to my parents."

Fallon looked at Margot. Somehow, Grayson knew then what Fallon would decide. Because she wouldn't let Margot do this alone.

And Grayson wouldn't back out if Fallon was part of it.

So when she stepped forward, he did, too. Sutter nodded, the hint of a smile at his lips.

"Let's go."

THIRTY-FIVE

Sutter

Sutter's heart raced as he clicked off his flashlight and approached Meddlehart Manor. In this moment, the grand double doors of the house seemed frightening—a massive, gaping mouth waiting to consume whoever stumbled through them.

The five of them congregated on the front steps, crouching beneath the windows. The house was quiet, asleep for the night, but they couldn't take any chances.

Sutter eyed the doorknob, the first obstacle of what would surely be many. Carefully, he wrapped his fingers around it. It only turned a fraction before coming to a halt.

Locked, of course. He hadn't expected anything less, but it was worth a try.

"How will we get in?" Carter whispered. "Is there a back door, a window . . . ?"

"Hold on," Margot said. She pulled a small, slender object out of her pocket and held it up. "I think I can pick it."

"That's a hair thing!" Grayson whispered, nudging Carter.

Margot scrunched up her nose, giving him a weird look. "A *what*? It's called a bobby pin, Grayson."

Carter smacked Grayson's chest. "A *bobby* pin, genius."

"How was I supposed to remember that?" Grayson hissed.

"Shut up, all of you," Sutter whispered.

Margot knelt before the doorknob, straightened the bobby pin, and slipped it into the keyhole. She started picking, a series of clicks sounding as she did.

Sutter's heart rate sped up. *It's working.*

"How are you doing that?" Grayson asked.

"It's not *too* hard," she mumbled. "You just have to find the pins in the lock and push them down . . ."

The lock gave a resounding *click*, and she grinned. "Like that."

"Damn, Margot!" Carter whispered, slapping her five. "Have you done this before?"

"Once," she said. "My mom grounded me and locked my phone in her desk. I picked the lock to get it back. I've never done it again, though."

"We could've used that trick the first time we searched this place," Sutter told her pointedly.

She shrugged. "It's probably best we *didn't*, which is exactly why I never mentioned it before."

She glanced at Fallon, and they grinned at each other.

Sutter shook his head. "You knew, Fallon, didn't you?"

She just shrugged. Her lips quirked up at the corners, and Sutter eyed them, grinning back. He wanted so badly to kiss her in that moment.

"What about at the tunnel entrance in the courtyard?" Carter asked. "Could you pick that lock?"

Margot frowned. "I don't think anyone could pick that lock with something as small as a bobby pin. It looked pretty intense, not to mention ancient."

Grayson stepped forward and reached for the knob. "Let's get this over with."

Sutter nodded, ignoring his interruption and turning toward the girls.

"Text us if you see anything," he said.

"Not me, though," Carter said quickly. He shrugged. "I left my phone back at Shepherd."

"We already know you never read your texts, Carter," Margot said.

Grayson opened the door slowly and crept inside, and then Carter entered. Sutter took one last look back at Fallon before following them.

The house was shrouded in darkness and silence. It was the quiet that made Sutter's skin prickle with goose bumps. The sound of their breathing already seemed too loud, not to mention the light creaking of the floorboards under their feet.

Sutter blinked as his eyes adjusted. He nodded at Carter, who returned the nod.

Grayson was already making his way upstairs, so Sutter followed. He practically held his breath with each painstaking step, sliding his hand against the wall for guidance.

Sutter's heart was thundering by the time they reached the landing. Down the hall, he could hear rumbling snores muffled by the closed master bedroom door. That comforted him a little—they hadn't woken anyone, hadn't drawn any suspicions yet. They just had to keep it that way.

Grayson eased open the door to Averell's study and they crept inside. Sutter pulled his cell phone out of his pocket and checked for texts from the girls. There were none, so he clicked the flashlight button and shone it around the room.

"It's gotta be in his desk," Sutter whispered, "or in the file cabinet."

"My money's on the file cabinet," Grayson replied, folding his arms across his chest. He stood by the door and peered into the hallway, keeping watch.

Sutter moved to the file cabinet. Each drawer was labeled alphabetically. He pulled gently on the *H* drawer and started thumbing through files.

"Hey, man," he whispered to Grayson, somewhat hesitantly. "Are you angry with me for some reason?" He paused, hoping Grayson might speak up, but he didn't. "I talked to Fallon already, but . . . I should've apologized for snapping at you after the last test."

"I mean, it's whatever, Sutter," Grayson said with a shrug. "I don't hold grudges, so don't worry about me. It's Fallon I'm worried about."

Sutter froze for a moment, frowning. "Why would you be worried about Fallon?"

"Just forget it, man."

"No, really. Tell me."

"It's just that she obviously cares a lot about you," Grayson said, not meeting Sutter's eyes, "and I don't want her to get hurt."

Sutter glared at him. "And you think *I'd* be the one to hurt her?"

"I didn't say that."

"You strongly implied." Sutter shook his head. "You have feelings for her, don't you?"

A muscle rippled in Grayson's jaw, and that was all the answer Sutter needed. His chest tightened.

"We can talk about this later," Grayson said sternly. "Find the file and let's *go*."

Sutter turned away—Grayson may have been pissing him off, but he was right. He focused on searching the files until he found what he was looking for.

Lawson Heyward. And behind it, he saw a file labeled with his own name.

Don't do it. It's not worth it. Just take Lawson's and go.

But Sutter was weak. He pulled both files from the drawer and set them gently on the desk. He opened his own first and began skimming.

"What are you doing?" Grayson hissed. "We can read them later, can't we?"

"Not if we have to deliver Lawson's file straight to Quincy," he said, and kept reading. His folder was the thinner of the two. There wasn't much in it, but he wilted when he saw the papers documenting what Nurse Fran called a "breakdown" the year before.

"What is it?" Grayson whispered.

Sutter shook his head. "Just . . . stuff about last year." He closed the folder. "Did I . . ." He swallowed thickly. "Did I seem—*crazy* to you all? Last year, when it all got really bad?"

Grayson frowned, shaking his head. "No, Sutter. None of us thought you were crazy. We were just . . . worried about you."

Sutter nodded, clearing his throat quietly. He slipped the folder back into the drawer and turned to Lawson's. After a deep breath, he flipped it open and began to read.

There was the usual stuff—report cards and transcripts, an incident report for when Lawson broke a finger on the school ski trip his sophomore year—and then thick packets of papers, all from when he went missing.

One caught Sutter's eye right away—a letter to Averell on thick white paper edged with gold foil:

Mr. Averell,

I know it's been some time since we've spoken. I've heard the terrible news about the Meddlehart student who disappeared last month, and I can't imagine the duress you're under as headmaster. I have no doubt you're working tirelessly to return this young man to his family.

I do have some concerns, however. I remember our time as students at Meddlehart Academy well, and while I'd like to say I have pleasant memories, I'm afraid my recollections are tainted by the endless cycle of bullying I experienced at your hands. People change, of course—I can acknowledge this—but I have not forgotten your self-centered nature and the tendency you had toward violence. It's truly unfortunate your ancestry protected you from any real consequences at the school.

My parents refused to remove me from the institution, and there were many nights where I pondered the unspeakable out of desperation to escape the daily fear you inflicted on me. This is why I've refrained from enrolling my own children at Meddlehart—because you're now the man in charge and I cannot fathom entrusting their care to a merciless bully.

Recently, I've considered sharing my experiences with the media. It troubles me greatly to know you're responsible for hundreds of young, impressionable students. Now that this boy has *vanished, I find it impossible to remain silent any longer. I suspect you may be responsible, to some degree.*

I would appreciate a private conversation about how you wish to handle this matter. I'm sure we can reach an agreement that will satisfy both of us. If you'd like to meet, you know where to find me.

Sincerely,
Joseph T. Rockwell

"Holy shit," Sutter murmured. He held the letter out to Grayson. "Look at this."

Grayson studied the letter in the light of Sutter's flashlight beam. As Grayson read, Sutter scanned Averell's desk. Something beneath it caught his eye.

There, in the wastebasket, was a discarded envelope. The return address was written in squat letters: *Kimberly Harker.*

That must be Alex's mom. Before he could think twice, Sutter began sifting through the other documents on the desk, searching for what had to be there . . .

And then he found it. On familiar creamy stationery was a short letter—not handwritten this time, but typed.

To whom it may concern,

I regretfully must remove my son, Alexander Harker, from Meddlehart Academy. I'm unable to afford tuition any longer due to the passing of my husband. I apologize for the suddenness of this decision. Alex is quite upset and asked me to bring him home as soon as possible to avoid embarrassment.

Thank you for the happy memories my son made as a Meddlehart student.

Sincerely,
Kim Harker

Quickly, Sutter searched the desk for anything else. The only thing left was Averell's weekly planner. Penciled meticulously next to his appointments for the past two days were the words *Call Kim Harker*. Beneath them in stark red letters: *NO RESPONSE*.

"Something's fishy," Sutter said. "Grayson, look at this."

Before Grayson could move, something shattered downstairs.

They froze, waiting for another sound. Sutter's mind raced. Had Carter broken something?

Instead, their phones buzzed with a text from Fallon: *Light on upstairs!!! SOS!!!*

"Shit," Sutter murmured. "We need to run."

Grayson said nothing. He bolted toward the stairs, and Sutter followed. They took the steps as quickly and quietly as they could, and when they reached the bottom, they found Carter kneeling beside a broken vase.

"It was an accident!" he whispered, eyes wide with panic.

"Leave it!" Sutter hissed. "Let's go!"

The three of them tumbled out the front door just as Averell's voice, groggy with sleep, called out, "Who's there?"

They pulled the door shut behind them, and then the five of them were flying across the lawn, straight for the courtyard.

Quincy smiled as they approached.

"What do you have for us?" he asked, extending his hand.

Reluctantly, Sutter handed over Lawson's file. Quincy skimmed through it, nodding. He raised his brows.

"I'm impressed," he told them. "Nicely done." He extended his hand for Sutter to shake.

"Well?" Margot said impatiently. "Are we in?"

Quincy smirked, glancing at the other Vipers. "We'll be in touch. The next time we meet, it'll be for you to claim your Viper pins."

They breathed a collective sigh of relief.

"You should get back to your dorms now, before the prefects catch you," Quincy warned.

Sutter nodded, and the five of them turned to go. They made it halfway to Shepherd before he turned to his friends.

"Great job, guys," he said. "Thank you for everything. Really."

"We did it," Carter said, pumping his fist. "We're almost Vipers!"

Sutter grinned. He wanted to celebrate, too, but there was something that didn't sit right after what he'd just read.

Fallon seemed to sense it. "Did you look through the file?"

Sutter nodded, glancing at Grayson. "Yeah. There was a letter . . . Apparently, someone suspected Averell of being involved in Lawson's disappearance."

The others came to a halt, staring wide-eyed at him. "Are you serious?" Margot asked.

"Hold on," Grayson said, stepping forward. "You're not giving them the whole story. The guy who wrote the letter claimed Averell bullied him in high school—said he was violent, and he suspected him of being guilty somehow—and threatened to take his accusations to the media." He held his hands up. "Averell's a wealthy guy, and Meddlehart is a wealthy school. Sounds like the guy just wanted a payout, and given we haven't heard anything about this in the news . . . he probably got one."

Sutter narrowed his eyes at Grayson. "Yeah, but what if he's right? What if Averell *did* have something to do with it? When I was in his office the other day, he said things that were odd. Something's up with him, guys. He knows something."

"But do you know for sure?" Grayson asked. "Or are you reaching for an answer here, Sutter?"

A spark of anger caught fire in Sutter's stomach, and he stepped forward. "What's your deal, Grayson? Why are you suddenly so angry?"

Grayson's eyes narrowed. "You really want to do this right now?"

"Yeah, I do."

"All right." Grayson's chest inflated, and he straightened. "I'm getting sick of following you around all the time, always doing what you want to do even if it's a stupid idea. Fallon said it herself—Sutter makes a plan, and we all follow along without question."

Sutter wagged a finger in the air. "*Fallon* said that, huh? Be honest—that's what this is really about. You're trying to take your frustration out on me because you've got a crush on Fallon and she doesn't feel the same way."

Grayson looked like he'd been slapped. Sutter caught Fallon's slack-jawed expression in the corner of his eye. Carter's eyes were wide, too, but he stayed silent. Margot stepped forward angrily, her eyes alight.

"Sutter," she warned.

"Shut up," Grayson said in a low voice. "You're one to talk."

"Or is it all about your dad?" Sutter went on, ignoring him. "Hate to break it to you, but you're not the only one with a shitty dad. My dad's a world-class asshole, and you don't see me moping around like you've been."

Grayson didn't wait for Sutter to say another word. He launched himself forward, tackling Sutter, and they landed on the ground with a thud. Suddenly, they were a tangle of flailing limbs, both throwing punches wildly. Grayson landed one to Sutter's ribs, and Sutter hit him back, hard, in the eye.

Within seconds, Carter had wedged himself between them, breaking the fight up. He shoved Sutter's chest, and when Sutter looked up, Margot and Fallon were both restraining Grayson, dragging him backward.

"Knock it *off*!" Carter shouted. "Both of you just *stop*!"

Sutter shoved himself up off the ground, ignoring the ache in his ribs, and dusted himself off. He spat in the dirt, still glaring at Grayson, whose jaw was clenched.

Fallon let go of him. Sutter saw tears in her eyes glinting in the moonlight. She shook her head and then took off running toward Shepherd.

"Fallon!" Margot called out, but she didn't stop. Margot looked at Sutter and Grayson, shaking her head.

"Way to go, guys," she muttered before chasing after Fallon. The second she was gone, Carter turned his glare on his friends.

"I don't know what your problems are," he said, "but you

two need to figure it out, like, *now*. I'm sick of this bullshit. *Figure it out.*"

He turned and stalked away, also toward Shepherd. Sutter turned to Grayson, but before he could speak, Grayson started walking in the other direction, away from the student houses.

Sutter didn't go after his friends. Instead, he found a bench and sat down, the quiet sounds of the early-morning hours chirping around him.

He was alone.

THIRTY-SIX

Fallon

The month of October passed like a ghost, and by Halloween, Fallon felt once again as though she hardly recognized her life at Meddlehart. Most students were busy preparing for the upcoming school events—the Halloween dance and the annual ski trip to Swallowtail Mountain. But she was distracted by the new awkwardness between her best friends.

Grayson and Sutter both apologized—briefly and separately—for what happened the night of the last test. She told them it was fine and tried to move on. They went back to having meals together in the dining hall, sitting together in class, all the things they'd always done before.

But things were different. Sutter and Grayson hardly acknowledged each other. They avoided laughing at the other's jokes, refused to make eye contact, wouldn't even sit on the same side of the table. And as much as Fallon hated to admit it, they almost treated her the same way.

It seemed like they were continuing to hang around each other simply for the convenience of it, not because they actually wanted to.

Fallon spent more time in her dorm, reading and drawing. She hoped it might keep her mind off everything, but it didn't. She felt an emptiness in her chest that grew by the day, and she was worried about Grayson.

She missed him. She could see in his eyes he was struggling, and she wanted nothing more than for him to talk to her about it. But he didn't seem comfortable doing that now.

She found herself drawing him sometimes, sketching the outlines of his jaw, his lips, his eyes, before setting her pencil down and shoving her sketch pad away. She thought about the Halloween dance coming up and if he might ask her, then felt foolish for even considering it—of course he wouldn't. Not now.

She couldn't stop replaying her conversation with Margot in her head, along with the question her friend had asked: *Do you have feelings for him, too?*

She did, didn't she? Fallon did everything she could to ignore the thought, smothering it like a flame in her heart. But it kept coming back to her, and she kept longing for him.

The worst part was, if she admitted that to him, she wasn't sure he'd care anymore.

Halloween arrived, and like every other weekday, she went to history class. She and Grayson used to walk together, but now she showed up on her own. He was already there, sitting at the desk beside hers, tugging at his Meddlehart uniform tie and avoiding her gaze.

Quincy was in their history class, too, which was not a thing Fallon would've noticed before joining the order. He took the seat directly behind hers and flashed his trademark grin.

"Boo," he said.

Grayson glanced at him over his shoulder, a questioning look in his eyes.

Quincy smirked. "Not in the Halloween spirit, I take it? Don't tell me you're *too cool* for it or some shit."

Grayson offered a stiff smile as Whittaker strolled into the room tapping his cane with each step, a bowl of Halloween candy balanced in his free hand. "Kind of forgot what day it was," Grayson said.

Fallon felt her heart shrink at the words. Was he not going to the dance with them tonight?

Whittaker was passing out graded papers—their essays from last week, a major chunk of their overall grade—and approached them, cutting the conversation short. He handed Fallon hers and then passed the next one to Grayson. She could see the *D* in bold red ink at the top of the page.

"I suggest we schedule that meeting now, Mr. Hendricks," Whittaker whispered gently before he walked back to the whiteboard and began writing.

Fallon glanced at Grayson, whose cheeks were blazing. He leaned his head on his hand, jaw clenched.

"Grayson," she whispered. She wanted nothing more than to reach out and take his hand.

But he just shook his head. "I don't really want to talk about it, Fallon, but thanks."

The words stung more than she could bear to admit, and she sank lower into her chair. It was only then she heard Quincy's whispered curse.

She turned around, frowning. Quincy's face had gone pale, his eyes wide and unfocused. She scanned the front of the room, looking for something out of the ordinary, but it was just Whittaker and the whiteboard, where he'd listed their upcoming assignments.

"Quincy?" she whispered.

"Oh my God," he murmured, running a shaky hand through his hair. "Oh, fuck. Oh, *fuck*."

Margot risked a glance down at the essay he'd just gotten back, wondering if it was a bad grade. But a bright red *A* was written at the top, paired with the message *Excellent work!*

Fallon noticed then that Quincy had his journal under his desk, open to a page she couldn't see.

"What's wrong?" she whispered.

"I can't believe I didn't realize," he said breathlessly, and she started to wonder if he might pass out.

"Quincy, you're freaking me out," she said. "What's going on?"

Grayson turned slightly in his chair. "Are you good, man?"

Quincy swallowed, shaking his head. "I think I know . . . I've got to go."

Without another moment's hesitation, he shoved loudly from his chair and rushed out of the classroom. Whittaker turned at the sound, startled, and watched Quincy go.

"Mr. Stiles?" he asked. When Quincy didn't stop, he set down his marker and followed him out. "Mr. Stiles, class isn't over!"

Grayson turned to Fallon, frowning. "What the hell was that?"

She shook her head. "I don't know." Her heart raced a little. Something was definitely wrong.

After a few minutes, Whittaker came back in and gave the students a confused shrug.

"Let's carry on with class," he said. "As long as no one else would like to leave without explanation?"

No one did, and class continued normally after that, but Fallon bounced one leg up and down the entire hour. She couldn't help but think of Lawson and how quickly he decided to leave campus that rainy night, only to vanish. When the bell rang, she grabbed her bag and hurried out, Grayson following behind her.

"Where are we going?" he asked.

"To find Quincy."

"Hold on." He reached for her arm, fingertips grazing her skin. The feel of them was enough to stop her in her tracks, her breath catching in her throat. "He seemed upset, Fallon. We might want to give him space."

Fallon frowned. "It seemed important, though. What if it has something to do with the Vipers?"

"If it does," Grayson said evenly, "Quincy will tell us when we meet to claim our pins. I'm sure of it. We should probably let it go and focus on enjoying Halloween."

She nodded. He was right. But then she looked up at him, nearly melting under his stare, and said, "Are you coming to the dance with us?"

He sighed. "Fallon—"

"I just want to have fun together," she said. "Like old times."

She regretted the words immediately because his eyes hardened, like he'd been surprised to hear that phrase—*like old times*. Like it *hurt* him to hear it.

But he nodded. "Yeah, all right. Like old times. For sure."

She nodded and they walked back to Shepherd together, though they didn't say another word.

Fallon's heart fluttered as she crossed campus with Margot. She wore a deep-purple gown, a sharp contrast to the striking red dress her roommate was wearing, and Margot had done their eye makeup in a spiderweb pattern in the spirit of Halloween.

Fallon felt beautiful in an edgy way, something she was unaccustomed to, but she could only think about how tonight would feel. She wanted nothing more than a normal, *good* night with her friends.

The dance was held on the lawn by the lake, and she could already see the purple and orange twinkle lights that had been strung to create a canopy of sorts over the grassy space. The temperature had chilled considerably as the sun went down, and she hoped there would be apple cider to drink so she could warm up.

Fallon's heart leaped when she spotted Carter, Sutter, and Grayson waiting at the entrance to the canopy of lights. Each of them wore suits—Carter's a snazzy emerald green, Sutter's navy, and Grayson's classic black and white. After the seemingly endless awkwardness between Sutter and Grayson, she was relieved they all showed up.

"Ladies," Carter said with a smile. "Beautiful as always."

Margot grinned. "Thanks, Carter. *Please* tell me they have hors d'oeuvres." She walked beneath the canopy, and he followed her, calling something about goat cheese crostini.

That left Fallon with Sutter and Grayson, a heavy silence draping over them.

She cleared her throat. "Hi."

The boys hesitated. After a moment, they both tried to speak, cutting across each other.

"You look—" Grayson started.

"Would you—" Sutter said.

They froze, glancing at each other before Grayson nodded. "You first."

Sutter turned to Fallon again, determination in those hazel eyes. "Would you like to dance?"

Fallon barely held back her surprise. "Oh, um . . . Yes."

Sutter extended his hand, and she took it, letting him lead her under the lights. Grayson's gaze dropped to the ground as they passed, and he gave a nod before stepping off to the side.

Fallon wondered if Sutter could feel her hand shaking as he pulled her out to where other students were dancing. The song was an easy beat, acoustic, and she tried to lean into it as Sutter placed one arm around her waist. Fallon was instantly taken back to the night after the memorial, his kiss. They swayed for a moment, neither speaking, before Sutter broke the silence.

"I wanted to tell you something," he said quietly. "If that's all right."

Her mouth went dry. "Okay," she whispered.

"Okay . . . I haven't been fair to you, Fallon. Or to Grayson." He kept his eyes steady on hers. "I know that. I've been so . . . *focused* on finding Lawson, and that's something I'll never apologize for, never regret. But I do regret how I've treated you."

Fallon couldn't stop the tears from welling in her eyes. "Sutter—"

"Please, let me say it," he murmured, but his voice caught on the words. He cleared his throat. "I still feel for you what I felt that night in the courtyard. I love you, Fallon—who you are, who I could be with you. And lately, if you've doubted even for a second how important you are to me . . . that's my fault. I just wanted to tell you that."

"Sutter . . ." Fallon could barely keep a grip on her voice. She placed her hand on his chest, wanting him to hear her words, to hold on to them. "You've had to bear the kind of burden most people can't even imagine. There's only so much you can expect of yourself. You're a human being. Do you understand?" She placed her palm gently on his cheek. "No matter what happens, I don't hold that against you—I *never* will."

Sutter's eyes shone, but he clenched his jaw, nodding. "Thank you, Winthrop."

The song ended then, and as though being pulled by a magnet, she turned to see Grayson standing alone at the edge of the canopy. His hands were in his pockets, his eyes downcast.

Her head spun with the words Sutter just said—*I love you, Fallon*—but she needed time before she could even think about what they meant to her. Slowly, she walked back to where Grayson stood. He looked up, waiting.

Before she could say a word, Margot and Carter approached, each with cups of apple cider in hand.

"Where's Sutter?" Carter asked.

"Here," Sutter said from behind them.

"Good," Margot said, "because there's a photo booth and we're . . ."

That's when Jeffrey emerged from the crowd and walked right toward them. His brows were furrowed deeply, his shoulders tense.

"Hey, Jeffrey," Sutter said. "What's up?"

"I haven't seen Quincy since this morning," he said. "He was supposed to meet me an hour ago. Have any of you seen him?"

Fallon's eyes found Grayson's immediately. Alarm flashed across his face.

"We saw him in history class this morning," she answered. "He left early. He seemed upset."

Jeffrey's already worried expression crumpled into panic. "What if something's happened to him?"

Sutter clapped a hand on Jeffrey's shoulder. "It's all right, man, we'll find him. I'm sure he just got caught up or something."

"Do you *know* of anything bad that could've happened?" Margot asked, somewhat pointedly.

But when Jeffrey shook his head, his expression was earnest. "It's not like him to flake on me. And he's usually good about answering his phone."

"Don't panic," Grayson said. "We'll go look for him. How about that?"

Jeffrey nodded. "Should we split up?"

"Yeah, that's smart," Carter agreed. "How about some of us go to his dorm, and the rest of us can check the tunnel?"

"I'll go to the tunnel," Jeffrey said. "You guys aren't supposed to be there alone until you're initiated."

Oh, Jeffrey, always a rule follower. But Fallon supposed she could relate.

"I'll go to the tunnel with you," Sutter offered.

"Me too," Carter said.

"So we'll check out his dorm," Margot said, gesturing to Grayson and Fallon, and they both nodded. "Meet you guys back here after?"

Jeffrey, Sutter, and Carter strode under the canopy of lights and toward the boathouse.

"Let's make this quick," Grayson said as they made their way in the opposite direction. "If he isn't there, we might need to get help."

Fallon's chest ached with a twinge of fear. "You think he might be in danger?"

Grayson shook his head. "No, I'm sure there's an explanation. It's just . . ." He shuddered in the cold night air. "He was acting really weird in class, is all."

Fallon heard the unspoken words clear as a bell: *And this*

wouldn't be the first time a student went missing at Meddlehart Academy.

They jogged back to Shepherd, Margot's dress rustling loudly with each hurried step until they reached the front doors. They took the stairs two at a time to the ninth door on the fourth floor.

"Quincy?" Margot called, rapping quickly on the door. "Anyone home?"

Silence.

"Should we try calling him again?" Margot asked. She pulled out her phone and scrolled to find his contact.

Fallon knocked this time, a little harder. "Quincy!"

No answer.

Grayson stepped up and slammed his fist against the door. "Quincy, it's us. We just want to know you're all right."

Still nothing. Finally he grabbed the knob and twisted, shoving his shoulder against the door, but it was locked. He shook his head. "It sounds like no one's there."

But then the silence on the other side of the door fractured. Something buzzed noisily in a repetitive pattern—the unmistakable sound of a vibrating cell phone.

Margot's eyes went wide. "His phone's in there, but he's not answering my call."

Fallon's blood ran cold. If Quincy's phone was in the room, chances were he was, too. Why wasn't he picking up?

"Should we find a prefect?" Fallon asked, heart skipping wildly. "They could unlock it."

"Or we could do this a lot faster," Margot said, "and use Grayson's ginormous football-player foot."

He sighed, eyeballing the door for a minute. Then he spread his arms out. "Stand back."

The girls retreated against the wall, and Grayson took a deep breath. In one swift motion, he kicked the door hard near the knob. The lock buckled instantly, and the door flew inward.

Fallon sucked in a sharp breath, the edges of her vision blurring as she took in the scene before them. Margot cried out, and Grayson gagged, stumbling away and retching.

Quincy was lying on the floor of his room, his skin gray, Meddlehart uniform covered in blood.

He was dead.

THIRTY-SEVEN

Sutter

Sutter sat in Fallon and Margot's dorm room in silence, surrounded by his friends. All Meddlehart students were ordered to their rooms after the discovery of Quincy's body. The five of them decided they'd rather be together than separated, so the boys joined the girls in their room, not caring if they got in trouble for doing so.

The mood was heavy and miserable. When Sutter and Carter returned with Jeffrey to find that Quincy had been dead for hours, Jeffrey became inconsolable and was led away to the infirmary. Sutter took one glance at Grayson, Margot, and Fallon, and saw the haunted look in their eyes.

They'd seen Quincy's body—that image would be branded into their brains forever. Somehow, all Sutter could feel was suffocating guilt, like it was his fault they had to bear that burden.

No, he told himself. *Whoever killed Quincy is responsible for this.*

And perhaps they were responsible for far more than that.

They opened the curtains in the girls' room to watch the snowflakes falling, as a little storm had blown through after dark. The remnants of the Halloween dance were all around them—the girls' makeup, ruined by sweat and tears; the boys' dress shoes in a pile by the door, ties cast aside. They were like shells of themselves, still reeling from what the night had become.

The school counselor showed up at some point to talk to Margot, Fallon, and Grayson separately. Sutter wasn't entirely sure what the counselor said to Fallon, but when she finally returned, she was crying.

Margot rushed to put her arms around her. "It's okay, Fallon. It's going to be okay."

Sutter's chest ached. He wished he could wrap her in his arms himself. But Fallon shook her head and pushed Margot away.

"No," she said, her eyes scanning everyone in the room. "You guys . . . I messed up. I . . ." She hesitated. "I took something from Quincy's room when we found his body."

Sutter leaned forward, eyes wide. "You *what*?"

She crossed the room to her backpack and revealed Quincy's notebook.

"It was on his desk," she said. "I didn't touch anything else, and I checked—there's nothing new written in it."

Sutter heard the hidden meaning in her words—*there wasn't a note*. Regardless, the authorities were already assuming it was a suicide. Quincy probably poisoned himself with pills that were missing from a container on his nightstand, they said, and the blood all over him was what he'd likely coughed up as a result.

Sutter didn't believe that, though. He might not have known Quincy well, but suicide didn't add up.

"He was looking through the notebook in history class, right before he got upset and left," Fallon explained, her voice thick. "He said he realized something, and I—just didn't want to lose this. I figured if we read it, we might figure out whatever he did before he . . ." Her face crumpled, and Margot hugged her again.

"I shouldn't have done it," Fallon cried. "I should give it to the police, shouldn't I? It's evidence, isn't it?"

"No," Sutter said before he could stop himself. "I mean, yes, it's probably evidence, even if he hadn't written anything new. But it would only get us into more trouble if we took it to them now."

The others were silent, but they nodded in agreement. To turn in the journal would create a domino effect—the police would find out about the order and everything the five of them had done while searching for answers.

"You did the right thing," Sutter told Fallon, and he really believed it. "You protected us—all of us. The other Vipers, too. Quincy wouldn't want that notebook to go to the cops."

"I've already looked through it," Fallon said, sniffling. "I couldn't find anything out of the ordinary, but . . . maybe we should all take a look. If we put our heads together, we could figure out what happened to Quincy."

Grayson sat up straighter. "You don't think he killed himself?"

She shook her head. "No . . . I mean, I hope not. But the alternative isn't great, either."

Fallon was right. Because if Quincy hadn't taken his own life . . . that meant someone else had.

Sutter shuddered.

"Who would've killed him, though?" Carter asked, standing up to pace the room. "Why would anyone do that?"

Grayson frowned. "Have we thought about Alex in all of this? He's supposedly gone, but I can't get his phone call out of my head. What if he was talking to Quincy that night? What if things went south and Alex snapped? We've seen him do it before."

Sutter considered this. Could Alex still be lurking around

campus, waiting to exact revenge on anyone who had crossed him? Sutter thought of Alex attacking him during Vipers and Mice, demanding to know what happened to Lawson and the treasure. And he thought of the creepy poems Alex left for him and his friends to find.

Alex was a threat, and if he truly was as unhinged as they'd seen . . . Would they be next?

Margot shook her head, her eyes teary. "This can't be happening."

"Listen, if we really think someone else is responsible for Quincy's death," Sutter said, "we need to watch our backs and look out for each other. It seems like the police have already done exactly what they did with Lawson's case—they've made up their minds about Quincy's death based on the little evidence they have. But we can figure this out, if we—"

His words were interrupted by a collective chirping. They all looked at their phones.

"Holy shit," Carter breathed. Sutter read the text on his own phone:

Bell tower at midnight. By the fangs of greed.

His blood chilled. He'd assumed the order might disband in the wake of Quincy's death . . . but he was wrong.

The Vipers had more in store for them.

Sutter wasn't sure what to expect when they arrived at the old bell tower, bundled in their thick coats. Would the order be there to congregate in the wake of Quincy's passing? Would they discuss their plans, what they would do without their leader, who would be taking his place?

But no one else was there as the five of them approached, footsteps crunching lightly in the snow. The night was cold and dark, and snowflakes still swirled down around them.

"What now?" Margot asked. "We're the only ones who showed."

Fallon walked up to the base of the bell tower, where a service door blended in with the bricks. There was a note stuck to the door.

Sutter had his phone flashlight on when she returned, and he shone it over the message:

> WE'VE PROMISED YOU SHALL CLAIM YOUR PIN,
> JUST AS THE BELL WILL SURELY CHIME.
> THE FINAL TEST AWAITS THEREIN—
> ALL VIPERS MUST KNOW HOW TO CLIMB.

A cold dread washed over Sutter as he craned his neck to look up at the bell tower.

"Fuck," Grayson whispered. "They don't mean . . . ?"

Fallon was shaking her head, panic bright in her eyes. "No. They *can't*. That tower is a hundred feet tall, at *least*. We can't climb it!"

Carter circled the base of the tower, searching for a solution. "There aren't any ropes or climbing gear. Surely that's not—"

Margot approached the service door, and when she pulled, it opened with a creak. She looked back at them. "Seems like someone left it unlocked for us."

The Vipers. There was no chance school staff would leave that door unlocked for nosy students to enter.

Sutter swallowed thickly. *"The final test awaits therein."*

He looked at Fallon, who was still wide-eyed and breathing

rapidly, trembling in the cold. Gently, he reached into the dark, took her hand, and squeezed it.

He meant what he said at the dance, every word of it. He was sorry. He wished he could redo so many parts of this semester—he wished he could tell her sooner that he loved her, wished he hadn't lashed out at Grayson, wished he'd known how much his friends would go through to help him find Lawson.

But he knew Fallon meant what she said, too—she didn't want him to carry the boulder that was his guilt. Her words had nearly cracked open his chest, because no one had ever said that to him before. Not a single person.

And so he would take that boulder that had grown in his heart and leave it at the door of this bell tower. He would not carry it forward into the final test, the final steps in this search for his brother.

Before he let go of Fallon's hand, Sutter could've sworn he saw a blur in the darkness—a figure in the shadows, slinking past. But the figure was gone before he could decide what—or who—he saw, and he wondered if it might be a figment of his imagination.

Sutter led his friends through the service door and into the bell tower. The passage was narrow and dark, lit only by lanterns hanging along the wall. The steps of the winding staircase were made of old, pale wood that groaned under their weight.

"The lanterns are a strange choice," Margot commented as they climbed single file. "They couldn't install electric lighting in here?"

"I'm sure this was part of its original design," Grayson replied. "You know how Averell is about 'maintaining the historical elements' of campus."

A shudder ran through Sutter. Everything about the tower

felt ancient and forbidden and altogether wrong for them to be there.

The stairs wound up and up, one turn after another, and Sutter felt a sort of dizzy anticipation as they neared the top. At the landing, he stepped through the doorway and aimed his phone flashlight on a ladder that rose straight upward to a platform, where the bell hung at the center.

He glanced back at his friends. "Shall we?"

"They left us no other choice, buddy," Carter said, patting his shoulder. Carter grabbed hold of the ladder and climbed, and Sutter let the others ascend first before he followed.

The platform surrounding the massive bronze bell was cramped and narrow, held aloft by several wooden rafters. The top of the tower was open to the frigid night air, and gusts of wind blew in with surprising force. A small chorus of chirps and clicks sounded from the roof—some kind of insect, maybe? Sutter wasn't sure.

The five of them gazed around, searching for some sign of what they were supposed to do. Sutter panned the light around the space, until it caught on the engraved surface of the bell.

In reverent memory of Franklin B. Thatcher
May his legacy ring clear and true for generations

And hanging from the clapper was a green velvet drawstring bag.

"There," he said, pointing. "Our pins must be in that bag."

Carter swore. "How the hell do we reach it?"

Sutter studied the platform and the rafters supporting it. Past a wooden railing, there was a single beam running beneath the bell. The beam was the only solid object protecting someone from a straight drop down, maybe twenty feet to the landing they'd just climbed from—a height Sutter didn't feel comfortable with in the slightest.

As if on cue, a slam sounded from below. Sutter looked to find that the door to the landing was firmly shut, a click echoing with an air of finality.

"Did we just get trapped up here?" Carter asked, not a hint of humor in his voice.

Because he was right, and they all knew it. Someone had followed them. They were locked up here until they completed the test.

"One of us has to get across on that beam," Sutter said with renewed urgency. The more he stared at it, the more narrow it looked. "Wide enough to crawl across if . . ."

He trailed off. Because he wouldn't finish that sentence—*couldn't*.

But Fallon did. "If they're small enough."

Sutter turned to her. "Fallon—"

"I have to do it," she said quietly, shakily. "I'm the smallest one. It's the least risky if I do it."

"*Fuck* no," Grayson said. "I'll do it." He pulled his coat off and stepped forward. Sutter could see him assessing the climb over the platform railing and how far he'd have to lower himself to reach the beam—but Fallon jumped in front of him.

"Grayson, stop," she said. "Your arm's still in a cast."

"My arm's fine—this thing's coming off next week. Let me go."

"No," she insisted. "Whoever does this needs to be able to grip the beam, and the cast won't let you. You're *not* doing it."

Grayson's chest heaved. His eyes were lit with what looked like anger, but Sutter knew better—he knew it was fear wearing a mask, and he felt it, too.

"There has to be another way," Margot spoke up, fighting the tremor in her voice.

Fallon shook her head. "I can do this, all right? I'll just go slow. It's not that far. Just . . . be there to help me get back on the platform."

Grayson looked like he might jump out of his skin. Carter put a hand on his shoulder, holding him back as Fallon grabbed the railing and eased herself over it. Slowly, she put one foot onto the beam, then crouched so she could grab it with both hands . . . and began a slow crawl across.

Sutter's heart was in his throat. He couldn't speak as he watched her move, inch by inch, closer to the bell, to the drawstring bag that held the end to all these games.

"You've got this, Fallon," Margot said. She had a white-knuckle grip on the railing. "Slow and steady. You can do it!"

Fallon didn't respond. She continued her trek, and Sutter swore he could hear her sharp breathing even over the gusts of wind that blew through the bell tower.

Sutter risked another glance at Grayson, who'd gone white as a sheet. He watched Fallon with wide eyes, frozen in place, Carter's hand still on his shoulder.

Finally, after minutes that felt like hours, Fallon reached the bell. Slowly, hands trembling hard enough that Sutter could see it from the platform, Fallon reached up and untied the bag from the clapper. She wrapped the drawstrings tight around her wrist, keeping her hands free for the journey back across.

Sutter breathed a sigh of relief.

"Holy shit, Fallon!" Carter cried. "Are you okay?"

"Y-yes," she managed. Her chin wobbled. "Fine. I'm fine."

"Yes!" Margot called. "You're halfway there, Fallon—all you need to do is crawl back!"

Fallon kept her concentration, and her grip, on the beam as she ever so slowly turned around. After taking a moment to breathe, she began inching back toward the platform.

Sutter watched, breath caught in his chest, until she was only a couple of feet from the platform. Grayson broke free of Carter's grasp then and stood beside Sutter so they could pull Fallon back over the railing. She was so close—so close, but then—

The bell rocked forward, then backward, then forward again. Its chime rattled Sutter's skull with the volume, and he clamped his hands over his ears.

His friends did the same, crying out in shock, and he looked at Fallon. She was frozen, eyes wide with fear, but still on the beam, still—

As the bell's toll faded, the chirps and clicks turned into a terrible symphony of shrieks. Out of nowhere, a barrage of flapping wings bore down on them. They all ducked low on the platform to avoid the frenzy, and Sutter could now see the source of what he'd mistaken for insects.

Bats—dozens of them—flying frantically out of the bell tower roof. He looked up in time to hear Fallon's startled scream, to see the dark wings flying past the bell, and then . . .

He witnessed the instant when she fell.

THIRTY-EIGHT
Grayson

A roar erupted from Grayson's throat as he saw Fallon tip sideways over the beam. He charged forward screaming her name and leaned over the railing.

His heart nearly stopped when he saw her hanging on to the beam, fingertips white with the effort to keep her grip as she dangled over the drop that would surely leave her body broken.

Grayson didn't wait. He threw himself to the floor of the platform and wedged himself through the posts of the railing. Desperately, he reached out for Fallon, pushing himself as far as he could without falling over the drop, until—

He felt a sturdy weight against the back of his leg, holding him steady. It was Sutter, shouting, "Grab her! *Hurry!*"

Carter grabbed Grayson's other leg. Grayson leaned farther until he could grab Fallon's arms. Her eyes locked with his, panicked and full of the kind of mind-numbing fear you have when you're about to die.

"I've got you," he promised her. "I've *got you*. Grab on to me!"

She had to trust him. She *had* to, or else—

Finally, she released one hand from the beam and latched on to his arm—the one with the cast. With all his strength, he pulled her up as Sutter and Carter dragged him backward until Fallon was on the platform and in his arms.

Quickly, he pushed up to sitting, cradling her to his chest. She was shaking like a leaf, her expression frozen with shock.

"I've got you," he whispered. He reached up to cup her cheeks, only to find his own hands were trembling. His heart thundered so hard, he felt like he might be sick.

Margot was sobbing. She fell to her knees beside them and wrapped her arms around them both—and then Sutter and Carter did the same, and for a moment, they were all huddled on the floor, rattled by the truth that they could've lost Fallon that easily.

But they hadn't. Grayson had to repeat the words over and over in his head to slow the racing of his heart—she was okay. She was *okay*.

Finally, the group let go of each other and Fallon sat up, tears staining her cheeks. Shakily, she untangled the drawstring bag from her wrist, loosened it, and emptied its contents onto the floor.

Five identical silver viper pins spilled out, gleaming under Sutter's flashlight. A brass key thudded out, too, and Sutter took it.

"Must be to unlock the door down there," he said. "So we can leave."

Grayson shuddered with the thought of how differently it could've ended—with only four of them leaving the bell tower in one piece.

Fallon fished in the bag and pulled out a small, thin slip of paper, stained with the familiar handwriting of the Vipers' messages. She read it silently, then said, "Initiation into the order will happen the night after we get back from the ski trip. We must bring our pins to gain entry into the tunnel."

Slowly, Sutter gathered the pins and passed them out. Grayson shoved his in his pocket. He wasn't sure he wanted this anymore, and he wondered if the others felt the same. He felt that if he saw Jeffrey or the other Vipers after tonight, all he'd want to do was throttle them.

He knew he wouldn't have survived losing Fallon. And going through with the initiation seemed like a terrible idea after what they'd just been put through. If they ever did find the treasure, he couldn't stand the thought of sharing a single bit of it with those people.

Margot touched Fallon's shoulder. "Are you okay?"

Fallon nodded. "Yeah . . . I am. Let's just go back to Shepherd."

So they stood, and one by one, they climbed down the ladder. In silence, they descended the stairs to the bottom of the bell tower. The snow had already covered their tracks.

Grayson glanced at Fallon as they walked. Her eyes were cloudy and distant, even as they gazed back at him. He wanted to reach for her so badly. He wanted to comfort her. He wanted to tell her he would never let anything bad happen to her, ever.

But they'd talked about that already, that day in the courtyard. They'd agreed to move on. To just be friends. And he would honor her wishes if it was the last damn thing he did.

So he focused on the dark, snowy night ahead until he saw the warm porch lights of Shepherd House before him.

THIRTY-NINE

Fallon

Fallon hadn't expected to be on the bus to Swallowtail Mountain Ski Resort this soon.

The annual ski trip was planned for later that month, but Headmaster Averell announced just a few days after the test in the bell tower that the trip was being moved up. He claimed it was so they could "come together as a school, grieve, and heal" after the tragic loss of their classmate.

"He's lying," Sutter insisted. "There's no chance Averell isn't hiding something."

"Maybe they're getting us off campus so the police have more space to investigate," Margot suggested. "Or they really just want to boost our spirits."

"I don't buy it for a second" was Sutter's only response.

Fallon tried not to overthink it as she packed her things. She was honestly relieved to be getting away—after finding Quincy's body in Shepherd House, and after nearly slipping from that beam in the bell tower, she was having a hard time sleeping without waking in a panic, feeling like she was falling, falling, *falling*. Maybe a getaway would do her some good.

She had to admit she felt a sense of pride, though, at being brave enough to do what she had done. Overcoming something so scary and surviving it. She avoided every thought of how badly that night could've ended and tried to focus on the good—on the strength she uncovered that had been dwelling dormant inside her until the moment she needed it most.

Before leaving campus, Fallon bundled Quincy's notebook in her heavy coat and shoved it into her suitcase. She had photos of everything they'd seen in the vault, but she wanted to keep investigating while they were at the resort. She asked Sutter to bring Lawson's notebook as well. Fallon wasn't much of a skier, and she spent most of her time on these trips reading by the fireplace at the warming house rather than out on the slopes. Her reading material just wouldn't be the usual this time.

The drive from Meddlehart Academy to Swallowtail Mountain wasn't long, just thirty or forty minutes, and they arrived before lunchtime. The students stepped off the bus and were welcomed by a smiling woman wearing a Swallowtail Mountain vest with the butterfly logo embroidered on the chest.

"Welcome, Meddlehart Academy," she said. "I'm Anna, and I'm thrilled to be the first to welcome you to Swallowtail Mountain. I'll give a brief tour of our resort, and then we'll get you all settled in your rooms!"

Fallon smiled. As horrible as the week had been, she loved Swallowtail Mountain, and it was already a massive relief to be there. She breathed in deep, taking in the crisp mountain air, and looked around at the snow-covered landscape.

"Right now, we're at the base of our ski slopes," Anna called out as the students ambled along through the snow. "Most of these slopes were first made when the resort was founded in 1948. Before that, this area was a hot spot for rich men to dig coal mines, but our founders sealed all the mines up so the resort could be built."

She pointed to the wide slope in front of them. "This big one here is what's commonly referred to as the bunny slope, which is perfect for beginners who are learning how to ski or snowboard. Many of our slopes are named after different types of swallowtail butterflies," she informed the students. "It might be interesting for you to try to guess which ones. Then you can Google it and find out if you were right."

Anna led the group through the warming house, where you could sit by the grand fireplace, eat chili, and drink hot cocoa—the *only* things Fallon felt were worth doing in the winter—and then to the resort lodge, where the students would find their rooms. They stopped in the lobby, where a giant grizzly bear statue stood by a streaming fountain.

"Your teachers have your room assignments," Anna said. "They'll pass out your keys. Oh, and one more thing." Her smile widened. "We heard your Halloween dance was canceled, and we thought it might be nice to host a make-up dance for you at the end of the week in the resort ballroom! Don't worry—it's not prom or anything, but if you'd like, you can get dressed up, smash some punch, and dance with your friends to end your visit here at Swallowtail!"

An excited buzz brought the somber group of students to life, and Fallon glanced at Margot.

"A dance," Margot said, eyebrows raised. "That's new."

Fallon turned to look at the boys, who were looking back at them.

"Will we need dates?" she asked quietly.

Margot smirked, and Fallon rolled her eyes.

"Never mind," she muttered. "Forget I said anything."

"Look, Fallon," Margot whispered, "I know you're not totally sure what you want, and things have been weird lately . . . but I hope you know it's not a bad thing to want him."

"Want who?" Fallon asked, but Margot was already strolling off to where the teachers stood passing out room keys. Fallon sighed.

She was pretty sure she knew the *him* Margot was talking about. She didn't have to say his name.

FORTY

Sutter

Skiing was a thing Sutter wanted to be good at. But every year, he showed up at Swallowtail again and felt like he had to relearn everything.

Luckily, he wasn't alone this year—Carter and the others were all skiers, but Carter talked Margot and Grayson into learning to snowboard, landing them right back on the beginner courses on the bunny hill. Normally by the end of the first day, they were taking off down the green- and blue-ranked runs, but not this time. They ended the day right where they started it—at the bottom of the bunny slope.

"Think we'll get to do the fun runs tomorrow?" Sutter asked as they ambled back to the warming house, sore and exhausted.

Grayson just grunted, and Margot pulled her goggles off to reveal her windburned cheeks.

"Doubtful," she muttered.

"Aw, come on, guys!" Carter said, somehow still his cheerful, energetic self. "We've got this. We did great today—we're learning a new skill together! Except Sutter."

Sutter rolled his eyes. "Yeah, and because of that I didn't wipe out eleven times in one day."

"It was actually twelve," Margot corrected, "but I got up every single time, didn't I?"

"We're proud of you, Margot," Grayson said. "Not you, Sutter."

"Thanks, pal."

When they made it inside, the warmth embraced them like a glorious hug. They spotted Fallon right away, the only one at a table for five.

"Well," she said. "Look at all you ski bunnies."

Sutter smiled, relieved to see her at ease again. She'd been really rattled after the bell tower, and he'd been worried about her. A trip to Swallowtail Mountain was good for the soul, though—it had always done wonders for him.

"Literally," he replied, "because we never made it off the bunny hill."

"Gotta start somewhere," she said, gesturing to the steaming cups of apple cider. "Drink up."

They sat down and gulped their drinks greedily. The hot cider burned Sutter's throat, but he didn't care. He took three full sips before Fallon spoke.

"So . . . I think I found something." She lifted Quincy's notebook. "I've spent the entire day flipping through the journals, looking for clues, and pretty much none of it is readable. It's almost like it's written in code."

"So's Lawson's," Sutter said. "All the Vipers probably did it for their own protection."

"Which makes sense," Fallon said. "But there's one part of Quincy's journal that's not in code." She turned to the note at the end, the note Lawson had left for Quincy—*Keep going.*

"And then I realized," Fallon said, turning back a few pages, "the handwriting doesn't match. In Lawson's journal, the letters are a little longer and thinner, and he writes his *e*'s funny. They almost look like little *c*'s. And . . . was Lawson left-handed?"

Sutter nodded. Fallon continued, "I figured, because sometimes the ink is smeared in his journal. But that doesn't happen in his note to Quincy."

Sutter frowned, heart skipping a beat. "So . . . was that last note in Quincy's handwriting, then?"

Fallon shook her head. "Quincy writes in cursive. See . . ." She flipped a few pages to where Quincy had written notes about the new initiates, the five of them included. Sure enough, the letters were loopy and slanting.

"Show us the note again," Grayson said. Fallon flipped back to the note, and Sutter stared at the letters, squared off and squat on the page. They weren't drastically different from Lawson's letters, but now that he was looking at them, he wanted to smack himself in the forehead.

"How did I not realize this before?" he murmured.

Fallon startled a little at his words, and she shuddered.

"That's what Quincy said in class the other day," she said. "I think this is what he realized, what upset him so much. The person who wrote this note wasn't Lawson."

"But who wrote it, then?" Margot asked.

Fallon shook her head. "That, I haven't figured out."

"Wait," Grayson spoke up. "The handwriting . . . it's the same as in the poems we found in my locker and in the cafeteria."

Margot's eyes widened. "Are you positive?"

Grayson took out his phone, removed the folded poem from the clear case, and handed it to Margot. They all leaned forward to compare it to the note left for Quincy, and Fallon gasped.

The handwriting looked identical.

Sutter felt a chill drip down his spine. This suddenly felt like an even more dangerous game than the one they'd been playing the past few months.

"So . . . if someone else wrote this note in Quincy's journal," Carter said, "and it's the same person who wrote the poems we found . . . could that also be the person who killed Quincy?"

Sutter was afraid to speak the words, but they were there, in his mind.

And maybe that person knows where Lawson is, too.

FORTY-ONE

Grayson

Grayson's favorite part of the ski trips to Swallowtail may have been the lift rides up the mountain. There was something about getting taken up high, where he could see everything from above—the other skiers and boarders making their runs down the slopes, the snow-dusted trees watching over them, the peak of the mountain, which looked to him like a massive chunk had been taken out of it ages ago by some ancient creature. He could almost picture a dragon crawling up the side of the mountain, the rocks crumbling beneath its weight as it roared a stream of fire.

Sounds like one of Fallon's books, he thought as he gazed up at the peak, the lift bouncing gently in the wind, and his heart ached.

Grayson had done his best to find a new normal with Fallon. He'd tried to ignore the way he felt, ignore the fact that he had told her he loved her and she'd turned him away. That was okay—she didn't have to love him back. Grayson just wanted her to be happy. But he couldn't pretend it didn't hurt him, like a wound that reopened every time he saw her, right when it had started to heal.

It doesn't matter, he told himself over and over. *It doesn't matter, it doesn't matter, it doesn't* matter.

But every day the gaping hole in his chest seemed to grow a little wider, and the ache burrowed a little deeper. He wasn't sure how much more he could take.

Maybe he hadn't realized it, but for so long his friends were all he had. His dad would never be the father he wanted—the father he *needed*—and his mom had been gone so long, he'd almost forgotten what it was like to be loved. His friends were *everything* to him.

But Fallon had become so much more, and no matter how badly he wanted to deny it . . . he couldn't.

Margot was on the lift with him. Carter and Sutter were on the seat behind theirs, several yards back. The trip was nearly over, and they'd spent most of their time on the green-ranked runs—Tiger's Tail was probably their favorite—but Sutter insisted it was time they test their skills on the blues near the top of the mountain, and maybe by the end they'd take on a black diamond run.

"How's it going, Grayson?" Margot asked, breaking the silence. Something about the lilt in her voice told Grayson she was curious about more than just how he was doing.

"Hanging in there," he said, trying to smile.

"Are you excited for the dance tomorrow night?"

He kept his gaze focused ahead. "Sure. Sounds like a fun time."

"Are you going to ask anyone?"

"I wasn't planning on it."

She nudged him. "Maybe you should think a little more about it."

He sighed. "Margot, I know what you're doing, and—"

"I'm not doing anything," she said. "I'm just chatting."

By then they were at the lift drop-off, and he didn't have time to retort. The two of them angled their boards just right and hopped off the lift, then glided down to the map of the slopes that was planted near the trees.

When Sutter and Carter got off the lift, Carter's board dug into the snow, and he face-planted hard. The lift operator stopped the lift and helped him to his feet, and Sutter's laughter practically echoed as they made their way toward Margot and Grayson.

"Shut *up*, Heyward," Carter grumbled, dusting snow off his coat.

Sutter's laughter waned, and he angled his skis to a stop at the sign. "Have you guys looked at our options yet?" he asked. "Which run do you want to try out first?"

"I haven't looked," Margot said.

"Me either, honestly," Grayson muttered. He'd kind of assumed Sutter had one in mind.

Sutter squinted, running a gloved finger over the trails on the map. Grayson followed Sutter's lead and read the slope names off in his mind. *Snowdrift, Goliath, Apollo . . .*

"Holy shit," Sutter murmured.

"What?" Carter asked, moving forward to look. "What's wrong?"

"Goliath," Sutter said, pointing. "Apollo. These were on the list of random words in Lawson's journal!"

Grayson's blood chilled. "You're not serious."

"I am," Sutter said. "What were the others on the list? Alex was one of them, right? Zebra, lime, Oregon . . ."

"Wait," Margot said, shaking her head. She pulled out her phone. "Do we have service up here?"

"In some spots," Carter said. "Depends."

She started typing, and her eyes went wide. She turned her phone to show them the web page she'd pulled up.

"Those are types of swallowtail butterflies," she said. "All of them."

"Holy *shit*," Carter breathed. "Hold on . . . What does that mean?"

Sutter's face had blanched, and he shook his head. "I . . . don't know." He looked up at them. "We need to go talk to Fallon. *Now.*"

Grayson's heart hammered the entire ride down the mountain. He didn't feel totally sure of the snowboard yet, and he wiped out twice in their race to get to the warming house. They found Fallon eating a steaming bowl of soup, Lawson's journal open in front of her.

"What's going on?" she asked as they approached.

Sutter didn't bother with words. He reached for Lawson's journal and flipped through the pages until he landed on the list.

"Swallowtail butterflies," he said, pointing the names out.

Fallon frowned as she looked over the list. Margot showed her the photos on her phone, and Fallon's eyes went wide.

"Butterflies," she said. "Wait . . . *wait* . . ."

She reached for her phone and scrolled, until finally she started reading.

"I'll go where the butterflies drift out west," she said. *"From the rabbit's home to the broken peak."*

"Oh my God," Grayson murmured.

Swallowtail Mountain was west of campus. And the broken peak . . .

"I'll move along from the old giant's rest," she read.

"Goliath," Margot whispered.

"And seek the place where the snowflakes sneak."

Sutter snapped his fingers. "Snowdrift. That's another one of the slopes!"

"Shit, shit, *shit*," Carter said, folding his hands on top of his head.

"I won't look high, but I'll get down low," Fallon went on, voice trembling. *"Though it's dark and cold, I'll knock on the door, for my heart is hidden there below . . ."*

"Where the past will lie forevermore," Grayson mumbled, recalling the last line. "That's Meddlehart's poem."

"They're instructions," Fallon said, looking up at them. "He wrote it in 1949, and this resort opened in 1948." She was shaking. "Do you think . . . ?"

"The treasure's hidden here," Sutter said breathlessly. "It was never on campus. All this time, it was here."

"How?" Carter cried. "How is that possible?"

Sutter shook his head. "I don't know. But we could find it. We *have* to try." He shook his head, eyes glistening. "Lawson figured it out, didn't he? He knew it was here."

"Okay, but how the hell are we going to find it without the teachers getting suspicious?" Margot asked. "A lot of them are out there on the slopes all day, monitoring us. What if one of them sees what we're doing?"

Grayson could practically see Sutter's wheels turning. "They won't, because we'll do what we do best," he said simply. "We'll sneak out."

"Sutter," Fallon groaned. "On a mountain, after dark? Really?"

"Tomorrow, after the dance," he said. "After everyone's gone back to their rooms and crashed for the night, we'll go."

"The lifts close after dark," Carter pointed out.

"Could we turn them on ourselves?" Sutter asked. "Or high-jack a snowmobile? I think Dr. Wilbur rented one—Whittaker, too."

"You're kidding, right?" Grayson asked him.

"He's not," Fallon answered, "but allow me to be the first to say *no*."

Sutter bit his lip, eyes unfocused. "Okay, so we go *during* the dance. Just before sundown, while everyone's occupied. And maybe not all of us together. We'll split up—two of us stay at the dance and three of us go search. That way it won't be as suspicious, and the two who stay can cover for the others."

Margot shook her head. "We're really doing this? We're going to find Meddlehart's fortune?"

Sutter grinned. "Hell yeah, we're doing this."

The next day crept by slower than molasses, and Grayson was an anxious, jittery mess the entire time.

Their plan was simple. Sutter, Grayson, and Margot volunteered to leave the dance and search for the treasure. That left Carter and Fallon with the job of covering for them at the dance.

Grayson followed Sutter and Margot up the mountain during the day, hoping maybe they'd find what they were looking for early and make their jobs that night easier. But Whittaker caught up to them on a snowmobile.

"My old knee can't handle the skis," he told them, "but the

resort has some excellent snowmobile rental options, so I can still supervise!"

Needless to say, they didn't get to do much searching with Whittaker zipping around, keeping an eye on the students. By the time they got back to their rooms, it was nearly time for the dance.

"I kind of wish they'd let us know about this whole dance thing *before* we left campus," Carter grumbled as he pulled a thin sweater over his head. "This is the fanciest thing I brought."

"I'm ready to go," Sutter said as he buttoned up a flannel shirt and then zipped his jeans. He headed for the door. "Gonna go check in at the dance so I've shown my face. Then we can get going."

He left, and Carter followed quickly after. Grayson was the last one left, fastening the buttons on his dress shirt and tying his tie around his neck. He brushed his fingers through his hair a few times, staring in the mirror like he might see something different if he messed with his hair long enough.

But he was just himself, and that wasn't going to change, no matter how many times he'd wished it might. He wished maybe one day he'd be enough for his father. He wished he could be what Fallon needed.

He'd wished a lot of things, and none of them had come true. Not yet.

His phone buzzed. He pulled it from his pocket and glanced at the screen.

It was a text from his dad. *Thought you'd want to hear this from me, before the news gets out.*

There was a picture attached. It was of his father holding

the hand of Hannah Grace James, a massive, glistening diamond ring on her fourth finger.

Grayson's chest seized with a brief wave of panic. No, no, *no*. This couldn't be real.

But the longer he stared at the image, the more the crushing reality sank onto his shoulders. White-hot anger and roiling disgust mingled with a heavy sense of dread that overwhelmed everything else.

His dad had proposed to this girl. He was going to *marry* her.

Grayson felt sick. He stood there, leaning against the wall until the room stopped spinning. When he looked at his phone again, there was a text from Margot in their group chat.

You coming, Grayson????

He swallowed thickly and straightened, trying to compose himself. His friends were waiting for him, and though that was suddenly the last place he wanted to go, he knew it might help get his mind off the news. He ran the faucet in the bathroom for a moment, splashing cool water on his face until he felt like he could manage showing up in the ballroom.

"Let's do this," he murmured.

The ballroom was a high-ceilinged, warm space with chandeliers and a large dance floor in the center. It was already full of students. Teachers lined the walls, sipping punch and laughing at each other's jokes.

Margot's words from earlier crossed his mind as he looked for his friends.

Are you going to ask anyone?

He thought about Fallon. Her arms around him in the infirmary, how much he'd longed for her embrace since the second she let him go. Her words that day he said he loved her, the ones he wanted so badly to be true.

I'm not going anywhere. I'm here. *I'm* with you.

And now, his heart aching once again, she was all he wanted—she was the only one he wanted to tell about what just happened, the only one who would really understand.

Maybe you should think a little more about it.

And he realized maybe Margot was right.

He let his eyes search for Fallon in the crowded room as he had so many times before. Every room he entered, he always looked for her. He didn't want to live a single day without the possibility of her being there, waiting for him.

It felt like ages before he found her. She was standing beside Margot, wearing a black dress and a burgundy cardigan. Her hair was pulled back—half up, half down—and she was laughing.

She was perfect, wasn't she? She was *perfect.*

That's when Grayson saw Sutter standing in front of her.

He realized with a sinking feeling that Sutter was the one making her laugh. And hadn't he always been? Grayson had denied it for so long, but it was clear as day—Fallon wanted *Sutter.* She always had.

And . . . that was okay. Wasn't that all Grayson really wanted? For Fallon to be happy, with a guy who was right for her?

That guy isn't me, he thought. *It's never been me.*

Grayson could accept that. He *would.* But right now . . . tonight of all nights . . .

He didn't want to stick around and watch. He *couldn't.*

He had just turned around when a hand landed on his arm, and he glanced over his shoulder. Carter was grinning at him, a cup of punch in his other hand.

"Hey," he said, but his grin faded when he saw the look on Grayson's face. "Where are you going, man?"

Grayson shook his head. "I can't do this, Carter."

"Do what?"

"Any of this," he said. "I can't keep pretending, all right?"

This isn't where I belong, he wanted to say. *I thought it was, but it's not.*

He didn't say that, though. Instead, he walked out of the ballroom and into the snow, and he didn't look back.

FORTY-TWO

Fallon

"I'm going to get more punch," Sutter called over the music. "Want any?"

"Sure," Fallon said. She could hardly hear the words come out of her own mouth.

He nodded at her, then at Margot. "We'll leave a few minutes after Grayson shows up, all right?"

"Got it," Margot said. Once Sutter was out of earshot, she turned back to Fallon, her smile ear to ear. "Fallon, you look *amazing*."

Fallon rolled her eyes. Margot had already said that a hundred times, as if she hadn't put the outfit together herself. "Thanks, Margot."

"He's going to *flip*," she squealed, grabbing Fallon's arm. "I can't wait to see his face!"

"Margot," Fallon groaned, but she couldn't help smiling. She silently hoped Margot was right. She wanted Grayson to see her in this dress, and she wanted to tell him—to *finally* tell him—how she felt.

Had she known all along? She wasn't sure. But she wanted

more than anything to say the words, to talk to him, to tell him everything she'd been avoiding in her own heart for so long.

Fallon kept thinking of that night in the bell tower—the terror that had taken her captive, and the sweeping sense of safety that surrounded her the moment she was in Grayson's arms.

For so long, he'd been that for her—safety that she felt with no one else. She had finally found the courage to tell him, and while she wished she had found it sooner, all she could do was look forward—look for *him*.

Carter reached them right as Sutter arrived with fresh cups of punch.

"Hey," he said. His smile was gone. "So, uh, I have some not-awesome news."

Margot grabbed him by the arm. "Is someone onto us?"

Carter shook his head. "No, it's not that . . . Grayson just left."

Fallon's heart dropped. *"What?"*

"What do you mean, he left?" Sutter pressed. "Like, he went back to our room?"

"He said he can't help us out anymore and he's got to go," Carter told them.

"So he's gone?" Margot cried. "You mean *gone* gone? He left the resort?"

"I don't know," Carter muttered, but the look on his face made it clear that was exactly what he meant.

"He can't just leave," Fallon said numbly, blood pulsing in her ears. "The teachers will freak."

"They probably don't even know he's going," Carter called over the music. "Aren't there hourly shuttles from here? What if he tries to catch a bus to West Fork?"

Fallon's head spun. "Oh my God."

"What do we do?" Margot asked.

"We don't have much time," Sutter said firmly. "If we don't go now, the lifts will close, and our last chance to find the treasure is gone."

Fallon shook her head. "You guys go find the treasure. I'll go after him."

"What?" Margot asked. "Fallon—"

"I *have* to do this," Fallon interrupted, and even though her voice shook—even though the idea of leaving the resort and chasing Grayson down was the furthest thing from comfortable to her—she knew it was the truth.

She had to do this. She had to stop him. She had to tell him.

Sutter was looking at her with a strange expression. *Is this it?*

She gave a slight nod. And he returned it.

Margot threw her arms around Fallon. She hugged Margot back, her eyes watering, but she blinked the tears away. Her hands were suddenly *very* shaky, and she balled them into fists.

"Stay in touch with me," she told the others. "Be careful. Don't do anything I wouldn't do."

"Unfortunately," Carter said, "this whole plan is something you wouldn't do."

Despite everything, that made Fallon smile.

"I love you guys," she said, and she felt choked up. Why did this feel so much like a goodbye?

"We love you too," Margot said.

Sutter gave a little wave. "Go get him, Winthrop."

And somehow, that gave her enough momentum to walk to the door and push out into the cold night.

Fallon raced back to the lodge and searched their rooms. Grayson wasn't there, and he wasn't in the dining room, either. The last place she checked was the warming house, which was nearly empty and about to close for the day.

"Have you seen a tall guy?" she asked one of the servers. "Dark hair, a little wavy? Grayish eyes?"

"Uh, no," the server said, shrugging. "Sorry."

Dread filled Fallon's stomach, but she knew where to go now. As fast as she could, she rushed to the bus stop at the front of the resort.

Her heart nearly stopped. The bus was already halfway down the road.

"Wait!" she shouted, and suddenly she was running. Her feet slipped a few times on the snowy ground, but she kept pushing forward against the sudden burning in her lungs. "Wait! *Stop!*"

The bus's brakes squealed loud enough that Fallon's ears ached. The bus came to a halt on the side of the road and Fallon rushed to the doors, which slid open. A bald man sat in the driver's seat, gazing down at her with a raised eyebrow, unamused.

"You know the bus stop is back that way," he grumbled, jerking his thumb over his shoulder. Then he sighed. "Ah, whatever. You need on?"

She swallowed—was she really doing this? Was she out of her damn *mind*?

"Yes," she said, hoisting herself up the two tall steps onto the bus. She fished in her purse for cash and handed it to the driver with trembling hands. He gave her a confused look for a second before shoving the money in his pocket. Then the doors closed, and before she'd even taken a seat, the bus was moving again.

Shivering, she scanned the rows of seats, which were empty . . . except for one at the back.

A familiar face looked over the seats at her, nose rosy, hair a mess. Fallon's chest ached with fondness and longing when she saw the tie around his neck—that meant Grayson *had* planned on coming to the dance. He was all by himself, looking at her like he was seeing her for the first time.

Grayson stood up shakily, the bus nearly knocking him over as it bumped along.

"Fallon?" he asked.

She rushed to him, and he moved over to let her take the aisle seat.

"What the *hell* are you doing here?" he asked, but she shook her head and reached up to touch his cheek.

"I'm so sorry," she said, eyes already blurred with tears. "I'm sorry I didn't realize it sooner. I was afraid, Gray, because I didn't want to mess everything up between us, but I love you, too. Actually, I adore you—I really do. It's always been you, hasn't it? Maybe it took me a while to realize it, but—"

She didn't get the chance to say another word, because he'd taken her face in his hands and pressed his lips to hers. She grabbed the front of his shirt and pulled him closer, then let her hands travel up to his hair. It was soft, and although the tip of his nose was cold, the rest of him was so warm. His palms braced the back of her neck, strong and sure. He held her like she was something precious that he'd searched forever to find.

And it was everything. *He* was her everything. He had been for a long time.

When they broke apart, they both looked around for a moment. They seemed to register that the bus was still moving. Grayson rested his hand on hers.

"You're so cold," he said. "What were you thinking, running down the road like that?"

She relished the warmth of his hands as she laced her fingers between his. "I needed you to know."

Those were the words he'd said to her that day, when he told her he loved her, and she saw the recognition in his eyes. He smiled a little, but there was something beneath it. A sadness of sorts.

"What's wrong?" she asked quietly.

He swallowed, Adam's apple bobbing. "My dad," he muttered. "He proposed to that girl."

Fallon let out a breath. "I'm so sorry, Gray."

He shook his head. "It doesn't matter."

"Of course it does," she whispered. She touched his cheek again, stroking her thumb across his skin.

She could hardly believe they were in this moment. She could hardly believe the look of awe in Grayson's eyes as he stared down at her, the words her heart whispered that she hoped he could hear—*I'm finally yours.*

They were quiet for a moment, the movement from the bus jostling them a little. Then Grayson shook his head, snapping out of it.

"Damn it, I shouldn't have bailed—I'm such an idiot," he said. "What about the others?"

"They went up the mountain," Fallon answered. "I told them to go, and I'd come find you."

"Shit," he murmured. "We need to get off this bus." He craned his neck and called out, "Excuse me, sir—"

"I am *not* stopping this bus again unless someone is bleeding or dying," the driver bellowed from the front. "We'll reach West Fork in just under thirty minutes. There'll be buses every hour until midnight, so you'll get back sometime, kid, but I have a feelin' you'll be in a hell of a lot of trouble when you do."

The driver chuckled bitterly. Grayson's jaw snapped shut, and he sank down into his seat.

"I guess we're going back to West Fork," he said.

Fallon sighed, leaning into his chest. He put his arm around her, and she gave a little shrug.

"It's all right," she told him. "We'll figure it out. We always do."

FORTY-THREE

Sutter

Sutter, Margot, and Carter made it to the lift just in time. The lift chair could safely hold four people, so the three of them fit with room to spare. Sutter carefully pulled out his phone and held it tightly as he scrolled to the photos of Meddlehart's poem.

I'll go where the butterflies drift out west,
From the rabbit's home to the broken peak . . .

"That line's talking about the bunny hill," he told Margot and Carter. "From the bottom of the mountain to the top."

After they hopped off the lift at the top, Sutter scanned the signposts showing which slopes were which. Goliath was to their left, Snowdrift to their right.

I'll move along from the old giant's rest
And seek the place where the snowflakes sneak . . .

"So we take Snowdrift down," Sutter said. Based on the map of the mountain, the Snowdrift run stopped midway down and turned into the Bigfoot's Bed run.

"And—what?" Carter asked. "The treasure will be there?"

Sutter shrugged, trying not to let the uncertainty of their mission bother him. "There are more instructions, so . . . I guess when we get there, we'll figure it out."

Sutter and the others slid over to the top of Snowdrift and peered down at it. Sutter's heartbeat faltered at the steepness and the short mounds carved out in the snow throughout the slope. It was one step below a straight drop, and bumpy the whole way down.

"Oh God," Margot mumbled. "This is a black diamond run, Sutter. I am not prepared for this in the slightest."

"You know," Carter said shakily, "me neither. I'm not feeling it. I think maybe we should find another way—"

"Guys," Sutter said. "This is what the poem said to do. We've got to try, right?" He swallowed, his throat suddenly dry. "We'll just take it nice and slow. Make big, wide turns, like they taught us."

"Why did we decide to learn to snowboard *this* year, of all years?" Carter asked Margot, scrunching his face anxiously.

"Um, wasn't that *your* idea?" Margot cried.

"Relax," Sutter told them as he pushed himself down a few feet. "Take it slow."

Almost immediately, though, Sutter's skis slid beneath him, and he fell sideways. He dug his mittens into the snow like he was hanging on for dear life.

"Would it be possible to just slide down on my ass?" Carter asked.

"I mean, sure, but you'll never live it down," Margot said.

"Honestly, I might be okay with that."

Sutter pushed back to standing, his knees wobbling, and he slid forward again. He skied across the slope, made a turn, and then skied back to the other side. He slid over the mounds, a tiny thrill rushing through him at the up-and-down feeling, and though his legs ached with the effort of staying upright on a surface this steep, he felt a little pride. He was doing it. He was going to make it.

They were halfway down when Carter lost his balance. One minute he was right behind Sutter, and the next he was tumbling down the slope. He landed at the bottom, covered in snow and clutching one knee.

Sutter and Margot rushed down, barely staying upright themselves. But they made it, and Sutter skidded to a halt beside Carter, unclipping his boots from his skis.

"You all right, Carter?" he asked.

"No," Carter groaned. "My knee . . . I messed it up bad. Oh *God*, this hurts."

Margot clamped her hand on his shoulder. "Breathe, Carter. Deep breaths. Can you stand?"

She and Sutter unbuckled his feet from the board and lifted him. His knee gave out immediately, and they caught him before he fell.

"Just give me a minute, guys," Carter said, sinking back to the ground. "Go look around. I'll wait here."

Sutter glanced at Margot and nodded before checking his phone again. He scanned the first lines of the poem, down to the second half.

"I won't look high, but I'll get down low," he read. *"Though it's dark and cold, I'll knock on the door."*

"For my heart is hidden there below," Margot continued. She

glanced up at the sky. "I mean, it makes sense not to look up high, because there's nothing but stars and trees. Obviously, if he hid anything here, it'll be down low."

"Underground," Sutter said, mind whirling. He looked at her. "Meddlehart and Thatcher made their money in coal mining before founding the school, right?" When she nodded, he said, "I bet Thatcher wasn't the only one who liked to dig tunnels."

Margot frowned. "You think he hid the treasure in a tunnel on Swallowtail Mountain?"

"You heard what the resort guide said, didn't you?" he asked. "People mined on this mountain before it was turned into a ski resort. They sealed up the mines so they could build this place."

Margot's eyes went wide. "Maybe Thatcher and Meddlehart had mines here."

A line from Meddlehart's message surfaced in Sutter's memory.

"*I hide my worth in my legacy*," Sutter murmured. "When he said *legacy*, he wasn't talking about the school . . ."

Margot completed his thought. "He was talking about the mines!"

Sutter nodded, his pulse like a jackhammer. "Let's look around."

The two of them started into the trees surrounding the Snowdrift run, their boots making deep imprints in the thick snow. The sun had dropped low behind the mountaintop, and the darkness was settling fast. Sutter turned his phone flashlight on and scanned the area, looking for anything out of the ordinary.

But there wasn't anything abnormal that he could see. Just trees, trees, and more trees. He walked up to a few of them and knocked, but the wood was solid. A few yards away, Margot was struggling to kick snow out of the way and searching the ground for whatever she could find.

"Not seeing any doors here, Sutter," she called.

"A door in the ground would be a little obvious," Sutter said. "I feel like if Meddlehart meant that literally, someone would've found the treasure a long time ago."

"What if someone did, though?" Margot asked. "What if they just didn't tell anyone?"

Sutter shook his head. "We would know," he said, but suddenly he wasn't so sure.

"Ugh," Margot huffed. "This snow is deep. I'm freaking exhausted." She struggled toward a small boulder up ahead. "Let me sit for a sec."

"We've got to hurry," Sutter told her. "The teachers will get suspicious when they realize all five of us are—"

When Margot sat on the boulder, it wobbled ever so slightly. Her head snapped up.

"Sutter," she said.

"I saw," he murmured. He hustled forward and she hopped up, turning to look down at the boulder. Sutter knelt beside it, shoveling snow away with his hands, until he saw them.

Two iron hinges, barely visible in the dirt and snow, holding the thing to the earth.

"Help me lift," he said. "On my count. One, two, *three*."

They pulled, and just like the bench, the boulder lifted out of the ground and landed on its side. It took a little more effort than the bench had—Sutter guessed this thing had been sealed shut for a long time. Beneath it was a deep hole and a ladder dropping straight down.

"Oh my God," Margot breathed.

"This is it," Sutter said, looking up at her.

"This seems dangerous," she said shakily.

He grabbed her shoulders. "You don't have to go down there, Margot. I can go."

She shook her head. "You can't go alone. I'll follow you."

"Hey!" Carter shouted from the bottom of the slope. "You guys find anything?"

"Yeah," Sutter called. "Can you walk, man?"

"Eh, probably not," he yelled back. "I'll just stay here and keep watch, how's that sound?"

"Good!" Margot shouted. "Text us if someone shows up, all right?"

"Um . . ." Carter paused. "Oh thank God, I didn't forget my phone! It's right here. Don't worry, I've got your back!"

Sutter lowered himself into the hole in the ground. But as he grabbed hold of the ice-cold rungs of the ladder and made the climb downward, he had a bad feeling they might not have cell service belowground.

It didn't matter. They'd come too far—no going back now.

The ladder might as well have been a mile long. Sutter felt like he'd been climbing for hours by the time he reached the bottom. His blood pulsed in his ears, nearly deafening. When Margot jumped down after him, she eyed him for a long moment. Finally, she grabbed his hand and squeezed.

"You're okay, Sutter," she said.

It wasn't a question. Something about it made him feel unsteady.

He nodded numbly. "I just can't believe we're here."

She gave him a reassuring smile, even though she looked scared out of her mind, too. "One step closer to finding Lawson, right?"

His throat tightened, but he cleared it and nodded. It was never about the treasure for Sutter, and his friends knew that. They'd risked everything to help him, and for some reason the full weight of that was just now crashing over him. "One step closer."

Sutter shined his flashlight around them and took in their surroundings. At the base of the ladder was a small, round room of sorts, with three tunnels branching out from it. They'd clearly been mines, and the space looked like it hadn't been touched in centuries—there were dusty crates stacked to the side and a cart on the tracks leading down one of the tunnels. Another tunnel looked like a dead end.

The third, though, was blocked off a few feet in by a rusted metal door.

"Holy shit," Sutter whispered. *This is it.* Even in the dim light, Sutter could see Margot was trembling.

He stepped forward, and gently he took the knob and turned it.

The door swung open, hinges squealing. Inside it was completely dark, and Sutter said a silent prayer of thanks for his little phone flashlight.

He took the first step inside, Margot following close behind. They kept their hands clasped, and though Sutter wouldn't admit it out loud, he was thankful he had someone's hand to hold on to. His heart hammered, and he swore he could hear the walls of the tunnel crumbling as they walked. Suddenly he wanted to talk about something, *anything* other than the long, dark abyss stretching ahead of them.

"Margot," he said. "I know I've made some mistakes the past few months."

"I mean," she said, voice trembling, "everybody makes mistakes, as my childhood role model Hannah Montana once said. But . . . yeah. You did."

"What would you say if I told you a few of those mistakes were made because of Fallon?"

She was silent. "You're not serious, right?"

He groaned. "That came out wrong. She's not to *blame* for them. It's more like—"

She didn't wait for him to finish. "You have feelings for her."

He cleared his throat. "Maybe. But I think I lost my chance."

Margot was quiet, and they took several steps forward before she said, "Yeah."

Sutter sighed. "That's okay."

"You know," she said carefully, "you could have been with her, though. She would have . . ." She trailed off for a moment. "She would've been with you in a heartbeat, before."

He cleared his throat again. "I blew it."

She squeezed his hand. "No, I don't think that's it. I think . . . it's about timing. Sometimes you're the right person at the wrong time. Or the wrong person at the . . . No, that wouldn't make sense." She paused. "What I'm trying to say is, things aren't always meant to be, you know?"

He nodded. "She deserves to be happy . . . They both do."

"We *all* do, Sutter," Margot whispered. "You included."

Sutter was glad for the darkness, because his eyes were prickling with the threat of tears.

Then, out of nowhere, Margot grabbed his arm.

And he saw it, glinting in the light of his flashlight.

The tunnel had come to an end. They stood in a cave with stalactites, and stalagmites . . .

And gold. Stacks of gold bars, sacks of gold coins, even a few small sculptures made from gold. A crate of gold nuggets sat in one corner—the sight made Sutter weak in the knees. There were jewels, too—some of them loose, in little piles, others placed carefully in jewelry pieces. Some of it was half-buried in dirt and dust and chunks of rock, but it was all there, laid out carefully like it had been meant for them all along.

Sutter picked up a gold compass that sat atop a stack of coins. Engraved on its case was the name *J. Meddlehart.*

"It's Meddlehart's," he murmured.

Margot stepped forward. Sutter could see her hands trembling as she reached out to touch a gold bar stacked along the wall nearest to her. The moment she touched it, she gasped.

"Is it real?" Sutter asked, hardly able to believe it himself.

Her face broke into a smile, and she laughed.

"Oh . . . my . . . God," she cried. "Oh my *God*, Sutter, look at all this! We found it. We *found* it!"

Sutter's eyes welled up. "We found it," he repeated weakly. *Lawson, we found it. We really found it.*

Margot jumped into his arms, wrapping him in a suffocating hug, and he held her back. Half his face was buried in her shoulder, muffling his shocked laughter.

A scuffling sound startled them.

Margot broke away from him. The excitement in her eyes was instantly replaced with panic. "Sutter," she whispered. "What was that?"

For a moment, they were frozen. Sutter's ears searched the silence, straining to locate the sound they'd just heard.

And then the silence shattered.

"No, no, no, *no*!" a voice cried. Out of the darkness, Carter stumbled, blood dripping down his forehead and into his eyes.

"Oh my God," Margot gasped. She and Sutter rushed to his side.

"What the hell happened to you?" Sutter asked.

"I'm so sorry, guys," Carter murmured, and it was only then Sutter saw the tears streaking down his face. "I'm *so sorry.*"

Then he heard it. The *tap, tap, tap* of a cane against the tunnel floor. The one he'd heard a thousand times before class as their beloved teacher entered the room.

He stepped into the flashlight beam, and the cold glare in his eyes made Sutter's heart drop like a stone.

Whittaker.

FORTY-FOUR

Grayson

Grayson felt like he was floating on air as he and Fallon approached Shepherd House, hand in hand. They didn't have much time before the next bus returned to Swallowtail Mountain, but until then, they were going to the boys' room to see if Carter had any of his fancy snacks hidden in his dresser. They were starving, and they needed to save their cash for the ride back.

"I'm pretty sure he hid gourmet mini doughnuts or something," Grayson told Fallon. "I've seen him shove snack packages in there when Sutter and I walk in. He thinks he's sneaky."

"It's worth a shot," Fallon said. She looked around at the quiet campus, then at Grayson. "It's kind of eerie out here with no one around."

Grayson nodded. "Yeah, it is. We'll be quick, though."

"I'm worried about the others," she said. "I want to get back soon, before something goes wrong."

"Do you think they'll find it?"

Fallon bit her lip. "I don't know. I mean, if they don't find it, based on everything we've found . . ." She shook her head. "Maybe the treasure really doesn't exist."

A moment later, Grayson unlocked the door to his room and opened it, flicking the light on. He went straight to Carter's dresser, and Fallon strolled to Grayson's desk and sat on the edge.

"Ha!" he cried, hoisting the snacks into the air triumphantly. "Found them."

But Fallon was frozen in place, staring down at Grayson's desk. He walked over.

"Hello?" he said. "Earth to Fallon."

"This paper," she said, pointing at the history test with Whittaker's note at the top—*Let's meet and discuss.* "This is Whittaker's handwriting?"

Grayson frowned. "Yeah, why?"

But then he saw it. The square, blocky letters.

Just like the note written for Quincy in his notebook. Just like the poems that had been left for them.

"Oh," he murmured. "Oh my God." How had they not realized the similarities before?

But then again, how could they have known? Grayson may have been in Whittaker's classes each week, but he didn't pay enough attention to any of his teachers' handwriting to recognize it without something to compare it to. Not to mention that it was impossible to believe . . . impossible to *accept* that—

"It was Whittaker," Fallon said, her face drained of color.

Grayson thought back to history class the other day, of Quincy staring straight ahead, in shock.

Grayson understood now that he'd been staring at the board, at what Whittaker was writing on it. Quincy had put the pieces together right there in class.

"Grayson," Fallon said, her voice strung with panic. "What if—what if this was all Whittaker, all along? What if—"

"We don't know what this means yet," Grayson said, because it couldn't be Whittaker, could it? That kind old man, the one they all loved the most, *trusted* the most.

"We have to figure it out," she said. "We have to do it now, while no one's here to catch us."

Grayson's heart thundered. "What do you want to do?"

Moments later, they were racing across campus, straight to Whittaker's classroom in Morland Hall. Grayson pulled on the doors, but they clanged in protest—locked.

He held out one hand. "Hair thing."

Fallon sighed, pulling one out of her hair. "Bobby pin."

He took it and tried to mimic what they'd seen Margot do at the headmaster's house. It definitely wasn't as easy as she'd made it look, but after a minute, he unlocked the door.

"Well done," Fallon said as they hurried inside. They went straight to Whittaker's room, and this time Grayson didn't waste time picking the lock. He kicked the door in, just like he'd done a few nights ago at Quincy's dorm.

"I didn't tell you this before," Fallon said, pushing past him to get inside, "but it's incredibly attractive when you do that."

He nodded. "Good to know."

Fallon rushed to Whittaker's desk, pointing out a filing cabinet to Grayson.

"You check those drawers," she said. "I'll check the desk."

Grayson started searching the file drawers, which were full of test templates and copies of graded essays.

"Bingo," Fallon said. She held up a ring of keys. They weren't your average house keys, either—they were heavy-duty metal keys that looked like they matched with very old-fashioned locks.

Grayson's blood turned to ice. "Do you think those go to . . . ?"

She nodded. "The tunnels."

Grayson took a deep breath and let it out slowly. "Are we doing this?"

Fallon's hand was shaking, the keys jingling lightly, but she nodded. "Let's go."

The two of them ran across campus. Grayson's lungs burned, but he kept pushing. They didn't hesitate when they reached the bench in the courtyard—they each took hold of one end and tipped it over, revealing the metal doors beneath it.

Fallon tested three of the keys before one worked and the lock clicked satisfyingly. Grayson pulled the doors open, revealing a long, dark climb down a narrow ladder.

He went first and Fallon followed, shining her phone light to guide their way. At the bottom, there was a cramped tunnel.

"Stay behind me," Grayson said. He took Fallon's phone and shone the flashlight ahead of them, and then, reluctantly, he moved forward. He couldn't tell how far the tunnel went, and that may have been what scared him the most.

They hadn't gotten far when the smell hit them.

Fallon gagged. Grayson pulled his shirt over his nose to try to block it, but it was no use.

"Gray, what is that smell?" she asked.

He didn't want to answer. He thought he knew, but God, if he was right . . .

"Stay behind me," he said again as they crept forward.

The tunnel opened ahead of them into a dead end, a square space that was dark and damp and reeked of rotten flesh. There was a dilapidated, twisting metal staircase in one corner—Grayson had a feeling it led to the top story of Meddlehart Manor, to the sealed-off entrance they'd found in Averell's office.

And on the floor . . .

He tried to push Fallon behind him, to keep her from seeing what was at the end of the tunnel, but she shoved past him.

"*Oh my God,*" she gasped.

The two bodies were unrecognizable, each one in a completely different state of decay, but Grayson knew without a doubt who they were.

One with strawberry-blond hair, his bloated face still showing remnants of the beating he took. *Alex.*

And one still in the letterman jacket he'd worn the night he disappeared. The one they'd been searching for all along.

Lawson.

Fallon screamed, and Grayson pulled her against his chest, holding her there. He turned away—he couldn't look at them, though the damage was already done. He'd seen everything. The truth was there in front of them, and it broke his heart.

Grayson wiped helplessly at the tears in his eyes as Fallon sobbed into his chest. He stroked her hair, fighting to not be sick, his mind reeling. What the hell were they going to do now?

And Sutter . . . Oh God, Sutter.

Sutter. Margot. Carter. They were hunting for the treasure on the mountain.

And Whittaker was on the mountain with them.

Quickly, he pulled Fallon away from him and knelt slightly to meet her eyes.

"Fallon," he said, his voice tight with panic. "Fallon, listen to me. We need to go."

"I can't," she cried. *"I can't—"*

She was panicking. He brushed the tears off her cheeks—it was all he could do to calm her. "Whittaker is on that mountain with our friends right now," he said, heart racing, "and they are in danger. We need to go. *Now.*"

A moment passed before Fallon stopped crying and sucked in a breath. She wiped her face with her sleeve. "You're right. Let's go."

He took her hand and they raced back the way they'd come, leaving the bodies of the missing boys—missing no longer—behind.

FORTY-FIVE

Sutter

"You know, I must admit," Whittaker said as he took a step toward the three of them, "I thought your brother was my ticket, Mr. Heyward. I thought if any of my students, past or present, were going to be the ones to find the treasure, it would be him."

Whittaker smiled. "He was a genius, wasn't he? Just the brightest kid you'd ever met. I thought he was going to lead me here and we'd get to share the fortune between us and leave all that Viper nonsense behind." He shook his head. "But here we are, son. It was you. You did what he couldn't do."

Sutter and Margot dragged Carter backward protectively, away from Whittaker. "Did you do this to him?" Sutter asked, pointing at the blood trickling down Carter's face. "Was this you?"

Whittaker frowned a little, and the expression was painfully familiar, like Sutter had brought him a particularly puzzling piece of homework. "It wasn't intentional," he said. "I'll admit, maybe I let things get out of hand. But we had a deal, didn't we, Carter? You tell me where your friends went, and I'll let you go."

Carter let out a strangled cry. Margot cowered, and suddenly Sutter's chest trembled with fear.

This wasn't happening. This *could not* be happening.

"Did you have any idea?" Whittaker asked. "Do you know why I'm here right now? I figured if you were as smart as your brother, you'd put the pieces together. Especially considering I did everything but take you by the hand and lead you to the Order of the Vipers myself."

The pieces clicked together in Sutter's mind. "You planted Lawson's phone for me to find?"

Whittaker smiled. "I simply left clues to light the way. I did the same for Quincy, of course. And dozens of students before that." He shrugged. "I knew eventually it would all pay off."

Clues to light the way. "Alex didn't write those poems, did he?"

Whittaker smirked—something Sutter had never seen him do. "He was merely the delivery boy. I must admit, though . . . he thought it was sabotage. He wouldn't have been so willing to assist me if he knew we were helping you all along."

"But *why*?" Margot asked. "I bet his mom never withdrew him from school. Is he dead, too?"

Sutter felt frozen. "Were you the one who killed Quincy?"

Whittaker let out a laugh, the same laugh that sounded so kind and warm in class. "Quincy. He had quite the ego. I could tell you never liked him."

Sutter was shaking. Whittaker had been watching them, putting the pieces in place so they could get him what he wanted.

The treasure. He wanted the fortune.

The news clippings in the vault made even more sense now.

"Those kids who got hurt searching for the treasure," Sutter said. "Were you manipulating them, too?"

"*Manipulating* is a harsh word, Sutter," Whittaker said.

"You saw the video Lawson made when he buried the time capsule," Carter said. "Why didn't you go dig it up yourself?"

Whittaker tapped his temple with his forefinger. "Smart question, Mr. Sterling. I knew Lawson well by the time he buried that capsule. I knew he would not hide secrets of great consequence with the intention of someone else digging them up. He wanted the treasure too much, and he certainly didn't want to share. He didn't hide the location of the treasure in the woods." He turned to Sutter. "Whatever he hid out there, he intended for someone smart enough—and dare I say, stubborn enough—to put together the puzzle pieces he left behind. Someone who could take the insurance of his time capsule and finish the job . . . And I knew I could use that when the time was right. When I needed *you*."

Sutter's spine tingled. He stared at this man he thought he'd known, who appeared to be a total stranger now.

"How did you get Lawson's phone in the first place?" Margot asked, her voice high-pitched like she was about to cry.

"Where do you think?" Whittaker asked, sounding impatient. "From him, of course."

Sutter's blood boiled. "You know where he is?"

Whittaker sighed. "You know I can't tell you that, Sutter."

"Why the hell not?"

"I'm here for one thing," he said. "I'm here to take what's rightfully mine."

Sutter's mind raced. "All your little nature walks," he spat. "You were hunting for it. Just like everyone else, you want the fortune."

"What makes you think it belongs to you?" Margot asked.

"Oh, girl," Whittaker said, tapping his cane on the ground a few times. "Because I'm the great-grandson of Jacob Meddlehart."

Sutter felt sick. *No*—there was no way he could be related

to this man, this monster. It couldn't be true, could it? It wasn't possible.

But Whittaker didn't seem to know the Heywards were related to Meddlehart. Sutter couldn't give him any hints—he needed to hear Whittaker explain himself.

So he laughed. "What a load of horseshit. Meddlehart didn't have any heirs, old man. His only child drowned."

"Did she?" Whittaker asked calmly, though Sutter could see a spark of anger in his eyes. "Or was she sent away by her villain of a father out of shame? Not shame of her own, mind you, but because *he* was ashamed of *her*."

"I'm not following," Carter muttered, his voice hoarse.

"My grandmother Amelia was pregnant," Whittaker said. "With Boone Thatcher's daughter—my mother. He denied that she was his child, of course, but that was a lie. They were unmarried teenagers, and back then, well, a pregnancy like that was unacceptable, especially to a man like Jacob Meddlehart. When Amelia began to show, he went into a rage. He sent her away, told her to never return, and faked her death. She changed her name and lived in shame, and she was dirt-poor until the day she died."

Sutter thought back to the poem Meddlehart had written—*my Amelia.* He'd said her sins mirrored his, and he could never find her now, no matter how hard he tried.

It wasn't just a poem. He'd meant it literally, every word. Amelia hadn't drowned—she'd been sent away like a criminal. And not long after, he would have a son with a woman he wasn't married to. The very thing he'd punished his daughter for.

With love and regret.

Meddlehart died a guilt-ridden man. His guilt was what had led them here to this tunnel, dug deep in a mountain.

Whittaker spat on the ground. "Meddlehart's actions were like a curse for my grandmother, my mother, and me. We had *nothing*, when we could've had everything. Every trial in my life—they could've all been solved if not for that wretched old man and his damned reputation." He gestured to his leg. "My knee is a perfect example. This happened when I was a child. It was an accident, and the doctors had a plan, but we couldn't afford the surgery to fix it." He paused. "What is it you Vipers always say? *Franklin Thatcher died by the fangs of greed.* Well, whose greed do you think that is? Thatcher's, or Meddlehart's?" He shook his head. "That man could've done so much with this fortune, but he buried it. And that's the biggest disgrace of all."

"They were both greedy men," Margot snapped. "Just like you."

Whittaker laughed. "The world is full of greedy men, but I'm not one of them. I'm simply trying to turn many, many wrongs into a right."

Sutter struggled to keep up with the flood of information, fighting the panic that threatened to drown him. "So you made it your life's mission to find the treasure," he said, heart galloping.

"Clever boy." Whittaker smiled. "But why stop there? My dear cousin is the headmaster, isn't he? The golden boy, the descendant of the school's founders, the one who grew up with *everything*. He has no idea we're related, and what he doesn't know can't hurt him." Whittaker tapped his cane a few more times on the ground. "The Thatchers are just as guilty as the Meddleharts. I'll never avenge my mother and my grandmother until I destroy the Thatchers, too."

"How do you know about the Vipers?" Margot pressed.

He laughed. "My plans have been in motion for ages, young lady. In my teenage years, I fought for a scholarship to

Meddlehart and just managed to snag it. I joined the order when I was your age."

The realization hit Sutter like a ton of bricks—there was someone whose face had been scratched out of one of the group pictures in the vault, someone who had wanted to hide that they were part of the order. Someone whose name started with *Je*.

Jensen Whittaker. He'd ensured his face was removed from the photograph, another step to cover his tracks.

"Joining didn't get me very far, obviously," Whittaker went on. "My year didn't find the treasure. But that's all right, because look at us! Every order of the past paved the way for this moment."

The treasure glittered around them, beautiful and enticing. It seemed to taunt them now. *Look what greed has done.*

"You went to school with Averell, then," Carter said numbly.

"Yes, I did," Whittaker said. "He was miserable to be around back then—arrogant, cruel, but oh so *popular*. I managed to stay on his good side, though. I landed this teaching job because of him—because he knew me." He grinned. "Put me in the perfect position to keep searching. Without this job, I would never have met your brother, Sutter, and I would never have met you." He chuckled. "I would never have had these bright youngsters to help me with the hard work."

"You manipulated Lawson, then?" Sutter asked, voice wobbling. "Like Alex and Quincy? Like *us*?" He wanted answers. He wanted this man to tell him where his brother was.

Whittaker rolled his eyes. "You and that word. I *mentored* him. Quite a bit more closely than I did with you, in fact . . . I let my guard down a little too quickly that year. I should've kept my distance. I knew better. But Lawson was smart. He figured me out, and by the end, well . . . I think he was wary of me."

The pages of Lawson's journal flashed through Sutter's mind, and suddenly he remembered the last one.

we hear in the trees a killer's
every rumination

Sutter's knees went weak. It was an acrostic, like the ones Lawson used to make up for him when they were little. It spelled it out clearly—*WHITTAKER.*

It was a message—a warning. Lawson had left it for him. The realization was like a knife straight to Sutter's heart.

"How did you know Lawson's journal was in his room?" Sutter asked, his voice crumbling. "You left us that poem telling us to search his room."

Whittaker hesitated. "I didn't know for certain. I could only assume . . . because of what he said to me that night."

Sutter could no longer conceal his tears. "The night he disappeared? You were there?"

"He told me I wouldn't get away with any of it," Whittaker said carefully, "because there was someone out there who always found the things he tried to keep hidden. I had to make a wild guess about who he was referring to . . . but you're my student, too, Sutter. It didn't take much thought for me to make that connection." He paused. "And I suppose Lawson was right about one thing—you did find everything he hid. Things I couldn't manage to find myself."

Sutter almost laughed, because he could practically hear the words in Lawson's voice.

Lawson knew he would look for him. Lawson knew Sutter would figure out the clues he'd left behind.

Lawson knew his little brother would *never* give up.

"But your brother was a *fool*," Whittaker continued, "who decided to find the treasure on his own. And he paid for it, didn't he?"

"What's that supposed to mean?" Sutter demanded, his voice trembling.

"He knew too much," Whittaker said, his eyes unfocused. "Like Alex, like Quincy . . . and a lot like you."

Sutter's stomach churned with nausea. He glanced at Margot, who'd gone completely pale, and Carter, covered in sweat and panting in pain.

He had to think of something, or they might not make it out of here.

"All right," Sutter said. "You want the treasure—fine. You can have it. Just let us go and we won't say a word."

Whittaker laughed and stepped forward. "Oh, sure. You think I'm that stupid, young man? No, I won't be falling for false promises."

Sutter's heart raced, and he took a step backward. "Whittaker, come on. Lawson was right—you'll never get away with this."

"Sure I will," he said. "I have a hundred times before, haven't I? I know what I'm doing, Mr. Heyward."

Whittaker took another step toward him. He was closing in, and—

Sutter hardly saw it coming when Margot lunged at Whittaker.

He sidestepped her, lifted his cane, and brought it down on her head in one swift motion. The cane cracked against her skull. She fell hard and rolled onto her back, moaning.

"Margot!" Sutter cried, stumbling backward.

"All right," Whittaker said. "Thought you three might make this easy for me."

Margot and Carter were both on the ground, injured. Sutter was their only shot. He swallowed the bile rising in his throat and scanned the space, looking for an opening—a point of weakness—

Sutter's eyes locked on the old man's knee. He hesitated for a moment too long—enough time for Whittaker to grab him by the hair and drag him to his knees. Sutter's shock was immediate—Whittaker was so much stronger than he looked. He pinned Sutter roughly to the cave wall, but Sutter was able to turn his head just enough to see what happened next.

Whittaker reached behind him, right at his belt, and pulled a gun from his waistband. Sutter hadn't even noticed it there before. Whittaker cocked the gun and held it out, the barrel aimed at Sutter's head. The cold metal dug into his skull, and pain splintered down his spine.

"You should've thought this through, son," Whittaker said. "This isn't what I wanted for you."

"D-don't do this," Sutter stammered. "Please don't do this."

"I hate to break it to you, Mr. Heyward," Whittaker said, "but it's already done."

His finger slid to the trigger. Sutter opened his mouth to speak, but it was too late. A sickening *crack* echoed off the cave walls . . .

Right before Whittaker collapsed.

FORTY-SIX

Fallon

Fallon held the rock high even as Whittaker sank to the ground, blood oozing from the back of his head. He muttered something before slipping into unconsciousness.

Grayson ran up behind Fallon and rested his hand on her back.

"That," he whispered, "was incredible."

"Oh my God," Margot cried. She pushed up from the floor, sobbing, and stumbled into Fallon's arms. "You're *here*!"

Fallon nearly dissolved into tears herself. It felt like they'd barely made it. The only reason she and Grayson were able to get there in time was because they found Dr. Wilbur's snowmobile rental parked outside the ballroom and managed to highjack it. And they saw Whittaker's own snowmobile parked outside the tunnel entrance, a beacon to where their friends were trapped.

It was almost comical, how one of their crazy ideas from before—one Fallon had outright rejected at first—came in handy at the last second.

Carter hobbled to his feet, and Fallon frowned.

"You're hurt," she said.

"I'm alive," he said shakily. Sutter reached to help Carter keep his balance. "That's all I care about."

Grayson grabbed the gun from Whittaker's limp hand.

"The police are on their way," he said evenly. "We already called."

Margot's jaw dropped. "How did you know? Did you hear his confession?"

Fallon glanced at Grayson, who clenched his jaw.

"Guys?" Sutter asked. "What's going on?"

They stayed silent for a long moment. Fallon had no idea how to tell them what happened. She had no words.

"We found Lawson," Grayson finally said, his eyes still on Whittaker. His voice was brittle.

The tension dropped from Sutter's shoulders, and his expression softened.

"You found him?" he asked. "Are you kidding? Where is he?"

Fallon's chin quivered, and she looked at Grayson again. His expression was grave.

Sutter's face fell. "Guys?"

"He's dead, Sutter," Grayson murmured. "Alex, too. They're gone. I'm so sorry."

Sutter dropped his phone, the flashlight beam casting wildly about the tunnel.

And then a stampede of footsteps came echoing down the tunnel, and Fallon knew the police had arrived.

It was all over.

One Week Later

FORTY-SEVEN

Sutter

Everyone had their reasons for attending Meddlehart Academy. Sutter's was ever evolving.

At first, he'd come because he had to. He didn't have another choice.

But that had changed pretty quickly. He found a family, something he'd never expected. And then, when he lost the person he loved the most, the person he admired more than anyone else, this was the only place that held answers.

Now, sitting on the makeshift stage at a press conference in the Meddlehart auditorium, his friends on either side of him, a woman with a microphone called out from the crowd.

"Will you stay at Meddlehart, Sutter?"

The others turned to look at him—Grayson and Fallon on his right, Margot and Carter on his left. They were all dressed up, the girls had their hair and makeup done, and they all looked . . . older. Like they were all suddenly grown and nothing would be the same anymore.

Sutter wasn't sure how to answer the question. He had the whole world in his hands—fame, fortune . . . it was all his. The five of them would split the treasure, and even then, it left them with more than enough.

With all that and more at his fingertips, why would he want to stay here—on the campus where his brother died, where they'd been dragged into a nightmare, where they'd met the teacher who would try to kill them?

Because this was where his friends were, wasn't it? This was where they could be together, where they could make their own memories and be their own people. It was where he'd met them, gotten to know them, grown to love them.

He leaned forward and answered, startling a little when his voice echoed through the speakers.

"Only if my friends do," he said, which warranted a chuckle from the crowd.

"How did it feel to finally get the answers you've been searching for?" a guy holding a voice recorder called out. "To learn the truth about your brother and find the treasure?"

Sutter swallowed at the mention of Lawson. He shifted in his seat, pondering the answer. When he didn't speak, someone else shouted out another question.

"Do you feel betrayed by your teacher, Mr. Jensen Whittaker?"

Sutter felt sweat surface on the back of his neck. He stammered for a moment before Headmaster Averell stepped up to the podium and tapped the mic.

"I think that's enough for now," he said. "Thank you, kids, for agreeing to speak to us today."

Before the five of them even managed to stand, a man called out, "Mr. Averell, is it true you didn't know about the tunnel connected to your home on campus?"

Averell cleared his throat. "I was unaware of the tunnel. It was sealed years ago, long before I took the position of headmaster, and no one informed me of its existence. We are investigating further to ensure that no other staff members knew about it other than Jensen Whittaker. We will not be holding classes until it is completely safe to do so. Now, kids . . ."

He ushered them offstage and they ducked their heads, ignoring the barrage of shouted questions and flashing cameras. They stumbled backstage, and Sutter saw his mother jump from a chair. His father stood behind her.

"Honey," she said, rushing to hug him. Her tears leaked onto his shirt. She'd done nothing but cry since she got here, and Sutter wasn't sure if she'd ever stop. "You did such a wonderful job."

Sutter's father hadn't been able to meet his gaze once since arriving at Meddlehart. Now, though, he looked at Sutter with unmasked shame and regret. "We're proud of you, champ. And . . . we're sorry, Sutter. *I'm* sorry."

Sutter's windpipe felt like it was closing. He could see the pain both his parents were in, and as much resentment as he held in his heart for them . . . maybe this was the start of healing. Maybe they could mend fences, now that they had some sort of closure.

Closure didn't mean much to Sutter, though. Not when his brother was gone.

"Thank you," he murmured. When his father pulled him into a one-armed hug, he let him. He didn't know what to say right now, but maybe later, he'd find the right words.

Sutter took a glance around. Fallon's aunt and uncle were there. The Sterlings had come, and Margot's parents had managed to show up, too.

Grayson stood alone in a corner. His dad was off shooting a movie, apparently. He hadn't bothered to come.

Sutter broke away from his parents and went to stand beside Grayson. "You all right, man?"

Grayson smiled. "Yeah, I'm good. Who needs parents when you have a bazillion dollars?"

Sutter clapped him on the shoulder. "I'm sorry."

He shrugged. "It's fine. My family's all here, anyway."

Sutter grinned. Fallon approached then and wrapped her arms around Grayson's torso. He rested his arm over her shoulders.

If Sutter had pictured a moment like this a few months ago, it might have felt like a knife in the chest. But seeing Fallon with Grayson this past week hadn't hurt like he'd expected it to. Maybe he was a little numb right now, after everything, but . . . it felt like there was a new sense of peace between them all. His friends were happy.

And he believed what Margot had said—he deserved happiness, too. He was looking forward to finding it, no matter what it looked like.

Margot came to stand with them, and Carter limped over, too—he was supposed to be using crutches, but he insisted he didn't need them. Their parents all stood awkwardly, chatting among themselves, and Carter lowered his voice to a whisper.

"Could we get the hell out of here?" he asked. "I'm sick of being smothered by everyone."

Sutter couldn't agree more. For the past week, it had been nothing but being screened by doctors and therapists, grilled by investigators, and relentlessly harassed by news crews, complete with cameras and microphones, looking for the perfect quote.

The story of their treasure hunt had spread like wildfire and captivated the country. The five of them had been thrust to instant fame, and it had been nothing short of madness. Sutter hoped the press conference would satisfy the public and shut them up for a while, but only time would tell.

Sutter nodded toward the other side of the backstage area. "I think there's roof access back there."

"Let's go," Fallon said, and they all filed toward the ladder installed against the wall.

"Where are you all going?" Margot's mom called out crisply.

"Just getting some air!" Margot answered, and she shoved the others forward. "Hurry—she *will* follow us."

They rushed for the ladder, climbing up one after the other. Sutter reached the hatch to the roof first and shoved it open, the cold, fresh mountain air gushing in.

They climbed onto the roof and strolled to the edge, then sat in a row. The view was something else up there, Sutter had to admit. The billowing clouds, the mountain peaks, and seeing the entire campus from above, sprawling out before them. He only wished he'd known about it sooner.

"I can't wrap my head around all this," Fallon said. "How did this happen? Weren't we just a bunch of kids the other day?"

"Technically, we're still kids," Carter said, and Fallon elbowed him.

"You know what I mean."

They went quiet for a moment before Margot said, "I didn't like that question . . . the one about whether we're staying at Meddlehart or not."

No one answered for a minute. Then Grayson spoke.

"I mean, have any of you thought about what you're going to do with the money?" he asked.

"Have you?" Fallon asked him.

He shrugged. "I mean . . . the only thing I really want to do is get my own house," he said. "Away from my dad."

"Hell yeah," Carter said. "You deserve it."

"I'm ditching my parents, too, and I'll ask my little sisters if they want to come with me," Margot said. She grinned at Fallon. "Want to be our roomie?"

Fallon grinned back. "Duh. Cashton sisters for life." She laughed and then turned to Carter. "You're going to culinary school, right?"

Carter grinned. "You bet. And maybe one day, I'll open my own restaurant. I've got to figure out what to call it, but I guess I have time for that. What about you, Fallon?"

She shrugged. "I don't know. Maybe donate most of it?" She sighed, and Sutter saw the glisten in her eyes. "I just don't want us to split up. Everything's going to change now, isn't it? We're all going to go in different directions, and . . ." She shook her head. "If I could, I'd spend every penny to keep us all in one place."

Grayson tucked a lock of her hair behind her ear. "Well, I'm not going anywhere."

"Yeah, Fallon," Carter said, squeezing her shoulder. "You can't get rid of us that easy."

She smiled, blinking at a few tears until they dropped down her cheeks. "Promise?"

"Promise," they said together, and Sutter joined the chorus.

They all turned to look at him.

"Your turn," Carter said. "What are you going to do?"

Sutter aimed his gaze toward the horizon. What was he going to do with the money? He hadn't thought about it, to be honest. All he'd thought about was Lawson.

On the run from Whittaker, chasing after the treasure he'd wanted so badly to find. And when Whittaker finally caught up to him . . .

The investigators were still working to determine what had

happened in that tunnel. They suspected Alex died from blunt force trauma shortly after being brought there, likely at gunpoint. It had all made sense to Sutter after learning more about Alex—his late father had been a Viper, but he'd never shared information about the order with his son.

Whittaker was the one who told Alex about his father's history with the secret society and lured him into the dangerous web of manipulation the teacher had weaved for his own gain.

It had been easy for Whittaker to stage Alex's withdrawal from school. His mother hadn't been well since her husband's passing and was difficult to reach in the first place, and Whittaker changed Alex's emergency contact info without Averell realizing. By the time Averell reached out to Kim Harker, he had no idea he was calling a number that would never be answered.

That was one of the few things Whittaker had done on his own, rather than making a student do the dirty work for him. It made sense he wouldn't want to risk being caught doing things like searching a student's dorm room—that would've likely gotten him fired, eliminating any chance he had of finding the treasure.

But locking Lawson in that tunnel, trapping him there until he died . . . that was something Whittaker believed he could do undetected.

The investigators told Sutter and his parents that while they weren't sure how long Lawson survived after being locked in the tunnel, there was evidence of starvation and possible torture. It didn't take long for Sutter to piece it together.

Lawson had finally figured out where the treasure was. The night of the dance, he made a break for Swallowtail Mountain, hoping to find it before Whittaker could stop him. At that point, Lawson knew what Whittaker was capable of—he knew if Whittaker realized he'd solved the riddle and found the treasure, he'd kidnap him, maybe even kill him, to make sure he kept every single piece of gold for himself.

Lawson wasn't just running toward the fortune when he snuck away from Meddlehart that night. He was running for his life.

But Whittaker was one step ahead. He kidnapped Lawson and imprisoned him in the sealed-off tunnel. When Lawson refused to tell Whittaker the location of the treasure, he let him starve, thinking he would break down and give in when the hunger became too much to bear. When that didn't work, he turned to torture.

Whittaker may have thought he knew Lawson, but he clearly hadn't known him well enough. He hadn't known Lawson would die before he ever gave in to a sick, twisted old man who was going to make sure he died either way.

Sutter shook his head a little, trying to rid his brain of the thoughts. But he couldn't banish them—they kept him up at night, pacing the floor, unable to sleep.

Had Lawson been afraid? Had he known, when Whittaker caught up to him, that it was the end of the line? Did he know he would die in that tunnel, right below the feet of everyone he knew—the brother he loved? Did he know the rest of the world would presume him dead and move along?

Not me, Lawson, he promised. *I never stopped looking. I found the treasure. I found* you.

Did he know how much Sutter loved him? Did he know how much his little brother would miss him—that every day, he would wake up and want to fall apart when he remembered all over again that Lawson was gone?

Sutter didn't have time to try to stop the tears. They came suddenly, racing hot and fast down his cheeks, and his shoulders shook. He hunched over, burying his face in his arms, and let the dam inside him break.

Margot slipped her arms around him first. Then Carter, then Fallon and Grayson. They didn't say a word, but they were there, and they let him cry until there was nothing left. When he finally sat up straight, wiping the tears off his face, they let go of him and he forced a weak smile.

"Sorry," he muttered.

"Don't be," Margot told him.

He shook his head a little. "I don't have a clue what I'll do with the money. I never . . . I never cared about finding it. I never thought we would." He swallowed, gazing out at the campus before them. "I'll just take the memories. That's all I care about."

They all nodded slowly. Fallon wiped away a few tears of her own, and Grayson hugged her under his arm.

"We'll always have that," Carter said. "The memories, they're ours. These were the good old days."

The good old days. Sutter shook his head.

"They're not over," he said. "Not yet."

He thought of the piece of paper in his pocket—the one he'd found slipped under the door of his room earlier that morning. Carefully, he pulled it from his pocket and scanned the handwritten words:

MAKE NO MISTAKE—WE WILL ARISE
TO SATE THE ENVY FOR OUR PRIZE.
YOU'LL EVADE EVERY THREAT
IF YOU DO NOT FORGET—
THE VIPERS WILL NEVER DIE.

Sutter folded the paper and put it back in his pocket, noting the curious glances his friends shared. Who'd left this message for him, what it meant . . . he didn't know. Perhaps he never would. But he *did* know that the good old days with his friends were far from over.

Maybe they'd only just begun.

Acknowledgments

To be writing these words is a dream in itself. I have longed to be an author for as long as I can remember, and now I finally have the privilege of thanking the many people who have helped me achieve this goal. Writing a book can feel quite solitary, but publishing a book takes a village. I thank God every day for this opportunity I've been given, and for each and every person in my life who played a part in getting this story into readers' hands.

Thank you to my agent, Rachel Beck, for taking a chance on me all those years ago. Rachel has been representing my work since I was eighteen, and ours is a partnership I am endlessly grateful for. Thank you for your honest guidance and passion for my stories. Thank you also to the team at Liza Dawson Associates, especially Liza Dawson, Havis Dawson, Eileen Larkin, and Anna Ange, for everything you do!

My editor, Kelsey Horton, has been so wonderful to work with on this book. It was important to me to find the right home for my Meddlehart Academy crew, and Kelsey took such great care in helping me elevate this story to the next level.

Thank you for loving these characters as much as I do and for all the work you've done to ensure their story is told!

The team at Penguin Random House deserves all the praise I have to offer. Special thanks to Emma Leynse, Ray Shappell, Joey Ho, Gabriella Murdoch, Michelle Campbell, Wendy Loggia, Mallory Loehr, Colleen Fellingham, Heather Lockwood Hughes, Tamar Schwartz, and Jinna Shin. You truly make magic happen!

There are so many educators who encouraged and influenced my writing over the years, and for my debut novel especially, I want to thank them. To the teachers who saw the love of writing spark in me at a young age and chose to fan the flame, thank you for instilling in me the belief that I could be an author one day—it has carried me in ways you will never know. To my college professors, especially Jennifer Lynn Barnes and Mel Odom, thank you for the endless hours you spent helping me hone my craft, preparing me to navigate the publishing process, and encouraging me, even when I faced rejection, that one day, the dream *would* come true. Thank you, thank you, thank you!

To the 2026 debut group—thank you for creating a space where I could meet other writers who were navigating the world of publishing for the first time. I have learned so much from each of you, and the support you've offered has carried me through some hard days. Never have I been so appreciative of goose memes. And to Megan Davidhizar, thank you for being one of the first authors to reach out to me after my book was announced—your kindness has meant so much to me!

I owe immense gratitude to Ashley Girard, who has been a fantastic beta reader for each of my manuscripts. I've lost count of how many drafts she has diligently read and provided comments on, for this book and others the world hasn't yet seen.

Ashley, you are one of a kind. I don't know how to thank you for all the encouragement and reassurance you have given me. A million times over, *thank you*!

To all the family, friends, former classmates, and coworkers who have shown excitement for my debut, or simply listened to me talk about the process of publishing this book—you have no idea how much it has meant to be surrounded by so much support and enthusiasm during this time. And to all the friends from years past who have read and enjoyed my stories before—thank you for helping a budding author feel confident enough to keep going. There are too many to name, but you all know who you are!

I dedicated this book to my grandmothers. Neither of them is here to hold this book today, but I have thought of them constantly through this process because they would have likely been the most excited of all. I desperately wish they could be here to share in this joy, but I am so thankful for two women who loved me so dearly and fostered my love of writing and reading when it mattered most.

To my brother and sister—thank you for making my childhood so precious. Our memories together are pure magic, and you both inspire my writing in ways that are invaluable to me. I consider myself lucky to be your big sister.

To my mom and dad—I would not be where I am today without both of you. You are the ones who taught me to be a person who never, ever gives up. Thank you for your steadfast support, for your genuine selflessness, for taking me to the book fair every year, and for crying tears of joy on the phone with me when I got the call that I was going to be an author.

To my sweet husband—I am so lucky to have you by my side through the ups and downs of this life. Thank you for the limitless confidence you have in me, for always being the first to celebrate my writing milestones, and for showing me that I can do the things I don't believe I can do. Your support is priceless.

And finally, I want to thank *you*, dear reader! Without you, none of this would be possible. Thank you for choosing to spend your time with my characters in their world. Reading was my refuge during the hardest parts of growing up, and I hope Meddlehart Academy offers an escape for those who need it.

About the Author

Emma Jackson is the author of *A House of Vipers*. She wrote her first story at eight years old and knew immediately she wanted to be an author one day. Emma studied professional writing at the University of Oklahoma, where she focused on growing her love of writing young adult fiction. When she is not writing her next story, she can be found spending time with friends and family, playing cozy video games, going on adventures with her husband, or reading on the couch with her orange tabby cat.

authoremmajackson.com
@authoremmajackson